STOVE BY A WHALE

OWEN CHASE

THOMAS FAREL HEFFERNAN

STOVE BY A WHALE
Owen Chase and the *Essex*

WESLEYAN UNIVERSITY PRESS
Published by
UNIVERSITY PRESS OF NEW ENGLAND
Hanover and London

THE UNIVERSITY PRESS OF NEW ENGLAND
is a consortium of universities in New England dedicated to publishing scholarly and trade works by authors from member campuses and elsewhere. The New England imprint signifies uniform standards for publication excellence maintained without exception by the consortium members. A joint imprint of University Press of New England and a sponsoring member acknowledges the publishing mission of that university and its support for the dissemination of scholarship throughout the world. Cited by the American Council of Learned Societies as a model to be followed, University Press of New England publishes books under its own imprint and the imprints of Brandeis University, Brown University, Clark University, University of Connecticut, Dartmouth College, Middlebury College, University of New Hampshire, University of Rhode Island, Tufts University, University of Vermont, Wesleyan University.

Printed in United States of America

∞

G
545
.H38
1990
June 1994

LIBRARY OF CONGRESS CATALOGING-IN-PUBLICATION DATA
Heffernan, Thomas Farel, 1933-
    Stove by a whale : Owen Chase and the Essex / Thomas Farel Heffernan.
      p.   cm.
    Includes bibliographical references and index.
    ISBN 0-8195-6244-0
    1. Chase, Owen.   2. Essex (Whale-ship)   3. Survival (after airplane accidents, shipwrecks, etc.)   I. Title.
    G545.H38 1990
    910.4'5—dc20   90-38190
                                                      CIP

5   4   3   2   1

I don't know when I was first in that kitchen—it was more than forty years ago—and I must have seen the maple chest then, but children don't pay attention to things like that. Children want to go out into the fields and find hedgerow blackberries and snakes. But my wife saw it the first time she was in the kitchen. "Oh," Irene Chase said, "that was Howard's great-grandfather's sea chest." "Sea chest?" I said, "—not Owen Chase's?" "No, it was Owen's brother's." But that was enough; the vessel had been rubbed and the genie came out, hardly waiting to be asked to tell the following story, which therefore demands to be dedicated to the people of the chest—to Carol and to Howard and Irene Chase and to Isabell Chase Burnett.

CONTENTS

ILLUSTRATIONS

PREFACE

In 1819 a Nantucket whaleship put to sea for a voyage from which
it never returned. Almost two years later a handful of its officers
and crew set foot again on Nantucket with a story that would distinguish their *Essex* from the countless other whaling ships that had
gone to the bottom of the world's wide oceans. For something had
happened to the *Essex* that had never happened to any ship before:
it had been attacked and sunk by a whale.

The story of the *Essex* belongs especially to its first mate, Owen
Chase, who became the historian of the disaster. Within a few
months of the *Essex* survivors' return to Nantucket, a New York
publisher brought out a thin volume under Owen Chase's name
that told the story of the *Essex* and its crew. Herman Melville tells
us how he came to read the book. The *Acushnet,* on which Melville
had sailed from Fairhaven on his first whaling voyage, had gammed
an unidentified Nantucket ship:

> In the forecastle I made the acquaintance of a fine lad of sixteen or
> thereabouts, a son of Owen Chace. I questioned him concerning his
> father's adventure; and when I left his ship to return again the next
> morning (for the two vessels were to sail in company for a few days)
> he went to his chest & handed me a complete copy . . . of the Narrative.
> This was the first printed account of it I had ever seen, . . . The reading
> of this wondrous story upon the landless sea, & close to the very
> latitude of the shipwreck had a surprising effect on me.[1]

When Melville turned to the writing of *Moby-Dick,* the little
book that William Henry Chase had lent him at sea was to provide
the ending of the novel. In chapter 45 of *Moby-Dick* Melville again
spoke of Owen Chase and quoted from Owen's book some passages
that are awesome enough in themselves but become more awesome
in Melville's eerily reverential reference to them.

Other authors learned the story and borrowed it. McGuffey's readers made the tale familiar to generations of school children, and popular writers on the sea have continued to recount accurate and inaccurate versions of the story.[2]

From some familiar and many new sources the story of Owen Chase and the *Essex* has been collected in the book that follows. At the appropriate point in the book the teller will become Owen Chase himself: his *Narrative of the Most Extraordinary and Distressing Shipwreck of the Whale-ship Essex* is a vivid and compelling account into which not a touch of quaintness has crept in a century and a half. It is the indispensable document on the *Essex*.

This study is indebted to so many people that I could not dedicate a page apiece to them. My very first thanks go to Owen Chase's collateral descendants, Mr. and Mrs. Howard Chase, Aurora, New York, and Mrs. Isabell Chase Burnett, Ithaca, New York. I would not even have started on this book without the documents, information, and encouragement they lent to the undertaking. Owen Chase's great-great-granddaughters, Isabelle and Margaret Tice, were also most kind and helpful.

Then come the Nantucketers: my debt to Edouard Stackpole, Louise Hussey, Helen Winslow, and Andre Aubuchon, accumulated over many long weeks spent in the Peter Foulger Museum, is massive.

From the descendants of the English captain who rescued three of the *Essex* survivors from Henderson Island I have received the most generous and painstaking attention to all inquiries: the Honourable E. P. T. Raine, C. B. E., E.D., his aunt Margaret Fane De Salis, and his brother Maxwell Raine.

At the National Archives I have had the help of many of the staff, of whom I must mention Kenneth Hall, Gibson Smith, William F. Sherman, James Harwood, and Terry Matchette; at the Library of Congress I am indebted to John McDonough, Manuscript Historian, and to the staff of the Manuscript Division.

I also thank Wilson Heflin; Louise Coulson; Charles Paddack, M.D.; Charlotte Giffin King; Douglass Fonda; Eugenio Pereira Salas; Patricia Reynolds, La Trobe Librarian, the State Library of Victoria; Suzanne Mourot, Mitchell Librarian, the State Library of New South Wales; D. Troy, Acting Senior Archivist of the Archives

Authority of New South Wales; Robert Langdon of the Pacific
Manuscripts Bureau; Irene Moran, University of California at
Berkeley; Mona L. Dearborn, National Portrait Gallery; Bruce
Barnes, formerly of the New Bedford Free Public Library; Marion
V. Bell, Enoch Pratt Free Library; V. J. Kite, Avon County
Library Service; G. D. Harraway, Office of the Governor of Pit-
cairn Island; the Earl of Dundonald; Mrs. Leroy T. Taylor; Mrs.
Mary K. Norton; the late Chester Simkin; Mr. and Mrs. Ray
Lewis; Carlos Lopez; Sonia Pinto Vallejos; Franklin Proud;
Eduardo Reyes; Mr. and Mrs. Archibald Davies; Nicholas Carbo;
Suzanne M. Zobel; William Omeltchenko; J. Stephen Taylor;
Rollo G. Silver, Claude L. Chappell; John Tebbel; Mr. and Mrs.
John Donahue; Frank Muhly and Bunny Harvey; and three
experts on a chemical question: Richard Rapp, Rutgers University;
G. H. Lording, the British Phosphate Commissioners; and Arthur
Notholt, Institute of Geological Sciences (London).

The help of the following institutions has been indispensable: the
New York Public Library, the New York Historical Society, the
International Marine Archives, Inc., the Nantucket Historical
Association, the Nantucket Atheneum, the Old Dartmouth His-
torical Society, the Harvard University Library, the Berkshire
Atheneum, the British Library, the Library of University College
(London), the Historical Society of Pennsylvania, the National
Maritime Museum (Greenwich), the Scottish Record Office, the
American Printing History Society, the Kendall Whaling Museum,
the National Library of Australia, the National Library of New
Zealand, the Devon Library Services, the Devon Family History
Society, the Devon Record Services, the Operational Archives of the
Naval History Department, the Explorers' Club, the Seaman's
Church Institute Library, and the Dukes County Historical Society.

Jay Leyda, from whom a word on the subject would be prized,
read the manuscript and had many words on it, for which I am
most grateful. Wilson Heflin and Helen Winslow were also kind
enough to read and advise. All have my thanks and my assurance
that the shortcomings of the book are no faults of theirs. Jeanne
Widmayer's help in preparing the manuscript went far beyond the
call of duty.

STOVE BY A WHALE

Chapter One

OWEN CHASE

I T L I E S so far out in the sea, that tiny sickle of land, that one wonders how the Indians ever found it. The old legend, retold in chapter 14 of *Moby-Dick,* that an Indian baby was carried out over the ocean in an eagle's talons and that the parents pursued it in a canoe until they fell upon Nantucket, seems to be a right myth for the island, even though one who has caught sight of Nantucket on a clear day from one of the modest elevations north of Hyannis knows there were more pedestrian—or remigian—ways of coming upon it.

The voyager who makes the crossing today steps onto an island that has, with some appropriateness, almost exactly the shape that Thomas More gave to his island of Utopia. But this island is a built-up desert, a sandbar, albeit one of the most enterprising and prosperous sandbars in history. Even saying it is a desert calls for some qualification. It is fertile for many plants—including secret patches of heather; Nantucketers do not import weeds, as Herman Melville facetiously suggested, or send overseas for wood to plug a hole. But what Melville said about the Nantucketers' energetic business with the whale needs no qualification: "And thus have these naked Nantucketers, these sea hermits, issuing from their ant-hill in the sea, overrun and conquered the watery world like so many Alexanders; parcelling out among them the Atlantic, Pacific, and Indian oceans."[1] When Melville wrote, Nantucket meant whaling wherever its name was spoken; the ant-hill was known in most nations that had ocean ports.

American whaling did not begin on Nantucket; it had already started on Long Island in the middle of the seventeenth century before Nantucket was settled.[2] Immemorially known to Indians and

by white men discovered in 1602, Nantucket was sold to a group of
partners in 1659, one of whom, Thomas Macy, became the island's
first white settler. Nantucketers, the old histories relate, began their
whaling business around 1668 when a whale entered their harbor
and stayed three days, long enough for them to fashion a harpoon
and kill it. In 1672 they engaged James Lopar to conduct whaling
in partnership with the town; in 1690 they brought over the—quite
literally—legendary Ichabod Paddack from Cape Cod to school
them in whaling. (Ichabod was real, but he is probably most
remembered for the yarn—now spun in children's books—about his
frequent Jonah-like visits to the bowels of a whale where he was
welcomed by an enticing mermaid.) Shore whaling yielded to the
fitting out of thirty-ton vessels for six-week cruises and seventy-ton
vessels for longer cruises down the Atlantic and to the Grand
Banks. In 1712 Christopher Hussey killed the first sperm whale,
and in 1745 the Nantucketers exported their first whale oil to England. By 1763 Nantucket ships were operating off the coast of
Africa and by 1774 off the coast of Brazil. On March 25, 1793, the
Beaver, Capt. Paul Worth, returned to Nantucket from the Pacific
with 1,300 barrels of oil, the first Nantucket ship to have rounded
Cape Horn. From that day on, Nantucket and the Pacific were
wedded. Today's visitor to Nantucket finds the Pacific Club at one
end of Main Street and the Pacific National Bank at the other,
while a map of the Pacific Ocean is dotted with Nantucket names
like Gardner's Island, Swain's Island, and—sure enough—New
Nantucket. There were even more Nantucket names in the Pacific
before the islands began, largely in this century, to be reclaimed by
their native names. There was, indeed, a Chase's Island, which is
now Arorae of the Gilberts.

The American whaling industry grew and prospered despite set-
backs from natural disasters, the revolutionary war, pirates, competition, legislative restraint, and market fluctuation. It was growing impressively at the end of the eighteenth century, and Nantucket
still had the primacy among whaling ports that it was not to lose to
New Bedford until late in the 1820s.

In 1763 a doggerel verse had listed all of Nantucket's then captains, seventy-five of them, drawn from twenty-eight families such

as the Coffins, Folgers, Starbucks, Gardners, Husseys, Swains, Myricks, Delanos, Colemans, Bocotts, Bunkers, and Barnards.[3] If the verse had been updated fifty years later, most of the old names would have remained in it, but a few new ones would have had to be added—Joy, Russell, Luce, Ray, Meader, and Chase.

There were a number of prominent Chase captains sailing out of Nantucket—Reuben, Shubael, and George B., to name but a few— and the Chases were a sizable clan. The islanders spoke of "the thousand Dunhams" and "the thousand Chases," quite a tribute when coming from a Coffin or a Folger whose own families seemed to have been granted the stellar multiplicity promised to Abraham in his descendants.

Most of the Nantucket Chases traced their lineage back to two brothers, Thomas and Aquila, who settled in Hampton, New Hampshire, in 1639. Through Lt. Isaac Chase of Martha's Vineyard their line descended to the majority of Nantucket Chases. But Owen Chase was not one of these.

A certain mystery has surrounded Owen Chase's origins. The ordinary genealogical instruments of Nantucket—the *Vital Records of Nantucket*, the Folger Records, and the Barney Records—all identify Owen's father, Judah, but at that point they stop, save to make provocative references to Judah's mother: "Judah . . . , s. —————— and Desire" and "Desire Chase ('a stranger')."[4] So mysterious does Grandmother Desire appear that one might wonder if that was her real name or if the historians had made her a personification like a classical goddess. Over a century after her death there were allusions to Desire at a Chase family reunion that made her still mysterious, Desire's great-great-grandson recalled.[5] One Nantucket historian says quite explicitly, "*Desire Chase*—was born ? date—Gave birth to *Judah* out of wedlock."[6] And that does seem to be the universal Nantucket oral tradition on the matter.

That tradition would have been more acceptable if it had come supported by evidence, especially since the evidence is abundantly available in vital records of the town that Desire came from, Yarmouth. Even some of the Nantucket records mention her Yarmouth origin.

Yarmouth, which is situated on Cape Cod right across the water from Nantucket, is as important a seat of the Chase family as Nantucket is, but the Yarmouth Chases are not from the line of Thomas and Aquila; they go back to William Chase, who was born around 1595, came to America in 1630 with Governor Winthrop, was a member of the first church in Roxbury, the minister of which was the celebrated John Eliot, and moved to Yarmouth in 1638.[7] His son William and grandson John brought the family down to the point where some light begins to be shed on Desire. And at this point a diagram is nearly indispensable (Appendix H), for John's son Isaac became the father of Desire, and John's son Thomas became the grandfather of Desire's husband, Archelus Chase. On its face the result is nothing more than the marriage of first cousins once removed, a relationship that was neither forbidden nor uncommon at the time.

Dates add something to the picture; those given in *The Chase Family of Yarmouth* indicate that Desire's father, Isaac, married his first wife, Mary Berry, on May 23, 1706, and his second wife, Charity O'Kelley (Desire's mother), August 3, 1727, and that Desire was born March 6, 1741.[8] Archelus Chase's birth date is given as May 17, 1740, and the year of his marriage to Desire as 1764.

These same records give Judah Chase's birth date as March 26, 1765, indicating that at least at the time of his birth his parents were married. But on this detail they are almost certainly wrong. Against their date of Judah's birth stands the March 26, 1764, given by the *Vital Records of Nantucket*, the Barney Records, the 1820 Nantucket census, and private records of Mrs. Charlotte Giffin King, a lifelong researcher into Owen Chase. So there is reason to support the Nantucket belief that Owen's father was born out of wedlock.

That is neither here nor there, of course, except that it would tend to explain why the Nantucket records fall silent at Desire. The puzzle presented by the marriage of the cousins, however, becomes more enticing the more that the diagram is filled in with dates, siblings, and their marriages. It opens to the genealogist "a vague field for . . . surmise," as did an unclear curriculum vitae in *Billy Budd*.

The genealogical appendix at the end of the book contains more detail on these generations of the family.

The place of Judah Chase's birth is even less clear than the date, the Pollard papers saying he was born off the island and Mrs. King's records indicating that he was born on it. But in any event Nantucket was the only place he was ever associated with. He was a farmer, not, as far as records indicate, a seaman.[9] In 1787 he married Phoebe Meader, daughter of a large and prominent Island family today commemorated in Nantucket's Meader Street.

Phoebe Meader was a distant cousin of Benjamin Franklin through her Wyer, Swain, and Folger ancestors. Owen Chase's precise relationship to Benjamin Franklin was first cousin four times removed.

Judah Chase settled in the Newtown section of Nantucket, an area south of the center of town, where for a while he owned a house jointly with David Wyer with whom he had family ties through the Meaders. He subsequently owned land closer to town between Beaver and Spring streets and owned other land as well. Whether he had a house on the Beaver Street property is not clear, but he also acquired other land including a lot and house two blocks from the Beaver Street property, which in time he sold to his son Owen.

To Judah and Phoebe Chase were born eight children. Benjamin, the first, died as a young man from drowning in the harbor in March 1809; his birth date has not been recorded. Eliza was born in 1791, William in 1794, Owen on October 7, 1796, Joseph M. in 1800, George G. in 1802, Alexander M. in 1805, and Susan in 1806.[10] In 1808 Judah's wife Phoebe died, and in the same year he married Ruth Coffin, forty years old, by whom he had one daughter, Maria, born in 1812.

All five of Judah's surviving sons turned to the sea, and all five in time became whaling captains, an accomplishment that would distinguish the family even in Nantucket. The rapid rise of all of them to captain suggests that they started their sea careers at the earliest possible ages—they were all captains in their late twenties, save Alexander who was thirty at the time of his first known captaincy.

Judah Chase had the satisfaction of seeing all of his sons rise to captain, complete their sailing careers, and retire from the sea before his death in 1846.

About Owen Chase's early years little is known. He clearly had some schooling, but it is hard to know where. Public schools were not founded on the Island until 1827, except for a short-lived effort in 1716 to establish one. There were some Quaker schools, dame schools, cent schools, and infant schools, but in 1818 a town committee reported that there were between three and four hundred children in the town between the ages of three and fourteen who could not afford private schooling.[11]

The soundest evidence we have of Owen's literacy is the 1836–40 log of the *Charles Carroll*.[12] Owen, the captain, kept the log himself, as is clear from his first-person references, and it demonstrates an adequate mastery of the written language in most matters save spelling. Whether or not we should read Owen's *Narrative* of the *Essex* shipwreck as coming from his pen is a question left for chapter 5.

Owen's religious upbringing cannot be determined from extant Nantucket church records. His name does not appear in surviving Baptist, Methodist Episcopal, or Congregational church records or in records of the Quaker Meetings.[13] But Owen's sister-in-law Winnifred, the wife of Joseph M. Chase, is on the Quaker records from 1834 to 1844 (the year that Joseph and family left Nantucket), and a tradition has been passed on in Joseph Chase's family that the Chases were Quakers.[14] If the text of Owen's *Narrative* accurately reflects his sentiments, he was a devout man; most likely these are accurate impressions, for a similar piety is manifest in a letter (quoted in chapter 4) of Joseph Chase.

What Owen's first ship was and how old he was when he sailed on it are not known, but what his second—or perhaps third—ship was is known. On June 11, 1817, at the age of twenty he sailed from Nantucket on a whaling voyage on the *Essex* under Capt. Daniel Russell and a first mate named George Pollard, Jr. However much sea experience he had had at that time he was certainly not a green hand, for he was hired as boatsteerer, and no one became boatsteerer on his first voyage.

The boatsteerer's, or harpooner's, duties are graphically described in chapter 62, "The Dart," of *Moby-Dick*: after the harpooner rises from his forward oar, pitches his harpoon into the whale, and stands back from the speeding line, the headsman comes forward, exchanges positions with the harpooner, and uses his lance to pierce the whale's vital organs.

Had Owen's first voyage or voyages been on the *Essex*? There is a suggestive continuity of service between the 1817 voyage of the *Essex* and its 1819 voyage: Captain Russell retired, the first mate moved up to captain, and the boatsteerer moved up to first mate. One is led to guess that Boatsteerer Chase and Mate Pollard had served each in a lower grade on the *Essex's* 1815 voyage. Owen would have been eighteen years old at that time. And before that? Owen's brother Joseph went to sea at the age of fifteen and Owen as captain of the *Winslow* was to have thirteen- and fourteen-year-olds serving under him.[15] It was common for boys to go out on whaling ships at this age. Owen's 1817 voyage may well have been his third.

In any event young Seaman Chase arrived back in Nantucket from the Pacific on April 9, 1819, after an almost two-year voyage on the *Essex,* a fairly prosperous voyage for a ship of that size, resulting in 160 barrels of whale oil and 1,260 barrels of the more valuable sperm whale oil. Owen's lay from the voyage was one sixty-second, that is, his pay was one sixty-second of the profits.[16]

This money gave him something to live on and something to get married on; on April 28, 1819, about three weeks after he returned from sea, he married Peggy Gardner. They had part of the spring and early summer together before Owen went to sea again on August 12, 1819, this time as first mate of the *Essex*. On April 16, 1820, while the *Essex* was cruising and taking whales off the coast of Chile, Owen's first child, Phebe Ann, was born back in Nantucket.

The *Essex,* which by this time Owen had gotten to know inside out, was not a new ship—it had been sailing for twenty years when Owen went out as first mate. The ship is described in its original register:

William Bartlet of Newburyport in the State of Massachusetts

Merchant, having . . . sworn that he is the only owner of the Ship or
vessel called the Essex of Newburyport whereof George Jenkins is at
present master, and is a citizen of the United States, as he hath sworn
and that the said ship or vessel was built at Amesbury in the said state
this present Year One thousand seven hundred and Ninety Nine, And
Michael Hodge surveyor of this District having certified that the said
ship or vessel has two decks and three masts and that her length is
eighty seven feet, seven inches her breadth twenty five feet her depth
twelve feet six inches and that she measures two hundred thirty eight
tons; and seventy two ninety fifths that she is a square sterned ship
has no Gallery and no figure head.[17]

Subsequent registers of the *Essex* make it possible to trace its history. On May 7, 1804, a temporary register was issued in
Newburyport indicating that the ship had been sold to David Harris
(who was also its master) and Sylvanus Macy of Nantucket.[18] Two
months after this temporary register was issued, the new Nantucket
owners brought the ship home to its new port, and on July 7, 1804,
a permanent Nantucket register was issued.[19] On June 21, 1815, a
permanent Nantucket register was issued for the *Essex* indicating
that the owners were Daniel Russell, Walter Folger, Gideon
Folger, David Harris, Philip H. Folger, Benjamin Barnard, Paul
Macy, and Tristram Starbuck, "all of Nantucket."[20] Some notations made on the back of this register indicate that a contemplated
change of captain after the 1815 voyage (which Owen Chase may
have been on) never took place: on November 19, 1816, the *Essex*
returned from its 1815 voyage; four days later Tristram Pinkham
replaced part-owner Daniel Russell as captain, but on May 26,
1817, two weeks before the ship was to sail on the voyage on which
Owen Chase was boatsteerer, Daniel Russell resumed the
captaincy. Another notation on this same register records George
Pollard's replacement of Daniel Russell as captain on April 5, 1819,
about four months before the *Essex* sailed on its last voyage. The
last register of the *Essex* was issued August 10, 1819, two days
before it sailed, and listed Paul Macy, Walter Folger, [Philip H.?]
Folger, Gideon Folger, David Harris, Job Smith, Benjamin Barnard, and Tristram Starbuck as owners.[21] On the back of this
register is written: "Surrender at Nantucket August 6, 1821. Ship
sunk at Sea."

The *Essex*'s new captain on its 1819 voyage, George Pollard, Jr., a whaling master for the first time, was twenty-eight years old and even more of a newlywed than First Mate Chase. Captain Pollard had married Mary C. Riddell on June 17, 1819, two months before his ship's sailing date. Apart from his earlier service on the *Essex*, little is known of George Pollard's early life. A report that he had been a member of the crew of the first steamboat, Robert Fulton's *North River* (later and more widely known as the *Clermont*) on its inaugural voyage is apparently unfounded.[22]

The crew was a dominantly Nantucket crew, as far as records indicate. Matthew P. Joy, the second mate, was a Nantucketer, twenty-six years old and two years married at the time of sailing. Obed Hendrix was twenty, Barzillai Ray seventeen, Owen Coffin sixteen. There were twenty-one in all on board when the *Essex* put out for its last voyage. One man was to leave the ship in the South American port of Tecamus. Of the twenty left on the ship all were to be victims of the most singular and unprecedented marine disaster whalemen had ever experienced; yet a month after their shipwreck all twenty were still alive. Three months after the shipwreck, eight were alive.

The story of the *Essex* is preeminently Owen Chase's story, for he is the only one who told it at length. He told it promptly; eight months after his rescue, four months after his return to Nantucket, the *Narrative of the Most Extraordinary and Distressing Shipwreck of the Whale-ship Essex* was published in New York. Every other account of the shipwreck is summary or fragmentary, touching the action at only one point or another. Those that were written later or at one or two removes from events are proportionately less trustworthy. But Owen's account is the fresh eyewitness account.

At this point, then, Owen Chase will take up the story of the *Essex*'s last cruise. The chapter that follows is the full and exact text of his *Narrative*.[23]

NARRATIVE OF THE MOST EXTRAORDINARY AND DISTRESSING SHIPWRECK OF THE WHALE-SHIP ESSEX, OF NANTUCKET; . . .

BY OWEN CHASE

TO THE READER

I AM AWARE that the public mind has been already nearly sated with the private stories of individuals, many of whom had few, if any, claims to public attention; and the injuries which have resulted from the promulgation of fictitious histories, and in many instances, of journals entirely fabricated for the purpose, has had the effect to lessen the public interest in works of this description, and very much to undervalue the general cause of truth. It is, however, not the less important and necessary, that narratives should continue to be furnished that have their foundations in fact; and the subject of which embraces new and interesting matter in any department of the arts or sciences. When the motive is worthy, the subject and style interesting, affording instruction, exciting a proper sympathy, and withal disclosing new and astonishing traits of human character:—this kind of information becomes of great value to the philanthropist and philosopher, and is fully deserving of attention from every description of readers.

On the subject of the facts contained in this little volume, they are neither so extravagant, as to require the exercise of any great credulity to believe, nor, I trust, so unimportant or uninteresting, as to forbid an attentive perusal. It was my misfortune to be a considerable, if not a principal, sufferer, in the dreadful catastrophe that befell us; and in it, I not only lost all the little I had ventured, but my situation and the prospects of bettering it, that at one time seemed to smile upon me, were all in one short moment destroyed with it. The hope of obtaining something of remuneration, by giving a short history of my sufferings to the world, must therefore constitute my claim to public attention.

PREFACE

The increasing attention which is bestowed upon the whale fishery in the United States, has lately caused a very considerable commercial excitement; and no doubt it will become, if it be not at present, as important and general a branch of commerce as any belonging to our country. It is now principally confined to a very industrious and enterprising portion of the population of the States, many individuals of whom have amassed very rapid and considerable fortunes. It is a business requiring that labour, economy, and enterprise, for which the people of Nantucket are so eminently distinguished. It has enriched the inhabitants without bringing with it the usual corruptions and luxuries of a foreign trade; and those who are now most successful and conspicuous in it, are remarkable for the primitive simplicity, integrity, and hospitality of the island. This trade, if I may so call it, took its rise amongst the earliest settlers, and has gradually advanced to the extended, important, and lucrative state in which it now is, without any material interruption, and with very little competition until the present time. The late war temporally, but in a great degree affected its prosperity, by subjecting numerous fine vessels with their cargoes to capture and loss; but in its short continuance, it was not sufficient to divert the enterprise of the whalemen, nor to subdue the active energies of the capatalists embarked in it.[1] At the conclusion of peace, those energies burst out afresh; and our sails now almost whiten the distant confines of the Pacific. The English have a few ships there; and the advantages which they possess over ours, it may be feared will materially affect our success, by producing in time a much more extensive and

NARRATIVE

OF THE

MOST EXTRAORDINARY AND DISTRESSING

SHIPWRECK

OF THE

WHALE-SHIP ESSEX,

OF

NANTUCKET;

WHICH WAS ATTACKED AND FINALLY DESTROYED BY A LARGE

SPERMACETI-WHALE,

IN THE PACIFIC OCEAN;

WITH

AN ACCOUNT

OF THE

UNPARALLELED SUFFERINGS

OF THE CAPTAIN AND CREW

DURING A SPACE OF NINETY-THREE DAYS AT SEA, IN OPEN BOATS

IN THE YEARS 1819 & 1820.

BY

OWEN CHASE,

OF NANTUCKET, FIRST MATE OF SAID VESSEL.

NEW-YORK:

PUBLISHED BY W. B. GILLEY, 92 BROADWAY.

J. SEYMOUR, Printer.

. . . .

1821.

FIRST EDITION

powerful competition. They are enabled to realize a greater profit from the demand and price of oil in their markets; and the encouragement afforded by parliament, not only in permitting the importation of it free of duty, but in granting a liberal bounty. It is to be hoped that the wisdom of Congress will be extended to this subject; and that our present decided supremacy will not be lost for the want of a deserved government patronage.

Recent events have shown that we require a competent naval force in the Pacific, for the protection of this important and lucrative branch of commerce; for the want of which, many serious injuries and insults have been lately received, which have a tendency to retard its flourishing progress, and which have proved of serious consequence to the parties concerned.

During the late war, the exertions and intrepidity of Capt. Porter, were the means of saving a great deal of valuable property, which otherwise must have fallen into the hands of the enemy. His skilful, spirited, and patriotic conduct, on all occasions where he was called upon to act, imparted a protection and confidence to our countrymen, which completely fulfilled their expectations of him, and without doubt those of the government in sending him there.

Our ships usually occupy from two to three years in making a voyage. Occasionally, necessity obliges them to go into port for provisions, water, and repairs; in some cases, amongst mere savages, and in others, inhospitable people, from whom they are liable to every species of fraud, imposition, and force, which require some competent power to awe and redress. As long as the struggle between the patriots and royalists continues, or even should that speedily end—as long as young and instable governments, as there naturally must be for many years to come, exist there, our whalemen will continue to require that countenance and support which the importance and prosperity of the trade to them, and to the country, eminently entitle them.[2] It is, undoubtedly, a most hazardous business; involving many incidental and unavoidable sacrifices, the severity of which it seems cruel to increase by the neglect or refusal of a proper protection.

The seamen employed in the fishery, and particularly those from Nantucket, are composed of the sons and connexions of the most respectable families on the island; and, unlike the majority of the class or profession to which they belong, they labour not only for their temporary subsistence, but they have an ambition and pride among them which seeks after distinguishment and promotion. Almost all of them enter the service with views of a future command; and submit cheerfully to the hardships and drudgery of the intermediate stations, until they become thoroughly acquainted with their business.

There are common sailors, boat-steerers, and harpooners: the last of these is the most honourable and important. It is in this station, that all the capacity of the young sailor is elicited; on the dexterous management of the harpoon, the line, and the lance, and in the adventurous positions which he takes alongside of his enemy, depends almost entirely the successful issue of his attack; and more real chivalry is not often exhibited on the deck of a battle-ship, than is displayed by these hardy sons of the ocean, in some of their gallant exploits among the whales. Nursed in the dangers of their business, and exposed to the continual hazards and hardships of all seasons, climates, and weathers, it will not be surprising if they should become a fearless set of people, and pre-eminent in all the requisites of good seamen. Two voyages are generally considered sufficient to qualify an active and intelligent young man for command; in which time, he learns from experience, and the examples which are set him, all that is necessary to be known.

While on this subject, I may be allowed to observe that it would not be an unprofitable task in a majority of our respectable shipmasters in the merchant service, to look into the principles of conduct, and study the economical management of the captains of our whale-ships. I am confident many serviceable hints could be gathered from the admirable system by which they regulate their concerns. They would learn, also, what respect is due to the character and standing of a captain of a whale-ship, which those of the merchant service affect so much to undervalue. If the post of danger be the post of honour; and if merit emanates from exemplary private character, uncommon intelligence, and professional gallantry, then is it due to a great majority of the shipmasters of Nantucket, that they should be held above the operations of an invidious and unjust distinction. It is a curious fact that one does exist; and it is equally an illiberal, as an undeserved reproach upon them, which time and an acquaintance with their merits must speedily wipe away.[3]

NARRATIVE

CHAPTER I

The town of Nantucket, in the State of Massachusetts, contains about eight thousand inhabitants; nearly a third part of the population are quakers, and they are, taken together, a very industrious and enterprising people. On this island are owned about one hundred vessels, of all descriptions, engaged in the whale trade, giving constant employment and support to upwards of sixteen hundred hardy seaman, a class of people proverbial for their intrepidity. This fishery is not carried on to any extent from any other part of the United States, except from the town of New-Bedford, directly opposite to Nantucket, where are owned probably twenty sail. A voyage generally lasts about two years and a half, and with an entire uncertainty of success. Sometimes they are repaid with speedy voyages and profitable cargoes, and at others they drag out a listless and disheartening cruise, without scarcely making the expenses of an outfit. The business is considered a very hazardous one, arising from unavoidable accidents, in carrying on an exterminating warfare against those great leviathans of the deep; and indeed a Nantucket man is on all occasions fully sensible of the honour and merit of his profession; no doubt because he knows that his laurels, like the soldier's, are plucked from the brink of danger. Numerous anecdotes are related of the whalemen of Nantucket; and stories of hair-breadth 'scapes, and sudden and wonderful preservation, are handed down amongst them, with the fidelity, and no doubt many of them with the characteristic fictions of the ancient legendary tales. A spirit of adventure amongst the sons of other relatives of those immediately concerned in it, takes possession of their minds at a very early age; captivated with the tough stories of the elder seamen, and seduced, as well by the natural desire of seeing foreign countries, as by the hopes of gain, they launch forth six or eight thousand miles from home, into an almost untraversed ocean, and spend from two to three years of their lives in scenes of constant peril, labour, and watchfulness. The profession is one of great ambition, and full of honourable excitement: a tame man is never known amongst them; and the coward is marked with that peculiar aversion, that distinguishes our public naval service. There are perhaps no people of superior corporeal powers; and it has been truly said of them, that they possess a natural aptitude, which seems rather the lineal spirit of their fathers, than the effects of any experience. The town itself, during the war, was (naturally to have been expected,) on the decline; but with the return of peace it took a fresh start, and a spirit for carrying on the fishery received a renewed and very considerable excitement. Large capitals are now embarked; and some of the finest ships that our country can boast of are employed in it. The increased demand, within a few years past, from the spermaceti manufactories, has induced companies and individuals in different parts of the Union to become engaged in the business; and if the future consumption of the manufactured article bear any proportion to that of the few past years, this species of commerce will bid fair to become the most profitable and extensive that our country possesses. From the accounts of those who were in the early stages of the fishery concerned in it, it would appear, that the whales have been driven, like the beasts of the forest, before the march of civilization, into remote and more unfrequented seas, until now, they are followed by the enterprise and perseverance of our seamen, even to the distant coasts of Japan.[4]

The ship Essex, commanded by captain George Polland [sic], junior, was fitted out at Nantucket, and sailed on the 12th day of August, 1819, for the Pacific Ocean, on a whaling voyage. Of this ship I was first mate. She had lately undergone a thorough repair in her upper works, and was at that time, in all respects, a sound, substantial vessel: she had a crew of twenty-one men, and was victualled and provided for two years and a half.[5] We left the coast of America with a fine breeze, and steered for the Western Islands.[6] On the second day out, while sailing moderately on our course in the Gulf Stream, a sudden squall of wind struck the ship from the

SW. and knocked her completely on her beam-ends, stove one of our
boats, entirely destroyed two others, and threw down the cambouse.
We distinctly saw the approach of this gust, but miscalculated
altogether as to the strength and violence of it. It struck the ship
about three points off the weather quarter, at the moment that the
man at the helm was in the act of putting her away to run before it.
In an instant she was knocked down with her yards in the water;
and before hardly a moment of time was allowed for reflection, she
gradually came to the wind, and righted. The squall was accompanied with vivid flashes of lighting, and heavy and repeated claps
of thunder. The whole ship's crew were, for a short time, thrown
into the utmost consternation and confusion; but fortunately the violence of the squall was all contained in the first gust of the wind,
and it soon gradually abated, and became fine weather again. We
repaired our damage with little difficulty, and continued on our
course, with the loss of the two boats. On the 30th of August we
made the island of Floros, one of the western group called the
Azores.[7] We lay off and on the island for two days, during which
time our boats landed and obtained a supply of vegetables and a few
hogs: from this place we took the NE. trade-wind, and in sixteen
days made the Isle of May, one of the Cape de Verds. As we were
sailing along the shore of this island, we discovered a ship stranded
on the beach, and from her appearance took her to be a whaler.
Having lost two of our boats, and presuming that this vessel had
probably some belonging to her that might have been saved, we
determined to ascertain the name of the ship, and endeavour to supply if possible the loss of our boats from her. We accordingly stood
in towards the port, or landing place. After a short time three men
were discovered coming out to us in a whale boat. In a few moments
they were alongside, and informed us that the wreck was the Archi-
medes of New-York, captain George B. Coffin, which vessel had
struck on a rock near the island about a fortnight previously; that
all hands were saved by running the ship on shore, and that the
captain and crew had gone home. We purchased the whale boat of
these people, obtained some few more pigs, and again set sail. Our
passage thence to Cape Horn was not distinguished for any incident
worthy of note. We made the longitude of the Cape about the 18th

of December, having experienced head winds for nearly the whole distance. We anticipated a moderate time in passing this noted land, from the season of the year at which we were there, being considered the most favourable; but instead of this, we experienced heavy westerly gales, and a most tremendous sea, that detained us off the Cape five weeks, before we had got sufficiently to the westward to enable us to put away. Of the passage of this famous Cape it may be observed, that strong westerly gales and a heavy sea are its almost universal attendants: the prevalence and constancy of this wind and sea necessarily produce a rapid current, by which vessels are set to leeward; and it is not without some favourable slant of wind that they can in many cases get round at all. The difficulties and dangers of the passage are proverbial; but as far as my own observation extends, (and which the numerous reports of the whalemen corroborate,) you can always rely upon a long and regular sea; and although the gales may be very strong and stubborn, as they undoubtedly are, they are not known to blow with the destructive violence that characterizes some of the tornadoes of the western Atlantic Ocean. On the 17th of January, 1820, we arrived at the island of St. Mary's lying on the coast of Chili, in latitude 36°59′ S. longitude 73°41′ W.[8] This island is a sort of rendezvous for whalers, from which they obtain their wood and water, and between which and the main land (a distance of about ten miles) they frequently cruise for a species of whale called the right whale. Our object in going in there was merely to get the news. We sailed thence to the island of Massafuera, where we got some wood and fish, and thence for the cruising ground along the coast of Chili, in search of the spermaceti whale. We took there eight, which yielded us two hundred and fifty barrels of oil; and the season having by this time expired, we changed our cruising ground to the coast of Peru. We obtained there five hundred and fifty barrels. After going into the small port of Decamas, and replenishing our wood and water, on the 2d October we set sail for the Gallipagos Islands.[9] We came to anchor, and laid seven days off Hood's Island, one of the group; during which time we stopped a leak which we had discoverd, and obtained three hundred turtle. We then visited Charles Island, where we procured sixty more. These turtle are a most delicious food, and average in weight generally about one hundred pounds, but many of them weigh upwards of eight hundred. With these, ships usually supply themselves for a great length of time, and make a great saving of other provisions. They neither eat nor drink, nor is the least pains taken with them; they are strewed over the deck, thrown under foot, or packed away in the hold, as it suits convenience. They will live upwards of a year without food or water, but soon die in a cold climate. We left Charles Island on the 23d of October, and steered off to the westward, in search of whales. In latitude 1°0′ S. longitude 118° W. on the 16th of November, in the afternoon, we lost a boat during our work in a shoal of whales. I was in the boat myself, with five others, and was standing in the fore part, with the harpoon in my hand, well braced, expecting every instant to catch sight of one of the shoal which we were in, that I might strike; but judge of my astonishment and dismay, at finding myself suddenly thrown up in the air, my companions scattered about me, and the boat fast filling with water. A whale had come up directly under her, and with one dash of his tail, had stove her bottom in, and strewed us in every direction around her. We, however, with little difficulty, got safely on the wreck, and clung there until one of the other boats which had been engaged in the shoal, came to our assistance, and took us off. Strange to tell, not a man was injured by this accident. Thus it happens very frequently in the whaling business, that boats are stove; oars, harpoons, and lines broken; ancles and wrists sprained; boats upset, and whole crews left for hours in the water, without any of these accidents extending to the loss of life. We are so much accustomed to the continual recurrence of such scenes as these, that we become familiarized to them, and consequently always feel that confidence and self-possession, which teaches us every expedient in danger, and inures the body, as well as the mind, to fatigue, privation, and peril, in frequent cases exceeding belief. It is this danger and hardship that makes the sailor; indeed it is the distinguishing qualification amongst us; and it is a common boast of the whaleman, that he has escaped from sudden and apparently inevitable destruction oftener than his fellow. He is accordingly valued on this account, without much reference to other qualities.

CHAPTER II

I have not been able to recur to the scenes which are now to become the subject of description, although a considerable time has elapsed, without feeling a mingled emotion of horror and astonishment at the almost incredible destiny that has preserved me and my surviving companions from a terrible death. Frequently, in my reflections on the subject, even after this lapse of time, I find myself shedding tears of gratitude for our deliverance, and blessing God, by whose divine aid and protection we were conducted through a series of unparalleled suffering and distress, and restored to the bosoms of our families and friends. There is no knowing what a stretch of pain and misery the human mind is capable of contemplating, when it is wrought upon by the anxieties of preservation; nor what pangs and weaknesses the body is able to endure, until they are visited upon it; and when at last deliverance comes, when the dream of hope is realized, unspeakable gratitude takes possession of the soul, and tears of joy choke the utterance. We require to be taught in the school of some signal suffering, privation, and despair, the great lessons of constant dependence upon an almighty forbearance and mercy. In the midst of the wide ocean, at night, when the sight of the heavens was shut out, and the dark tempest came upon us; then it was, that we felt ourselves ready to exclaim, "Heaven have mercy upon us, for nought but that can save us now." But I proceed to the recital.—On the 20th of November, (cruising in latitude 0°40′ S. longitude 119°0′ W.) a shoal of whales was discovered off the lee-bow. The weather at this time was extremely fine and clear, and it was about 8 o'clock in the morning, that the man at the mast-head gave the usual cry of, "there she blows." The ship was immediately put away, and we ran down in the direction for them. When we had got within half a mile of the place where they were observed, all our boats were lowered down, manned, and we started in pursuit of them. The ship, in the mean time, was brought to the wind, and the main-top-sail hove aback, to wait for us. I had the harpoon in the second boat; the captain preceded me in the first. When I arrived at the spot where we calculated they were, nothing was at first to be seen. We lay on our oars in anxious expectation of discovering them come up somewhere near us. Presently one rose, and spouted a short distance ahead of my boat; I made all speed towards it, came up with, and struck it; feeling the harpoon in him, he threw himself, in an agony, over towards the boat, (which at that time was up alongside of him,) and giving a severe blow with his tail, struck the boat near the edge of the water, amidships, and stove a hole in her. I immediately took up the boat hatchet, and cut the line, to disengage the boat from the whale, which by this time was running off with great velocity. I succeeded in getting clear of him, with the loss of the harpoon and line; and finding the water to pour fast in the boat, I hastily stuffed three or four of our jackets in the hole, ordered one man to keep constantly bailing, and the rest to pull immediately for the ship; we succeeded in keeping the boat free, and shortly gained the ship. The captain and the second mate, in the other two boats, kept up the pursuit, and soon struck another whale. They being at this time a considerable distance to leeward, I went forward, braced around the mainyard, and put the ship off in a direction for them; the boat which had been stove was immediately hoisted in, and after examining the hole, I found that I could, by nailing a piece of canvass over it, get her ready to join in a fresh pursuit, sooner than by lowering down the other remaining boat which belonged to the ship. I accordingly turned her over upon the quarter, and was in the act of nailing on the canvass, when I observed a very large spermaceti whale, as well as I could judge, about eighty-five feet in length; he broke water about twenty rods off our weather-bow, and was lying quietly, with his head in a direction for the ship. He spouted two or three times, and then disappeared. In less that two or three seconds he came up again, about the length of the ship off, and made directly for us, at the rate of about three knots. The ship was then going with about the same velocity. His appearance and attitude gave us at first no alarm; but while I stood watching his movements, and observing him but a ship's length off, coming down for us with great celerity, I involuntarily ordered the boy at the helm to put it hard up; intending to sheer off and avoid him. The words were scarcely out of my mouth, before he came down upon us with full speed, and struck the ship with his head, just forward of the fore-chains; he gave us such an

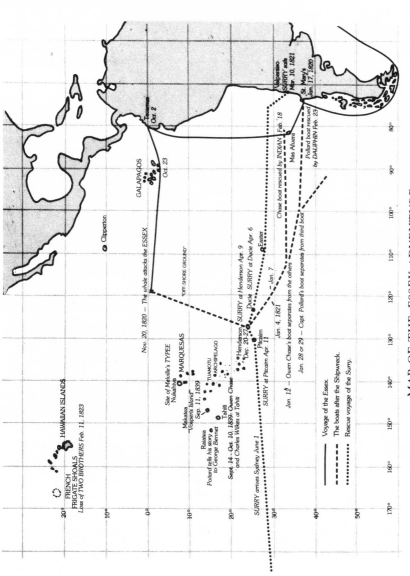

MAP OF THE *ESSEX* ADVENTURE
and later events in the lives of Owen Chase and Captain Pollard

appalling and tremendous jar, as nearly threw us all on our faces. The ship brought up as suddenly and violently as if she had struck a rock, and trembled for a few seconds like a leaf. We looked at each other with perfect amazement, deprived almost of the power of speech. Many minutes elapsed before we were able to realize the dreadful accident; during which time he passed under the ship, grazing her keel as he went along, came up alongside of her to leeward, and lay on the top of the water, (apparently stunned with the violence of the blow,) for the space of a minute; he then suddenly started off, in a direction to leeward. After a few moments' reflection, and recovering, in some measure, from the sudden consternation that had seized us, I of course concluded that he had stove a hole in the ship, and that it would be necessary to set the pumps going. Accordingly they were rigged, but had not been in operation more than one minute, before I perceived the head of the ship to be gradually settling down in the water; I then ordered the signal to be set for the other boats, which, scarcely had I despatched, before I again discovered the whale, apparently in convulsions, on the top of the water, about one hundred rods to leeward. He was enveloped in the foam of the sea, that his continual and violent thrashing about in the water had created around him, and I could distinctly see him smite his jaws together, as if distracted with rage and fury. He remained a short time in this situation, and then started off with great velocity, across the bows of the ship, to windward. By this time the ship had settled down a considerable distance in the water, and I gave her up as lost. I however, ordered the pumps to be kept constantly going, and endeavoured to collect my thoughts for the occasion. I turned to the boats, two of which we then had with the ship, with an intention of clearing them away, and getting all things ready to embark in them, if there should be no other resource left; and while my attention was thus engaged for a moment, I was aroused with the cry of a man at the hatchway, "here he is—he is making for us again." I turned around, and saw him about one hundred rods directly ahead of us, coming down apparently with twice his ordinary speed, and to me at that moment, it appeared with tenfold fury and vengeance in his aspect. The surf flew in all directions about him, and his course

towards us was marked by a white foam of a rod in width, which he
made with the continual violent thrashing of his tail; his head was
about half out of water, and in that way he came upon, and again
struck the ship. I was in hopes when I descried him making for us,
that by a dexterous movement of putting the ship away
immediately, I should be able to cross the line of his approach,
before he could get up to us, and thus avoid, what I knew, if he
should strike us again, would prove our inevitable destruction. I
bawled out to the helmsman, "hard up!" but she had not fallen off
more than a point, before we took the second shock. I should judge
the speed of the ship to have been at this time about three knots,
and that of the whale about six. He struck her to windward, directly
under the cathead, and completely stove in her bows. He passed
under the ship again, went off to leeward, and we saw no more of
him. Our situation at this juncture can be more readily imagined
than described. The shock to our feelings was such, as I am sure
none can have an adequate conception of, that were not there: the
misfortune befel us at a moment when we least dreamt of any
accident; and from the pleasing anticipations we had formed, of
realizing the certain profits of our labour, we were dejected by a
sudden, most mysterious, and overwhelming calamity. Not a
moment, however, was to be lost in endeavouring to provide for the
extremity to which it was now certain we were reduced. We were
more than a thousand miles from the nearest land, and with nothing
but a light open boat, as the resource of safety for myself and companions. I ordered the men to cease pumping, and every one to
provide for himself; seizing a hatchet at the same time, I cut away
the lashings of the spare boat, which lay bottom up, across two
spars directly over the quarter deck, and cried out to those near me,
to take her as she came down. They did so accordingly, and bore
her on their shoulders as far as the waist of the ship. The steward
had in the mean time gone down into the cabin twice, and saved
two quandrants, two practical navigators, and the captain's trunk
and mine; all which were hastily thrown into the boat, as she lay on
the deck, with the two compasses which I snatched from the bin-
nacle. He attempted to descend again; but the water by this time
had rushed in, and he returned without being able to effect his pur-

pose. By the time we had got the boat to the waist, the ship had
filled with water, and was going down on her beam-ends: we
shoved our boat as quickly as possible from the plant-shear into the
water, all hands jumping in her at the same time, and launched off
clear of the ship. We were scarcely two boat's lengths distant from
her, when she fell over to windward, and settled down in the water.

Amazement and despair now wholly took possession of us. We
contemplated the frightful situation the ship lay in, and thought
with horror upon the sudden and dreadful calamity that had
overtaken us. We looked upon each other, as if to gather some
consolatory sensation from an interchange of sentiments, but every
countenance was marked with the paleness of despair. Not a word
was spoken for several minutes by any of us; all appeared to be
bound in a spell of stupid consternation; and from the time we were
first attacked by the whale, to the period of the fall of the ship, and
of our leaving her in the boat, more than ten minutes could not certainly have elapsed! God only knows in what way, or by what
means, we were enabled to accomplish in that short time what we
did; the cutting away and transporting the boat from where she was
deposited would of itself, in ordinary circumstances, have consumed
as much time as that, if the whole ship's crew had been employed in
it. My companions had not saved a single article but what they had
on their backs; but to me it was a source of infinite satisfaction, if
any such could be gathered from the horrors of our gloomy situation, that we had been fortunate enough to have preserved our compasses, navigators, and quadrants. After the first shock of my feelings was over, I enthusiastically contemplated them as the probable
instruments of our salvation; without them all would have been
dark and hopeless. Gracious God! what a picture of distress and
suffering now presented itself to my imagination. The crew of the
ship were saved, consisting of twenty human souls. All that
remained to conduct these twenty beings through the stormy terrors
of the ocean, perhaps many thousand miles, were three open light
boats. The prospect of obtaining any provisions or water from the
ship, to subsist upon during the time, was at least now doubtful.
How many long and watchful nights, thought I, are to be passed?

How many tedious days of partial starvation are to be endured, before the least relief or mitigation of our sufferings can be reasonably anticipated. We lay at this time in our boat, about two ship's lengths off from the wreck, in perfect silence, calmly contemplating her situation, and absorbed in our own melancholy reflections, when the other boats were discovered rowing up to us. They had but shortly before discovered that some accident had befallen us, but of the nature of which they were entirely ignorant. The sudden and mysterious disappearance of the ship was first discovered by the boat-steerer in the captain's boat, and with a horror-struck countenance and voice, he suddenly exclaimed, "Oh, my God! where is the ship?" Their operations upon this were instantly suspended, and a general cry of horror and despair burst from the lips of every man, as their looks were directed for her, in vain, over every part of the ocean. They immediately made all haste towards us. The captain's boat was the first that reached us. He stopped about a boat's length off, but had no power to utter a single syllable: he was so completely overpowered with the spectacle before him, that he sat down in his boat, pale and speechless. I could scarcely recognise his countenance, he appeared to be so much altered, awed, and overcome, with the oppression of his feelings, and the dreadful reality that lay before him. He was in a short time however enabled to address the inquiry to me, "My God, Mr. Chase, what is the matter?" I answered, "We have been stove by a whale." I then briefly told him the story. After a few moment's reflection he observed, that we must cut away her masts, and endeavour to get something out of her to eat. Our thoughts were now all accordingly bent on endeavours to save from the wreck whatever we might possibly want, and for this purpose we rowed up and got on to her. Search was made for every means of gaining access to her hold; and for this purpose the lanyards were cut loose, and with our hatchets we commenced to cut away the masts, that she might right up again, and enable us to scuttle her decks. In doing which we were occupied about three quarters of an hour owing to our having no axes, nor indeed any other instruments, but the small hatchets belonging to the boats. After her masts were gone she came up about two-thirds of the way upon an even keel. While we were employed about the masts the captain took his quadrant, shoved off from the ship, and got an observation. We found ourselves in latitude 0°40′ S. longitude 119° W. We now commenced to cut a hole through the planks, directly above two large casks of bread, which most fortunately were between decks, in the waist of the ship, and which being in the upper side, when she upset, we had strong hopes was not wet. It turned out according to our wishes, and from these casks we obtained six hundred pounds of hard bread. Other parts of the deck were then scuttled, and we got without difficulty as much fresh water as we dared to take in the boats, so that each was supplied with about sixty-five gallons; we got also from one of the lockers a musket, a small canister of powder, a couple of files, two rasps, about two pounds of boat nails, and a few turtle. In the afternoon the wind came on to blow a strong breeze; and having obtained every thing that occurred to us could then be got out, we began to make arrangements for our safety during the night. A boat's line was made fast to the ship, and to the other end of it one of the boats was moored, at about fifty fathoms to leeward; another boat was then attached to the first one, about eight fathoms astern; and the third boat, the like distance astern of her. Night came on just as we had finished our operations; and such a night as it was to us! so full of feverish and distracting inquietude, that we were deprived entirely of rest. The wreck was constantly before my eyes. I could not, by any effort, chase away the horrors of the preceding day from my mind: they haunted me the live-long night. My companions—some of them were like sick women; they had no idea of the extent of their deplorable situation. One or two slept unconcernedly, while others wasted the night in unavailing murmurs. I now had full leisure to examine, with some degree of coolness, the dreadful circumstances of our disaster. The scenes of yesterday passed in such quick succession in my mind that it was not until after many hours of severe reflection that I was able to discard the idea of the catastrophe as a dream. Alas! it was one from which there was no awaking; it was too certainly true, that but yesterday we had existed as it were, and in one short moment had been cut off from all the hopes and prospects of the living! I have no language to paint out the horrors of our situation. To shed tears was indeed altogether unavailing, and withal unmanly; yet I was not able to deny myself the relief they served to afford me. After several hours of idle sorrow and repining I began to reflect upon the accident, and endeavoured to realize by what unaccountable destiny or design, (which I could not at first determine,) this sudden and most deadly attack had been made upon us: by an animal, too, never before suspected of premeditated violence, and proverbial for its insensibility and inoffensiveness. Every fact seemed to warrant me in concluding that it was any thing but chance which directed his operations; he made two several attacks upon the ship, at a short interval between them, both of which, according to their direction, were calculated to do us the most injury, by being made ahead, and thereby combining the speed of the two objects for the shock; to effect which, the exact manoeuvres which he made were necessary. His aspect was most horrible, and such as indicated resentment and fury. He came directly from the shoal which we had just before entered, and in which we had struck three of his companions, as if fired with revenge for their sufferings. But to this it may be observed, that the mode of fighting which they always adopt is either with repeated strokes of their tails, or snapping of their jaws together; and that a case, precisely similar to this one, has never been heard of amongst the oldest and most experienced whalers. To this I would answer, that the structure and strength of the whale's head is admirably designed for this mode of attack; the most prominent part of which is almost as hard and as tough as iron; indeed, I can compare it to nothing else but the inside of a horse's hoof, upon which a lance or harpoon would not make the slightest impression. The eyes and ears are removed nearly one-third the length of the whole fish, from the front part of the head, and are not in the least degree endangered in this mode of attack. At all events, the whole circumstances taken together, all happening before my own eyes, and producing, at the time, impressions in my mind of decided, calculating mischief, on the part of the whale, (many of which impressions I cannot now recall,) induce me to be satisfied that I am correct in my opinion. It is certainly, in all its bearings, a hitherto unheard of circumstance, and constitutes, perhaps, the most extraordinary one in the annals of the fishery.

CHAPTER III

NOVEMBER 21st. The morning dawned upon our wretched company. The weather was fine, but the wind blew a strong breeze from the SE. and the sea was very rugged. Watches had been kept up during the night, in our respective boats, to see that none of the spars or other articles (which continued to float out of the wreck,) should be thrown by the surf against, and injure the boats. At sunrise, we began to think of doing something; what, we did not know: we cast loose our boats, and visited the wreck, to see if any thing more of consequence could be preserved, but every thing looked cheerless and desolate, and we made a long and vain search for any useful article; nothing could be found but a few turtle; of these we had enough already; or at least, as many as could be safely stowed in the boats, and we wandered around in every part of the ship in a sort of vacant idleness for the greater part of the morning. We were presently aroused to a perfect sense of our destitute and forlorn condition, by thoughts of the means which we had for our subsistence, the necessity of not wasting our time, and of endeavouring to seek some relief wherever God might direct us. Our thoughts, indeed, hung about the ship, wrecked and sunken as she was, and we could scarcely discard from our minds the idea of her continuing protection. Some great efforts in our situation were necessary, and a great deal of calculation important, as it concerned the means by which our existence was to be supported during, perhaps, a very long period, and a provision for our eventual deliverance. Accordingly, by agreement, all set to work in stripping off the light sails of the ship, for sails to our boats; and the day was consumed in making them up and fitting them. We furnished ourselves with masts and other light spars that were necessary, from the wreck. Each boat was rigged with two masts, to carry a flying-jib and two sprit-sails; the sprit-sails were made so that two reefs could be taken in them, in case of heavy blows. We continued to watch the wreck for any serviceable articles that might float from her, and kept one man during the day, on the stump of her foremast, on the look out for vessels. Our work was very much impeded by the increase of the wind and sea, and the surf breaking almost continually into the boats, gave us many fears that we should not be able to prevent our provisions from getting wet; and above all served to increase the constant apprehensions that we had, of the insufficiency of the boats themselves, during the rough weather that we should necessarily experience. In order to provide as much as possible against this, and withal to strengthen the slight materials of which the boats were constructed, we procured from the wreck some light cedar boards, (intended to repair boats in cases of accidents,) with which we built up additional sides, about six inches above the gunwale; these, we afterwards found, were of infinite service for the purpose for which they were intended; in truth, I am satisfied we could never have been preserved without them; the boats must otherwise have taken in so much water that all the efforts of twenty such weak, starving men as we afterwards came to be, would not have sufficed to keep her free; but what appeared most immediately to concern us, and to command all our anxieties, was the security of our provisions from the salt water. We disposed of them under a covering of wood, that whale-boats have at either end of them, wrapping it up in several thicknesses of canvass. I got an observation to-day, by which I found we were in latitude 0°6′ S. longitude 119°30′ W. having been driven by the winds a distance of forty-nine miles the last twenty-four hours; by this it would appear that there must have been a strong current, setting us to the NW. during the whole time. We were not able to finish our sails in one day; and many little things preparatory to taking a final leave of the ship were necessary to be attended to, but evening came and put an end to our labours. We made the same arrangements for mooring the boats in safety, and consigned ourselves to the horrors of another tempestuous night. The wind continued to blow hard, keeping up a heavy sea, and veering around from SE. to E. and E.SE. As the gloom of night approached, and obliged us to desist from that employment, which cheated us out of some of the realities of our situation, we all of us

again became mute and desponding: a considerable degree of
alacrity had been manifested by many the preceding day, as their
attention had been wholly engaged in scrutinizing the wreck, and in
constructing the sails and spars for the boats; but when they ceased
to be occupied, they passed to a sudden fit of melancholy, and the
miseries of their situation came upon them with such force, as to
produce spells of extreme debility, approaching almost to fainting.
Our provisions were scarcely touched—the appetite was entirely
gone; but as we had a great abundance of water, we indulged in
frequent and copious draughts, which our parched mouths seemed
continually to need. None asked for bread. Our continued state of
anxiety during the night, excluded all hopes of sleep; still, (although
the solemn fact had been before me for nearly two days,) my mind
manifested the utmost repugnance to be reconciled to it; I laid down
in the bottom of the boat, and resigned myself to reflection; my
silent prayers were offered up to the God of mercy, for that protection which we stood so much in need of. Sometimes, indeed, a light
hope would dawn, but then, to feel such an utter dependence on and
consignment to chance alone for aid and rescue, would chase it
again from my mind. The wreck—the mysterious and mortal attack
of the animal—the sudden prostration and sinking of the vessel—
our escape from her, and our then forlorn and almost hapless
destiny, all passed in quick and perplexing review in my imagination; wearied with the exertion of the body and mind, I caught, near
morning, an hour's respite from my troubles, in sleep.

November 22d. The wind remained the same, and the weather
continued remarkably fine. At sunrise, we again hauled our boats
up, and continued our search for articles that might float out. About
7 o'clock, the deck of the wreck began to give way, and every
appearance indicated her speedy dissolution; the oil had bilged in
the hold, and kept the surface of the sea all around us completely
covered with it; the bulk-heads were all washed down, and she
worked in every part of her joints and seams, with the violent and
continual breaking of the surf over her. Seeing, at last, that little or
nothing further could be done by remaining with the wreck, and as
it was all important that while our provisions lasted, we should
make the best possible use of time, I rowed up to the captain's boat,

and asked him what he intended to do. I informed him that the ship's decks had bursted up, and that in all probability she would soon go to pieces; that no further purpose could be answered, by remaining longer with her, since nothing more could be obtained from her; and that it was my opinion, no time should be lost in making the best of our way towards the nearest land. The captain observed, that he would go once more to the wreck, and survey her, and after waiting until 12 o'clock for the purpose of getting an observation, would immediately after determine. In the mean time, before noon all our sails were completed, and the boats otherwise got in readiness for our departure. Our observation now proved us to be in latitude 0°13′ N. longitude 120°00′ W. as near as we could determine it, having crossed the equator during the night, and drifted nineteen miles. The wind had veered considerably to the eastward, during the last twenty-four hours. Our nautical calculations having been completed, the captain, after visiting the wreck, called a council, consisting of himself and the first and second mates, who all repaired to his boat, to interchange opinions, and devise the best means for our security and preservation. There were, in all of us, twenty men; six of whom were blacks, and we had three boats. We examined our navigators, to ascertain the nearest land, and found it was the Marquesas Islands. The Society Islands were next; these islands we were entirely ignorant of; if inhabited, we presumed they were by savages, from whom we had as much to fear, as from the elements, or even death itself. We had no charts from which our calculations might be aided, and were consequently obliged to govern ourselves by the navigators alone; it was also the captain's opinion, that this was the season of the hurricanes which prevail in the vicinity of the Sandwich Islands, and that consequently it would be unsafe to steer for them. The issue of our deliberations was, that, taking all things into consideration, it would be most advisable to shape our course by the wind, to the southward, as far as 25° or 26° S. latitude, fall in with the variable winds, and then, endeavour to get eastward to the coast of Chili or Peru. Accordingly, preparations were made for our immediate departure; the boat which it was my fortune, or rather misfortune to have, was the worst of the three; she was old and patched up, having been stove a number of times, during the cruise. At best, a whale-boat is an extremely frail thing; the most so of any other kind of boat; they are what is called clinker built, and constructed of the lightest materials, for the purpose of being rowed with the greatest possible celerity, according to the necessities of the business for which they are intended. Of all species of vessels, they are the weakest, and most fragile, and possess but one advantage over any other—that of lightness and buoyancy, that enables them to keep above the dash of the sea, with more facility than heavier ones. This qualification is, however, preferable to that of any other, and, situated as we then were, I would not have exchanged her, old and crazy as she was, for even a ship's launch. I am quite confident, that to this quality of our boats we most especially owed our preservation, through the many days and nights of heavy weather, that we afterwards encountered. In consideration of my having the weakest boat, six men were allotted to it; while those of the captain and second mate, took seven each, and at half past 12 we left the wreck, steering our course, with nearly all sail set, S.SE. At four o'clock, in the afternoon we lost sight of her entirely. Many were the lingering and sorrowful looks we cast behind us.

It has appeared to me often since to have been, in the abstract, an extreme weakness and folly, on our parts, to have looked upon our shattered and sunken vessel with such an excessive fondness and regret; but it seemed as if in abandoning her we had parted with all hope, and were bending our course away from her, rather by some dictate of despair. We agreed to keep together, in our boats, as nearly as possible to afford assistance in cases of accident, and to render our reflections less melancholy by each other's presence. I found it on this occasion true, that misery does indeed love company; unaided, and unencouraged by each other, there were with us many whose weak minds, I am confident, would have sunk under the dismal retrospections of the past catastrophe, and who did not possess either sense or firmness enough to contemplate our approaching destiny, without the cheering of some more determined countenance than their own. The wind was strong all day; and the sea ran very high, our boat taking in water from her leaks continually, so that we were obliged to keep one man constantly bailing. During the night the weather became extremely rugged, and the sea every now and then broke over us. By agreement, we were divided into two watches; one of which was to be constantly awake, and doing the labours of the boat, such as bailing; setting, taking in, and trimming the sails. We kept our course very well together during this night, and had many opportunities of conversation with the men in the other boats, wherein the means and prospects of our deliverance were variously considered; it appeared from the opinions of all, that we had most to hope for in the meeting with some vessel, and most probably some whale ship, the great majority of whom, in those seas, we imagined were cruising about the latitude we were then steering for; but this was only a hope, the realization of which did not in any degree depend on our own exertions, but on chance alone. It was not, therefore, considered prudent, by going out of our course, with the prospect of meeting them, to lose sight, for one moment, of the strong probabilities which, under Divine Providence, there were of our reaching land by the route we had prescribed to ourselves; as that depended, most especially, on a reasonable calculation, and on our own labours, we conceived that our provision and water, on a small allowance, would last us sixty days; that with the trade-wind, on the course we were then lying, we should be able to average the distance of a degree a day, which, in 26 days, would enable us to attain the region of the variable winds, and then, in thirty more, at the very utmost, should there be any favour in the elements, we might reach the coast. With these considerations we commenced our voyage; the total failure of all which, and the subsequent dismal distress and suffering, by which we were overtaken, will be shown in the sequel. Our allowance of provision at first consisted of bread; one biscuit, weighing about one pound three ounces, and half a pint of water a day, for each man. This small quantity, (less than one third which is required by an ordinary person,) small as it was, we however took without murmuring, and, on many an occasion afterwards, blest God that even this pittance was allowed to us in our misery. The darkness of another night overtook us; and after having for the first time partook of our allowance of bread and water, we laid our weary bodies down in the boat, and endeavoured to get some repose.

Nature became at last worn out with the watchings and anxieties of the two preceding nights, and sleep came insensibly upon us. No dreams could break the strong fastenings of forgetfulness in which the mind was then locked up; but for my own part, my thoughts so haunted me that this luxury was yet a stranger to my eyes; every recollection was still fresh before me, and I enjoyed but a few short and unsatisfactory slumbers, caught in the intervals between my hopes and my fears. The dark ocean and swelling waters were nothing; the fears of being swallowed up by some dreadful tempest, or dashed upon hidden rocks, with all the other ordinary subjects of fearful contemplation, seemed scarcely entitled to a moment's thought; the dismal looking wreck, and the horrid aspect and revenge of the whale, wholly engrossed my reflections, until day again made its appearance.

November 23d. In my chest, which I was fortunate enough to preserve, I had several small articles, which we found of great service to us; among the rest, some eight or ten sheets of writing paper, a lead pencil, a suit of clothes, three small fish hooks, a jack-knife, a whetstone, and a cake of soap. I commenced to keep a sort of journal with the little paper and pencil which I had; and the knife, besides other useful purposes, served us as a razor. It was with much difficulty, however, that I could keep any sort of record, owing to the incessant rocking and unsteadiness of the boat, and the continual dashing of the spray of the sea over us. The boat contained, in addition to the articles enumerated, a lantern, tinderbox, and two or three candles, which belonged to her, and with which they are kept always supplied, while engaged in taking whale. In addition to all which, the captain had saved a musket, two pistols, and a canister, containing about two pounds of gunpowder; the latter he distributed in equal proportions between the three boats, and gave the second mate and myself each a pistol. When morning came we found ourselves quite near together, and the wind had considerably increased since the day before; we were consequently obliged to reef our sails; and although we did not apprehend any very great danger from the then violence of the wind, yet it grew to be very uncomfortable in the boats, from the repeated dashing of the waves, that kept our bodies constantly wet with the salt spray. We, however, stood along our course until twelve o'clock, when we got an observation, as well as we were able to obtain one, while the water flew all over us, and the sea kept the boat extremely unsteady. We found ourselves this day in latitude 0°58′ S. having repassed the equator. We abandoned the idea altogether of keeping any correct longitudinal reckoning, having no glass, nor log-line. The wind moderated in the course of the afternoon a little, but at night came on to blow again almost a gale. We began now to tremble for our little barque; she was so ill calculated, in point of strength, to withstand the racking of the sea, while it required the constant labours of one man to keep her free of water. We were surrounded in the afternoon with porpoises that kept playing about us in great numbers, and continued to follow us during the night.

November 24th. The wind had not abated any since the preceding day, and the sea had risen to be very large, and increased, if possible, the extreme uncomfortableness of our situation. What added more than any thing else to our misfortunes, was, that all our efforts for the preservation of our provisions proved, in a great measure, ineffectual; a heavy sea broke suddenly into the boat, and, before we could snatch it up, damaged some part of it; by timely attention, however, and great caution, we managed to make it eatable, and to preserve the rest from a similar casualty. This was a subject of extreme anxiety to us; the expectation, poor enough of itself indeed, upon which our final rescue was founded, must change at once to utter hopelessness, deprived of our provisions, the only means of continuing us in the exercise, not only of our manual powers, but in those of reason itself; hence, above all other things, this was the object of our utmost solicitude and pains.

We ascertained, the next day, that some of the provisions in the captain's boat had shared a similar fate during the night; both which accidents served to arouse us to a still stronger sense of our slender reliance upon the human means at our command, and to show us our utter dependence on that divine aid which we so much the more stood in need of.

November 25th. No change of wind had yet taken place, and we experienced the last night the same wet and disagreeable weather of the preceding one. About eight o'clock in the morning we discovered that the water began to come fast in our boat, and in a few minutes the quantity increased to such a degree as to alarm us considerably for our safety; we commenced immediately a strict search in every part of her to discover the leak, and, after tearing up the ceiling or floor of the boat near the bows, we found it proceeded from one of the streaks or outside boards having bursted off there; no time was to be lost in devising some means to repair it. The great difficulty consisted in its being in the bottom of the boat, and about six inches from the surface of the water; it was necessary, therefore, to have access to the outside, to enable us to fasten it on again: the leak being to leeward, we hove about, and lay to on the other tack, which brought it then nearly out of water; the captain, who was at the time ahead of us, seeing us manoeuvring to get the boat about, shortened sail, and presently tacked, and ran down to us. I informed him of our situation, and he came immediately alongside to our assistance. After directing all the men in the boat to get on one side, the other, by that means, heeled out of the water a considerable distance, and, with a little difficulty, we then managed to drive in a few nails, and secured it, much beyond our expectations. Fears of no ordinary kind were excited by this seemingly small accident. When it is recollected to what a slight vessel we had committed ourselves; our means of safety alone consisting in her capacity of endurance for many weeks, in all probability, yet to come, it will not be considered strange that this little accident should not only have damped our spirits considerably, but have thrown a great gloominess over the natural prospects of our deliverance. On this occasion, too, were we enabled to rescue ourselves from inevitable destruction by the possession of a few nails, without which (had it not been our fortune to save some from the wreck,) we would, in all human calculation, have been lost: we were still liable to a recurrence of the same accident, perhaps to a still worse one, as, in the heavy and repeated racking of the swell, the progress of our voyage would serve but to increase the incapacity and weakness of our boat, and the starting of a single nail in her bottom would most assuredly prove our certain destruction. We wanted not this additional reflection, to add to the miseries of our situation.

November 26th. Our sufferings, heaven knows, were now sufficiently increased, and we looked forward, not without an extreme dread, and anxiety, to the gloomy and disheartening prospect before us. We experienced a little abatement of wind and rough weather to-day, and took the opportunity of drying the bread that had been wet the day previously; to our great joy and satisfaction also, the wind hauled out to E.NE. and enabled us to hold a much more favourable course; with these exceptions, no circumstance of any considerable interest occurred in the course of this day.

The 27th of November was alike undistinguished for any incident worthy of note; except that the wind again veered back to E. and destroyed the fine prospect we had entertained, of making a good run for several days to come.

November 28th. The wind hauled still further to the southward, and obliged us to fall off our course to S. and commenced to blow with such violence, as to put us again under short sail; the night set in extremely dark, and tempestuous, and we began to entertain fears that we should be separated. We however, with great pains, managed to keep about a ship's length apart, so that the white sails of our boats could be distinctly discernable. The captain's boat was but a short distance astern of mine, and that of the second mate a few rods to leeward of his. At about 11 o'clock at night, having laid down to sleep, in the bottom of the boat, I was suddenly awakened by one of my companions, who cried out, that the captain was in distress, and was calling on us for assistance. I immediately aroused myself, and listened a moment, to hear if any thing further should be said, when the captain's loud voice arrested my attention. He was calling to the second mate, whose boat was nearer to him than mine. I made all haste to put about, ran down to him, and inquired what was the matter; he replied, "I have been attacked by an unknown fish, and he has stove my boat." It appeared, that some large fish had accompanied the boat for a short distance, and had suddenly made an unprovoked attack upon her, as nearly as they could determine, with his jaws; the extreme darkness of the night prevented them from distinguishing what kind of animal it was, but they judged it to be about twelve feet in length, and one of the killer-fish species. After having struck the boat once, he continued to play about her, on every side, as if manifesting a disposition to renew the attack, and did a second time strike the bows of the boat, and split her stem. They had no other instrument of offence, but the sprit-pole, (a long slender piece of wood, by which the peak of the sail is extended,) with which, after repeated attempts to destroy the boat, they succeeded in beating him off. I arrived, just as he had discontinued his operations, and disappeared. He had made a considerable breach in the bows of the boat, through which the water had began to pour fast; and the captain, imagining matters to be considerably worse than they were, immediately took measures to remove his provisions into the second mate's boat and mine, in order to lighten his own, and by that means, and constant bailing, to keep her above water until daylight should enable him to discover the extent of the damage, and to repair it. The night was spissy darkness itself; the sky was completely overcast, and it seemed to us as if fate was wholly relentless, in pursuing us with such a cruel complication of disasters.[10] We were not without our fears that the fish might renew his attack, some time during the night, upon one of the other boats, and unexpectedly destroy us; but they proved entirely groundless, as he was never afterwards seen. When daylight came, the wind again favoured us a little, and we all lay to, to repair the broken boat; which was effected by nailing on thin strips of boards in the inside; and having replaced the provisions, we proceeded again on our course. Our allowance of water, which in the commencement, merely served to administer to the positive demands of nature, became now to be insufficient; and we began to e✓perience violent thirst, from the consumption of the provisions that had been wet with the salt water, and dried in the sun; of these we were obliged to eat first, to prevent their spoiling; and we could not, nay, we did not dare, to make any encroachments on our stock of water. Our determination was, to suffer as long as human patience and endurar. ˗ would hold out, having only in view, the relief that would be afforded us, when the quantity of wet provisions should be exhausted. Our extreme sufferings here first commenced.

The privation of water is justly ranked among the most dreadful of the miseries of our life; the violence of raving thirst has no parallel in the catalogue of human calamities. It was our hard lot, to have felt this in its extremest force, when necessity subsequently compelled us to seek resource from one of the offices of nature. We were not, at first, aware of the consequences of eating this bread; and it was not until the fatal effects of it had shown themselves to a degree of oppression, that we could divine the cause of our extreme thirst. But, alas! there was no relief. Ignorant, or instructed of the fact, it was alike immaterial; it composed a part of our subsistence, and reason imposed upon us the necessity of its immediate consumption, as otherwise it would have been lost to us entirely.

November 29th. Our boats appeared to be growing daily more frail and insufficient; the continual flowing of the water into them, seemed increased, without our being able to assign it to any thing else, than a general weakness, arising from causes that must in a short time, without some remedy or relief, produce their total failure. We did not neglect, however, to patch up and mend them, according to our means, whenever we could discover a broken or weak part. We this day found ourselves surrounded by a shoal of dolphins; some, or one of which, we tried in vain a long time to take. We made a small line from some rigging that was in the boat, fastened on one of the fish-hooks, and tied to it a small piece of white rag; they took not the least notice of it, but continued playing around us, nearly all day, mocking both our miseries and our efforts.

November 30th. This was a remarkably fine day; the weather not exceeded by any that we had experienced since we left the wreck. At one o'clock, I proposed to our boat's crew to kill one of the turtle; two of which we had in our possession. I need not say, that the proposition was hailed with the utmost enthusiasm; hunger had set its ravenous gnawings upon our stomachs, and we waited with impatience to suck the warm flowing blood of the animal. A small fire was kindled in the shell of the turtle, and after dividing the blood, (of which there was about a gill,) among those of us who felt disposed to drink it, we cooked the remainder, entrails and all, and enjoyed from it an unspeakably fine repast. The stomachs of two or three revolted at the sight of the blood, and refused to partake of it; not even the outrageous thirst that was upon them could induce them to taste it; for myself, I took it like a medicine, to relieve the extreme dryness of my palate, and stopped not to inquire whether it was any thing else than a liquid. After this, I may say exquisite banquet, our bodies were considerably recruited, and I felt my spirits now much higher than they had been at any time before. By observation, this day we found ourselves in latitude 7°53′ S. our distance from the wreck, as nearly as we could calculate, was then about four hundred and eighty miles.

December 1st. From the 1st to the 3d of December, exclusive, there was nothing transpired of any moment. Our boats as yet kept admirably well together, and the weather was distinguished for its mildness and salubrity. We gathered consolation too from a favourable slant which the wind took to NE. and our situation was not at that moment, we thought, so comfortless as we had been led at first to consider it; but, in our extravagant felicitations upon the blessing of the wind and weather, we forgot our leaks, our weak boats, our own debility, our immense distance from land, the small-ness of our stock of provisions; all which, when brought to mind, with the force which they deserved, were too well calculated to dishearten us, and cause us to sigh for the hardships of our lot. Up to the 3d of December, the raging thirst of our mouths had not been but in a small degree alleviated; had it not been for the pains which that gave us, we should have tasted, during this spell of fine weather, a species of enjoyment, derived from a momentary forgetful-ness of our actual situation.

December 3d. With great joy we hailed the last crumb of our damaged bread, and commenced this day to take our allowance of healthy provisions. The salutary and agreeable effects of this change were felt at first in so slight a degreee, as to give us no great cause of comfort or satisfaction; but gradually, as we partook of our small allowance of water, the moisture began to collect in our mouths, and the parching fever of the palate imperceptibly left it. An accident here happened to us which gave us a great momentary spell of uneasiness. The night was dark, and the sky was completely overcast, so that we could scarcely discern each other's boats, when at about ten o'clock, that of the second mate was suddenly missing. I felt for a moment considerable alarm at her unexpected disappearance; but after a little reflection I immediately hove to, struck a light as expeditiously as possible, and hoisted it at the mast-head, in a lantern. Our eyes were now directed over every part of the ocean, in search of her, when, to our great joy, we discerned an answering light, about a quarter of a mile to leeward of us; we ran down to it, and it proved to be the lost boat. Strange as the extraordinary interest which we felt in each other's company may appear, and much as our repugnance to separation may seem to imply of weakness, it was the subject of our continual hopes and fears. It is truly remarked, that misfortune more than any thing else serves to endear us to our companions. So strongly was this sentiment engrafted upon our feelings, and so closely were the destinies of all of us involuntarily linked together, that, had one of the boats been wrecked, and wholly lost, with all her provisions and water, we should have felt ourselves constrained, by every tie of humanity, to have taken the surviving sufferers into the other boats, and shared our bread and water with them, while a crumb of one or a drop of the other remained. Hard, indeed, would the case have been for all, and much as I have since reflected on the subject, I have not been able to realize, had it so happened, that a sense of our necessities would have allowed us to give so magnanimous and devoted a character to our feelings. I can only speak of the impressions which I recollect I had at the time. Subsequently, however, as our situation became more straightened and desperate, our conversation on this subject took a different turn; and it appeared to be an universal sentiment, that such a course of conduct was calculated to weaken the chances of a final deliverance for some, and might be the only means of consigning every soul of us to a horrid death of starvation. There is no question but that an immediate separation, therefore, was the most politic measure that could be adopted, and that every boat should take its own separate chance: while we remained together, should any accident happen, of the nature alluded to, no other course could be adopted, than that of taking the survivers into the other boats, and giving up voluntarily, what we were satisfied could alone prolong our hopes, and multiply the chances of our safety, or unconcernedly witness their struggles in death, perhaps beat them from our boats, with weapons, back into the ocean. The expectation of reaching the land was founded upon a reasonable calculation of the distance, the means, and the subsistence; all which were scanty enough, God knows, and ill adapted to the probable exigences of the voyage. Any addition to our own demands, in this respect, would not only injure, but actually destroy the whole system which we had laid down, and reduce us to a slight hope, derived either from the speedy death of some of our crew, or the falling in with some vesel. With all this, however, there was a desperate instinct that bound us together; we could not reason on the subject with any degree of satisfaction to our minds, yet we continued to cling to each other with a strong and involuntary impulse. This, indeed, was a matter of no small difficulty, and it constituted, more than any thing else, a source of continual watching and inquietude. We would but turn our eyes away for a few moments, during some dark nights, and presently, one of the boats would be missing. There was no other remedy than to heave to immediately and set a light, by which the missing boat might be directed to us. These proceedings necessarily interfered very much with our speed, and consequently lessened our hopes; but we preferred to submit to it, while the consequences were not so immediately felt, rather than part with the consolation which each other's presence afforded. Nothing of importance took place on the 4th of December; and on the 5th, at night, owing to the extreme darkness, and a strong wind, I again separated from the other boats. Finding they were not to be seen in any direction, I loaded my pistol and fired it twice; soon after the second discharge they made their appearance a short distance to windward, and we joined company, and again kept on our course, in which we continued without any remarkable occurrence, through the 6th and 7th of December. The wind during this period blew very strong, and much more unfavourably. Our boats continued to leak, and to take in a good deal of water over the gunwales.

December 8th. In the afternoon of this day the wind set in E.SE. and began to blow much harder than we had yet experienced it; by twelve o'clock at night it had increased to a perfect gale, with heavy showers of rain, and we now began, from these dreadful indications, to prepare ourselves for destruction. We continued to take in sail by degrees, as the tempest gradually increased, until at last we were obliged to take down our masts. At this juncture we gave up entirely to the mercy of the waves. The sea and rain had wet us to the skin, and we sat down, silently, and with sullen resignation, awaiting our fate. We made an effort to catch some fresh water by spreading one of the sails, but after having spent a long time, and obtained but a small quantity in a bucket, it proved to be quite as salt as that from the ocean: this we attributed to its having passed through the sail which had been so often wet by the sea, and upon which, after drying so frequently in the sun, concretions of salt had been formed. It was a dreadful night—cut off from any imaginary relief—nothing remained but to await the approaching issue with firmness and resignation. The appearance of the heavens was dark and dreary, and the blackness that was spread over the face of the waters dismal beyond description. The heavy squalls, that followed each other in quick succession, were preceded by sharp flashes of lightning, that appeared to wrap our little barge in flames. The sea rose to a fearful height, and every wave that came looked as if it must be the last that would be necessary for our destruction. To an overruling Providence alone must be attributed our salvation from the horrors of that terrible night. It can be accounted for in no other way: that a speck of substance, like that which we were, before the driving terrors of the tempest, could have been conducted safely through it. At twelve o'clock it began to abate a little in intervals of two or three minutes, during which we would venture to raise up our heads and look to windward. Our boat was completely unmanageable; without sails, mast, or rudder, and had been driven, in the course of the afternoon and night, we knew not whither, nor how far. When the gale had in some measure subsided we made efforts to get a little sail upon her, and put her head towards the course we had been steering. My companions had not slept any during the whole night, and were dispirited and broken down to such a degree as to appear to want some more powerful stimulus than the fears of death to enable them to do their duty. By great exertions, however, towards morning we again set a double-reefed mainsail and jib upon her, and began to make tolerable progress on the voyage. An unaccountable good fortune had kept the boats together during all the troubles of the night: and the sun rose and showed the disconsolate faces of our companions once more to each other.

December 9th. By twelve o'clock this day we were enabled to set all sail as usual; but there continued to be a very heavy sea running, which opened the seams of the boats, and increased the leaks to an alarming degree. There was, however, no remedy for this but continual bailing, which had now become to be an extremely irksome and laborious task. By observation we found ourselves in latitude 17°40′ S. At eleven o'clock at night, the captain's boat was unexpectedly found to be missing. After the last accident of this kind we had agreed, if the same should again occur, that, in order to save our time, the other boats should not heave to, as usual, but continue on their course until morning, and thereby save the great detention that must arise from such repeated delays. We, however, concluded on this occasion to make a small effort, which, if it did not immediately prove the means of restoring the lost boat, we would discontinue, and again make sail. Accordingly we hove to for an hour, during which time I fired my pistol twice, and obtaining no tidings of the boat, we stood on our course. When daylight appeared she was to leeward of us, about two miles; upon observing her we immediately ran down, and again joined company.

December 10th. I have omitted to notice the gradual advances which hunger and thirst, for the last six days, had made upon us. As the time had lengthened since our departure from the wreck, and the allowance of provision, making the demands of the appetite daily more and more importunate, they had created in us an almost uncontrollable temptation to violate our resolution, and satisfy, for once, the hard yearnings of nature from our stock; but a little reflection served to convince us of the imprudence and unmanliness of the measure, and it was abandoned with a sort of melancholy effort of satisfaction. I had taken into custody, by common consent, all the provisions and water belonging to the boat, and was determined that no encroachments should be made upon it with my consent; nay, I felt myself bound, by every consideration of duty, by every dictate of sense, of prudence, and discretion, without which, in my situation, all other exertions would have been folly itself, to protect them, at the hazard of my life. For this purpose I locked up in my chest the whole quantity, and never, for a single moment, closed my eyes without placing some part of my person in contact with the chest; and having loaded my pistol, kept it constantly about me. I should not certainly have put any threats in execution as long as the most distant hopes of reconciliation existed; and was determined, in case the least refractory disposition should be manifested, (a thing which I contemplated not unlikely to happen, with a set of starving wretches like ourselves,) that I would immediately divide our subsistence into equal proportions, and give each man's share into his own keeping. Then, should any attempt be made upon mine, which I intended to mete out to myself, according to exigences, I was resolved to make the consequences of it fatal. There was, however, the most upright and obedient behaviour in this respect manifested by every man in the boat, and I never had the least opportunity of proving what my conduct would have been on such an occasion. While standing on our course this day we came across a small shoal of flying fish: four of which, in their efforts to avoid us, flew against the mainsail, and dropped into the boat; one, having fell near me, I eagerly snatched up and devoured; the other three were immediately taken by the rest, and eaten alive. For the first time I, on this occasion, felt a disposition to laugh, upon witnessing the ludicrous and almost desperate efforts of my five companions, who each sought to get a fish. They were very small of the kind, and constituted but an extremely delicate mouthful, scales, wings, and all for hungry stomachs like ours. From the eleventh to the thirteenth of December inclusive, our progress was very slow, owing to light winds and calms; and nothing transpired of any moment, except that on the eleventh we killed the only remaining turtle, and enjoyed another luxuriant repast, that invigorated our bodies, and gave a fresh flow to our spirits. The weather was extremely hot, and we were exposed to the full force of a meridian sun, without any covering to shield us from its burning influence, or the least breath of air to cool its parching rays. On the thirteenth day of December we were blessed with a change of wind to the northward, that brought us a most welcome and unlooked for relief.

We now, for the first time, actually felt what might be deemed a reasonable hope of our deliverance; and with hearts bounding with satisfaction, and bosoms swelling with joy, we made all sail to the eastward. We imagined we had run out of the trade-winds, and had got into the variables, and should, in all probability, reach the land many days sooner than we expected. But, alas! our anticipations were but a dream, from which we shortly experienced a cruel awaking. The wind gradually died away, and at night was succeeded by a perfect calm, more oppressive and disheartening to us, from the bright prospects which had attended us during the day. The gloomy reflections that this hard fortune had given birth to, were succeeded by others, of a no less cruel and discouraging nature, when we found the calm continue during the fourteenth, fifteenth, and sixteenth of December inclusive. The extreme oppression of the weather, the sudden and unexpected prostration of our hopes, and the consequent dejection of our spirits, set us again to thinking, and filled our souls with fearful and melancholy forebodings. In this state of affairs, seeing no alternative left us but to employ to the best advantage all human expedients in our power, I proposed, on the fourteenth, to reduce our allowance of provisions one half. No objections were made to this arrangement: all submitted, or seemed to do so, with an admirable fortitude and forbearance. The proportion which our stock of water bore to our bread was not large; and while the weather continued so oppressive, we did not think it adviseable to diminish our scanty pittance; indeed, it would have been scarcely possible to have done so, with any regard to our necessities, as our thirst had become now incessantly more intolerable than hunger, and the quantity then allowed was barely sufficient to keep the mouth in a state of moisture, for about one-third of the time. "Patience and long-suffering" was the constant language of our lips: and a determination, strong as the resolves of the soul could make it, to cling to existence as long as hope and breath remained to us. In vain was every expedient tried to relieve the raging fever of the throat by drinking salt water, and holding small quantities of it in the mouth, until, by that means, the thirst was increased to such a degree, as even to drive us to despairing, and vain relief from our own urine. Our sufferings during these calm days almost exceeded human belief. The hot rays of the sun beat down upon us to such a degree, as to oblige us to hang over the gunwale of the boat, into the sea, to cool our weak and fainting bodies. This expedient afforded us, however, a grateful relief, and was productive of a discovery of infinite importance to us. No sooner had one of us got on the outside of the gunwale than he immediately observed the bottom of the boat to be covered with a species of small clam, which, upon being tasted, proved a most delicious and agreeable food. This was no sooner announced to us, than we commenced to tear them off and eat them, for a few minutes, like a set of gluttons; and, after having satisfied the immediate craving of the stomach, we gathered large quantities and laid them up in the boat; but hunger came upon us again in less than half an hour afterwards, within which time they had all disappeared. Upon attempting to get in again, we found ourselves so weak as to require each other's assistance; indeed, had it not been for three of our crew, who could not swim, and who did not, therefore, get overboard, I know not by what means we should have been able to have resumed our situations in the boat.

On the fifteenth our boat continued to take in water so fast from her leaks, and the weather proving so moderate, we concluded to search out the bad places, and endeavour to mend them as well as we should be able. After a considerable search, and, removing the ceiling near the bows, we found the principal opening was occasioned by the starting of a plank or streak in the bottom of the boat, next to the keel. To remedy this, it was now absolutely necessary to have access to the bottom. The means of doing which did not immediately occur to our minds. After a moment's reflection, however, one of the crew, Benjamin Lawrence, offered to tie a rope around his body, take a boat's hatchet in his hand, and thus go under the water, and hold the hatchet against a nail, to be driven through from the inside, for the purpose of clenching it. This was, accordingly, all effected, with some little trouble, and answered the purpose much beyond our expectations. Our latitude was this day 21°42′ South. The oppression of the weather still continuing through the sixteenth, bore upon our health and spirits with an amazing force and severity. The most disagreeable excitements were produced by it, which, added to the disconsolate endurance of the calm, called loudly for some mitigating expedient,—some sort of relief to our prolonged sufferings. By our observations to day we found, in addition to our other calamities, that we had been urged back from our progress, by the heave of the sea, a distance of ten miles; and were still without any prospect of wind. In this distressing posture of our affairs, the captain proposed that we should commence rowing, which, being seconded by all, we immediately concluded to take a double allowance of provision and water for the day, and row, during the cool of the nights, until we should get a breeze from some quarter or other. Accordingly, when night came, we commenced our laborious operations: we made but a very sorry progress. Hunger and thirst, and long inactivity, had so weakened us, that in three hours every man gave out, and we abandoned the further prosecution of the plan. With the sunrise the next morning, on the seventeenth, a light breeze sprung up from the SE. and, although directly ahead, it was welcomed with almost frenzied feelings of gratitude and joy.

December 18th. The wind had increased this day considerably, and by twelve o'clock blew a gale; veering from SE. to E.SE. Again we were compelled to take in all sail, and lie to for the principal part of the day. At night, however, it died away, and the next day, the nineteenth, proved very moderate and pleasant weather, and we again commenced to make a little progress.

December 20th. This was a day of great happiness and joy. After having experienced one of the most distressing nights in the whole catalogue of our sufferings, we awoke to a morning of comparative luxury and pleasure. About 7 o'clock, while we were sitting dispirited, silent, and dejected, in our boats, one of our companions suddenly and loudly called out, "there is land!" We were all aroused in an instant, as if electrified, and casting our eyes to leeward, there indeed, was the blessed vision before us, "as plain and palpable" as could be wished for. A new and extraordinary impulse now took possession of us. We shook off the lethargy of our senses, and seemed to take another, and a fresh existence. One or two of my companions, whose lagging spirits, and worn out frames had begun to inspire them with an utter indifference to their fate, now immediately brightened up, and manifested a surprising alacrity and earnestness to gain, without delay, the much wished for shore. It appeared at first a low, white, beach, and lay like a basking paradise before our longing eyes. It was discovered nearly at the same time by the other boats, and a general burst of joy and congratulation now passed between us. It is not within the scope of human calculation, by a mere listener to the story, to divine what the feelings of our hearts were on this occasion. Alternate expectation, fear, gratitude, surprise, and exultation, each swayed our minds, and quickened our exertions. We ran down for it, and at 11 o'clock, A.M. we were within a quarter of a mile of the shore. It was an island, to all appearance, as nearly as we could determine it, about six miles long, and three broad; with a very high, rugged shore, and surrounded by rocks; the sides of the mountains were bare, but on the tops it looked fresh and green with vegetation. Upon examining our navigators, we found it was Ducie's Island, lying in latitude 24°40′ S. longitude 124°40′ W.[11] A short moment sufficed for reflection, and we made immediate arrangements to land. None of us knew whether the island was inhabited or not, nor what it afforded, if any thing; if inhabited, it was uncertain whether by beasts or savages; and a momentary suspense was created, by the dangers which might possibly arise by proceeding without due preparation and care. Hunger and thirst, however, soon determined us, and having taken the musket and pistols, I, with three others, effected a landing upon some sunken rocks, and waded thence to the shore. Upon arriving at the beach, it was necessary to take a little breath, and we laid down for a few minutes to rest our weak bodies, before we could proceed. Let the reader judge, if he can, what must have been our feelings now! Bereft of all comfortable hopes of life, for the space of thirty days of terrible suffering; our bodies wasted to mere skeletons, by hunger and thirst, and death itself staring us in the face; to be suddenly and unexpectedly conducted to a rich banquet of food and drink, which subsequently we enjoyed for a few days, to our full satisfaction; and he will have but a faint idea of the happiness that here fell to our lot. We now, after a few minutes, separated, and went different directions in search of water; the want of which had been our principal privation, and called for immediate relief. I had not proceeded far in my excursion, before I discovered a fish, about a foot and a half in length, swimming along in the water close to the shore. I commenced an attack upon him with the breach of my gun, and struck him, I believe, once, and he ran under a small rock, that lay near the shore, from whence I took him with the aid of my ramrod, and brought him up on the beach, and immediately fell to eating. My companions soon joined in the repast; and in less than ten minutes, the whole was consumed, bones, and skin, and scales, and all. With full stomachs, we imagined we could now attempt the mountains, where, if in any part of the island, we considered water would be most probably obtained. I accordingly clambered, with excessive labour, suffering, and pain, up amongst the bushes, roots, and underwood, of one of the crags, looking in all directions in vain, for every appearance of water that might present itself. There was no indication of the least moisture to be found, within the distance to which I had ascended, although my strength did not enable me to get higher than about 20 feet. I was sitting down at the height that I had attained, to gather a little breath, and ruminating upon the fruitlessness of my search, and the consequent evils and continuation of suffering that it necessarily implied, when I perceived that the tide had risen considerably since our landing, and threatened to cut off our retreat to the rocks, by which alone we should be able to regain our boats. I therefore determined to proceed again to the shore, and inform the captain and the rest of our want of success in procuring water, and consult upon the propriety of remaining at the island any longer. I never for one moment lost sight of the main chance, which I conceived we still had, of either getting to the coast, or of meeting with some vessel at sea; and felt that every minute's detention, without some equivalent object, was lessening those chances, by a consumption of the means of our support. When I had got down, one of my companions informed me, that he had found a place in a rock some distance off, from which the water exuded in small drops, at intervals of about five minutes; that he had, by applying his lips to the rock, obtained a few of them, which only served to whet his appetite, and from which nothing like the least satisfaction had proceeded. I immediately resolved in my own mind, upon this information, to advise remaining until morning, to endeavour to make a more thorough search the next day, and with our hatchets to pick away the rock which had been discovered, with the view of increasing, if possible, the run of the water. We all repaired again to our boats, and there found that the captain had the same impressions as to the propriety of our delay until morning. We therefore landed; and having hauled our boats up on the beach, laid down in them that night, free from all the anxieties of watching and labour, and amid all our sufferings, gave ourselves up to an unreserved forgetfulness and peace of mind, that seemed so well to accord with the pleasing anticipations that this day had brought forth. It was but a short space, however, until the morning broke upon us; and sense, and feeling, and gnawing hunger, and the raging fever of thirst then redoubled my wishes and efforts to explore the island again. We had obtained, that night, a few crabs, by traversing the shore a considerable distance, and a few very small fish; but waited until the next day, for the labours of which, we considered a night of refreshing and undisturbed repose would better qualify us.

December 21st. We had still reserved our common allowance, but it was entirely inadequate for the purpose of supplying the raging demand of the palate; and such an excessive and cruel thirst was created, as almost to deprive us of the power of speech. The lips became cracked and swollen, and a sort of glutinous saliva collected in the mouth, disagreeable to the taste, and intolerable beyond expression. Our bodies had wasted away to almost skin and bone, and possessed so little strength, as often to require each other's assistance in performing some of its weakest functions. Relief, we now felt, must come soon, or nature would sink. The most perfect discipline was still maintained, in respect to our provisions; and it now became our whole object, if we should not be able to replenish our subsistence from the island, to obtain, by some means or other, a sufficient refreshment to enable us to prosecute our voyage.

Our search for water accordingly again commenced with the morning; each of us took a different direction, and prosecuted the examination of every place where there was the least indication of it; the small leaves of the shrubbery, affording a temporary alleviation, by being chewed in the mouth, and but for the peculiarly bitter taste which those of the island possessed, would have been an extremely grateful substitute. In the course of our rambles too, along the sides of the mountain, we would now and then meet with tropic birds, of a beautiful figure and plumage, occupying small holes in the sides of it, from which we plucked them without the least difficulty. Upon our approaching them they made no attempts to fly, nor did they appear to notice us at all. These birds served us for a fine repast; numbers of which were caught in the course of the day, cooked by fires which we made on the shore, and eaten with the utmost avidity. We found also a plant, in taste not unlike the peppergrass, growing in considerable abundance in the crevices of the rocks, and which proved to us a very agreeable food, by being chewed with the meat of the birds. These, with birds' nests, some of them full of young, and others of eggs, a few of which we found in the course of the day, served us for food, and supplied the place of our bread; from the use of which, during our stay here, we had restricted ourselves. But water, the great object of all our anxieties and exertions, was no where to be found, and we began to despair of meeting with it on the island. Our state of extreme weakness, and many of us without shoes or any covering for the feet, prevented us from exploring any great distance; lest by some sudden faintness, or over exertion, we should not be able to return, and at night be exposed to attacks of wild beasts, which might inhabit the island, and be alike incapable of resistance, as beyond the reach of the feeble assistance that otherwise could be afforded to each. The whole day was thus consumed in picking up whatever had the least shape or quality of sustenance, and another night of misery was before us, to be passed without a drop of water to cool our parching tongues. In this state of affairs, we could not reconcile it to ourselves to remain longer at this place; a day, and hour, lost to us unnecessarily here, might cost us our preservation. A drop of the water that we then had in our possession might prove, in the last stages of our debility, the very cordial of life. I addressed the substance of these few reflections to the captain, who agreed with me in opinion, upon the necessity of taking some decisive steps in our present dilemma. After some considerable conversation on this subject, it was finally concluded, to spend the succeeding day in the

further search for water, and if none should be found, to quit the
island the morning after.

December 22d. We had been employed during the last night in
various occupations, according to the feelings or the wants of the
men; some continued to wander about the shore, and to short
distances in the mountains, still seeking for food and water; others
hung about the beach, near the edge of the sea, endeavouring to take
the little fish that came about them. Some slept, insensible to every
feeling but rest; while others spent the night in talking of their
situation, and reasoning upon the probabilities of their deliverance.
The dawn of day aroused us again to labour, and each of us
pursued his own inclination, as to the course taken over the island
after water. My principal hope was founded upon my success in
picking the rocks where the moisture had been discovered the day
before, and thither I hastened as soon as my strength would enable
me to get there. It was about a quarter of a mile from what I may
call our encampment; and with two men, who had accompanied me,
I commenced my labours with a hatchet and an old chissel. The
rock proved to be very soft, and in a very short time I had obtained
a considerable hole, but, alas! without the least wished-for effect. I
watched it for some little time with great anxiety, hoping that, as I
increased the depth of the hole, the water would presently flow; but
all my hopes and efforts were unavailing, and at last I desisted from
further labour, and sat down near it in utter despair. As I turned
my eyes towards the beach I saw some of the men in the act of
carrying a keg along from the boats, with, I thought, an extraordinary spirit and activity; and the idea suddenly darted across my
mind that they had found water, and were taking a keg to fill it. I
quitted my seat in a moment, made the best of my way towards
them, with a palpitating heart, and before I came up with them,
they gave me the cheering news that they had found a spring of water.
I felt, at that moment, as if I could have fallen down and thanked God
for this signal act of his mercy. The sensation that I experienced was
indeed strange, and such as I shall never forget. At one instant I felt
an almost choking excess of joy, and at the next I wanted the relief of
a flood of tears. When I arrived at the spot, whither I had hastened as
fast as my weak legs would carry me, I found my companions had all

taken their fill, and with an extreme degree of forbearance I then satisfied myself, by drinking in small quantities, and at intervals of two or three minutes apart. Many had, notwithstanding the remonstrances of prudence, and, in some cases, force, laid down and thoughtlessly swallowed large quantities of it, until they could drink no more. The effect of this was, however, neither so sudden nor bad as we had imagined; it only served to make them a little stupid and indolent for the remainder of the day.

Upon examining the place from whence we had obtained this miraculous and unexpected succour, we were equally astonished and delighted with the discovery. It was on the shore, above which the sea flowed to the depth of near six feet; and we could procure the water, therefore, from it only when the tide was down. The crevice from which it rose was in a flat rock, large surfaces of which were spread around, and composed the face of the beach. We filled our two kegs before the tide rose, and went back again to our boats. The remainder of this day was spent in seeking for fish, crabs, birds, and any thing else that fell in our way, that could contribute to satisfy our appetites; and we enjoyed, during that night, a most comfortable and delicious sleep, unattended with those violent cravings of hunger and thirst, that had poisoned our slumbers for so many previous ones. Since the discovery of the water, too, we began to entertain different notions altogether of our situation. There was no doubt we might here depend upon a constant and ample supply of it as long as we chose to remain, and, in all probability, we could manage to obtain food, until the island should be visited by some vessel, or time allowed to devise other means of leaving it. Our boats would still remain to us: a stay here might enable us to mend, strengthen, and put them in more perfect order for the sea, and get ourselves so far recruited as to be able to endure, if necessary, a more protracted voyage to the main land. I made a silent determination in my own mind that I would myself pursue something like this plan, whatever might be the opinion of the rest; but I found no difference in the views of any of us as to this matter. We, therefore, concluded to remain at least four or five days, within which time it could be sufficiently known whether it would be adviseable to make any arrangement for a more permanent abode.

December 23d. At 11 o'clock, A.M. we again visited our spring: the tide had fallen to about a foot below it, and we were able to procure, before it rose again, about twenty gallons of water. It was at first a little brackish, but soon became fresh, from the constant supply from the rock, and the departure of the sea. Our observations this morning tended to give us every confidence in its quantity and quality, and we, therefore, rested perfectly easy in our minds on the subject, and commenced to make further discoveries about the island. Each man sought for his own daily living, on whatsoever the mountains, the shore, or the sea, could furnish him with; and every day, during our stay there, the whole time was employed in roving about for food. We found, however, on the twenty-fourth, that we had picked up, on the island, every thing that could be got at, in the way of sustenance; and, much to our surprise, some of the men came in at night and complained of not having gotten sufficient during the day to satisfy the cravings of their stomachs. Every accessible part of the mountain, contiguous to us, or within the reach of our weak enterprise, was already ransacked, for birds' eggs and grass, and was rifled of all that they contained: so that we began to entertain serious apprehensions that we should not be able to live long here; at any rate, with the view of being prepared, as well as possible, should necessity at any time oblige us to quit it, we commenced, on the twenty-fourth, to repair our boats, and continued to work upon them all that and the succeeding day. We were enabled to do this, with much facility, by drawing them up and turning them over on the beach, working by spells of two or three hours at a time, and then leaving off to seek for food. We procured our water daily, when the tide would leave the shore: but on the evening of the twenty-fifth, found that a fruitless search for nourishment had not repaid us for the labours of a whole day. There was no one thing on the island upon which we could in the least degree rely, except the peppergrass, and of that the supply was precarious, and not much relished without some other food. Our situation here, therefore, now became worse than it would have been in our boats on the ocean; because, in the latter case, we should be still making some progress towards the land, while our provisions lasted, and the chance of falling in with some vessel be considerably increased. It was certain that we ought not to remain here unless upon the strongest assurances in our own minds, of sufficient sustenance, and that, too, in regular supplies, that might be depended upon. After much conversation amongst us on this subject, and again examining our navigators, it was finally concluded to set sail for Easter Island, which we found to be E.SE. from us in latitude 27°9′ S. longitude 109°35′ W. All we knew of this island was, that it existed as laid down in the books; but of its extent, productions, or inhabitants, if any, we were entirely ignorant; at any rate, it was nearer by eight hundred and fifty miles to the coast, and could not be worse in its productions than the one we were about leaving.

The twenty-sixth of December was wholly employed in preparations for our departure; our boats were hauled down to the vicinity of the spring, and our casks, and every thing else that would contain it, filled with water.

There had been considerable talk between three of our companions, about their remaining on this island, and taking their chance both for a living, and an escape from it; and as the time drew near at which we were to leave, they made up their minds to stay behind. The rest of us could make no objection to their plan, as it lessened the load of our boats, allowed us their share of the provisions, and the probability of their being able to sustain themselves on the island was much stronger than that of our reaching the main land. Should we, however, ever arrive safely, it would become our duty, and we so assured them, to give information of their situation, and make every effort to procure their removal from thence; which we accordingly afterwards did.

Their names were William Wright of Barnstable, Massachusetts, Thomas Chapple of Plymouth, England, and Seth Weeks of the former place. They had begun, before we came away, to construct a sort of habitation, composed of the branches of trees, and we left with them every little article that could be spared from the boats. It was their intention to build a considerable dwelling, that would protect them from the rains, as soon as time and materials could be provided. The captain wrote letters, to be left on the island, giving information of the fate of the ship, and that of our own; and stating that we had set out to reach Easter Island, with further particulars, intended to give notice (should our fellow-sufferers die there, and the place be ever visited by any vessel,) of our misfortunes. These letters were put in a tin case, enclosed in a small wooden box, and nailed to a tree, on the west side of the island, near our landing place. We had observed, some days previously, the name of a ship, "The Elizabeth," cut out in the bark of this tree, which rendered it indubitable that one of that name had once touched here. There was, however, no date to it, or any thing else, by which any further particulars could be made out.

December 27th. I went, before we set sail this morning, and procured for each boat a flat stone, and two arms-full of wood, with which to make a fire in our boats, should it become afterwards necessary in the further prosecution of our voyage; as we calculated we might catch a fish, or a bird, and in that case be provided with the means of cooking it; otherwise, from the intense heat of weather, we knew they could not be preserved from spoiling. At ten o'clock, A.M. the tide having risen far enough to allow our boats to float over the rocks, we made all sail, and steered around the island, for the purpose of making a little further observation, which would not detain us any time, and might be productive of some unexpected good fortune. Before we started we missed our three companions, and found they had not come down, either to assist us to get off, nor to take any kind of leave of us. I walked up the beach towards their rude dwelling, and informed them that we were then about to set sail, and should probably never see them more. They seemed to be very much affected, and one of them shed tears. They wished us to write to their relations, should Providence safely direct us again to our homes, and said but little else. They had every confidence in being able to procure a subsistence there as long as they remained: and, finding them ill at heart about taking any leave of us, I hastily bid them "good-bye," hoped they would do well, and came away. They followed me with their eyes until I was out of sight, and I never saw more of them.[12]

On the NW. side of the island we perceived a fine white beach, on which we imagined we might land, and in a short time ascertain if any further useful discoveries could be effected, or any addition made to our stock of provisions; and having set ashore five or six of the men for this purpose, the rest of us shoved off the boats and commenced fishing. We saw a number of sharks, but all efforts to take them proved ineffectual; and we got but a few small fish, about the size of a mackerel, which we divided amongst us. In this business we were occupied for the remainder of the day, until six o'clock in the afternoon, when the men, having returned to the shore from their search in the mountains, brought a few birds, and we again set sail and steered directly for Easter Island. During that night, after we had got quite clear of the land, we had a fine strong breeze from the NW.; we kept our fires going, and cooked our fish and birds, and felt our situation as comfortable as could be expected. We continued on our course, consuming our provisions and water as sparingly as possible, without any material incident, until the thirtieth, when the wind hauled out E.SE. directly ahead, and so continued until the thirty-first, when it again came to the northward, and we resumed our course.

On the third of January we experienced heavy squalls from the W.SW. accompanied with dreadful thunder and lightning, that threw a gloomy and cheerless aspect over the ocean, and incited a recurrence of some of those heavy and desponding moments that we had before experienced. We commenced from Ducies Island to keep a regular reckoning, by which, on the fourth of January, we found we had got to the southward of Easter Island, and the wind prevailing E.NE. we should not be able to get on to the eastward, so as to reach it.[13] Our birds and fish were all now consumed, and we had begun again upon our short allowance of bread. It was necessary, in this state of things, to change our determination of going to Easter Island, and shape our course in some other direction, where the wind would allow of our going. We had but little hesitation in concluding, therefore, to steer for the island of Juan Fernandez, which lay about E.SE. from us, distant two thousand five hundred miles. We bent our course accordingly towards it, having for the two succeeding days very light winds, and suffering excessively from the intense heat of the sun. The seventh brought us a change of wind to the northward, and at twelve o'clock we found ourselves in latitude 30°18′ S. longitude 117°29′ W. We continued to make what progress we could to the eastward.

January 10th. Matthew P. Joy, the second mate, had suffered from debility, and the privations we had experienced, much beyond any of the rest of us, and was on the eighth removed to the captain's boat, under the impression that he would be more comfortable there, and more attention and pains be bestowed in nursing and endeavouring to comfort him. This day being calm, he manifested a desire to be taken back again; but at 4 o'clock in the afternoon, after having been, according to his wishes, placed in his own boat, he died very suddenly after his removal. On the eleventh, at six o'clock in the morning, we sewed him up in his clothes, tied a large stone to his feet, and, having brought all the boats to, consigned him in a solemn manner to the ocean. This man did not die of absolute starvation, although his end was no doubt very much hastened by his sufferings. He had a weak and sickly constitution, and complained of being unwell the whole voyage. It was an incident, however, which threw a gloom over our feelings for many days. In consequence of his death, one man from the captain's boat was placed in that from which he died, to supply his place, and we stood away again on our course.

On the 12th of Jan. we had the wind from the NW. which commenced in the morning, and came on to blow before night a perfect gale. We were obliged to take in all sail and run before the wind. Flashes of lightning were quick and vivid, and the rain came down in cataracts. As however the gale blew us fairly on our course, and our speed being great during the day, we derived, I may say, even pleasure from the uncomfortableness and fury of the storm. We were apprehensive that in the darkness of this night we should be separated, and made arrangements, each boat to keep an E.SE. course all night. About eleven o'clock my boat being ahead a short distance of the others, I turned my head back, as I was in the habit of doing every minute, and neither of the others were to be seen. It was blowing and raining at this time as if the heavens were separating, and I knew not hardly at the moment what to do. I hove my boat to the wind, and lay drifting about an hour, expecting every moment that they would come up with me, but not seeing any thing of them, I put away again, and stood on the course agreed upon, with strong hopes that daylight would enable me to discover them again. When the morning dawned, in vain did we look over every part of the ocean for our companions; they were gone! and we saw no more of them afterwards. It was folly to repine at the circumstances; it could neither be remedied, nor could sorrow secure their return; but it was impossible to prevent ourselves feeling all the poignancy and bitterness that characterizes the separation of men who have long suffered in each other's company, and whose interests and feelings fate had so closely linked together. By our observation, we separated in lat. 32°16′ S. long. 112°20′ W.[14] For many days after this accident, our progress was attended with dull and melancholy reflections. We had lost the cheering of each other's faces, that, which strange as it is, we so much required in both our mental and bodily distresses. The 14th January proved another very squally and rainy day. We had now been nineteen days from the island, and had only made a distance of about 900 miles: necessity began to whisper us, that a still further reduction of our allowance must take place, or we must abandon altogether the hopes of reaching the land, and rely wholly on the chance of being taken up by a vessel. But how to reduce the daily quantity of food, with any regard to life itself, was a question of the utmost consequence. Upon our first leaving the wreck, the demands of the stomach had been circumscribed to the smallest possible compass; and subsequently before reaching the island, a diminution had taken place of nearly one-half; and it was now, from a reasonable calculation, become necessary even to curtail that at least one-half; which must, in a short time, reduce us to mere skeletons again. We had a full allowance of water, but it only served to contribute to our debility; our bodies deriving but the scanty support which an ounce and a half of bread for each man afforded. It required a great effort to bring matters to this dreadful alternative, either to feed our bodies and our hopes a little longer, or in the agonies of hunger to seize upon and devour our provisions, and coolly await the approach of death.

We were as yet, just able to move about in our boats, and slowly perform the necessary labours appertaining to her; but we were fast wasting away with the relaxing effects of the water, and we daily almost perished under the torrid rays of a meridian sun; to escape

which, we would lie down in the bottom of the boat, cover ourselves
over with the sails, and abandon her to the mercy of the waves.
Upon attempting to rise again, the blood would rush into the head,
and an intoxicating blindness come over us, almost to occasion our
suddenly falling down again. A slight interest was still kept up in
our minds by the distant hopes of yet meeting with the other boats,
but it was never realized. An accident occurred at night, which gave
me a great cause of uneasiness, and led me to an unpleasant rumi-
nation upon the probable consequences of a repetition of it. I had
laid down in the boat without taking the usual precaution of securing the lid of the provision-chest, as I was accustomed to do, when
one of the white men awoke me, and informed me that one the
blacks had taken some bread from it. I felt at the moment the
highest indignation and resentment at such conduct in any of our
crew, and immediately took my pistol in my hand, and charged him
if he had taken any, to give it up without the least hesitation, or I
should instantly shoot him!—He became at once very much
alarmed, and, trembling, confessed the fact, pleading the hard
necessity that urged him to it: he appeared to be very penitent for
his crime, and earnestly swore that he would never be guilty of it
again. I could not find it in my soul to extend towards him the least
severity on this account, however much, according to the strict
imposition which we felt upon ourselves it might demand it. This
was the first infraction; and the security of our lives, our hopes of
redemption from our sufferings, loudly called for a prompt and
signal punishment; but every humane feeling of nature plead in his
behalf, and he was permitted to escape, with the solemn injunction,
that a repetition of the same offence would cost him his life.

I had almost determined upon this occurrence to divide our provisions, and give to each man his share of the whole stock; and should
have done so in the height of my resentment, had it not been for the
reflection that some might, by imprudence, be tempted to go beyond
the daily allowance, or consume it all at once, and bring on a premature weakness or starvation: this would of course disable them
for the duties of the boat, and reduce our chances of safety and
deliverance.

On the 15th of January, at night, a very large shark was observed swimming about us in a most ravenous manner, making attempts every now and then upon different parts of the boat, as if he would devour the very wood with hunger; he came several times and snapped at the steering oar, and even the stern-post. We tried in vain to stab him with a lance, but were so weak as not to be able to make any impression upon his hard skin; he was so much larger than an ordinary one, and manifested such a fearless malignity, as to make us afraid of him; and our utmost efforts, which were at first directed to kill him for prey, became in the end self-defence. Baffled however in all his hungry attempts upon us, he shortly made off.

On the 16th of January, we were surrounded with porpoises in great numbers, that followed us nearly an hour, and which also defied all manoeuvres to catch them. The 17th and 18th proved to be calm; and the distresses of a cheerless prospect and a burning hot sun, were again visited upon our devoted heads.

We began to think that Divine Providence had abandoned us at last; and it was but an unavailing effort to endeavour to prolong a now tedious existence. Horrible were the feelings that took possession of us!—The contemplation of a death of agony and torment, refined by the most dreadful and distressing reflections, absolutely prostrated both body and soul. There was not a hope now remaining to us but that which was derived from a sense of the mercies of our Creator. The night of the 18th was a despairing era in our sufferings; our minds were wrought up to the highest pitch of dread and apprehension for our fate, and all in them was dark, gloomy, and confused. About 8 o'clock, the terrible noise of whale-spouts near us sounded in our ears: we could distinctly hear the furious thrashing of their tails in the water, and our weak minds pictured out their appalling and hideous aspects. One of my companions, the black man, took an immediate fright, and solicited me to take out the oars, and endeavour to get away from them. I consented to his using any means for that purpose; but alas! it was wholly out of our power to raise a single arm in our own defence. Two or three of the whales came down near us, and went swiftly off across our stern, blowing and spouting at a terrible rate; they, however, after an hour or two disappeared, and we saw no more of them. The next day, the 19th of January, we had extremely boisterous weather, with rain, heavy thunder and lightning, which reduced us again to the necessity of taking in all sail and lying to. The wind blew from every point of the compass within the twenty-four hours, and at last towards the next morning settled at E.NE. a strong breeze.

January 20. The black man, Richard Peterson, manifested to day symptoms of a speedy dissolution; he had been lying between the seats in the boat, utterly dispirited and broken down, without being able to do the least duty, or hardly to place his hand to his head for the last three days, and had this morning made up his mind to die rather than endure further misery: he refused his allowance; said he was sensible of his approaching end, and was perfectly ready to die: in a few minutes he became speechless, the breath appeared to be leaving his body without producing the least pain, and at four o'clock he was gone. I had two days previously, conversations with him on the subject of religion, on which he reasoned very sensibly, and with much composure; and begged me to let his wife know his fate, if ever I reached home in safety. The next morning we committed him to the sea, in latitude 35°07′ S. longitude 105°46′ W. The wind prevailed to the eastward until the 24th of January, when it again fell calm. We were now in a most wretched and sinking state of debility, hardly able to crawl around the boat, and possessing but strength enough to convey our scanty morsel to our mouths. When I perceived this morning that it was calm, my fortitude almost forsook me. I thought to suffer another scorching day, like the last we had experienced, would close before night the scene of our miseries; and I felt many a despairing moment that day, that had well nigh proved fatal. It required an effort to look calmly forward, and contemplate what was yet in store for us, beyond what I felt I was capable of making; and what it was that bouyed me above all the terrors which surrounded us, God alone knows. Our ounce and a half of bread, which was to serve us all day, was in some cases greedily devoured, as if life was to continue but another moment; and at other times, it was hoarded up and eaten crumb by crumb, at regular intervals during the day, as if it was to last us for ever. To add to our calamities, biles began to break out upon us, and our imaginations shortly became as diseased as our bodies. I laid down at night to catch a few moments of oblivious sleep, and immediately my starving fancy was at work. I dreamt of being placed near a splendid and rich repast, where there was every thing that the most dainty appetite could desire; and of contemplating the moment in which we were to commence to eat with enraptured feelings of delight; and just as I was about to partake of it, I suddenly awoke to the cold realities of my miserable situation. Nothing could have oppressed me so much. It set such a longing frenzy for victuals in my mind, that I felt as if I could have wished the dream to continue for ever, that I never might have awoke from it. I cast a sort of vacant stare about the boat, until my eyes rested upon a bit of tough cow-hide, which was fastened to one of the oars; I eagerly seized and commenced to chew it, but there was no substance in it, and it only served to fatigue my weak jaws, and add to my bodily pains. My fellow sufferers murmured very much the whole time, and continued to press me continually with questions upon the probability of our reaching land again. I kept constantly rallying my spirits to enable me to afford them comfort. I encouraged them to bear up against all evils, and if we must perish, to die in our own cause, and not weakly distrust the providence of the Almighty, by giving ourselves up to despair. I reasoned with them, and told them that we would not die sooner by keeping up our hopes; that the dreadful sacrifices and privations we endured were to preserve us from death, and were not to be put in competition with the price which we set upon our lives, and their value to our families: it was, besides, unmanly to repine at what neither admitted of alleviation nor cure; and withal, that it was our solemn duty to recognise in our calamities an overruling divinity, by whose mercy we might be suddenly snatched from peril, and to rely upon him alone, "Who tempers the wind to the shorn lamb."

The three following days, the 25th, 26th, and 27th, were not distinguished by any particular circumstances. The wind still prevailed to the eastward, and by its obduracy, almost tore the very hopes of our hearts away: it was impossible to silence the rebellious repinings of our nature, at witnessing such a succession of hard fortune against us. It was our cruel lot not to have had one bright anticipation realized—not one wish of our thirsting souls gratified. We had, at the end of these three days, been urged to the southward as far as latitude 36° into a chilly region, where rains and squalls prevailed; and we now calculated to tack and stand back to the northward: after much labour, we got our boat about; and so great was the fatigue attending this small exertion of our bodies, that we all gave up for a moment and abandoned her to her own course.—Not one of us had now strength sufficient to steer, or indeed to make one single effort towards getting the sails properly trimmed, to enable us to make any headway. After an hour or two of relaxation, during which the horrors of our situation came upon us with a despairing force and effect, we made a sudden effort and got our sails into such a disposition, as that the boat would steer herself; and we then threw ourselves down awaiting the issue of time to bring us relief, or to take us from the scene of our troubles. We could now do nothing more; strength and spirits were totally gone; and what indeed could have been the narrow hopes, that in our situation, then bound us to life?

January 28. Our spirits this morning were hardly sufficient to allow of our enjoying a change of the wind, which took place to the westward.—It had nearly become indifferent to us from what quarter it blew: nothing but the slight chance of meeting with a vessel remained to us now: it was this narrow comfort alone, that prevented me from lying down at once to die. But fourteen days' stinted allowance of provisions remained, and it was absolutely necessary to increase the quantity to enable us to live five days longer: we therefore partook of it, as pinching necessity demanded, and gave ourselves wholly up to the guidance and disposal of our Creator.

The 29th and 30th of January, the wind continued west, and we made considerable progress until the 31st, when it again came ahead, and prostrated all our hopes. On the 1st of February, it changed again to the westward, and on the 2d and 3d blew to the eastward; and we had it light and variable until the 8th of February. Our sufferings were now drawing to a close; a terrible death appeared shortly to await us; hunger became violent and outrageous, and we prepared for a speedy release from our troubles; our speech and reason were both considerably impaired, and we were

reduced to be at this time, certainly the most helpless and wretched
of the whole human race. Isaac Cole, one of our crew, had the day
before this, in a fit of despair, thrown himself down in the boat, and
was determined there calmly to wait for death. It was obvious that
he had no chance; all was dark he said in his mind, not a single ray
of hope was left for him to dwell upon; and it was folly and madness to be struggling against what appeared so palpably to be our
fixed and settled destiny. I remonstrated with him as effectually as
the weakness both of my body and understanding would allow of;
and what I said appeared for a moment to have a considerable
effect: he made a powerful and sudden effort, half rose up, crawled
forward and hoisted the jib, and firmly and loudly cried that he
would not give up; that he would live as long as the rest of us—but
alas! this effort was but the hectic fever of the moment, and he
shortly again relapsed into a state of melancholy and despair. This
day his reason was attacked, and he became about 9 o'clock in the
morning a most miserable spectacle of madness: he spoke
incoherently about every thing, calling loudly for a napkin and
water, and then lying stupidly and senselessly down in the boat
again, would close his hollow eyes, as if in death. About 10 o'clock,
we suddenly perceived that he became speechless; we got him as
well as we were able upon a board, placed on one of the seats of the
boat, and covering him up with some old clothes, left him to his
fate. He lay in the greatest pain and apparent misery, groaning
piteously until four o'clock, when he died, in the most horrid and
frightful convulsions I ever witnessed. We kept his corpse all night,
and in the morning my two companions began as of course to make
preparations to dispose of it in the sea; when after reflecting on the
subject all night, I addressed them on the painful subject of keeping
the body for food!! Our provisions could not possibly last us beyond
three days, within which time, it was not in any degree probable
that we should find relief from our present sufferings, and that
hunger would at last drive us to the necessity of casting lots. It was
without any objection agreed to, and we set to work as fast as we
were able to prepare it so as to prevent its spoiling. We separated
his limbs from his body, and cut all the flesh from the bones; after
which, we opened the body, took out the heart, and then closed it

again—sewed it up as decently as we could, and committed it to the sea. We now first commenced to satisfy the immediate craving of nature from the heart, which we eagerly devoured, and then eat sparingly of a few pieces of the flesh; after which, we hung up the remainder, cut in thin strips about the boat, to dry in the sun: we made a fire and roasted some of it, to serve us during the next day. In this manner did we dispose of our fellow-sufferer; the painful recollection of which, brings to mind at this moment, some of the most disagreeable and revolting ideas that it is capable of conceiving. We knew not then, to whose lot it would fall next, either to die or be shot, and eaten like the poor wretch we had just dispatched. Humanity must shudder at the dreadful recital. I have no language to paint the anguish of our souls in this dreadful dilemma. The next morning, the 10th of February, we found that the flesh had become tainted, and had turned of a greenish colour, upon which we concluded to make a fire and cook it at once, to prevent its becoming so putrid as not to be eaten at all: we accordingly did so, and by that means preserved it for six or seven days longer; our bread during the time, remained untouched; as that would not be liable to spoil, we placed it carefully aside for the last moments of our trial. About three o'clock this afternoon a strong breeze set in from the NW. and we made very good progress, considering that we were compelled to steer the boat by management of the sails alone: this wind continued until the thirteenth, when it changed again ahead. We contrived to keep soul and body together by sparingly partaking of our flesh, cut up in small pieces and eaten with salt-water. By the fourteenth, our bodies became so far recruited, as to enable us to make a few attempts at guiding our boat again with the oar; by each taking his turn, we managed to effect it, and to make a tolerable good course. On the fifteenth, our flesh was all consumed, and we were driven to the last morsel of bread, consisting of two cakes; our limbs had for the last two days swelled very much, and now began to pain us most excessively. We were still, as near as we could judge, three hundred miles from the land, and but three days of our allowance on hand. The hope of a continuation of the wind, which came out at west this morning, was the only comfort and solace that remained to us: so strong had our desires at last reached in this respect, that a high

fever had set in, in our veins, and a longing that nothing but its continuation could satisfy. Matters were now with us at their height;
all hope was cast upon the breeze; and we tremblingly and fearfully
awaited its progress, and the dreadful development of our destiny.
On the sixteenth, at night, full of the horrible reflections of our
situation, and panting with weakness, I laid down to sleep, almost
indifferent whether I should ever see the light again. I had not lain
long, before I dreamt I saw a ship at some distance off from us, and
strained every nerve to get to her, but could not. I awoke almost
overpowered with the frenzy I had caught in my slumbers, and
stung with the cruelties of a diseased and disappointed imagination.
On the seventeenth, in the afternoon, a heavy cloud appeared to be
settling down in an E. by N. direction from us, which in my view,
indicated the vicinity of some land, which I took for the island of
Massafuera. I concluded it could be no other; and immediately
upon this reflection, the life blood began to flow again briskly in my
veins. I told my companions that I was well convinced it was land,
and if so, in all probability we would reach it before two days more.
My words appeared to comfort them much; and by repeated
assurances of the favourable appearance of things, their spirits
acquired even a degree of elasticity that was truly astonishing. The
dark features of our distress began now to diminish a little, and the
countenance, even amid the gloomy bodings of our hard lot, to
assume a much fresher hue. We directed our course for the cloud,
and our progress that night was extremely good. The next morning,
before daylight, Thomas Nicholson, a boy about seventeen years of
age, one of my two companions who had thus far survived with me,
after having bailed the boat, laid down, drew a piece of canvass over
him, and cried out, that he then wished to die immediately. I saw
that he had given up, and I attempted to speak a few words of
comfort and encouragement to him, and endeavoured to persuade
him that it was a great weakness and even wickedness to abandon a
reliance upon the Almighty, while the least hope, and a breath of
life remained; but he felt unwilling to listen to any of the consolatory suggestions which I made to him; and, notwithstanding the
extreme probability which I stated there was of our gaining the land
before the end of two days more, he insisted upon lying down and

giving himself up to despair. A fixed look of settled and forsaken despondency came over his face: he lay for some time silent, sullen, and sorrowful—and I felt at once satisfied, that the coldness of death was fast gathering upon him: there was a sudden and unaccountable earnestness in his manner, that alarmed me, and made me fear that I myself might unexpectedly be overtaken by a like weakness, or dizziness of nature, that would bereave me at once of both reason and life; but Providence willed it otherwise.

At about seven o'clock this morning, while I was lying asleep, my companion who was steering, suddenly and loudly called out *"There's a Sail!"* I know not what was the first movement I made upon hearing such an unexpected cry: the earliest of my recollections are, that immediately I stood up, gazing in a state of abstraction and ecstasy upon the blessed vision of a vessel about seven miles off from us; she was standing in the same direction with us, and the only sensation I felt at the moment was, that of a violent and unaccountable impulse to fly directly towards her. I do not believe it is possible to form a just conception of the pure, strong feelings, and the unmingled emotions of joy and gratitude, that took possession of my mind on this occasion: the boy, too, took a sudden and animated start from his despondency, and stood up to witness the probable instrument of his salvation. Our only fear was now, that she would not discover us, or that we might not be able to intercept her course: we, however, put our boat immediately, as well as we were able, in a direction to cut her off; and found, to our great joy, that we sailed faster than she did. Upon observing us, she shortened sail, and allowed us to come up to her. The captain hailed us, and asked who we were. I told him we were from a wreck, and he cried out immediately for us to come alongside the ship. I made an effort to assist myself along to the side, for the purpose of getting up, but strength failed me altogether, and I found it impossible to move a step further without help. We must have formed at that moment, in the eyes of the captain and his crew, a most deplorable and affecting picture of suffering and misery. Our cadaverous countenances, sunken eyes, and bones just starting through the skin, with the ragged remnants of clothes stuck about our sun-burnt bodies, must have produced an appearance to him affecting and revolting in the highest degree. The sailors commenced to remove us from our boat, and we were taken to the cabin, and comfortably provided for in every respect. In a few minutes we were permitted to taste of a little thin food, made from tapiocha, and in a few days, with prudent management, we were considerably recruited. This vessel proved to be the brig Indian, captain William Crozier, of London; to whom we are indebted for every polite, friendly, and attentive disposition towards us, that can possibly characterize a man of humanity and feeling. We were taken up in latitude 33°45´ S. longitude 81°03´ W. At twelve o'clock this day we saw the island of Massafuera, and on the 25th of February, we arrived at Valparaiso in utter distress and poverty. Our wants were promptly relieved there.

The captain and the survivers of his boat's crew, were taken up by the American whale-ship, the Dauphin, Captain Zimri Coffin, of Nantucket, and arrived at Valparaiso on the seventeenth of March following: he was taken up in latitude 37° S. off the island of St. Mary. The third boat got separated from him on the 28th of January, and has not been heard of since. The names of all the survivers, are as follows:—Captain George Pollard, junr. Charles Ramsdale, Owen Chase, Benjamin Lawrence, and Thomas Nicholson, all of Nantucket. There died in the captain's boat, the following: Brazilla Ray of Nantucket, Owen Coffin of the same place, who was shot, and Samuel Reed, a black.

The captain relates, that after being separated, as herein before stated, they continued to make what progress they could towards the island of Juan Fernandez, as was agreed upon; but contrary winds and the extreme debility of the crew prevailed against their united exertions. He was with us equally surprised and concerned at the separation that took place between us; but continued on his course, almost confident of meeting with us again. On the fourteenth, the whole stock of provisions belonging to the second mate's boat, was entirely exhausted, and on the twenty-fifth, the black man, Lawson Thomas, died, and was eaten by his surviving companions.[15] On the twenty-first, the captain and his crew were in the like dreadful situation with respect to their provisions; and on the twenty-third, another coloured man, Charles Shorter, died out of the same boat, and his body was shared for food between the crews of both boats.

On the twenty-seventh, another, Isaac Shepherd, (a black man,) died in the third boat; and on the twenty-eight, another black, named Samuel Reed, died out of the captain's boat. The bodies of these men constituted their only food while it lasted; and on the twenty-ninth, owing to the darkenss of the night and want of sufficient power to manage their boats, those of the captain and second mate separated in latitude 35° S. longitude 100° W. On the 1st of February, having consumed the last morsel, the captain and the three other men that remained with him, were reduced to the necessity of casting lots. It fell upon Owen Coffin to die, who with great fortitude and resignation submitted to his fate.[16] They drew lots to see who should shoot him: he placed himself firmly to receive his death, and was immediately shot by Charles Ramsdale, whose hard fortune it was to become his executioner. On the 11th Brazilla Ray died; and on these two bodies the captain and Charles Ramsdale, the only two that were then left, subsisted until the morning of the twenty-third, when they fell in with the ship Dauphin, as before stated, and were snatched from impending destruction. Every assistance and attentive humanity, was bestowed upon them by Capt. Coffin, to whom Capt. Pollard acknowledged every grateful obligation. Upon making known the fact, that three of our companions had been left at Ducies Island, to the captain of the U.S. frigate Constellation, which lay at Valparaiso when we arrived, he said he should immediately take measures to have them taken off.

On the 11th of June following I arrived at Nantucket in the whale-ship the Eagle, Capt. William H. Coffin. My family had received the most distressing account of our shipwreck, and had given me up for lost. My unexpected appearance was welcomed with the most grateful obligations and acknowledgements to a beneficent Creator, who had guided me through darkness, trouble, and death, once more to the bosom of my country and friends.

SUPPLEMENT.

The following is a list of the whole crew of the ship, with their arrangements into the three several boats upon starting from the wreck: the names of those who died, were left on the island, or shot—with those also who survived, and who were in the third or second mate's boat at the time of separation—and whose fate is yet uncertain:—

Capt. James Pollard, jun.[17]	1st boat	survived
Obed Hendricks,	do.	put in 3d boat
Brazilla Ray,	do.	died
Owen Coffin,	do.	shot
Samuel Reed, (black)	do.	died
Charles Ramsdale,	do.	survived
Seth Weeks,	do.	left on the island
Owen Chase,	2nd boat	survived
Benjamin Lawrence,	do.	do.
Thomas Nicholson,	do.	do.
Isaac Cole,	do.	died
Richard Peterson, (black)	do.	do.
William Wright,	do.	left on the island
Matthew P. Joy,	3d boat	died
Thomas Chapple,	do.	left on the island
Joseph West,	do.	missing
Lawson Thomas, (black)	do.	died
Charles Shorter, (black)	do.	do.
Isaiah Shepherd, (black)	do.	do.
William Bond, (black.)	do.	missing

FINIS.

Chapter Three

NE CEDE MALIS

C OULD IT have been otherwise? Is there any way that the survivors, who stayed alive for a month, could have stayed alive to
the end? Yes, if they had had better luck or if they had known what
we know today about the Pacific.

Chance could have brought them into contact with any of a
number of ships in the area, the names of some of which are known.
Three Nantucket ships were not far away—the *Governor Strong*,
the *Thomas*, and the *Globe*, the same *Globe* which three years later
was to be the stage of the bloodiest mutiny in the history of the
American whaling industry. Also in the area were the *Balaena*, the
Persia, and the *Golconda* of New Bedford and the English ship
Coquette of London.[1] Some of these ships may even have been
spoken by the *Essex* shortly before the whale's attack. But luck of
this kind was long in abeyance.

If we spread our modern maps of the Pacific before us and call
upon a century and a half of information gained by Pacific island
explorers, we will have no end of good suggestions for the *Essex*
survivors. But the *Essex* is not sinking today, and what was known
of the Pacific in 1820 is considerably less than what is known—
often even by the layman—today.

We see at a glance that the nearest land to the site of the *Essex*
disaster was Clipperton Island (10° N/109° W), but winds and
currents would have been against the *Essex* boats if they had tried
to reach it; moreover, that obscure guano island was probably
unknown to the people of the *Essex*. The Marquesas were the next
nearest bits of land, and after them some islands in the Tuamotu
Archipelago like Puka-Puka, Fakaina, and Tatakoto. These were

ominous names to seamen in 1820, however, and even today we
cannot say that their fears were altogether unjustified.

The Marquesas have been especially well studied, for it was in
the harbor of Nukahiva of the Marquesas that Herman Melville,
twenty-two years after the sinking of the *Essex*, jumped ship and set
out to live among the natives. Melville had been out a year and a
half on his first whaling voyage when he deserted; his sojourn
among the Marquesans gave him the material for his first novel,
Typee. The climactic action of the novel is that of the narrator's
escape from the clutches of the natives after he discovered that his
friendly hosts had been cherishing him not out of hospitality but out
of animal husbandry and that he was destined to become a succulent
bit of "long pig." Naturally the Melville scholar wants to know
how autobiographical this part of the story is. Charles Roberts
Anderson, who has collected important sources on the question of
Marquesan cannibalism, says after an extensive survey of the evidence, "There is no authenticated instance on record of human flesh
being eaten as a delicacy, according to my discoveries, nor any reliable record of a white man being eaten by Polynesians for any reason
whatever; finally, I have not been able to find a single unequivocal
eyewitness account of a Marquesan eating the flesh of even a native
enemy slain in battle, though in all likelihood this custom did exist
at one time."[2] The threat of just plain murder is another matter, of
course, and this was real enough in the islands.[3] Still, the odds were
against meeting a violent death at anyone's hands in the Marquesas, the Tuamotus, or the Society Islands; the fears of the men of
the *Essex* were exaggerated but not really irrational.

After these islands the nearest land would have been the coast of
Mexico near Manzanillo, and then the Galapagos, but here, too,
winds and currents would have been unfavorable, at least for a
direct course. The survivors actually did consider the Sandwich
Islands but were put off, Owen Chase tells us, by the thought of
hurricanes. That is probably true, but, one may add, Hawaii and
the other islands in the group were great unknowns to Nantucketers. At the time the *Essex* left its home port no American
whaler had ever visited the Sandwich Islands; the *Equator* and the
Balaena, the first two to touch at Hawaii, arrived there September

17, 1819. This fact will seem surprising if one is aware only of the role that the Sandwich Islands were shortly afterward—within ten or fifteen years—to play as victualing stops for Nantucket ships, but that development was an overnight one.[4]

The easiest way to see how the *Essex* people envisioned their Pacific is to examine the book that they had with them in their boats, Nathaniel Bowditch's *New American Practical Navigator*.[5] The part that would have been most useful to them would have been table 46, "Latitudes and Longitudes": "This table contains the LATITUDES and LONGITUDES of the most remarkable harbours, islands, shoals, capes, &c. in the WORLD, founded on the latest and most accurate Astronomical observations, surveys and charts." One of the subdivisions of this table is "Friendly and Other Islands in the Pacific Ocean." Here a number of Pacific islands lying in west longitude are listed along with their positions (see Appendix G). This is obviously a selective list of Pacific islands—there are, for example, only seven islands named in the Tuamotu Archipelago— and many of the latitudes and longitudes are slightly wrong. There is no knowing which edition of the *Navigator* was carried on the *Essex,* probably a fairly current one, possibly that of 1817. The edition is unimportant, though, since the list of Pacific islands had remained unrevised for ten years before the 1817 edition, and any fairly recent edition would have contained the same information. Even the 1802 *Navigator* differs little from the 1817 one as far as the data in this table go. It goes without saying that experienced officers and seamen knew much about the Pacific that was not down on paper and were not completely at the mercy of their *Navigators*. Nonetheless, the terror of the moment and the gravity of the decisions to be made by the officers of the *Essex* would have rendered any authority somewhat more reverend than usual. The survivors seemed to count heavily on their *Navigators*.

For one thing, their erroneous identification of the island they came upon after a month in the boats is explainable by reliance on the *Navigator*: Ducie is listed in the *Navigator* at 24°40′ S/ 124°40′ W, exactly the latitude and longitude that Owen Chase gives in his *Narrative*. This is the correct latitude and almost the correct longitude (it should be 124°47′) for Ducie. But the *Essex* boats had not come to Ducie Island, and they were not at 24°40′ S/124°40′ W. Instead they had come ashore at 24°20′ S/128°18′ W on an island whose name they could not be expected to know since the name had been bestowed on the island just a few months before the *Essex* had left Nantucket.

Four islands, today known as Ducie, Henderson, Pitcairn, and Oeno, make up the Pitcairn Island group. Henderson, the island on which the survivors came ashore, is the largest of the four, but only Pitcairn is inhabited and only Pitcairn has a real history.

Ducie and Henderson islands had been discovered January 26 and 29, 1606, by Pedro Fernandez de Quiros and named, respectively, La Encarnación and San Juan Bautista.[6] Ducie was given its present name by Capt. Edward Edwards of the *Pandora,* the ship that had been sent out from England in 1790 to hunt down and capture the *Bounty* mutineers. Captain Edwards, after stopping at Ducie and naming it for Lord Ducie, sailed on to Tahiti, passing north of the relatively nearby Pitcairn where his prey actually lurked.

Henderson Island was renamed—and unsuccessfully re-renamed— two years before the *Essex* survivors landed on it: in January 1819 Capt. James Henderson of the *Hercules,* out of Calcutta, rediscovered San Juan Bautista and gave it his own name; about three months later Capt. Henry King of the *Elizabeth* visited the island and, unaware of the visit of the *Hercules,* named the island after his ship. Since, however, the name of the *Elizabeth* had been left carved on a tree on the island and had been seen by the people of the *Essex,* the name Elizabeth Island was passed on in some secondhand and garbled accounts of the *Essex* story where it has been, to the increase of confusion, treated as another name for Ducie Island. The only serious consequence of the mistake the survivors made about their island was that the rescue ship sent to pick up the three who stayed on the island was misdirected to the real Ducie—only the decision of its captain to try Henderson too averted an additional tragedy.

Even if Owen Chase had given neither name nor position of the island, there would be no question from his description that it was Henderson Island that he had landed on. The most interesting descriptions of Ducie and Henderson islands fairly contemporary with the *Essex* survivors' stopover are found in a book by the British navy captain Frederick William Beechey, who visited both of them five years after the *Essex* survivors had been at Henderson. Captain Beechey described Ducie Island as he found it in November 1825:

Ducie's Island is of coral formation, of an oval form, with a lagoon or lake, in the centre, which is partly inclosed by trees, and partly by low coral flats scarcely above the water's edge. The height of the soil upon the island is about twelve feet, above which the trees rise fourteen more, making its greatest elevation about twenty-six feet from the level of the sea. The lagoon appears to be deep, and has an entrance into it for a boat, when the water is sufficiently smooth to admit of passing over the bar. It is situated at the south-east extremity, to the right of two eminences that have the appearance of sandhills. The island lies in a north-east and south-west direction,—is one mile and three quarters long, and one mile wide. No living things, birds excepted, were seen upon the island; but its environs appeared to abound in fish, and sharks were very numerous. The water was so clear over the coral, that the bottom was distinctly seen when no soundings could be had with thirty fathoms of line; in twenty-four fathoms, the shape of the rocks at the bottom was clearly distinguished. The coarallines were of various colours, principally white, sulphur, and lilac, and formed into all manner of shapes, giving a lively and variegated appearance to the bottom; but they soon lost their colour after being detached.

By the soundings round this little island it appeared, for a certain distance, to take the shape of a truncated cone having its base downwards. The north-eastern and south-western extremities are furnished with points which project under water with less inclination than the sides of the island, and break the sea before it can reach the barrier to the little lagoon formed within. It is singular that these buttresses are opposed to the only two quarters whence their structure has to apprehend danger; that on the north-east, from the constant action of the trade-wind, and that on the other extremity, from the long rolling swell from the south-west, so prevalent in these latitudes; and it is worthy of observation, that this barrier, which has the most powerful enemy to oppose, is carried out much farther, and with less abruptness, than the other.

The sand-mounds raised upon the barrier are confined to the eastern and north-western sides of the lagoon, the south-western part being left low, and broken by a channel of water. On the rocky surface of the causeway, between the lake and the sea, lies a stratum of dark rounded particles, probably coral, and above it another, apparently composed of decayed vegetable substances. A variety of evergreen trees take root in this bank, and form a canopy almost impenetrable to the sun's rays, and present to the eye a grove of the liveliest green.[7]

After observing Ducie, Captain Beechey sailed very slowly westward and on December 3, 1825, arrived at Henderson Island, which he also described:

We found that the island differed essentially from all others in its vicinity, and belonged to a peculiar formation, very few instances of which are in existence. Wateo and Savage Islands, discovered by Captain Cook, are of this number, and perhaps also Malden Island, visited by Lord Byron in the Blonde. The island is five miles in length, and one in breadth, and has a flat surface nearly eighty feet above the sea. On all sides, except the north, it is bounded by perpendicular cliffs about fifty feet high, composed entirely of dead coral, more or less porous, honeycombed at the surface, and hardening into a compact calcareous substance within, possessing the fracture of secondary limestone, and has a species of millepore interspersed through it. These cliffs are considerably undermined by the action of the waves, and some of them appear on the eve of precipitating their superincumbent weight into the sea; those which are less injured in this way present no alternate ridges or indication of the different levels which the sea might have occupied at different periods, but a smooth surface, as if the island, which there is every probability has been raised by volcanic agency, had been forced up by one great subterraneous convulsion. The dead coral, of which the higher part of the island consists, is nearly circumscribed by ledges of living coral, which project beyond each other at different depths; on the northern side of the island the first of these had an easy slope from the beach to a distance of about fifty yards, when it terminated abruptly about three fathoms under water. The next ledge had a greater descent, and extended to two hundred yards from the beach, with twenty-five fathoms water over it, and there ended as abruptly as the former, a short distance beyond which no bottom could be gained with 200 fathoms of line. Numerous *echini* live upon these ledges, and a variety of richly coloured fish play over their surface, while some cray-fish inhabit the deeper sinuosities. The sea rolls in successive breakers over these ledges of coral, and renders landing upon them extremely difficult. It may, however, be effected by anchoring the boat, and veering her close into the surf, and then, watching the opportunity, by jumping upon the ledge, and hastening to the shore before the succeeding roller approaches. In doing this great caution must be observed, as the reef is full of holes and caverns, and the rugged way is strewed with sea-eggs, which inflict very painful wounds; and if a person fall into one of these hollows, his life will be greatly endangered by the points of coral catching his clothes and detaining him under water. The beach, which appears at a distance to be composed of a beautiful white sand, is wholly made up of small broken portions of the different species and varieties of coral, intermixed with shells of testaceous and crustaceous animals.

Insignificant as this island is in height, compared with others, it is extremely difficult to gain the summit, in consequence of the thickly interlacing shrubs which grow upon it, and form so dense a covering, that it is impossible to see the cavities in the rock beneath. They are at the same time too fragile to afford any support, and the traveller often sinks into the cavity up to his shoulder before his feet reach the bottom. The soil is a black mould of little depth, wholly formed of decayed vegetable matter, through which points of coral every now and then project.

The largest tree upon the island is the pandanus, though there is another tree very common, nearly of the same size, the wood of which has a great resemblance to common ash, and possesses the same properties. We remarked also a species of budleia, which was nearly as large and as common, bearing fruit. It affords but little wood, and has a reddish bark of considerable astringency: several species of this genus are to be met with among the Society Islands. There is likewise a long slender plant with a stem about an inch in diameter, bearing a beautiful pink flower, of the class and order hexandria monogynia. We saw no esculent roots, and, with the exception of the pandanus, no tree that bore fruit fit to eat.[8]

Sizable and varied as it was, it was clear to all that Henderson Island was not a long-inhabitable place. The three *Essex* survivors who chose to remain apparently hold the occupancy record for the island, 111 days. Twentieth-century Pitcairn Islanders visit Henderson to collect the hard red miro wood they use for carving their artifacts, and there are scattered reports of other brief visits to the island. A U.S. Naval Intelligence report indicates that there were signs that the island had been visited in 1937 by Japanese pearlers. The same report goes on to say:

There are a very limited number of coconut trees but no lime or orange trees. Fish and lobsters are reported to be plentiful.

Fresh water is found in small pools. In 1933 good fresh water was found at half ebb, running from a cleft in the rocks at the N. end of the island; this was not visible at high water.[9]

That is the old *Essex* spring rediscovered. Another *Essex* discovery was rediscovered in the twentieth century, too: Thomas Chapple in his Account (Appendix C) describes the skeletons found in one of Henderson Island's caves by the three *Essex* men who had chosen to stay on the island. The subsequent history of the skeletons and some other details of Henderson Island history are recounted by Robert McLoughlin:

Although the survivors of the "Essex" told of the discovery of some skeletons in a cave on Henderson Island, this fact appears to have been overlooked as on their first visit to the island on the whaling ship "Joseph Meigs" in August, 1851, a party of twelve Pitcairners reported the discovery of a human skeleton in a cave adjacent to the beach near the landing point. Later in the same year a party of thirty-eight Pitcairners again visited Henderson in the whaling ship "Sharon" and on further search found eight more human skeletons in the same cave. As pieces of wreckage were found on the beach it was assumed that the skeletons were the remains of seamen from an unidentified wreck. The skeletons, the origin of which still remains an unsolved mystery were again "discovered" by Messrs. George Ellis and J. D. Arundel of the Pacific Phosphate Company who visited the island briefly in 1907 for the purpose of investigating the island's phosphate mining potential. Although the Pitcairn Islanders visited the island on a number of occasions no further mention was made of the skeletons until they were again "discovered" by a party of Pitcairners who visited the island to collect miro wood in March, 1958. The latter discovery sparked off an inquiry into the origin of the skeletons until a search of the official records revealed the previous discovery of them and a medical examination of some of the bones revealed that they were of Caucasian origin confirming the belief that they were the remains of shipwrecked seamen from an unidentified wreck. Although buried in shallow graves by the Pitcairners on their visit to the island in 1958 the remains were again investigated by a United States survey party in 1966 and after examination of the bones the skeletons were given final burial in five coffins which were placed in the far left hand corner of the cave in which they had been found with a six foot cross jammed hard between the rock floor and roof of the cave entrance. From this examination it was revealed that the skeletons were of five or six people, of whom one was a child aged between three and five years; that they were most probably survivors

of a shipwreck; and that the primary cause of death was lack of
water.

Other visits to the island have been made in 1937 by a landing
party from H.M.S. "Leander" who reported finding the remains of
huts and names carved on trees together with an arrow and flagon
carved on one tree, which was interpreted as meaning that water was
to be found in that direction. Although no running streams have been
observed on the island puddles of fresh water were observed by the
"Leander" party in a small hollow between the crest of the beach and
the base of the cliffs and fresh water was seen spouting from the roof
of the cave containing the skeletons only fifty yards from those puddles. A damp depression was also observed in the hollow in front of
that cave. Like the survivors of the "Essex" the Pitcairners obtain
their water supplies when visiting the island from a spring which
seeps out on the beach at the half-tide level.

The only other significant visit which is known to have been made
to the island was that of Captain Webster in H.M.C.S. "Awahou"
over the period from 31st July to 10th August, 1948, when an auto-
matic light house was erected after considerable difficulty on the
Northwest point. The lighthouse equipment was hauled up the cliff
face by means of a breeches buoy and the light tower erected only a
few hundred yards North of the Northwest landing place. Although
thoroughly tested and left operating the gas operated light actuated by
a sun valve soon became extinct and has not since been re-activated.
The difficulty of exploration of the island was demonstrated on this
visit by the fact that the lighthouse party in an attempt to reach the
Northeast point from the Northern landing place succeeded in making
only a little over half a mile in five hours during which they received
so many cuts and bruises from falls on the sharp coral hidden in the
dense undergrowth that they were forced to give up.

The island was briefly in the news again in 1957 when an
American named Robert Tomarchin and his chimpanzee Moko were
landed there from a yacht and dramatically rescued by a passing
vessel some three weeks later and taken to Pitcairn Island.[10]

The biggest single "if only" of the whole *Essex* story arises when
one realizes how near Henderson Island is to Pitcairn—about a
hundred miles. Capt. Joseph Mitchell II of the *Three Brothers*
wrote in his journal for July 18, 1847:

at 5 PM saw Elizabeth? Isle bearing SW by S 40 miles through the
night light airs latter part Sent two boats on shore this is the Island
that some of the Essex? Crew landed on what a pitty that they did not

know of Pitcairn's Island for they might of been to it in a few days or even one day with a good breeze.[11]

So indeed they could have, as Chapple, Wright, and Weeks, the three survivors left on Henderson, were to find out after their rescue ship bore them to Pitcairn in a day. But Pitcairn was not in the *Navigator,* and in the 1820s even among those who knew of the existence of Pitcairn there was confusion over its precise position, Carteret, its discoverer, having recorded it as being farther west than it really was.

There is no question that the *Essex* survivors would have been cordially welcomed by the Pitcairners and their patriarch, John Adams. Adams, who had been known as Alexander Smith at the time of the *Bounty* mutiny, was now the last of the mutineers left alive and he ruled over the large *Bounty* family like a benevolent Homeric king. The island's turbulent days were past, and the people were now exemplary for their sober, devout, and kindly way of life. One need only read the accounts of the island, cited later in this chapter, which the rescuers of Thomas Chapple, William Wright, and Seth Weeks wrote after their stopover to realize what tender solicitude and care would have been waiting for the *Essex* boats if they had made the one-day trip to the west. The fact that the survivors were from a Nantucket ship would have added more excitement to their welcome, for it was a Nantucketer, Capt. Mayhew Folger of the *Topaz,* out of Boston, who had discovered the *Bounty* colony in 1808 and announced the fact to the world.

But this was not to be. The *Essex* boats were put in the water once again, and Henderson Island dropped behind them in the west, not in the east. Missing Easter Island must have been the result of faulty navigation due to weakness or to bad observations; it was not due to inaccuracy in Bowditch, for the *Navigator's* latitude and longitude for Easter Island were near enough to correct to bring ships within sight of the island: 27°9′ S/109°35′ W (should be 109°20′ W).

If the boats' course had been north by about three hundred miles, they would have arrived at Easter Island around January 15, nineteen days out from Henderson. This would have been after the death of Second Mate Joy and around the time that a crewman died in the second mate's boat, but these two might have been the only dead. The conclusion that they could not reach Easter Island seems premature if the dates and subsequent observations are correct. Judging by the position given later in the same paragraph for January 7 (30°18′ S/117°29′ W), they must have been about 28°35′ S/120° W on January 4. Since Easter Island is 27°9′ S/ 109°20′ W, reaching it even in the face of east-northeast winds would not have been extremely difficult for ships and boats under ordinary circumstances. The necessary tacking may have seemed too much of a strain, however, for the weakened men.

The fear of hostile natives that made the survivors leery of the Society Islands and other unknown spots would, perhaps, have been the right attitude to approach Easter Island with if they had stayed on course and had been able to approach it. Some reports suggest that the natives could be threatening. The explorer La Perouse was well received on Easter Island in 1786, and Captain Raine's meeting with the natives aboard the *Surry* on March 24, 1821, was uneventful, but Captain Beechey received a less reassuring welcome in 1825.[12] On his way to the Ducie and Henderson visits already described, Beechey called at Easter Island and was met by a clamorous but not initially hostile reception. The mood turned ugly, though, when the natives began an energetic exercise of pilferage from the visitors. When this became outrageous, Beechey ordered a departure, something which so angered the natives that they unleashed a hail of one-pound stones on their visitors, injuring some of them. The crew fired warning shots, which had no effect, over the heads of the natives and finally followed with a shot that struck a chief. This produced some remission in the stone throwing, and the crew reached their ship. There is some suggestion that it was the very gift giving of the visitors, and of others before them, that encouraged the natives' playful, rowdy plundering. Such behavior may be no indication of how the natives would have treated distressed shipwreck survivors, but that whole question is moot.

The separation of the boats was foreseeable. The wonder is that they were able to stay together as long as they did. What happened to the third boat after it separated from the captain's can only be guessed. Captain Beechey discussed the *Essex* adventure and made an interesting, but almost certainly wrong, guess about what happened to that boat: "The third [boat] was never heard of; but it is not improbable that the wreck of a boat and four skeletons which were seen on Ducie's Island by a merchant vessel were her remains and that of her crew."[13] This could hardly be the case: at the time of separation the third boat had already covered half the distance to South America; it would not have turned about and retraced over a thousand miles to Ducie Island, nor would winds and currents have been likely to carry a drifting boat there.

It was the morning of the ninety-first day since the whale's attack when Benjamin Lawrence called out, "There's a Sail!" The awesome feat had now grown to proportions proper to fantasy. How defiant of limits can the human organism be? The three men in one boat and two in the other were breathing and moving and talking. One can see Owen Chase and his companions trying to climb on board the *Indian* by their own power and, almost apologetically, acknowledging that they needed help. Thirty years before, Captain Bligh's survival in a crowded open boat had been talked about around the world; the *Essex* survivors were out twice as long as Bligh had been.

If one were to diagnose the condition of the survivors in strict medical terms, one would have to be somewhat tentative, for their symptoms were reported in a spotty fashion in the records that have come down to us, but one might observe at the start that, in the light of the rapid physical deterioration of the men, they probably had started out in a somewhat precarious nutritional balance. Shipboard fare was not varied and was usually chosen more for its imperishability than its nutrients. The boils described may reflect a chronic vitamin deficiency and the swelling of the limbs a protein deficiency.

The water shortage that afflicted the men in the boats for the first month after the wreck is the classic hazard of the shipwrecked. While it may seem that expedients such as holding salt water in one's mouth or drinking urine were nothing worse than disagreeable, the fact is that they were positively harmful. Both fluids contain a high percentage of minerals in solution, and these, if taken into the body, leech water out of the body and produce dehydration, the exact opposite of the effect desired. On the other hand, drinking blood would have relieved dehydration not merely by the intake of liquid but by taking advantage of the other animal's "sodium pump," which takes minerals out of the blood and other body fluids. When considering the dehydration problem, one wonders whether it was not aggravated to some extent by the very bread that kept the men alive, for the bread may have had a high salt content.

Not all of the deaths were caused by starvation. Matthew Joy was in poor health before the shipwreck. Isaac Cole seems to have died of some febrile-delirium disorder, with an infection of the nervous system or perhaps just electrolyte imbalance accounting for the convulsions. Several seem to have died from hopelessness and despair, abandoning their efforts to survive when the body still had the resources for more life.[14]

When the first three *Essex* survivors arrived in Valparaiso, their story spread rapidly through the city, especially among members of the English-speaking community, who raised a sum of money for them. The story probably would have been an even bigger sensation at another time, though, for Chile was in a distracted state in 1821. The five fragile men from the *Essex* fell into the midst of the war that the united patriot forces were waging for the liberation of Chile and Peru. Most of Chile had been permanently wrested from the royalists, and the attack, largely financed by Chile, on the forces of the viceroy of Peru was reaching a climax. Everyone in Chile hung on news from the north.

The *Gazeta ministerial de Chile* (April 28, 1821) reported:

Dicho dia [March 16, 1821] Ha dado fondo la fragata americana ballenera dos Hermanos de porte de 217 tonelados, su capitan D. Jorge Worth procedente de su pesca. Y en la latitud 37 grados Sur tomaron á un bote de la fragata ballenera Essea [*sic*] con el capitan de ella D. Juan Pollard y su muchacho Carlos Ramsen, los que se perdieron de dicha fragata siguiendo á una ballena en la latitud Sur, un grado, y estaban perdidos en la mar 93 dias.

And that was all it had to say about the *Essex*. Even though the *Gazeta* featured maritime news and had a flair for exciting reports, this was the wrong time to expect much coverage of anything but the war.

There is no visualizing the circumstances that Owen Chase and the others found themselves in without taking into account the revolution, which was everybody's business in one way or another. The sites of the survivors' convalescence and the time of their return were affected by it, and it was the main thing on the minds of the United States Navy personnel who took care of Owen and his companions.

The revolution against Spanish authority was not in its origins like the revolution of the thirteen colonies.[15] In North America rebellion against the mother country was in the blood of the earliest settlers; the revolution against England could have taken place in the earliest years of the Massachusetts Bay Colony. But in South America, especially in Chile, it was a different story. The whole question of revolting against the Spanish throne arose only when Spain temporarily ceased to be Spanish—when Napoleon I usurped the Spanish throne in 1808. Colonial Spaniards who would have remained unquestioningly loyal to Ferdinand VII, were he on the throne, were uncertain about where their loyalties lay if Napoleon were to remain in power. Within a year factions emerged, and the division of Chile into "patriot," the advocates of independence, and "royalist" was born. Once ignited, the passion for independence continued to burn, even after Ferdinand VII returned to the throne in 1814 and on the face of things took away from the patriots their rationale for rebelling against the distant Spanish authority.

A succession of revolutionary leaders brought Chile nearer and nearer to authentic independence, only to have their cause receive a decisive defeat at Rancagua in 1814, after which the royalists resumed control of Chile. Bernardo O'Higgins and other revolutionary leaders fled to Argentina, where O'Higgins formed an alliance with Gen. José de San Martín, the brilliant strategist of Argentina's struggle for independence. O'Higgins and San Martín marched on Chile, and by 1817 O'Higgins, who had accepted the directorate of the new nation after San Martín had turned it down, was able to proclaim a threatened but eventually secure independence.

The main thrust of the liberation movement once the war in Chile had been more or less won was against the forces of the viceroy of Peru. The army moved north under the command of

General San Martín, and the newly formed Chilean navy operated under the command of one of the most colorful naval figures of the century, Thomas Cochrane, tenth earl of Dundonald. By his early thirties Lord Cochrane had become a legend in the British navy for success with bold and original maneuvers against overwhelming odds. His career, which was promising in spite of a spasmodic irreverence toward superiors, was interrupted by his unfortunate and apparently thoroughly innocent relationship to some participants in a dramatic stock exchange fraud. He was fined and imprisoned and, after an escape and recapture, subjected to harsh treatment. In 1817 after his release the Chilean patriots offered him the command of their navy; this he assumed the following year. In the service of Chile he distinguished himself by such feats as personally leading a boarding party against a Spanish ship—it was not the first time he had done that—and by a brilliant opportunism in operations up and down the Chilean coast. He had also made himself a nuisance to the shipping of neutral nations like the United States and England whenever he suspected that their traffic was advantageous to the royalists. The very ship that rescued Owen Chase, the *Indian*, came into port as one of Lord Cochrane's prizes.

At the time that the *Essex* boats were drifting closer to the continent, Lord Cochrane's and General San Martín's forces were closing in on Lima. The conquest of that city was completed about three months after Owen Chase reached South America.

If Lord Cochrane was the most colorful figure on the side of the patriots, the most colorful on the side of the royalists had to be the pirate Benavides. Originally in the patriot army, he had deserted to the royalists, was captured by the patriots at the battle of Maypo in 1818, sentenced to death, and very nearly executed. Stories vary on how he managed to survive a firing squad and a saber cut on the throat. Recovered, he offered his services to General San Martín, betrayed him, and rejoined the royalists in the south of Chile. Commanding an army of Araucanian Indians, he alternately presented himself under the Spanish flag and his own private flag. He was a ruthless barbarian, ready to kill and devastate for light reasons or no reasons; yet he was not wanting in the organizational skills of a general. He was a particular threat to the neutral ships off the Chilean coast, for he preyed on them to collect his own little navy and to force their crews into his army. His center of operations, Arauco, stood on the mainland facing St. Mary's Island, a favorite watering place of whalers using the off-shore ground, as Owen Chase mentioned in his *Narrative*. Readers of Melville's *Benito Cereno* will recognize St. Mary's as the setting of that tense story. The *Essex* had stopped at St. Mary's January 17, 1820; it was about a year later that Benavides began to prey on the whalers coming to the island.

On February 26, 1821, the day after the *Indian* arrived in Valparaiso with Owen Chase and his two companions, and three days after Pollard and Ramsdell were picked up off St. Mary's Island, another Nantucket ship, the *Hero*, Capt. James Russell, tied up at St. Mary's to cut into a whale it had taken. What happened to the *Hero* has been told in many versions, of which one of the most precise is one apparently never quoted before, a first-person account in the *Gazeta ministerial de Chile* for March 24, 1821: "Sucesos ocurridos con los españoles á bordo de la fragata 'Herrio, dada por su Piloto." The Herrio was the *Hero* (carefree spelling of foreign names was a rule with the *Gazeta*), and the Piloto apparently the ship's young first mate, Obed Starbuck, who gave a similar account of the *Hero*'s troubles, as we shall see, to the senior American naval officer in Valparaiso. Mate Starbuck gives the story as follows:

The Encounter with the Spanish on board the ship Hero, as
Recounted by its First Mate

Anchored February 26, 1821 at seven o'clock in the bay of Santa Maria in ten fathoms of water. . . . The captain took his boat and went to the island, saw a whale and killed it. At three o'clock he got it to the ship and we began to cut in. At that moment two boats from Arauco came to see who we were and ordered the captain to go and see the governor.

On the 27th we finished cutting into the whale; the captain went to Arauco, and his boat and its whole crew were detained there. At ten o'clock three armed Spanish boats came alongside and fired at the ship at close range without doing it any harm. They took possession of the ship and began to rob the crew and loot the baggage.

On the 28th of February they raised sail on the ship and took us back to Arauco. On March 1st they took out twenty barrels of meat, twelve barrels of flour, four quarter casks of ship's biscuits and three barrels of rum. These were taken ashore as was the whole crew except for the first and second officers and six seamen.

On March 2nd the pirates came aboard at 4 o'clock and returned half the provisions and the third officer and three crewmen. They raised anchor and took the ship to Tubul, anchored in four fathoms of water and put ashore four boats loaded with provisions.

On March 3rd it was very foggy and was raining quite heavily when we spotted a schooner that was coming straight toward us. The pirates took the captain's trunks where all the ship's papers were and looted them at will. Then they cut the cables and took all the ship's boats except one.

After they left the ship we came on deck and found that the ship was drifting toward the beach and was lying in just three fathoms of water. We immediately set the sails to save the ship. At this point the pirates came out again in two boats, but the wind was so favorable to us that they could not give chase; we decided to head for Valparaiso.

On March 5th we spoke the ship Two Brothers, Captain George Worth, of Nantucket; the Dauphin, Captain Zimri Coffin, of Nantucket; and the Diana, Captain Aaron Paddack, of New York.

On the sixth we saw land and spotted a brigantine off to the north. The Spaniards had taken from us all kinds of sail and rigging.[16]

At that March 5 meeting with the *Two Brothers*, the *Dauphin*, and the *Diana*, the remnant of the *Hero*'s crew learned of the rescue of Captain Pollard and Charles Ramsdell. Of these four ships, the *Hero*, hastening to Valparaiso for relief and repairs, was the first to come into port. It was, therefore, the pillaged *Hero*, struggling down the coast with no captain, that by fitting coincidence brought to shore the first news that the captain of the *Essex* along with one of his men had been rescued. All four of the ships that were parties to the March 5 gam spread the news of Captain Pollard's rescue over the seas as well as in port; the incompleteness of their knowledge of the *Essex* people's fate eventually led to a tragic but short-lived misunderstanding back in Nantucket when the very first reports arrived.

The sequence of events surrounding Captain Pollard's rescue are the following: on February 23 Pollard and Ramsdell were picked up by the *Dauphin* of Nantucket, Capt. Zimri Coffin. The *Dauphin* happened to have on board a seaman, Charles Murphey, who was a nautical poet on the order of Lemsford in Herman Melville's

White-Jacket—very much like Lemsford, to judge by his verses—
and who had been keeping a verse journal of the cruise of the *Dauphin*. Captain Pollard was to be memorialized fifty-five years later
in Herman Melville's monumental poem, *Clarel*, but his first
appearance in verse, thanks to Seaman Murphey, took place
immediately after his rescue. Murphey writes:

> The second month, quite early on
>   The three-and-twentieth day,
> From our mast-head we did espy
>   A boat to leeward lay.
>
> Hard up the helm, and down we went
>   To see who it might be.
> The Essex boat we found it was,
>   Been ninety days at sea.
>
> No victuals were there in the boat,
>   Of any sort or kind,
> And two survivors, who did expect
>   A watery grave to find.
>
> The rest belonging to the boat
>   Ah! shocking to relate,
> For want of food and nourishment,
>   Met an unhappy fate.
>
> We rounded to, and hove aback;
>   A boat was quickly lowered;
> We took the two survivors out,
>   And carried them on board.
>
> At sunrise on the third of March,
>   We then did plainly see
> A shoal of spermaceti whales
>   Lie spouting off our lee.[17]

Here the poem returns for three stanzas to routine accounts of
whaling. Then a meeting of the *Dauphin* and the *Two Brothers* is
described along with the transfer of the two survivors to the latter
ship:

> Same day, while cutting in our whale,
>   About the hour of three,
> The ship Two Brothers then we spoke,
>   And kept her company.

We cruised together off and on
   Till March the thirteenth day.
Our two survivors went on board;
   Next morn they bore away.

To Valparaiso they were bound,
   Provisions for to buy,
Cruise one more month, and then they were
   Bound home immediately.[18]

The result of the transfer was to get the two survivors into Valparaiso about a week earlier than they would have arrived if they had stayed on the *Dauphin*.

Another account of the *Essex* story may have been written around the same time as the Murphey poem. A letter, which will be quoted and discussed later (Appendix E) and which is attributed to Capt. Aaron Paddack of the *Diana*, tells the story in a few pages. It adds little to Owen Chase's account, but its main importance lies in the part it or its assumed author played in getting the *Essex* story back to Nantucket.

The letter speaks of the *Diana* gamming the *Dauphin* the day it picked up Pollard and Ramsdell and recounts in considerable detail the tale that Pollard told. The letter contains a probably perfect abstract of the rescue story that was now to be put in circulation. The circulation of Captain Pollard's news proceeded as follows: first, the *Diana* learned it on February 23; then, on March 3 the *Two Brothers* learned it when it gammed the *Dauphin* which had Pollard and Ramsdell on board. Two days later, on March 5, the *Hero* spoke all three of the ships involved in the Pollard rescue, the *Dauphin*, the *Two Brothers*, and the *Diana*. Every one of these four ships now had Captain Pollard's story, and every one of them assumed, for want of any evidence to the contrary, that Pollard's boat was the only one to have survived. Where did the four ships go now with their story?

The *Dauphin* kept sailing for whales. The *Diana* headed home to New York. On the way the *Diana* encountered the *Triton*, Capt. Zephaniah Wood, which was on its way back to New Bedford, and Captain Paddack repeated the story, apparently adding a few details not recorded in the letter presumed to be his. This meeting of Captain Paddack and Captain Wood (a darkly coincidental one, for both captains were to die in pursuit of whales on their next voyages) is documented, for Captain Wood, arriving in New Bedford either June 7 or June 9, told the story to the *New Bedford Mercury*, which carried it in its issue of June 15, 1821.[19] The story, of course, circulated by word of mouth at once and doubtless reached Nantucket the same day that the *Triton* arrived in New Bedford, or the next day at the latest. And the story was that the wreck of the *Essex* left only two survivors, or possibly five if the men on the island were alive. For several days this is what Nantucket believed.

The other two ships from the March 5 gam headed for Valparaiso. The *Hero* arrived March 9 with news of the Pollard rescue. The *Two Brothers* arrived March 17 carrying Pollard and Ramsdell.

At this point we may turn back to Owen Chase and the two seamen rescued with him. Owen and his companions had been brought into Valparaiso February 25, one week after their rescue. They had, therefore, been in port almost two weeks when the *Hero* arrived with news of Captain Pollard's rescue and three weeks when the captain himself arrived on the *Two Brothers*.

There was no American consul in Valparaiso when the *Essex* survivors arrived. Up until shortly before Owen Chase was brought into port there had been an American diplomatic officer in charge of business at Santiago and Valparaiso: Henry Hill was a businessman, missionary, and Mark Twainesque model of frontier enterprise who had been given his government post in 1818 and kept it until early 1821.[20] The U.S. frigate *Macedonian* was completing its tour of duty and returning to the United States at that time, and its commander, Commodore Downes, invited Hill to return with him. Hill accepted the invitation but did not wait for the *Macedonian* to sail; instead, he set out across the Andes and was on hand to meet the *Macedonian* in Rio de Janeiro when the ship arrived there. He started out on his trek from Santiago on March 12. He may have been in Santiago for several weeks before his departure, or he may not have been approached with the news of Owen Chase's arrival in Valparaiso because he had given up his post. William Hogan, the next American consul in Valparaiso, did not arrive to take up his duties until after the *Essex* survivors had left.

COMMODORE CHARLES GOODWIN RIDGELY
Painted by J. W. Jarvis.

U.S.S. *CONSTELLATION* OFF PORT MAHON, MINORCA, IN 1831

Painted by Nicola Cammillieri. The *Constellation*, which was a much rebuilt ship, had more or less this appearance at the time that it participated in the *Essex* rescue.

Diplomatic duties, as was usual in such cases, devolved on the senior United States naval officer in the area. The new head of the Pacific station, replacing Commodore Downes, was Commodore Charles Goodwin Ridgely, commanding the U.S. frigate *Constellation*.[21] Word of the *Essex* survivors was brought to him and, as he tells us, he attended to them at once. The survivors were fortunate to come under the care of Captain Ridgely: from the story of his life and from his own writings there emerges a picture of a courageous and reliable officer (he had won a congressional medal for bravery in the battle of Tripoli), a firm disciplinarian, and at the same time, a sensitive and humane person. Commodore Ridgely wrote of the *Essex* survivors in letters and in his Journal. His Journal account contains two of the most vivid pictures of the survivors:

On the 9th March the American ship Hero of Nantucket arrived, the chief Mate reports that a few days previous, while lying at anchor off the Island of St Marys, near Conception that the ship was taken possession by a party of Spaniards & Indians under the command of a Spaniard named Benevides having previously induced the Captain Russell & ten men, to land, whom they made prisoners, that after plundering the ship of a number of articles of provisions &c they got the Ship underway for the purpose of proceeding to some other place that about the same instant a strange sail came in sight which they believed to be a cruiser from Valp.[o] that the plunderers immediately fled in their boats, & that he took advantage of it & immediately made sail for this port leaving the Captain and ten men in possession of the plunderers—the Hero brings the pleasing acct. that the Master of the Essex, Pollard & one boy have been picked up by a Whale ship from New York. They were ninety two days in the boat & were in a most wretched state, they were unable to move when found sucking the bones of their dead Mess mates, which they were loth to part with. On the 15 the English Brig India arrived a prize to Lord Cochrane, she brought in the Mate one man & a Boy of the Ship Essex of Nantucket Pollard master, they stated that ninety two days previous while some of the boats were about striking whale, the ship then in Lat[d]   Long: a large whale attacked the ship stove in her bows, that they had been in the boat eighty six days, a great part of which time they had subsisted on the flesh of those that died, they separated from the Cap[t] in lat[d]   long: in a squally night that it was their intention to endeavour to reach Esther Island and presumed the Cap[t] had gone there that a few days after the accident they all reach'd and landed on an island called Ducies in lat[d] 24°40′ S

long: 124°40′ W that it was not inhabited and only water to be had
there, they left it with the exception of three, who prefered remaining
alth? the island afforded no article whatever of sustenance & the whole
hope left was, the surf might occasionally throw on shore a dead fish,
they had no boats it was the opinion of the mate they could not have
survived many days—the Indian picked up those that were in the boat
within half a degree of Juan Fernandes, the Captain had showed them
every kind attention, but their appearance / bones working through
their skins their legs & feet much smaller & the whole surface of their
bodies one entire ulcer / was truly distressing—I took them on board
my ship, supplied them with every article they required and by the
attention of my surgeon they entirely recovered—The English ship
Surry Cap.ᵗ Raines now lying here being on the eve of sailing for New
Holland[22] I applied to him to know if he would call at Esther Island &
the Island of Ducies & endeavour to relieve these unfortunate men; he
consented, and I paid him for his trouble four hundred & thirty
dollars—from the character of this gentleman, and having given me
security for the performance of his engagement, I have no doubt but he
will do so. I should not omit to mention that a subscription was
immediately put on foot by the American & English residents of Valp:
for the relief of those poor fellows that were brought in & between three
& four hundred dollars was procured them, beside which my crew with
that thoughtless liberality which is peculiar to seamen, subscribed each
a months pay, but as that would have amounted to between two and
three thousand Dollars & as these men were not then in want of any
thing, & I intended sending them home in the Macedonian where they
would have every comfort & no expence I would allow no more than
one dollar from each man to be given them—The Macedonian arrived
on the 4ᵗʰ March & informed me that the Ship Chesapeake of Baltimore & Brig Warrior of New York were detained at Coquimbo by the
Govt. & their situation a very critical one, I therefore determined on
going to their relief. After having landed a quantity of surplus stores &
spars, and the Purser who was very sick, caulked & painted Ship, sent
the arrested officers on board the Macedonian to be carried to the U.
States—and also those unfortunate men of the Essex & requesting Capᵗ
Downes to go to Aurauco to the assistance of Capᵗ Russell & men of the
Hero. On the 11ᵗʰ March I sailed for Coquimbo—[23]

If there is a single image that lingers in the imagination after one
has heard Captain Ridgely's story of the *Essex*, it is that of the two
skeletal, rag-clad men in the boat sucking on the bones of their dead
crewmates—and clutching them to themselves, fearful that giving
them up to their very rescuers would somehow sever them from the

earth's last nutrients. That was Pollard and Ramsdell who were so described, and the description was passed on to Captain Ridgely by Obed Starbuck who obviously heard it from someone on the *Two Brothers, Dauphin*, or *Diana*.

What Captain Ridgely says of Owen Chase, Benjamin Lawrence, and Thomas Nickerson, however, is from firsthand observation, not from report. That means that when they were brought to him, perhaps the same day that they were brought into Valparaiso, February 25, he found their bones pressing through their skin, their legs and feet shrunken, and their skin "one ulcer." That would have been a week after their rescue.

The ship's surgeon was Dr. Leonard Osborn; the surgeon's mate was Dr. William D. Babbit.[24] If the survivors were kept in sick bay on the *Constellation*, they would have been in the forward part of the berth deck. This was the third deck down of four: spar deck, gun deck, berth deck, and orlop deck. It was a cramped and airless corner of the ship, probably heaven to the men of the *Essex* but not a spot that the delicate would pick for convalescence. Today the visitor can go into sick bay and walk over the same decks of the *Constellation* that Owen Chase did, for the *Constellation*, the oldest ship in the U.S. Navy and the oldest ship in the world continuously afloat, is tied up at Constellation Dock in Baltimore harbor.

Captain Ridgely wrote to the secretary of the navy on March 7 about the rescue of Owen Chase and his two companions—his letter is reprinted in Appendix D—two days before he heard about the rescue of Captain Pollard. At that time he was simply planning to put the three survivors he was attending to onto the *Macedonian* for their return home. In the end, none of the survivors returned on the *Macedonian*; all but Captain Pollard returned on the whaleship *Eagle*, which had arrived in Valparaiso March 11 and sailed for Nantucket March 22 or 23, a few days after the *Macedonian* sailed for home on March 19.[25] Doubtless the advantages of having a direct passage home were decisive in the selection of the *Eagle* over the *Macedonian*.

The only *Essex* survivors to have been on the *Constellation*, of course, were Owen Chase, Benjamin Lawrence, and Thomas Nickerson. The *Constellation* was gone from Valparaiso before

Pollard and Ramsdell arrived. As Captain Ridgely makes clear, Chase, Lawrence, and Nickerson were transferred to the *Macedonian*, still at anchor and waiting to start home when the *Constellation* had to leave for Coquimbo. That means that they had about two weeks on the *Constellation* and were to have about one week on the *Macedonian*.

If the three recuperated fast enough to begin paying attention to the shipboard life around them and to absorb some of the scuttlebutt, they would have learned that the *Constellation* was tense from the acting out of a singular little drama that had reached its climax just before the *Essex* men came on board. It is worth pausing to examine, for it affected everyone on the ship.

Captain Ridgely in assuming his new station inherited the onerous duty of rescuing and protecting American ships and the delicate duty of saving them from seizure by Lord Cochrane without offending the patriot government. And Captain Ridgely was not too happy that the duties were dropped so indifferently on him by the departing Commodore Downes; "flagrant dereliction of his duty," Ridgely said of Downes in a letter to the secretary of the navy, for it seemed to Ridgely that if American ships were in distress, it did not make a whit of difference that one's tour of duty had expired.[26] But all of these concerns were basically routine navy business.

In addition to all of them, however, Captain Ridgely had to contend with an unusual and exacerbated discipline problem which had arisen from the presence on board his ship of a sinister and manipulative civilian passenger. The action, worthy of a Eugene O'Neill sea play, is described by Commodore Ridgely:

> On my passage from New York to Montivideo Mr. Dan! S. Griswold with the consent and approbation of the Secretary of the Navy was born a passenger in this ship & lived in my Cabin. during the passage this gentleman became intimate with my youngest Commissioned officers, was frequently in the Gun room with them and occasionally mentioned to me the strange things as he considered them which he heard there until I suppressed a course which I considered so improper by the dissatisfied manner in which I listened to him.[27]

Although Captain Ridgely would tolerate no more talebearing by Griswold, he did send word by one of his lieutenants that he was apprised of disrespectful talk in the gun room "and would recommend to the Officers to be more circumspect and decorous in speaking of their superior Officers in their absence. This produced a great foment of good and bad feeling amongst them of which I was kept in ignorance."

In Valparaiso and subsequently in Santiago Captain Ridgely received from citizens of those cities more reports about Griswold, including one that Griswold had shocked and mortified the community by a scandalous public quarrel and another report that Griswold had defrauded an American merchant in Santiago of $2,500. Ridgely concluded that Griswold was not a healthy influence on the ship and diplomatically sent word from Santiago through one of Griswold's friends that he would not be permitted to reboard the ship. Returning to Valparaiso, Captain Ridgely learned that Griswold had been seen around the city in public with four or five officers of the *Constellation* who "appeared devoted to him" and "were unremitted in their attentions to him with every mark of respect & evidently making a display of their personal regard for a man, who was thought ill of by the people whom he was amongst." The captain summoned his gun room officers to his cabin and advised them not to consider Griswold a proper acquaintance. Detailing Griswold's abuses, the captain explained that Griswold had been boasting on shore that he had stirred up quarrels between the captain and the officers and that four duels were now depending among the officers in vindication of Griswold's character. (Ridgely had months before made clear to his officers his vehement opposition to dueling.) The captain had no sooner explained the intent of his orders when three junior officers interrupted him and

> as if by one consent . . . contradicted & challenged & defied & threatened in a tone and spirit of perfect equality, without the least show of respect or regard for me as their superior Officer. . . . All of which was rendered more outrageous and insufferable by the frequent repetition of the profane asseverations of by God I shall do so, by God I will, and the low & vulgar imprecation, of damn me if I dont.

The three officers were Lt. John P. Cambreleng, Lt. Robert B. Randolph, and Lt. Joseph P. Hall, the last named a member of the Marine Corps. Captain Ridgely heard them out in turn—they spoke of hearing of charges against Griswold, looking into them, and satisfying themselves that Griswold was an injured man. They tended to use the same language, sometimes saying "we," and gave the impression that their defiant and vituperative confrontation had been rehearsed. Lieutenant Cambreleng after an insolent speech was ordered out of the cabin. The other two carried on with mounting threats and disrespect, Hall even trying to arrange a duel with another officer right in front of the captain. Hall said they would disobey the captain's orders to avoid Griswold and would continue to associate with him. Captain Ridgely had the three arrested and ordered them sent home "to be dealt with as the Government may think proper."

To understand Owen Chase's proximity to the Griswold drama it is sufficient to note the following dates. The *Constellation* anchored in Valparaiso February 6; four days later on February 10 Ridgely went to Santiago with five lieutenants and midshipmen. They arrived the eleventh and were received "with much polite attention by the Supreme Director O'Higgins" and stayed in the capital for the independence anniversary celebrations. On February 21 Ridgely returned to Valparaiso and his ship.[28] On February 25 Owen Chase, Benjamin Lawrence, and Thomas Nickerson were brought into Valparaiso. Ridgely's meeting in his cabin with his officers and confrontation with the three vituperative ones were separated by only a few days from his reception of Owen Chase on board. On March 7 Randolph and Hall were put on board the *Macedonian* with instructions for their delivery to authorities.

Cambreleng's case is the most interesting. Writing the same day that Randolph and Hall were transferred from the ship, Captain Ridgely said,

> Since the arrest of these officers Lt. Cambreleng has become deranged. if he should not get better I will not send him home by this conveyance, he is quite a youth, just promoted & I thought very promising, I have always had a regard for him, and regret extremely the course he has persisted in.[29]

On March 10, the day before the *Constellation* sailed for Coquimbo, Lieutenant Cambreleng was transferred to the *Macedonian*. Owen Chase, Benjamin Lawrence, and Thomas Nickerson were likewise transferred to the *Macedonian* some time that week, at the very latest March 10, the same day that Lieutenant Cambreleng was taken over. Five days later, on March 15, while the *Macedonian* was still at anchor in Valparaiso harbor, Lieutenant Cambreleng died. The *Macedonian* log for March 16 reads: "10.30 the remains of Lieut John P. Cambrelind [*sic*] were taken on Shore & interred in the grounds of the Military Hospital at the Almendral with every honor due his rank."[30] A mysterious and unforeseen conclusion to the tense weeks on the *Constellation*.

If by the time of his transfer to the *Macedonian* Owen Chase was *au courant* of the Griswold affair—and it is hard to see how he could not have been—the whole thing must have seemed surreal to him. Snatched from months in a setting where the elements of the visible and imaginable world were stripped of all meaning except succor and threat, he must have blinked long before his gaze could readjust to take in the world of leisure good and leisure evil, where right and wrong were done not to meet a need but merely because the doer wanted to do them. Now, stirring from the lovely world of helping hands and bowls of tapioca, he was forced to focus on a scene of suggestive viciousness as if he had awoken in a cave with lurid and distorted pictures on the wall. His bunk may even have adjoined that of the dying Cambreleng.

But this was just a fragment of the scene before him. Naval life was still intense on the homebound *Macedonian*. The same day that Lieutenant Cambreleng died, a distinguished visitor came on board the *Macedonian*. The British ships *Creole* and *Glendower* had come into Valparaiso, and their captains were guests of Commodore Downes.[31] The captain of the *Creole* was Sir Thomas Hardy, one of England's most famous nineteenth-century naval officers. Best remembered for his attendance on the dying Lord Nelson and for Nelson's legendary last words, "Kiss me, Hardy," he was now the commander of Britain's Pacific station, the British counterpart of Commodore Ridgely. There is no telling whether news of the *Essex* survivors' adventure and their presence on the *Macedonian* ever came to Hardy's ears, but his visit added something to the pageantry of shipboard life and to the spectacle unfolding before the survivors.

The survivors were, in any event, soon to change ships again. On

Saturday, March 17, two days after Hardy's visit to the *Mace-donian*, the *Two Brothers* came into port carrying Captain Pollard and Charles Ramsdell. It was time for making plans: the *Mace-donian* was to sail on Monday. The decision was made, and all but Captain Pollard went on board the *Eagle*, Capt. William H. Coffin, which sailed from Valparaiso March 22 (or 23, if we again correct a date given in the *Gazeta ministerial de Chile*). An anonymous Australian source says, "Capt. Pollard was advis'd by the faculty to continue a short time longer, for the further establishment of his health."[32] Whatever "faculty" means precisely, there is a suggestion in the statement that Pollard and perhaps the others were receiving the attention of a group of doctors. Pollard did stay on in Valpa-raiso and came home about two months after the others in the *Two Brothers*, the ship that had brought him into port and the ship that was to play—no one would have dreamed of predicting such a thing at the time—a bigger role in his life than even the *Essex* did.

Now there were only three *Essex* men still in trouble. While the five in Valparaiso had been recovering, William Wright, Seth Weeks, and Thomas Chapple were eating birds' eggs and pep-pergrass on Henderson Island.

As Captain Ridgely had made clear, the most immediate steps were taken to rescue the remaining three. Capt. Thomas Raine, whom Captain Ridgely approached with the request for help for the three island survivors was a twenty-seven-year-old English captain with considerable experience in crossing the Pacific and in dealing with emergencies. He had been taking the *Surry* back and forth between England and Australia for at least seven years. In 1814 he had been a junior officer on the ship when a typhus epidemic swept through crew and passengers, a group of convicts being brought over from England. Raine was the only officer to survive; he assumed command, brought the ship to Australia, and then, retain-ing command, sailed to China to collect a homebound cargo and returned to England with it. Arrived in England, the twenty-two-year-old acting captain was made full captain and stayed with the *Surry* for years. He eventually settled in Australia and became prominent in the business world of the new country—including the whaling business.[33]

CAPT. THOMAS RAINE

Captain Raine had brought the *Surry* to South America on an emergency mission. A grave shortage of wheat caused by torrential rains ruining the harvest was impending in Australia, and Captain Raine had offered to make, at his own risk, a voyage to Chile to purchase wheat. He had left Sydney in mid-December and anchored in Valparaiso Bay February 1; he would be about five and a half weeks in Valparaiso buying and loading 15,000 bushels of wheat.

One of the minor ironies of the *Essex* adventure is that Captain Raine was sailing east to South America at the same time that the *Essex* survivors were. Had it not been for the more southerly route of the *Surry*, the ship might have found the *Essex* boats. Owen Chase's observations of latitude and longitude compared to the positions of the *Surry* given in its Abstract Log indicate that the *Surry* did, in fact, "pass" the survivors on January 13, the day after Owen's boat became separated from the other two, but the *Surry* was about ten degrees to the south.

Whatever reports Captain Raine had received of the war in Peru and the disruption of neutral shipping were enough to convince him to arm his ship. "Getting the guns ready for fighting the Spanish Patriots," reads the log entry for January 16. And on January 22: "quite equipped for Action—mounting six Guns and 42 Hands—plenty of Muskets etc."[34]

The *Surry* arrived in Valparaiso February 1 and spent five weeks loading wheat. The *Constellation* arrived a few days later and was to be in the port until the day after the *Surry* sailed, so there was ample opportunity for Captain Ridgely and Captain Raine to become acquainted and for Captain Ridgely to learn the other's plans for returning to Australia. When Owen Chase came into Valparaiso February 25, the *Surry,* because of its sailing plans, would have seemed one of the most logical ships to approach with the request for a rescue effort for the three men left on the island. At that time no one ashore knew what had happened to Captain Pollard's boat, so the suggestion was made to Captain Raine that he stop at Easter Island before going on to Ducie on the chance that Pollard's boat had made it to that island. It is clear from Captain Ridgely's March 7 letter that Captain Raine was expected to make both stops. That plan was obviously modified when on March 9 the

Hero arrived with the news that Pollard had been found. The *Surry* was to leave the next day, March 10, and the *Constellation* the day after that, but there must have been time to pass on to Captain Raine the news that he now had only one set of survivors to look for. The main reason for assuming that this message was given to Captain Raine is that when the *Surry* did actually make a brief stop at Easter Island there is no indication that the stop had been made for the sake of finding survivors; rather, its purpose appears to have been trading with the natives—and that on board the ship, not even on shore.

Perhaps the last-minute news about Pollard's rescue may also explain the contradiction in figures quoted for the payment made by Captain Ridgely to Captain Raine. In his March 7 letter (when he still assumed that a stop at Easter Island would be wise) Captain Ridgely speaks of paying Captain Raine $500 for his efforts. In his Journal, however, which was written later, he speaks of giving Captain Raine $430. The reduction of the mission may have led to the captains' agreeing on the smaller sum. One of the figures, of course, may simply be an error.

Leaving Valparaiso on March 10, the *Surry* was at Easter Island two weeks later and at Ducie Island April 6. The dates given in the *Surry* accounts of the rescue conflict with the dates in the Chapple narrative (Appendix C), where the rescue is described as being completed April 5, at which time the *Surry* would not, by its own records, have reached either Ducie or Henderson. The *Surry*'s records are more reliable, for the day-to-day notations of date, position, and so on, on board the ship are less likely to err, while the survivors' recollections could be imprecise, and Chapple, the only one of the three quoted on this part of the adventure, told his story through someone else. There are three *Surry* documents that tell the rescue story: the Abstract Log of the *Surry;* an account written by Dr. David Ramsay, surgeon on the *Surry;* and an anonymous manuscript in the Mitchell Library, Sydney, designated A131.[35] Dr. Ramsay in his Journal describes the *Surry*'s arrival at Ducie and the subsequent search:

Lat. 24. 37 S
Long. 124.27 Ducie's Island

A low flat appearance of shells, corals—coral reefs—it's shape resembles

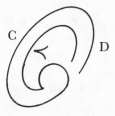

surrounded by coral reefs & breakers, had great difficulty landing—
went in the gig with the Capt—the second mate in the cutter—took
an observation & found it according to Norrie's Epitome viz
Long   Lat.

There is only one kind of tree, which almost covers the island also a
small bush like myrtle and a few tufts of grass was all that could be
seen although we went round the island. We landed at C. The Cap^{ts}
party [   ] into the lake. The other party went round to D by the
beach & returned by the lake . . . so that the ship sailed round it,
the boats sailed round it & we walked round it. There was no marks
of any person having been there before,—it is completely occupied by
birds (all of the sea kind) in many places one can—scarcely walk
without treading on them—they had no nests but layed their eggs (for
they have only one) in any little hollow a small white bird I called a
whale bird was observed to place its egg on the branch of a tree only a
little hollow chipped for it—The birds were the Man of War kind—
gannets—. The lake or bay is pretty deep has a reef of coral extending across its mouth—two springs could be seen—one brought off a
great many birds, eggs, corals, shells eggs.

Sunday 9th April 1821   Lat 24.26 S
                         Long 128.20 W

Saw the Island at 2 Oclock and soon got up with it—fired two guns &
a little after the second gun Mr Hall saw the three men running along
the beech We hove to, got our boats out & went ashore for them but
[on account] of the coral [could] not land—one swam off to us & told
us that the others could not swim—but we with great risk got close
into the rocks & got the other two in the gig—only one had a pair of
trousers, they all had shirts one waistcoat among them had a book
with his certificate and his [   ], also the days of the month correctly kept—I kept off all night and in the morning went ashore to get
off a little tin box & 3 letters in it—one was to the Cap^{ts} wife, one to
the Mate's wife & the other to the public. We learned that the ship

Essex an American whaler was attacked by a whale in Lat. 00.47 S
Long 11[6]°—

That the men took to the boats put what bread & water they could
carry and intended to get to the Gallipagos Island but the wind continuing from the N.E. and S.E. they after 24 days without seeing any
other sight of land arrived at —————— Island now called Henderson's
but which they took to be Ducies. They had three boats, the Capt and
[   ] men in one, cheif [sic] mate 6 & the second mate 7 men—
although no springs on the island they got as much rain water as
filled up their casks and after a week they set sail for Easter Island
excepting the three men we picked up who would not trust themselves
in the boats—

When the whale struck the ship it was under the main [   ] &
the stroke knocked off the keel, she then lay along side the ship &
tried to bite some part of it, but could get no hold, she then took a
sweep round about the distance of half a mile & came dead on to the
ship which was going about 6 knots, the chief mate then [   ] &
put the harpoon up but it was too late she drove her head into the
bow & then left the ship—when the boats left the ship she had not
gone down, all the starboard side was out of the water perhaps from
the oil in her but there was no possibility of repairing her her bows
being completely stove in—they scuttled the deck & to[ok] what they
wanted. The men on the Island fared very poorly living on shell fish,
birds & a few berries—& very much dis[tressed] for water. The
Island seems to be the produce of some Volcanic eruption—it consists
entirely of coraline matter & shells no soil and few trees of different
kinds.

All round it is very steep & difficult of access, with a great many
caverns in the rocks formed by the sea it appears but on the top it is
about 160 feet above the sea we seen a very few land birds—brought
off a great many peices of coral, small shells, sea eggs—

The report of the shipwreck that Dr. Ramsay passes along in this
account is presumably taken from conversation with the three men
just rescued from the island and perhaps from one or more of the
letters found in the tin box on the island. But Dr. Ramsay was
already partially informed on the *Essex*'s history, for he had been in
Valparaiso with the *Surry* and must have learned whatever Commodore Ridgely passed on to Captain Raine about the disaster.
Captain Raine or Dr. Ramsay or someone else from the *Surry* like
Edward Dobson, who is quoted below, may even have interviewed
Owen Chase or Benjamin Lawrence or Thomas Nickerson. These
circumstances are worth noting, for the account of the shipwreck

presented by Dr. Ramsay contains some elements not yet encountered, two of which—the absence of water on Henderson Island
and the survivors' intention of going to the Galapagos—are hard to
accept, the spring on the beach being so well attested to and Owen
Chase's description of the survivors' plans so specific. The other
new details in the account—Owen's trying to use a harpoon against
the whale and the whale's trying to bite the ship—are plausible and
contradict nothing known from other sources.

Mitchell Ms. A131 covers the same events and introduces some
additional description of the call at Henderson Island. The
considerations just expressed about new details in the Ramsay
Journal apply to Ms. A131 as well. The author, presumably
Edward Dobson, describes the fruitless visit to Ducie and then goes
on to the rescue. He says of Ducie:

> They found it a most barren Spot, the Beaches lined with Coral
> Rocks and Shells, there were a few Bushes among which an immense
> number of Birds, kept their nests—there was a large Lagoon in the
> Middle.—there was not the least appearance of any one ever having
> landed in this place before no appearance of fire, no Trees cut, and
> indeed no Sign whatever—they found a piece of a Spar on the Beach
> with notches at the ends.—which apparently had been a fender to
> some Ship.—
> Capt. Raine took a Meridian observation and found the Latitude of
> the N.E. end 24°38′ S.—and its Long: 124°24′ W.—being 13 Miles
> more to the Eastw.ᵈ than laid down in charts.—
> Capt. Raine not finding the 3 Men, thinks this Island has been
> mistaken for one, More to the Westw.ᵈ and accordingly intends to
> touch at it.—at 5 P.M. made Sail with a pleasant breeze.—
> 7ᵗʰ Pleasant breeze and fine Weather—70 ᵐⁱˡᵉˢ
> 8ᵗʰ Light Winds and cloudy Weather. Sea Smooth 4 P.M. Long.
> [by Obs.] 126°1′ W. chro. 125°48′ W.—Lat. 24°26′ S.—Keeping
> a good look out for the Supposed Ducies Island. 119 ᵐⁱˡᵉˢ
> 9ᵗʰ Fresh breezes and cloudy Weather, a man at the Mast Head
> who at 2 P.M. announced the intelligence of Land a head, we
> immediately steered for the Centre of it and being close in fired a
> Gun, but not seeing any one hauled on the Starboard tack and stood
> to the North End, on rounding of which, we opened a Spacious Bay
> and fired another Gun, in a few minutes to our very great joy we saw
> the "three poor fellows" come down to the Beach out of the Bush.—
> Shorten.ᵈ Sail and lowered the Boats down immediately lowered

down. Capt.ⁿ & Doctor, went in the Gig, and Mr. Powers in Cutter, in about an hour they returned with the Men they found the Surf very high and of course impracticable to land. but having Worked the Boats as close in as possible, the Men then Waded through the Surf, but with great difficulty they were got into the Gig, one of them being very much bruised, by the sharp coral Rocks that line the shore; they were very weak and thin and Capt.ⁿ Raine supposes they would not have weathered it another Month.—their names are Thomas Chappel, Will.ᵐ Wright and Seth Weeks—as soon as they came on board, they were taken into the Cabin and treated with every attention and kindness their situation demanded.—

They told Capt.ⁿ Raine there were some Papers on shore, left by their Captain,—determined on laying on and off the Island for the Night and in the Morning to go on shore again.—

April 10ᵗʰ This Morning at Day light found ourselves something to leeward of the Island, made all Sail and beat up, at Noon being close too, both Boats again went on shore and landed in another Bay, through a very nasty Surf, between a small Crack in the Rocks—they got the Letters (one addressed to the Public, one to the Capt.ⁿˢ Wife and one to the Brother of the Chief Mate). Capt.ⁿ Raine having taken the Letters, left one in their place, giving particulars of the above transactions, he also ordered the name of the ship and his own name, with the date to be cut on some trees,—he having seen the name of a Ship which it seems had touched there before these unhappy Men had landed on this desolate place—the name was the "Elizabeth' Capt.ⁿ H. King"—these Men say in a cave on another part of the Island— they found the skeletons of 8 Men who it appears (as they say) must have been there some time.—

at 4 P.M. both Boats having come on board again quite safe, made Sail from the Island, which Capt.ⁿ Raine calls "Incarnation Island" its Long. 128°20′ West and Lat. obs. 24°26′ South.—The above place is larger than Ducies Island and the top is level like a plain with, here and there a Bush or so, it affords very little Water and less food, they were obliged to live on a kind of Berry called a palm and such Sea Birds which they could catch asleep in the Night—they were partaking of a Bird they had just caught and cooked, when they heard the report of our Gun, one run out to see what it was, and the poor fellow told me himself when he saw the Ship, he was so overpowered with the emotions such a sight excited in his breast, he could not go to tell his companions the joyful intelligence—but when they all saw the Ship and knew they were once more on the point of seeing some of their fellow beings—their emotions and feelings at such a time may be better imagined than described.—

The following is the Account they give of their Shipwreck, and subsequent misfortunes.—They sailed from Nantucket, in the American
Whaler Essex, of 260 Tons comm^d by Captn Pollard, on the 12th
August 1819.—On a Whaling Voyage—they arrived in the South
Seas and were pretty fortunate, having procured 750 Barrels of Oil
and where [were] in the Lat 00°47′ S.—and Long. 118°0′ W. on
the 20th Novr 1820. on which day, they were among many Whales
and their Boats were all down, the 2nd Mates Boat had got stove and
had returned on board to be repaired, shortly after his being on
board, a very large Whale what Whalers term of the 1st Class Struck
the Ship and knock^d part of her false keel off, just abreast of her main
channels—the Whale there lay along side the Ship, endeavoring to lay
hold with her jaws, but could not accomplish it, she then turned and
went round the Stern and came up on the otherside—went away
ahead, turned short round, and again came with great velocity for the
Ship—the vessel at this time was going on at about 5 knots, but such
was the force say these Men—she had stern way. the Men on Deck
all knock^d down and the Water came dashing in the Cabin Windows,
and worst of all, the Bows were stove in, under the cathead on the
Starboard side, and in less than 10 Minutes, the vessel filled, and
went on her Beam ends.—

The Captain and Chief Mate had each got fast to a Whale but
upon the misfortune of the Ship—they cut from them and came on
board—the Captn ordered the masts to be cut away, upon which she
righted.—they then Scuttled the upper Deck, and got some Bread and
some Water, which they put in the Boats they staid by the Ship, three
days, during which time they made Sails for the Boats.—having taken
in the compasses and some Nautical Instruments—they left the Ship
and stood away to the Southw^d in hopes of getting into the variables
and fine Weather, but the Winds being right in their teeth, they made
much leeway. on the 20th Dec. 1820.—they made this Island, from
which through the humanity of Captn Raine, they have just been
taken.—

Captn Pollard remained here one Week, who finding the Island
afforded hardly any nourishment of any Description—they all (excepting the above three who preferred staying here to risking their
lives again) determined upon venturing to the Coast of S. America in
their Boats, and the sequel of their melancholy Story ends, with the
Boats Crews suffering unheard of hardships—two of which were
pick^e up—one Boat with the Captn and a Boy was brought into
Valparaiso—the other was taken on board some other Ship.

From the Appearance of the Island, it is wonderfull how these poor
Men have subsisted for such a period nearly 4 Months from the Cap-

tain's leaving them.—the whole Island says Captⁿ Raine appears to be a rock of Volcanic Matter and is full of caves of considerable length.—

The following is the letter addressᵉ to the Public and left there by Captⁿ Pollard.—

"Account of the Loss of the Ship Essex of Nantucket in North America commanded by Captⁿ Pollard Junʳ—which shipwreck happened on the 20.ᵗʰ day of November 1820.—in Long 118°0′ W on the Equator, by a large Whale striking her in the Bow with the head, which caused her to fill with Water. we got what Provisions etc the Boats would carry and left on the 22.ⁿᵈ Nov. & arrived here this day with all hands—we intend to leave here to morrow which will be the 26.ᵗʰ Decʳ— for the Continent.—I shall leave with this a letter for my Wife and who ever finding it, will have the goodness to forward it, will oblige an unfortunate man and receive his sincere Wishes.— Ducies Island 25.ᵗʰ Decʳ 1820."³⁶

As the *Surry* set out to the west, Henderson Island was left deserted for the first time in almost four months. It was an overnight cruise to Pitcairn Island, a stormy one with thunder and lightning, but by eight o'clock in the morning the skies had cleared and Pitcairn was in sight fifty-five miles away, and by the afternoon the ship was close to it. A canoe came alongside, and the *Surry* was hailed by a cheery, "How you all do?" That greeting from Edward Quintal and George Young began the *Surry*'s memorable brief visit to Pitcairn Island. Captain Raine's account of the visit was published shortly after the *Surry*'s arrival in Sydney; Dr. Ramsay's has also been subsequently published.³⁷

The accounts of both men show them completely stunned and charmed by the paradise they had stepped into. The natives were beautiful to look at, physically agile and physically fearless, warmhearted, devout, and triumphantly hospitable. They feasted their guests on roast pig and brought out their island whiskey, which was found very good by the Europeans. They prevailed on their visitors to stay overnight—the visitors awoke in the morning to the sound of singing coming from all the houses of the village, as the people began their day with psalms and prayer. John Adams, though unwell, received the visitors and talked with them at length, even going through the whole *Bounty* story for them. The islanders' desire to have a missionary sent out to them was a frequent subject

116   STOVE BY A WHALE

of conversation as was their longing for more skill in reading and
more books to read.

One anecdote recounted by Captain Raine catches the spirit of
the island that he found so enchanting:

> There is one remark I cannot omit, respecting the eagerness the
> women manifested to see an Englishwoman. I told them Captain
> Henderson, of the Hercules, would call there, and that he was mar-
> ried and had children. At this their joy was truly excessive, and
> though only two heard me relate the fact, it was soon spread amongst
> them all. Some said, "O! I so like to see an Englishwoman! Suppose
> I see an Englishwoman, I kiss her suppose I die directly after."

Raine and Ramsay, the two sophisticated and experienced
mariners, took their departure in a reluctant and looking-over-the-
shoulder fashion. One of the last sights to fascinate them was an
exhibition of an original Pitcairn water sport, which they described
in detail, thereby putting on record the first known description of
surfboarding:

> The women [and subsequently the men] . . . then amused themselves
> with *sliding,* as they term it; one of the strangest, yet most pleasing
> performances I ever saw. They have a piece of wood, somewhat
> resembling a butcher's tray, but round at one end and square at the
> other, and having on the bottom a small keel; with this they swim off
> to the rocks at the entrance, getting on which they wait for a heavy
> surf, and, just as it breaks, jump off with the piece of wood under
> them, and thus, with their heads before the surf, they rush in with
> amazing rapidity, to the very head of the bay; and although amongst
> rocks, &c. escape all injury. They steer themselves with their feet,
> which they move very quickly.

To fully appreciate the enthusiasm of the *Surry* people and the
Bounty people at this visit, one must realize that this was one of the
earliest visits of any ship to the island. Captain Raine assumes that
the *Surry* was just the seventh ship to visit Pitcairn:

> It was in 1808 that the Topaz touched here; the next was the Briton,
> English frigate, commanded by Sir Thomas Staines, in September,
> 1814; and since then the Sultan, Captain Reynolds, an American
> whaler; the Hercules, Captain Henderson, a country ship from
> Valparaiso on her return to India; the Elizabeth, Captain King,
> English South Seaman; the Stanton, Captain Birch, an American

whaler; the Elizabeth, Captain Douglas; and, lastly, ourselves, the Surry,—making in all seven, counting the Elizabeth's second visit.[38]

This calculation may be correct; it includes ships whose visits are not mentioned in the *Pitcairn Island Register Book* (where, as a matter of fact, the *Surry*'s visit is not recorded).[39] Even if other unrecorded visits had taken place before the *Surry* arrived, they were few, for the Pitcairners' conversation made it clear what an exceptional event the ship's arrival was.

William Wright, Seth Weeks, and Thomas Chapple, one can be sure, did not go ashore. They would have been much too weak for that, and even if they had not been, there would have been a touch of black humor in their setting foot on any island, even an island paradise. Their idea of paradise at the moment was doubtless most easily satisfied by life on shipboard.

Weak as they were when taken on the *Surry,* their recovery was evidently rapid. Chapple tells us in his narrative that they were able before the end of the voyage to do their share of the ship's work. Even if lighter duties were apportioned them, such a restoration of powers is impressive, for there were only seven more weeks to the voyage—the *Surry* moored in Sydney Cove on June 1.

From this point it is possible to follow two of the three survivors. William Wright and Seth Weeks became crew members of the *Surry.* Apparently ashore in Sydney for the winter months of June, July, and August, they went out on the *Surry*'s next voyage September 5, 1821, to Macquarie Island.[40] They were back in Sydney on December 6, 1821. A little over two months later, on February 15, 1822, Weeks and Wright were members of the crew when the *Surry* sailed for England, this time with Gov. Lachlan Macquarie on board. The ship stopped at Bahia, from which it sailed May 6, and arrived at Gravesend July 3, 1822. In England, Weeks and Wright left the *Surry* and arranged their passage back to the United States.

About Thomas Chapple nothing more is known save that, as he tells us in his narrative, he returned to London in June 1823 "and furnished the details from which this account has been drawn up." He must have been interviewed soon after his return, for the Religious Tract Society had his shipwreck tale (see Appendix C) on sale in 1824.⁴¹ Whether he returned to sea from his hometown of Plymouth or any other port is not known. A Thomas Chapple was known to be living on Bedford Street in Plymouth in 1834.⁴² That would have been a reasonable year for him to be retiring from the sea, but, on the other hand, Chapple is not an unusual name in Devon.

With the return of Wright and Weeks to Massachusetts, all that could be restored of the *Essex* was restored, save for a little leather-covered chest from the ship, which bobbed on the waves over the sunken *Essex* like Queequeg's coffin and was picked up and passed about until it too came home to Nantucket seventy-five years after its ship went down.⁴³

On the crest of one branch of the Chase family is the motto, *Ne cede malis,* "Do not give in to evils." It could have been inscribed there in anticipation of Owen—one would wonder indeed what feat had once occurred in the family's history to prompt the phrase that could have matched Owen's for endurance and fortitude. But, the motto once vindicated, what then? The survivors of the *Essex* were young men, and the question for all of them was what to do with their favored lives.

Chapter Four

NEXT LOWERING

OWEN CHASE AFTER THE *ESSEX*

IN CHAPTER 23 of *Moby-Dick,* "The Lee Shore," a seaman named Bulkington, just in from a four-year voyage, signs up within days to ship out again. Melville exalts him for repudiating all havens and comforts and realizing that it is only in the storm that he can survive the storm. Bulkington's gesture is abruptly romantic and seems to be larger than life, but many seamen without a romantic bone in their bodies have done what Bulkington did, not always within a few days but fairly soon after coming back from the sea. Just how many of the *Essex* survivors returned to sea we cannot be sure, but the two about whom we know most, the first mate and the captain, did. They were Bulkingtons in behavior if not in motive—the sea was what they lived from, and it would take more than a dramatic shipwreck to keep them away from it.

On June 11, 1821, the *Eagle,* Capt. William H. Coffin, arrived in Nantucket and disembarked half of the eight *Essex* survivors, Owen Chase, Benjamin Lawrence, Thomas Nickerson, and Charles Ramsdell.[1] At the moment the ship docked, as we have seen in chapter 3, no one on Nantucket had reason to assume that Chase, Lawrence, or Nickerson was alive. These three getting off the ship were walking up out of a watery grave into the arms of their startled, mourning families.

Phebe Ann Chase, fourteen months old now, saw her father for the first time. The little family went off to its home; the other three seamen, all of them unmarried, were taken home by their families; and Nantucket ingested the news. A melodramatic tale about the survivors' return appeared in a magazine article years later; it told of a large hushed throng on shore meeting the *Eagle* and parting like the crowd at the prison door for Hester Prynne as the survivors passed, stared at and ungreeted, to trudge alone to their homes.[2] *Non è vero ma è ben trovato,* one might say, if only it were *ben trovato.*

When on August 5 the *Two Brothers* arrived in Nantucket with Captain Pollard, all the living Nantucketers from the Essex were home. It is clear that both Captain Pollard and First Mate Chase were making preparations to go to sea again—before the year was out each of them would be back on a ship with his old rank. But Owen Chase used the summer months to write the story of the *Essex* that we have read. The literary history of this *Narrative* is saved for chapter 5, but it may be observed that, whatever else is known or unknown about it, the book was written quickly: by October 31 the printer registered the title with the court clerk for the Southern District of New York.

Owen had a half-year with his wife and daughter before going back to sea. When he did sail it was not from Nantucket but from New Bedford. He signed on the whaler *Florida,* Capt. Simeon Price, as first mate and sailed from New Bedford around December 20, 1821. For the first time on extant records there appears a physical description of Owen Chase: the crew list of the *Florida* describes Owen as twenty-four years old, five feet, ten inches tall, dark complexioned and brown haired.

The crew was about the same size as the crew of the *Essex;* no one on the ship but Owen was from Nantucket. The ship was out just short of two years, returning on November 26, 1823, with 2,000 barrels of oil. It had cruised the off-shore ground, had stopped at Coquimbo and Payta, at each of which it had had a desertion; it probably touched other ports as well. On August 11, 1823, it spoke the *Triton* off Tumbes, the same ship that had brought back the first reports of the loss of the *Essex.*[3]

When the *Florida* discharged its crew and officers in New Bedford, Owen crossed over to Nantucket and rejoined his family.

Phebe Ann was three and a half now, and there was once again a tot in the house who had never seen her father, year-and-a-half-old Lydia. This time Owen stayed in Nantucket almost two years. On September 14, 1824, his son William Henry was born, but the happiness of the event was quickly eclipsed by the first major domestic tragedy to affect Owen: less than two weeks after William Henry's birth, the baby's mother died. Peggy was twenty-six at the time of her death; her husband, who was twenty-seven was left to care for a four-year-old, a two-year-old, and a newborn baby.

Nine months later on June 15, 1825, Owen remarried. The marriage had a special poignancy, for it was an *Essex* marriage. Owen took as his wife Nancy Slade Joy, widow of Matthew Joy, the second mate of the *Essex* and first of the survivors to die. Nancy had been married to Matthew Joy for about two years before he signed on the *Essex* and had had no children by the marriage. Now she not only had three children to care for but was soon to be doing it single-handed, for Owen was to go to sea again within two months. First, however, was the matter of a new house. On June 29, 1825, about two weeks after getting married, Owen bought from his father the house on the northeast corner of what is now Orange and York streets but in his day was the corner of Orange and Maiden Lane. This was to be his house for the rest of his life.[4]

With Nancy and the children settled in the new house, Owen crossed over to New Bedford to make his first voyage as captain. In August 1825, twenty-eight years old, he sailed as master of the *Winslow*, a ship of 222 tons, just smaller than the *Essex,* and carrying a crew of fifteen. Owen's first mate, Josiah Smith, was a Nantucketer and the second mate, Polfrey Collins, a Vineyarder. Apart from one Sandwich Islander, all the crew members were Americans. The first week in August 1825 the *Winslow* sailed for the Pacific; by July of the following year it had reached the Japan ground and apparently met with success. By November 1826 it had crossed the Pacific eastward and had come into San Francisco. There among other ships it met the *Franklin,* Capt. Thaddeus Coffin, of Nantucket, a happy surprise for Owen, for his brother Joseph was then first mate of the *Franklin.* This was not the last time the brothers would meet at sea. Leaving San Francisco the

Winslow headed south to the off-shore ground, which it worked for a few months before returning home to New Bedford on July 20, 1827, with 1,440 barrels of oil. The crew was down to fourteen now, Seaman Amos Simon having been lost overboard off Japan.[5]

Owen was never more of a Bulkington than at this point in his life; in from his first cruise on the *Winslow,* he was on shore for less than a month before he went out on the ship again. He crossed over from New Bedford to Nantucket and was briefly reunited with Nancy and the children. On August 2 he paid off the $500 mortgage held by his father on his house and about a week and a half later was back in New Bedford to resume command of the *Winslow.*[6] He was joined on this voyage by Josiah Smith, his first mate on the previous voyage, and by two of the crewmen who had sailed with him then. This voyage was not to be to the Pacific but "on Brazil Banks & elsewhere."[7]

The *Winslow* never got that far. On September 18, following a course familiar to outbound whalers, it had come to 30°W/22°N, a point south of the Canary Islands, north of the Cape Verdes and a bit to the west of both, when a severe gale struck the ship. Owen had seen severe storms before—the *Essex* on its last voyage had been only two days out of Nantucket when it had been laid on its beam ends by a surprise storm—but this gale was nearly the end of the *Winslow.* It blew through September 18, 19, and 20, carrying away the whole mainmast and mizzenmast, leaving the foremast tottering, and sweeping away four of the boats. The ship was saved after exertions that pushed the sailors to their limits. It began to limp back home; five days after the gale abated, the ship had reached 23°N/40°20′W, having covered a distance that it could ordinarily have made in two days at most. The summer of 1827 had been an especially stormy one on the North Atlantic. The *Nile,* Captain Foster, was lost in a gale September 7, the schooner *Shylock,* Captain Minot, on August 29. The *Rufus* of Newburyport lost its spars in a hurricane August 21, and the *Eliza* of New York was severely damaged August 25.

After three weeks of agonizing progress, the *Winslow* was at a point just west of Bermuda and was still encountering rough weather. Between October 10 and October 14 the *Winslow* tried to speak three ships, the brig *Albert* from Portland, the schooner *Economy* from Philadelphia, and the schooner *Mary-Ann* from Warren, Rhode Island, but could get nothing more than the identifications; the wind was too strong to hear the ships' destinations.[8]

By October 19 the *Winslow* was back in New Bedford. The repairs called for were massive, and the owners took advantage of the work to have some major alterations made in the ship. By the time the *Winslow* was ready to go to sea again it was no longer a 222- but a 263-ton vessel.

The involuntary interlude in Owen's sea career while he waited for his ship to be repaired was a long one—nine months. Whatever feelings it left him with, it must have been a boon to his family, for of the twenty-eight months that Nancy had been married to Owen she had had him at home for only three.

In mid-July 1828 the *Winslow* was ready to sail again. The crew had been completely disbanded, and a new one had to be signed on. One sailor from the *Winslow*'s gale-ended cruise, George Smith, a Sandwich Islander, signed on for the next, and a Nantucket sailor, John R. Beard, who had sailed with Owen in 1825, also signed on. This cruise to the Pacific was to take two years almost to the day. This time Owen returned with 1,800 barrels of sperm oil, an amount, very likely, which the ship had been enabled to carry as a result of the alterations affecting its cargo capacity and increasing its tonnage; this was 400 barrels more than it had brought back in 1825. The *Winslow* returned July 7, 1830.[9]

Owen was now going to stay on Nantucket for more than two years. He was occupied with domestic concerns and with something else that was going on in Nantucket, the construction in the Brant Point shipyards of a new whaling ship. It was the first whaleship built at Brant Point, that little promontory forming a corner of the Nantucket harbor, and the builder was David Joy, second cousin of Matthew Joy of the *Essex,* Owen's wife's first husband. The ship was the *Charles Carroll,* and it was being built for Owen Chase. It was a larger ship than Owen had ever served on before, 376 tons, and therefore built for longer voyages.

On October 10, 1832, Owen Chase sailed as captain of the *Charles Carroll* on its maiden voyage. This was the first time he had sailed from Nantucket since he had gone out on the *Essex*. The ship was out three and a half years, returning early in March 1836 with the gratifying cargo of 2,610 barrels of sperm oil, one of the largest returns of oil by any whaler to any port that year.

Owen was eminently successful as a whaling captain. He was not an "unlucky man," as George Pollard had called himself—at least not at sea—but at home his fortunes were mixed. In July 1833— none of the records gives the precise date—Owen's daughter Adeline was born. Then on August 11, 1833, a few weeks—maybe only two—after Adeline's birth, Nancy Slade Joy Chase died at the age of thirty-four. Owen was only one-fourth of the way into his voyage when his daughter was born and his wife died. How the news reached him we can only speculate, but this was not news that need have been consigned to a letter—it would have circulated through both of the ports with which Owen was associated and would have been waiting for him at some gam or in some Pacific port.

The log for this voyage of the *Charles Carroll* is not extant, but Owen's brother Joseph, then captain of the *Catherine,* was sailing on the off-shore ground at the same time that the *Charles Carroll* was in the Pacific, and he noted in his log for June 28, 1834, "At 8 p.m. Spoake the Addaline 7 months out. got Distressing news for my self."[10] Since there is no evidence of any tragedy in Joseph's own family or in any other branch of the Chase family anywhere near this date, it is reasonable to guess that Joseph had received word of his sister-in-law's death ten months before. The *Adeline,* Captain Buckley, had sailed from New Bedford on November 13, 1833, three months after Nancy's death, and could well have carried the news. Any of several dozen ships sailing around the same time could have brought word of the death to Owen, but if no one had told Owen by August 13, 1834, and if the assumption is correct that Joseph Chase had learned of the death, then we know how the news came to Owen, for on August 13, about six weeks after Joseph Chase recorded his "Distressing news," the *Catherine* spoke the *Charles Carroll,* and Joseph and Owen had some time together. Joseph Chase's log for the days of this gam is all business with not a hint that he is with Owen; he merely notes that his brother's ship now has 1,700 barrels and that he is transferring to the *Charles Carroll* a seaman named Braddock Bears.

When the *Charles Carroll* did return to Nantucket in 1836 little Adeline Chase was two and a half; orphaned almost from birth, she was now only half an orphan. The other children were growing up: Phebe Ann was almost sixteen, Lydia was thirteen, and William Henry was eleven. Raised for more than two years by guardians, they must have felt their father's return keenly. He in turn seems to have come home pondering the family's plight, for he acted quickly to end his widowhood. On April 5, 1836, a month after the *Charles Carroll* docked, Owen married twenty-seven-year-old Eunice Chadwick.

This was another marriage in the interlude, this time a seven-month interlude, between voyages. Owen had the spring and summer with Eunice before the *Charles Carroll* was fitted out and ready to sail again. When the sailing date of August 30 came around, Owen was gone on a voyage which, as anyone familiar with Owen's ship would have predicted, was to last as long as the preceding voyage had, three and a half years. Eunice had had a few months to get to know the four children and to assume the most pressing task, the care of Adeline; now Eunice was nurse, housekeeper, and voice of authority, and alone in the big house, even more alone, perhaps, because of the presence of her husband's children but not her husband. Fall and winter and spring came around.

"These things happen," they would say in Nantucket, "and everyone understands." On January 17, 1838, sixteen months after Owen went to sea, a son, Charles Frederick, was born to Eunice.

There is some reason to believe that this unhappy news reached Owen at sea, as the tragic news about his second wife had probably reached him on his previous voyage. Herman Melville writes in his copy of Owen's *Narrative:*

> The miserable pertinaciousness of misfortune which pursued Pollard the Captain, in his second disastrous & entire shipwreck did likewise hunt poor Owen, tho' somewhat more dilatory in overtaking him the second time.
>
> For, while I was in the Acushnet we heard from some whaleship that we spoke, that the Captain of the "Charles Carroll"—that is

Owen Chace—had recently received letters from home, informing him
of the certain infidelity of his wife, the mother of several children, one
of them being the lad of sixteen, whom I alluded to as giving me a
copy of his father's narrative to read. We also heard that this receipt
of this news had told most heavily upon Chace, & that he was prey to
the deepest gloom.

Melville was wrong about which wife had been unfaithful—the
story could hardly be told many times over without some error
creeping in—but he may have been right about the rest. Just how
Owen was told the upsetting news we will consider shortly.

Of all of Owen's voyages this one on the *Charles Carroll,* his last,
is the one we know most about, for it is the only one the log of
which is extant. The log, which is today in the Peter Foulger
Museum in Nantucket, was kept by the captain, Owen himself, not
by the first mate. This we know from Owen's first-person references
("This is my Birth day"). It is as businesslike an account as the
average whaling log, but curiosities and suggestive details surface
throughout it. And the eye is caught by a graphic detail in the notation of whales taken: Owen, like most log keepers, used marginal
drawings of whales to record his kills, but he added the refinement
of making the drawings specific so that finbacks, sperm whales, and
so on, were distinguishable.

The voyage started with a good omen, a sixty-barrel whale taken
just a few days out of Nantucket, and a bad omen, Seaman
Benjamin Hayney falling from under the main top and breaking his
left arm and right thigh. Owen took him below and set the bones.
Hayney, who was fortunate not to have been killed in that all-too-
familiar shipboard accident, was never able to return to duty
without difficulty. Twenty months later, on May 18, 1838, Hayney
was put ashore in the Sandwich Islands "in care of the Consul on
account of lameness." Owen replaced Hayney with Emery
Goodrich, a young sailor he found in Hilo who may have been there
in consequence of desertion or discharge from the *Ansell Gibbs,*
Capt. Tristram D. Pease, of New Bedford.[11]

The *Charles Carroll* moved quickly to the Pacific and spent most
of its time on the off-shore ground. On August 9, 1837, the *Charles
Carroll* spoke the Nantucket whaler, *Charles and Henry,* Capt.

George Joy, a meeting which is of interest because the *Charles and Henry* on its next voyage out was to have for six months a boatsteerer whom it shipped in Eimeo named Herman Melville. This detail can be added to other pieces in the puzzle of Melville's claimed glimpse of Owen Chase at sea discussed in the next chapter.

On March 14, 1838, off the coast of Ecuador Owen spoke the famous *Hero,* the ship pillaged by the pirate Benavides and whose survivors had reached Valparaiso at the same time as the *Essex*'s seventeen years before. Now the captain of the *Hero* was Reuben Joy, second cousin of the owner of the *Charles Carroll* and, more important, brother of Matthew Joy of the *Essex,* Nancy Chase's first husband.

The contact between these two ships is more protracted than any other in the course of this whole voyage of the *Charles Carroll.* From March 14 to May 19 the two ships sailed in company. The practice of sailing in company was common; fortuitous encounters between ships were often prolonged for days or even for two or three weeks, and it was not merely ships that were already known to each other that chose to sail together. Sometimes the companion ships were of some assistance to each other, but most of the time they were simply company. The taste for this practice seems to have been keener in remote parts of the ocean like the Japan ground.

What distinguishes the two-month society of the *Charles Carroll* and the *Hero* is not just its length but the constant reference to the *Hero* in the *Charles Carroll*'s log. The ships were together sixty-seven days, thirteen of which were spent in the harbor of Hawaii (there are no entries for these days) and fifty-four at sea. On thirty-two of these fifty-four days the *Hero* is spoken of: "Hero in sight," "Hero in Co." On May 1 the *Hero* is mentioned twice in the same entry, and on April 4 occurs the telling and singular entry: "Hero out of sight."

If we seek to verify the statement that Melville makes in his annotation of Owen's *Narrative* about Owen being informed at sea about his wife's infidelity, one has to ask which ship of all those he encountered could have been the bearer of such delicate intelligence. Any captain could have compassionately passed on word about a wife's death, but most strangers would not be bearers of tidings about a wife's conduct. A letter could have been carried on any ship, of course, but there is something suggestive in the long contact between the two captains, almost relatives, and the extraordinary repeated mention of the *Hero*'s remaining in sight—and even passing out of sight for one day.

Reuben Joy had taken the *Hero* out of Nantucket before Charles Frederick was born to Eunice on January 17, but she was three months pregnant when the *Hero* left on August 16, 1837, and someone with Joy's ties to the family could easily have known the story.

On March 2, 1839, Owen recorded an experience frequently enough reported by ships off the Chilean and Peruvian coasts and even more frequently by American seamen in the ports of those countries: "At 10 AM this day felt the ship to tremble all over with A Sevear Shock of An Earth quake Accompanyed with A rumbling Noys Sunding like distant thunder Experienced Severall light Shocks after-wards the Swell Arose very much directly Afterwards." Earthquakes were a way of life along the Pacific coast of South America, and unreconstructed ruins greeted the visitor to city after city.[12] Owen's brother, Joseph Chase, records a similar earthquake in the log of the *Catherine* February 2, 1838, off the coast of Mexico.

On May 15, 1839, the *Charles Carroll* anchored in Nukahiva. Although this beautiful island of the Marquesas had become one of the major victualing stops for ships in the South Pacific, and although the Marquesas Islands were in time to become known as a paradigm of medical and social disaster thanks to the disease imported from Europe and America, nothing was to make Nukahiva better known than the novel *Typee* and the sojourn, already referred to in chapter 3, of *Typee*'s author, Herman Melville, on the island. It was three years after Owen Chase brought the *Charles Carroll* into Nukahiva that the *Acushnet* would anchor there and lose Seaman Melville by desertion.

A cursory survey of logs suggests that in the 1830s there was probably no place in the whole Pacific where desertion was more to be expected than on Nukahiva. An Irish crimp of some renown, Jimmy Fitz, lured sailors off ships in Nukahiva and then found them employment on other ships. Nor was Jimmy alone in the business, as we learn from Owen Chase's brother Joseph, who wrote in the log of the *Catherine* for April 25, 1836, while in Nukahiva: "At night Came of[f] Joseph Whiting Diserted to Day francis linch 2 Days since & Charles Brigdon & the Cook Diserted 4 in All intist [enticed] away by Jack and Tom Natives of this Island So bad frotune to them All." The Joseph Whiting mentioned by Joseph Chase, incidentally, was to reappear a few years later as a shipmate of Herman Melville's on the *Charles and Henry*. Whiting and Melville were both discharged from the *Charles and Henry* on May 2, 1843, in Lahaina. Whether Melville learned anything about Owen Chase from the man who served under Owen's brother is unknown. Whiting could have been the conduit of some of the more gossipy bits of news Melville records about Owen.

While in Nukahiva Owen had his share of desertions. George Coffin, James Malcolm, Emery Goodrich, John Cummins, James Henry, and Thomas Burdett all chose the island over the ship, and five of them succeeded in escaping. Emery Goodrich, the sailor recruited in Hilo to replace the lame Benjamin Hayney, was caught on shore and brought back to the ship.

Leaving Nukahiva in the beginning of June, the *Charles Carroll* stayed in the vicinity of the equator for about three months but considerably west of the place where the *Essex* was sunk. At no time during this voyage did the *Charles Carroll* come near the equator and 119° W.

On July 13, 1839, Owen noted, "This day lost my favourit Dog over board and was Drownd what a pity." Around the beginning of September he set course more or less for Tahiti and made the whalehunter's slow, meandering progress toward the island. He had taken four whales during August, and the ship was nearly full; he was, in fact, to take only one more whale before arriving back in Nantucket.

On his way to Tahiti Owen came through the northern tip of the Tuamotus and noted in his log for September 11, 1839: "A 4 of the West End of Deans island steed by to South B W prince of wails island in Sight to leward middle lay under short Sail at Day light Saw an island Baring South Calm Caled the island Vosperis Island

Lattd 15-40 [S] Longtd 148-25 [W]'' There is no Vosperis Island in
the Pacific, and the position of the ship makes it clear that the
island so named is in fact Makatea, also known as Aurora Island.
That is enough to explain the name Owen gave it, for Makatea is
one of the three major phosphate islands of the Pacific. "Vosperis"
Island is Phosphorus Island. This identification of the island is
noteworthy for one reason: it anticipates by roughly seventy years
the commercial discovery and exploitation of the phosphates on the
island. It poses, naturally, the question of how Owen came to be
aware of the phosphates. Certain phosphate deposits, those from
bone deposits or vegetable mold or those from avian excreta, could
be spotted by telescope, but it would have taken a trained crystallo-
grapher to detect natural phosphate rock. Whether Owen or some
other mariner from whom Owen eventually heard the story discovered the island's distinctive mineral, one marvels at the popular
circulation of this information for so long while the French phosphate interests that were eventually to establish the Compagnie
Française des Phosphates de l'Océanie were only beginning to
"suspect" the existence of phosphates on Makatea in 1907.[13]

On September 14, 1839, Owen Chase arrived at Tahiti.
Although the *Charles Carroll*'s log has little to say about the ship's
stopover of nearly a month at the island, it is possible to gain
some impression of Owen's experiences there from the numerous
contemporary descriptions of Tahiti and its more prominent people;
from the published recollections of one visitor whose stay in Tahiti
coincided almost to the day with Owen Chase's comes a good picture of what the visiting captain must have found on the island.
That chronicler was Lt. Charles Wilkes, commander of the
important United States Exploring Expedition.

Wilkes, forty-one years old, was already known in naval circles
for his scientific work, especially that performed as head of the
Depot of Charts and Instruments, the forerunner of the Naval
Observatory and the Hydrographic Office. Always a controversial
figure, Wilkes was to face in the course of his career more than one
court martial but was in time to be best remembered for two things,
the scientific publications resulting from the Exploring Expedition,
and his responsibility for the *Trent* affair. His stopping of the

British steamer *Trent* and seizure of the two Confederate commissioners to Britain, James Mason and John Slidell, created one of the gravest crises the Union faced in the course of the Civil War; readers of *The Education of Henry Adams* know how close the episode came to triggering England's entry into the Civil War on the side of the South.

Wilkes had arrived at Tahiti shortly before Owen Chase with four of the expedition's ships, the *Vincennes,* the *Porpoise,* the *Peacock,* and the *Flying Fish,* and had anchored off Point Venus, the northernmost point on the island, about eight miles east of the principal harbor, Papeete. His days were spent in meetings with native and European and American dignitaries, in explorations of the island, especially the inland mountain areas, and in observation of the daily life of Tahiti.[14]

Tahiti was ruled at the time by Queen Pomare IV but was an object of contention between the English and the French. The contention, which never acceded to military proportions, focused in 1839 on the case of two French missionaries expelled by the native authorities under pressure from the British consul Pritchard and on the subsequent amends exacted by the French admiral Dupetit-Thouars. This had taken place the year before Owen Chase arrived at Tahiti and was a prelude to the French domination of the island that had been effectively completed when Herman Melville arrived there three years after Owen Chase. In *Omoo,* probably the most autobiographically precise of his novels, Melville presents a succession of Tahiti vignettes, some of them depicting people whom Wilkes mentions and whom Owen Chase very likely met.

It is almost certain that Owen met one of the most talked about native characters in the Pacific, Jim, the Papeete harbor pilot. Jim or "English Jim" or "James Mitchell" was a crusty, colorful, and, as captain after captain testifies, competent pilot. An amusing episode in *Omoo* is that in which the narrator's ship is brought into Papeete unannounced and unauthorized to the great outrage of Jim, who rows out to meet it cursing and shouting and boards to take command for the brief remainder of its entry into the harbor.

> Jim turned out to be the regular pilot of the harbor; a post, be it
> known, of no small profit; and, in *his* eyes, at least, invested with

immense importance. Our unceremonious entrance, therefore, was regarded as highly insulting, and tending to depreciate both the dignity and lucrativeness of his office.

The old man is something of a wizard. Having an understanding with the elements, certain phenomena of theirs are exhibited for his particular benefit. Unusually clear weather, with a fine steady breeze, is a certain sign that a merchantman is at hand; whale-spouts seen from the harbor, are tokens of a whaling vessel's approach; and thunder and lightning, happening so seldom as they do, are proof positive that a man-of-war is drawing near.

In short, Jim, the pilot, is quite a character in his way; and no one visits Tahiti without having some curious story about him.[15]

Owen Chase doubtless had his tale of Jim. He brought the *Charles Carroll* up to Papeete on September 14 and signaled for the pilot, who was not able to come out until the next day because of high winds. On September 15 the *Charles Carroll* anchored in the harbor. The ships of the Wilkes expedition were still anchored off Point Venus and were not to come into Papeete harbor for about a week: Owen's log has the *Vincennes* coming in September 21 and the *Flying Fish* the next day; Wilkes says the *Vincennes* came in September 22 and the *Peacock* and the *Flying Fish* September 24. The *Vincennes* left Papeete for neighboring Eimeo on September 25.

Owen Chase and Charles Wilkes were on Tahiti at one anchorage or another for periods that overlapped by about a week and a half. After Wilkes took the *Vincennes* out, Owen was in port until October 10 with the *Flying Fish* and the *Peacock*. Wilkes does not mention, either in his chronicle of the expedition or in his *Autobiography*, the *Charles Carroll* or any other whaleship tied up in the port, for American whalers in Pacific ports were too common to note unless there was something special about them. It is likely, however, that the two captains met, for conventional courtesy would have called for such a meeting. The meeting is of interest not merely because of the particular distinctions of the two men but because of a roundabout *Essex* connection. Wilkes had heard the *Essex* story and was extremely taken with it; as we shall later see, he had met Captain Pollard and learned the details of the shipwreck firsthand from him. But the Melvillean will be even more interested in the meeting of Wilkes and Chase if he accepts David Jaffe's thesis that Wilkes was Melville's main model for Captain Ahab.[16] Nothing follows from the circumstance to alter literary history, but it would make a good engraving, the suddenly materialized captain of the *Pequod* and the mate of the *Pequod*'s prototype standing and talking on a spot where the *Pequod*'s creator was shortly to stand.

One other detail about the *Charles Carroll*'s stop in Tahiti is noteworthy: it may have been the only occasion on which Owen Chase saw a play. The *Flying Fish* was detained in Papeete by repairs until October 10, which was also the day that Owen was to sail, and the *Peacock* also remained in order to sail in company with the *Flying Fish* and to complete its survey of the island's harbors. Wilkes reports:

> In the interval of leisure which was thus afforded them, the crew of the Peacock asked and obtained permission to get up a theatrical entertainment, for the amusement of the natives and themselves. The council-house was placed at their disposal for the purpose by the native authorities. The play chosen was Schiller's "Robbers," the parts of which had been rehearsed at sea, in the afternoons—a task which had been the source of much amusement. An opportunity was now presented of getting it up well: the dresses having been prepared, the day was appointed, and when it arrived the piece was performed; the acting was thought by the officers very tolerable, and finally gave great delight to the natives. The latter, however, were somewhat disappointed in the early parts of the performance, for they had expected an exhibition of juggling, such as had been given for their · entertainment on board of a French frigate. While under this feeling, they were heard to say there was too much "parau" (talk). After they began to enter into the spirit of the performance, the murders took their fancy; and they were diverted with the male representatives of the female characters.
>
> A number of comic songs, which formed the relief of the more serious play, were exceedingly applauded; among others they laughed heartily at "Jim Crow" sung in character, and could not be persuaded that it was a fictitious character.[17]

Finally replenished for its return home, the *Charles Carroll* left Tahiti on October 10. It sped home as if it had been launched from a spring. Its route was an unusual southern one, straight down from Tahiti to about forty degrees and then east, rounding the Cape about six weeks after leaving Tahiti. It did not make the ordinary stops at Peruvian or Chilean ports; it did not, in fact, enter any port until it was home, but as it rounded the northeastern shoulder of South America it paused to send a boat into Pernambuco. On Saturday, February 15, 1840, the *Charles Carroll* stopped in Holmes Hole. Owen Chase had finished his last voyage.

It is hard to dissociate Owen's haste in coming home from the business he attended to once he got there. His arrival was on a weekend; on the following Tuesday, February 18, he filed for divorce:

To the Honorable Justices of the Supreme Judicial Court holden at Nantucket in and for the County of Nantucket on the first Tuesday of July A.D.1840.

Owen Chase of Nantucket, in said County master mariner, libels and gives this honorable Court to be informed that on the fifth day of April in the year of our Lord one thousand eight hundred and thirty-six, at Nantucket aforesaid he was lawfully married to Eunice Chase and has always behaved towards her as a chaste and faithful husband—Yet the said Eunice neglecting her marriage vows and duty since the marriage aforesaid, at said Nantucket has committed the crime of adultery with divers persons to this libellant unknown— Wherefore the said libellant prays that he may be divorced from the bonds of Matrimony, between him and the said Eunice.

                                                             Owen Chase

Nantucket Feb 18-1840[18]

The divorce was duly granted on July 7 by the judge then sitting, Lemuel Shaw, who seven years later was to become Herman Melville's father-in-law.

And now in this present term the Libellant appears, and the said Eunice Chase being called to come into Court, it appearing to the Court that she had been duly notified according to law, did not appear but made default—whereupon the evidence in support of the libel produced being seen, heard and understood, the facts alledged to sustain the charge of adultery are satisfactorily proved—It is therefore considered by the Court here, that the bonds of matrimony heretofore entered into between the said Owen Chase and Eunice Chase, be and hereby are dissolved, of which all persons concerned, are to take notice and govern themselves accordingly.

                                                    Attest Geo. Cobb, Clerk[19]

Eunice had been married to Owen Chase almost four years when he filed for divorce. She had been together with him less than six months of that time. For the first year and a half of her marriage she was mother to Owen's four children, Phebe Ann, Lydia, William Henry, and Adeline. On November 28, 1837, while her father was cruising off the coast of Ecuador, seventeen-year-old Phebe Ann Chase married Gardner Coffin and reduced the household by one. Phebe Ann had entered and left the household while her father was away. He had been at home for one-third of her seventeen years. The family's previous quorum was restored two months after Phebe Ann's marriage by Eunice's giving birth to Charles Frederick.

For two years Eunice raised the baby and took care of the older children. Lydia waited until her father returned before getting married; on March 15, 1840, one month after Owen arrived home and started his divorce proceedings, Lydia became the wife of William H. Tice. Divorced, Eunice left the family and, surprisingly, seems to have left behind her own son, Charles Frederick. Nantucket census records show him to have been part of Owen's family even at the age of twenty-seven. Eunice remained in Nantucket. Little is known of her subsequent life. Tax assessment records show her living on a modest but apparently safe income some twenty years after her divorce. Her life was to be a long one—she died of cancer at the age of eighty in 1888, outliving all but two of the Chases of her generation.

Two months after his divorce was granted, Owen married for the fourth time. Susan Coffin Gwinn, thirty-three years old, had married James Gwinn in 1827 and had been a widow since 1835. She and Owen were married September 13, 1840. She was childless by both her marriages and outlived Owen by twelve years, dying October 31, 1881.

The family in the house on Orange Street was getting smaller. William Henry would be going to sea in a few months, leaving seven-year-old Adeline and two-year-old Charles Frederick the only children in the house. It is possible that there was one other member of the household by this time. Joseph P. Chase was a Portuguese boy born in Fayal, the Azores, in 1831 who was formally or informally adopted by Owen and grew up with the family. Records do not show when the adoption took place, but some details of his later life are known. The *Inquirer and Mirror* reported at the time of his death:

> He was a native of Fayal, and when a youth came to Nantucket and made his home with Owen Chase. He made a number of whaling voyages, sailing in the Herald, Planter and several other vessels, rising to the rank of second officer under Captain William Beebe.
>
> In 1863 he crossed the isthmus and went to San Francisco, being employed by the Cutting Packing Co. He later became a longshoreman and for 35 years was foreman for Charles Haseltine & Co., holding th[a]t position up to the time of death.
>
> On February 21, 1854, he married Judith, daughter of Edward and Eunice Pinkham, and niece of Capt. Henry C. Pinkham, and two years ago Mr. and Mrs. Chase celebrated their golden wedding. The latter died in December, 1904. The couple were blessed with three sons, two of whom are now living.[20]

The adoption of Portuguese children was a familiar practice of Nantucket sea captains at this time. Some of the old Nantucket family names, all of them English or Irish, have survived on the island to this day through Portuguese branches. Nantucket names also turn up on natives of the Pacific islands—like the Hawaiian seaman Jack Chase who sailed under Owen on the 1828 voyage of the *Winslow*—but the Azores more than any other place seemed to supply Nantucket with permanent immigrants.

In January 1841 Owen became a grandfather. Daughter Lydia, the wife of William Tice, gave birth to Mary Anna. The Tices were to reside in Albany, and Mary Anna at twenty-one would marry Garret Van Iderstine in Albany. Mary Anna died at the age of twenty-two on June 29, 1863.

Owen Chase settled down to life ashore at this point. He had his property to attend to and apparently had an eye for real estate and investment. In the next twenty or so years he would buy and sell a variety of properties on Nantucket and invest in municipal bonds, the Pacific National Bank, the Indiana Central Railroad, and one booming business that attracted a number of Nantucket investors, Wamsutta Mills in New Bedford.[21]

The sea careers of all the Chase brothers were soon to be ended.

LYDIA CHASE TICE, DAUGHTER OF OWEN CHASE,
AND HER HUSBAND, CAPT. WILLIAM HARVEY TICE

George G. Chase completed his last voyage about the same time that Owen did his. Alexander, as far as records indicate, was the last of the five brothers at sea, bringing home the *Eliza Starbuck* on May 2, 1841. Several in the family settled down within a stone's throw of Owen's house on Orange Street: brother William lived on Orange Street, brother Alexander on Beaver Lane, sister Eliza, married to Ariel Cathcart, on Orange Street.

The five brothers had all survived their numerous voyages and had done well at sea. Their father was still alive and living near them. For over twenty years their interwoven arrivals and departures in Nantucket, their meetings at sea, exchange of news from home when out at sea and news of the sea when back at home had been the substance of their own lives and had wedded their wives and children to the sea. In Owen's case we can speculate that that was not at all times a happy union, but by and large the Chases were inured to the whaling family's fate. A letter written by Owen's brother Joseph offers a touching glimpse of the whaleman's feelings about his separation from his family; what Joseph wrote to his wife could probably have been written by any of the brothers and by countless other Nantucket whalemen, at least by those who were as open with their emotions:

> (November the 1—1837 Mawi
> Dear wife I am seated this eavning to communicate with my Dear wife in this way for it is Amoast 12 months since I have had this pleasure befoar but Dear wife will Excuse me for I have not had A oppitunity be, foar in that time I Arived hear the 2.9 of october from Japam my health is very good At this time I hope that my Dear wife & Children is in As good I have 2300 bbls of sperm oil good & woant About 6 or 7 hundred moar to fill my Ship I shall sail from this in About 10 Days for the Coast of California & line & of Shoar ground & if I shood be fortunate I hope to be At home in 12 or 14 months but if I shood not meate with good fortune perhaps not so soone my Crew and officers are All in good health & ship tite & in good order I have provision to last 16 or 18 months [   ] well fitted. I have taken 750 bbls. this Cruise to Japan and that is lowe for me but when I look Around & sea so many poor ships I doant complane of our fortune but think we have been very much favored & blest and triye to be thankfull to the good giver of so many Blessings to me this time & past favors that I feel not worthy of I have been favor in All things

thru life & hope to be favor thru this voyage & blest to meate my
Dear wife & Dear Children in health Again Oh happy Day to me &
my dear wife. I think & hope it will be the last time that we Are sep-
prated by these longe tegus voyages if we Are spaired to meate again,
I have as good A ship as I ever shood woant & well fitted And A fine
set of officers and All things as pleasant as these voyages can be I have
not enjoyed my health very well this some time back A Distress in my
stumark but am now As well as I was at home I shall wright A
number moar letters to be left at woahoo for thair will be some ships
thair bound home I shant wright by this ship to Mr Coffin so you
cam tell him the mews this I shall send by Capt. winslows I have
receaved A good many kind letters from dear wife & that is very
pleasing in Deade to me thair is good many ships At mowe & some
very [   ] I woant Dear wife to give my love to All our freinds I
want Dear wife to name the little girl Winifred for that is my Chois
let others sawe what thay. will About it I doant woant Dear wife to
have Any moar insurance Dun this time tell Mr. Coffin that I shall
wright At woahoo to him & like wise to Dear wife I hope to sea
Brother George on peruce it is getting late so I must bid Dear wife &
children good night with wishing health & poase to Attend Dear wife
& children.
J M Chase[22]

Joseph, who after Owen is the Chase brother about whom most is
known, is every bit as interesting a captain as Owen and wants only
one extraordinary adventure like Owen's to set him in relief against
the wide background of Nantucket's many unchronicled whalemen.
Such an adventure, as far as we know, never came, but even
Joseph's run-of-the-mill experiences often provide good stories:

At 4AM one of oure Boatsterers Jumped over board Loard A boat &
took him up & put him in Irons in A few Minits, got of his Irons &
went overboard Again Loard A boat & took him up hee is Crazy in
Consicus of being Drunke At Payta in those groge Shops & weants to
Drowne him Silfe hee thinks that all my Crew woants to kill him & I
had to Chane him fast to prevent him from Distroying him Silfe.[23]

Melville makes a good episode out of such an event in *Redburn*.
Joseph writes again:

At 7P.M. herd murdar cride in the foarcastol found pete F[ridingburg]
& Lyman mansfield A fitting [fighting] the Latter with his head cut
open very bad cold [called] them both Aft & flogd put peter in Irons
& Drest the others head we thout thair waas A grate chance of his

bleading to Death At 11 hold [hauled] up North hade up N by E At Dalight NNE At 7AM put those 2 men in the riggin & give them thair Diserts.[24]

And that could have come from *White-Jacket*—a little Melville drollery, in fact, would help out the account of the rapid succession of medical treatment and punishment.

Joseph did not, incidentally, get to see his brother George, who was then captain of the *Henry,* off the coast of Peru, as he had told his wife in the letter above that he hoped to do. He had already come close, however, to seeing his brother Alexander, but that near encounter was not happy news to send home and he did not mention it in his letter. On January 3, 1837, he spotted a ship aground on the coast of Mexico and on sending in a boat found it to be Alexander's ship, the *Swift,* which had parted its chains and drifted ashore: "my brothers Ship hee left hear 8 Days since for . . . the other side of the gulfe I wrote to hime & wish I Cood of seane hime."[25]

When Joseph did retire from the sea he briefly entertained the Barnumesque idea of making a road tour exhibiting an enormous whale's jaw. His partner in the enterprise was to be Capt. Henry B. Phelon, as Obed Macy, that inveterate chronicler and Nantucketer of all interests, relates:

Ship Three Brothers, Capt. Felon brought home the Jaw bone of a Spermaceti whole and intre, the length of which is 15 feet, and the number teeth it contained is 44. The whale was caught by him and made a 100 barrels of Oil. Capt. Felon and Capt. Joseph Chase are about to take it off into various parts of the country for a Show. Whih [*sic*] probably will be a great curiosity to those who never had an opportunity to see any thing of the kind.[26]

This would not have been the first whale's jaw taken on tour. Whether or not anything came of the plans of Captain Phelon and Captain Chase, Joseph had made an investment in the project, as some marginal notes in a log describing his expenditures on a case for the whale's jaw and related materials show. The bond between Joseph Chase and Henry Phelon that led them to consider show business may have had its origin in an episode that happened south

CAPT. JOSEPH CHASE

of the Galapagos on March 14, 1838. Joseph Chase writes that day
in the log of the *Catherine:*

> At 8 PM saw A number of lights set on board the Three Brothers
> [whose captain was Henry Phelon] At 9 tack for hur At 12 spaoke
> one of her boats found that the mate & boats crew were lost thay
> thinke stove by A black fish that thay loard for gist At Darke we loard
> All 4 boats & looked for them. At 4 the boats returned with out find-
> ing them took up the boats and made Shorte tacks At Dalight Saw the
> boat took them up All well thanks be to our preserver set them on
> board the Three brothers & boat Stood to the SE

A marginal note reads: "Thanks be to our Creator & Preserver of
that boats Crewe for his greate murcy."[27]

Probably the two captains had other ties than those created by
the boat crew's rescue. If their plans about the whale's jaw ever
were realized, it was not for long, for Joseph Chase moved to
Aurora, New York, in 1844, built a house that overlooked not an
ocean but a lake, and settled into the yeoman's life that had been his
father's. Cayuga County, New York, was at this time one of the
main migratory targets for Nantucketers, representing one further
step away from the sea than that other Nantucket settlement,
Hudson, New York. Nantucket names like Hussey, Howland,
Gardner, Swain, Folger, Coffin, Barney, Myrick, and others began
appearing in Auburn and the surrounding Finger Lakes villages in
the 1820s. "They didn't want their children to go to sea" was a
popular explanation for this inland movement of the old seamen. A
more likely explanation is the richness of the soil.

In 1846 Judah Chase, the patriarch of the extraordinary whaling
clan, died. This was thirty-eight years after the death of Phoebe
Meader Chase, his first wife and the mother of eight of his nine
children. His widow, Ruth Coffin Chase, was to live for another ten
years.

About the last years of Owen Chase's life relatively little is
known. An 1845 census record shows that Charles Frederick,
Eunice's son raised by Owen, had gone to sea. In 1847 Owen's son
William Henry married Mary Jane Morris; they would have one
son, Walter Nelson, who would become renowned on Nantucket for

his lifesaving work—in those days of frequent coastal shipwrecks lifesaving stations dotted the New England coastline. Daughter Adeline, the only child Owen had by Nancy Joy, married Francis S. Worth and had two children, Nancy and George.

And the Nantucket in which Owen was living was changing; it now held a very distant second place to New Bedford in volume of whaling, and it had been visibly depleted of young men by the gold rush. The population of Nantucket in the last few years of Owen Chase's life was less than half of what it had been when he retired from the sea. And the first signs of tourist interest in the island were detectable—even during Owen's last year at sea, Obed Macy had lamented in his Journal the harm done to the island's morals by visits of the pleasure steamer *Narraganset* from New York; now tourism had reached hopeless proportions.[28]

The last year of Owen's life is illuminated by a single letter, dated November 15, 1868, from Phoebe B. Chase to Owen's former sister-in-law, Winnifred Battie, the remarried widow of Owen's brother Joseph. The writer of the letter is Owen's first cousin, but—another example of Nantucket's Gordian genealogies—not on the Chase side; she is the daughter of Susan Meader Allen, the sister of Owen's mother. After talking of her own children, and by way of apparent reply to a question in a previous letter of Winnifred Battie's, she writes:

> In regard to said cousins, it was my intention to call on them before writing, but have not been well consequently failed to do so, they never called to see us, in our troubles as sickness, indeed have seldom seen them since you left the island, well, they never showed the interest Joseph and George did (for us.) William has been very sick but is now improving Owen is insane (will eventually be carried to the insane hospital) they now, have a man to take care of him I met with him last summer at Ariels (Phoebe visits us,) he called me cousin Susan (taking me for sister Worth) held my hand and sobbed like a child, saying O *my head, my head* it was pitiful to see the strong man bowed, then his personal appearance so changed, didn't allow himself decent clothing, fear's he shall come to want.[29]

The letter is the only known written description of Owen in his last years. Reports of his insanity had been passed down in

Nantucket tradition, and so had the tale, memorable for its graphicness, whether it was true or not, that Owen in his last days hid food in the rafters of his house as protection against starvation. Owen's great-great-granddaughters, Isabelle and Margaret Tice, recall a tale passed down in family tradition that Owen in his late years wanted food purchased in double quantities—not a ham but two hams, and so on. Certainly if fantasies of starvation are going to come back after almost fifty years, there are few people whom they should so reasonably trouble. Less than four months after the letter was written, Owen died on March 7, 1869. The Nantucket *Inquirer and Mirror* wrote six days later:

Another Member Gone

Died, in this town, on Sunday evening, March 7th, Capt. Owen Chase, aged 73 years, 5 months.

We suppose the cause from which Captain Chase died, can be traced back to the time he so suffered from starvation in an open boat, when the whale stove a hole in the ship "Essex," causing her to capsize and sink in the Pacific Ocean, in November, 1820. He always complained of pain and difficulty about his head, from that time to his death, particularly so after a long voyage. . . .

Captain Chase has since [the *Essex* shipwreck] been more favored, and has gathered up many fine voyages in the Pacific Ocean and elsewhere, without accident to his ship, or any of his officers or crews that have been engaged in these hazardous enterprises with him.

It is pleasant for us to look upon so firm and amiable a character as his has been through so eventful a life.

Owen Chase's will was probated May 13, 1869. Susan, his widow, was left the house in Orange Street and its furnishings as well as the income on $3,600. Son William Henry was given $25, but William Henry's wife and son were left the income on $1,000. The rest of the estate was divided between the other children, Phebe Ann, Lydia, Adeline, and Charles Frederick. Charles Frederick, Eunice's illegitimate son, was left, in addition to his share of the other property, Owen's gold watch and chain.[30]

On New Lane in Nantucket between Main Street and West Chester Street is the North Cemetery, its west side known as Old North and its east side as New North. It is an easy walk from the heart of town, a little more than ten minutes from the wharves and from Orange Street, but it seems part of the unsettled, scrub-covered Nantucket, not the active town. The ground rises slightly and creates a little vista; it is quiet even when the sparse traffic passes. Owen Chase is buried in New North; near him in the same lot lie three of his wives, Peggy, Nancy, and Susan. Death, with practiced irony, has assembled what was so long dispersed and impressed repose on what was so often anxious and haggard and pained.

GEORGE POLLARD, JR.

Captain Pollard's reputation as a master was not jeopardized by so freakish an accident as his ship being attacked by a whale, so it is not surprising to find him engaged a few months after his return to command another Nantucket whaler. The dramatic thing about the second command, however, was the ship he was chosen for—the *Two Brothers,* the same ship that had brought him back from Valparaiso. The circumstance, which from a remote viewpoint seems to have a touch of the ironic or sentimental to it, was probably not lost on contemporary Nantucketers.

Sailing from Nantucket in the latter part of 1821, Captain Pollard took the *Two Brothers* around Cape Horn and down the South American coast past the scenes of his rescue not one year before. Off the Ecuadorian coast he encountered the U.S. Navy schooner *Waterwitch,* on board which was the then midshipman Charles Wilkes, whom we have already met at a later period of his life at Tahiti. The meeting between the *Two Brothers* and the *Waterwitch* occurred seventeen years before Wilkes and the Exploring Expedition were to visit Tahiti and, as we have assumed, meet Owen Chase; at the moment Wilkes was an energetic and curious twenty-four-year-old midshipman pretty thoroughly contemptuous of the commanding officer he was serving under. It was the day before he saw the *Two Brothers,* he tells us in his *Autobiography,* that he had been reading the story of the *Essex.* What the precise date was he does not mention, but it must have been in mid-August 1822.

His account of the meeting with Captain Pollard was put down on paper a half-century later and contains some obvious inaccu-

racies, the most obvious his misnaming of Captain Pollard.
Nonetheless, it is a vivid and valuable account, for the impression
that Pollard made on Wilkes was a strong one, seemingly as strong
a one as Pollard made on Herman Melville in 1852. To Melville,
Pollard was "the most impressive man, tho' wholly assuming, even
humble—that I ever encountered," but Melville told us most of
what he had to say about Pollard indirectly in *Clarel*. Wilkes tells
the story:

We ran down the coast with the trade winds and when off Payta we
fell in with the whale ship Two Brothers Captain Potter, I went on
board and was kindly received he was just out from Payta the day
before; I had been reading the account of a whale ship that had been
struck by a whale and so much injured that she was wrecked, the
blow having started some planks; On finding the Capt^s name to be
Potter I asked him naturally if he was any relation to the one who
met with the disaster, he at once said he was the person; this made a
great impression on me and then he gave me a full account of the
disaster, which I will now attempt to give in his own language as
nearly as I could recollect it. He had discovered a large school of
whales and had lowered all his boats including his own for the pursuit
and capture leaving but three men on board the cook, steward and a
seaman. The weather was very fine and the sea smooth while engaged
in the exciting occupation of capturing as many of the whales he had
his attention called to the ship which was heeling over very
considerably became assured that some accident had happened called
his boats off and all made for the ship at great speed, before he
reached the ship she had turned over on her side and by the time he
got to her she was lying bottom up and the Cook Steward and seamen
on the hull. He described himself as almost appalled by the situation
in the middle of the East Pacific and far removed from any land. On
reaching his ship the boats were unprovided with every thing, they
had no provisions, no clothing, no instruments, no water, the ship lay
turned bottom up. These necessaries were to be got at and the only
thing to be done was to scuttle the bottom of the ship and to make
their way into the hull to obtain anything, this without any tools,
through the energy of Capt. Potter they succeeded in tearing off the
planking and making an entrance, and in this measure they succeeded
in obtaining provisions, tools for repairs of the Boats but the boats
were unable to take all they needed; Can any situation be conceived in
such circumstances that require so much thought and action as was
required within the short space of time allotted to them, to say noth-

ing of the untoward disappointment of the interruption of a successful issue of their hazardous employment, interrupted when their fondest hopes were about to be realised? a well appointed vessel, crew in all respects efficient and the fondest hopes indulged in of providing for themselves and families—in a short hour to be wrecked and left to grapple for their lives on the broad ocean. Through the example of Captn Potter all were encouraged the boats well stored and ready equipped, their ship filling fast before taking her final plunge into the deep, deep sea. She finally went down before their eyes, and then came the thought followed by the determination to seek the nearest land suposed to be some 150 miles distant, for this they lost no time in starting for, and reached it in three days. but little did it ameliorate their condition it was uninhabited, and moreover little was to be found on it to sustain life, it was evident they could not remain there some thirty in number with five boats; these they set about putting in complete repair from the materials they had brought with them, and when complete took the determination to embark in hopes of reaching the shores of South America. of the boats, only one was ever heard of, that of the captains who was picked up on the coast of Chili after being 32 days at sea the only two saved was the Captn and a boy. They had twice or thrice drawn lots and intense suffering ensued, I cannot state the narrative of this, it is too horrible to be related as it was told me. The Captain and boy were scarcely alive when picked up and reached port, their boat was nearly in pieces and all hope had long before passed from them. The Annals of wrecks at sea never has given so disastrous a case; it fairly in contemplation causes one's heart almost to cease beating, but when narrated by one who had undergone it all and miraculously as it were been preserved, I could not convey an idea of my feelings. I expressed myself how he could think of again putting his foot on board ship to again pursue such a calling, or hazard another voyage. He simply remarked that it was an old adage that the lightning never struck in the same place twice. he had recovered and returned home to Nantucket or New Bedford I forget which, and was offered the Two Brothers for another voyage which he accepted, and there he was bound probably for the same Area of Ocean where he had encountered so much. It was to be expected that some effect of his former cruise would have been visible in his manner or conversation, but not so, he was cheerful and very modest in his account, and very. desirous to afford us all the aid we might be in want of, presented us with some vegetables & potatoes especially of which he had a large store in nettings affixed to his cabin ceiling—I took leave of him with hearty wishes for his success and a feeling of respect that I had by accident become acquainted with a hero, who did not even consider that he had overcome obstacles which would have crushed 99 out of a hundred. There was a vividness about his description of the scenes, he had gone through which recurs to me often, and scarcely can believe that the actor could have been the narrator so modest and unassuming was his account and I feel satisfied most truthful. At the time I saw him I suppose he was about 35 years of age. I have not been able to trace him since although I have made many inquiries, he was one of three brothers who followed the whaling business. It is now some fifty years ago and there is little doubt but he is long since dead & regret that I did not pursue the short account in the paper which first attracted my notice of him, as I have not been able to find any account of the wreck if ever published.[31]

The modest dignity and openness that Wilkes saw in Pollard seem to be part of what appealed to Melville. One of the most revealing things about Pollard—something that we could easily overlook as we focus on the story he is telling—is the fact that Pollard actually *told* it. And he told it to a perfect stranger, not palliating the cannibalism or even the death of Owen Coffin. The reticence—legendary in Nantucket—of some of the survivors and their families to talk of the *Essex* was not shared by its captain. The story that Pollard was later to tell to George Bennet was an even more painful one coming as it did after the loss of the *Two Brothers,* but he told it all, even though rehearsing Owen Coffin's death finally wrung from him the cry, "I can tell you no more—my head is on fire at the recollection."

Looking on at the meeting of these two men, one is once again moved to entertain David Jaffe's thesis that Wilkes was the model for Captain Ahab. Now the captain of the *Pequod* is gamming the captain of the *Essex*—would that either one of them knew the rareness of the moment.

When Midshipman Wilkes asked Captain Pollard the question that would have come so readily to a landlubber, but which we may be surprised to find in the mouth of a seaman, Why return to sea after such an experience? he may have been satisfied by Pollard's equanimity and his affirmation that lightning does not strike twice in the same place. One can imagine Wilke's reaction if he had learned that lightning was as a matter of fact going to strike twice in the same place. Leaving the coast of Ecuador and the off-shore ground, the *Two Brothers* headed west-northwest; it may have even passed the spot where the whale had struck the *Essex* just about two years before. By early February 1823 the *Two Brothers* was west of the Sandwich Islands on a course that would have taken it to the Japan ground. On the afternoon of February 11, 1823, a gale began to rise, sail was taken in, and the course changed. Eben Gardner, the first mate, tells what happened then:

February 11th 182[3]

First part Came in with Strong gales from west & thick Squally Weather Latt^d by Obs 25°34^m North & Long. 168°40^m West at 4 PM took in our Waist Boat & turned up Our quarter Boats at 5 PM the gale Increasing Sent down our Fore & Mizzen topgallant yards, & Close Reeft the fore & main topsails & took in the Mizzen topsail & foresails Changed our course from NE to NE by N. Set the watch third & third at 7 PM Saw large Breakers Ahead, the helm was Put Aweather Imediately in that moment the Ship struck on A Reef of Rocks the Topsails were hove Aback the Ship Apeared to float once her Length & Then Struck Again so heavy As Shattered her Whole Stern, the Sea made A Road over us & in a few Moments the Ship was full of Water. The oil began to float Around us & It Apeared that the ships Bottom was stove In, The only Way for us to Escape from the Wreck was In our Boats, & they being turned up & Lashed It took some time To get them Clear We succeded in getting two of them Clear With 4 Oars & Each A Sail, one quadrant one Compass Two Practical Navigators no Cloths But those We stood In, Nither Water Nor Provisions Except two small piggs that Was Washed Into my Boat in getting Clear from the ship, I Rowed to Leward & soon fell in With Capt Pollard Who left the Wreck A few moments before me, he now got Into my boat & advised me to row to Windward In hopes to obtain Something from the Wreck in the Morning at 11 PM saw A Rock 50 feet High, It being verry Dark. We took it to be the Ship Capt Pollard wished for me to Row up & see What it Was as I had the best boat It came on A verry hevy squall & I lost sight of Capt^t Pollard & the Rock also Saw no more of them for the knight It continued thick & hevy squalls of Rain so that We Were Obliged to bail the boat continually, We soon Found ourselves near A Reef that Roared Trimendiously, We let the Boat drive A While & saw Another Reef to the Leward of us We then Rowed In A South Direction shipt A great Quantity of Water & Was near sinking several times, the long Wished for Daylight at length appered & opened to our vew A Dismal Seen, nothing but A Compleet Boddy of Rocks &

shoals Incompased us about on Every Side that thretened us With
Distruction, We saw at a Distance A Large Rock supposing it to be A
ship to the Northward, We found A blanket in the Boat & With It
Made A tolerable sail, With that & our oars We made towards the
supposed ship but soon found it to be A high Rock 50 feet Above the
surface of the sea With heavy Breakers all Round it, We then headed
to the southward & saw A ship supposed it to be the Wreck drove
uppon the rocks We saw 3 small Islands, As the Reefs Extended far
to the Westward of the ship & to Windward of the Islands, We
Resolved to Cross the Reef & hazerd our lives as they had Become of
No great value to us We Were rowing to leward & found A small
opening in the Reef 8 or 10 feet Wide We succeeded in going threw to
leward of the South Islands landed on It, Found Turtle sea foul &
some sea Elephant, The Island Was verry small but had the
Apearance of being Once lerger, We found the stump of A large tree
With the Roots fast in the ground to all Apperence it grew there. The
land was about 6 or 8 feet above the surface of the sea, From It We
saw the supposed wreck to be A ship at anchor There was no chance
of reaching her With only Two Oars We Turned up our boat & built
A fire, We then saw the ship get under Weigh & Was soon out of
Our sight We then lay$\underline{d}$ Down & made our selves Contented With our
Lot, Our Piggs strayed to the sea side, & one of our men Went after
them & soon Returned With the Welcome tidings of the ships Being
Aback at the leward of the Island, We got our Boat Down took in one
turtle & Rowed towards the Ship Hard, at 1 PM We got onboard of
the Marther & found Capt$\underline{n}$ Pollard safe With all his Crew we had 11
men In Each Boat, We found the Marther had discovered the Rocks In
the Night & anchored, at 10 AM She Parted her Cable & When We
Thot her Aback She was Aground on the Rocks But Received no
Damage so she makes no Water, We are Now in sight of the Bird
Islands & by the account of Our Vew we ware Wrecked in Latt$\underline{d}$ 24°4^m
N & Longt$\underline{d}$ 168° W

                                                    Eben Gardner[32]

Gardner's calculation of where the wreck occurred is slightly off.
There is nothing to run aground on at the point he identifies, but
the well-known French Frigate Shoals directly to the east at
23°45′N/166°15′ W are the only place in that part of the Pacific
fitting his description. They include the La Perouse Pinnacle and
are the site of a present-day loran tower.

The *Martha,* which rescued the survivors of the *Two Brothers,*
was a Nantucket whaler less than three months out from home and
under the command of Capt. John H. Pease. That it should have

been Captain Pease is involutedly and curiously coincidental, at least when one pursues Herman Melville's manifold ties to the *Essex* story. Captain Pease had a son, William C., who in time entered the Revenue Cutter Service, the forerunner of the present day Coast Guard; William C, also in time married his namesake, Miss Serena Pease, the daughter of Capt. Valentine Pease, Melville's captain on the *Acushnet*. In December 1853, when captain of the revenue cutter *Jefferson Davis,* William C. Pease made an unsuccessful attempt off the coast of South Carolina to rescue the shipwrecked crew of the revenue cutter *Hamilton*. Among those lost on the *Hamilton* was Lt. Ephraim Curtiss Hine, Melville's old shipmate from the *United States* and the real-life model for Lemsford the poet in Melville's *White-Jacket*.[33]

By mid-April Captain Pollard had been transferred to the United States brig *Pearl,* Captain Chandler. In the harbor of Raiatea on April 16, 1823, George Bennet, who had just arrived from Bora Bora, came upon the *Pearl,* met Captain Pollard, and gained the interview that he subsequently published. It is reprinted in Appendix B.

Pollard was only thirty-one years old when he described himself as an unlucky man who would never be trusted with command again. The only occupation that he is known to have had in subsequent years is that of night watchman, whether for the town of Nantucket or for a private employer is unclear.[34] That was his job when Melville met him almost thirty years after the loss of the *Two Brothers*—and one year after the publication of *Moby-Dick*. The impression that he made on Melville as a man of combined nobility and humility was as enduring a one as he had made on Charles Wilkes. We shall see shortly how Melville articulated his impression.

THE OTHER SURVIVORS

About the other survivors of the *Essex* less is known than about the captain and first mate. Records are fewer and more ambiguous, and their interpretation is as much hindered as aided by the wisps of oral tradition that float around them.

Charles Ramsdell, who was sixteen at the time of the shipwreck, married twice and, if one accepts the most extensive records on his family, had eight children.[35] Conclusions about his subsequent sea career rest on the assumption that he was captain of the whaler *General Jackson,* presumably on its voyage from Bristol, Rhode Island, January 23, 1842, to October 24, 1845, but the captain may have been another Ramsdell, for the birth of Charles Ramsdell's son James, whether it was in 1884 as the *Vital Records of Nantucket* say or 1845 as the Folger Records say, is in conflict with the dates of the *General Jackson* voyage.[36] Both birth records, of course, could be wrong. The Nantucket *Vital Records* consistently refer to Ramsdell as "mariner," not "master mariner."

One of the reasons for believing that Ramsdell, Nickerson, and Lawrence stayed with the sea and eventually became captains is a statement in Nickerson's obituary in the *Inquirer and Mirror,* February 10, 1883: "notwithstanding the terrible sufferings through which they passed, these five men all continued to follow the sea, all rose to the command of vessels, and all lived to a good old age." The five referred to are the five survivors picked up in the boats. One can only say the statement is possibly true but still undocumented. The obituary article itself does not cite any instance of Nickerson's going to sea, and it contains some clear inaccuracies. Reportage in the *Inquirer* and in the *Inquirer and Mirror* was not consistently reliable; it is usually a good source for arrivals, departures, records of ships spoken, and the week's events in town but not so good for biography and history.

The most interesting statement, nonetheless, in the Nickerson obituary is that

> Capt. Nickerson had prepared all the materials for a narrative of his thrilling adventures on that remarkable voyage, and some six years ago, disposed of his manuscripts to Leon Lewis, the novelist, then visiting our island, who proposed to edit and publish them in book form. The forthcoming volume was announced in our advertising columns, but Mr. Lewis abandoned the enterprise, and the book has not yet seen the light.

But, then again, maybe it has. Leon Lewis, who died in 1920, was a prolific popular and juvenile author who produced under his own name and under the pseudonyms F. Clinton Barrington and

Illion Constellano an almost uncatalogable avalanche of books like
The Boy Whaler, The Young Castaways, and so on. It is nearly
impossible to ascertain whether some of Thomas Nickerson's
recollections have not become part of one Lewis adventure tale or
another.

Benjamin Lawrence was twenty-one at the time of the shipwreck.
He married in 1824 and had, if a pooling of records can be trusted,
seven children, one of whom died as an infant, one at sea, and five
of whom moved to California. The *Inquirer and Mirror* in a two-
part article on the *Essex,* November 30 and December 7, 1935, says
of Lawrence:

> After making several voyages in ships of his native island, he became
> master of the bark *Huron,* of Hudson, N.Y. From 1839 to 1841, he
> commanded the *Dromo.* Following this voyage he retired from the sea
> and bought a little farm at 'Sconset. One son was lost at sea, while
> three daughters and two sons went to California to live. Mrs. Phillip
> Holmes, who passed away only a few weeks ago, was a daughter of
> Capt. Lawrence.[37]

Starbuck gives a Captain Lawrence as master of the *Dromo* out
of Hudson for the voyage mentioned in the article and notes,
"Reported late in 1839 with 200 sperm. Condemned 1840." Starbuck also gives a B. Lawrence as captain of the *Dromo* on an
earlier voyage, 1832–36.

The three survivors from Henderson Island have been followed in
the preceding chapter through their Australian experiences and on
to England. About Thomas Chapple nothing is known after his
return to England except for his contact with the Religious Tract
Society and the appearance of his story in one of their publications
(see Appendix C).

Seth Weeks and William Wright returned to the United States
but not when the *Inquirer and Mirror* said they did. In Seth
Week's obituary, September 24, 1887, the *Inquirer and Mirror*
stated that Weeks and Wright after arriving in London from
Sydney "took passage in the ship 'London Packet,' and arrived in
Boston in June, 1822." But the *Surry,* which sailed from Sydney
with Weeks and Wright as members of the crew, arrived at
Gravesend July 3, 1822. So the two men had not even arrived in

England on the date that the *Inquirer and Mirror* gives for their arrival in Boston. If it was the *London Packet* that they crossed the Atlantic in, they could not have sailed until August 8, 1822.[38] In any event they did get back. One can weigh the evidence of their having gone to sea again. Several times on New Bedford crew lists the names Seth Weeks and William Wright appear, in one instance on the same ship, but are they our survivors? There are reasons to believe they are not. And was Seth Weeks the master of the *George Howland,* New Bedford, 1838–41, the *March,* Barnstable, 1846–47, and the *March,* Yarmouth, 1849–50? The evidence is not adequate. The *Inquirer and Mirror* obituary cited above has Seth Weeks living out his last years in blindness and dying September 12, 1887. The last of the survivors had survived by two-thirds of a century.

Chapter Five

TELLING THE STORY

THE AUTHORSHIP AND
PUBLICATION OF
OWEN CHASE'S *NARRATIVE*

NO ONE doubts that the *Narrative* is Owen's story, but most would agree with Herman Melville that

> There seems no reason to suppose that Owen himself wrote the Narrative. It bears obvious tokens of having been written for him; but at the same time, its whole air plainly evinces that it was carefully & conscientiously written to Owen's dictation of the facts.—It is almost as good as tho' Owen wrote it himself.[1]

If Melville had seen the log of the *Charles Carroll,* he would have been sure that Owen did not do the actual writing of the *Narrative.* One may add that it would be safe to assume that no Nantucket whaling captain would be up to writing such a book.

The question arises, then: Who was the ghostwriter? It had to be someone who was in Nantucket during the summer of 1821 and free to give the composition of the book enough time to have the whole text ready for the printer in the fall. Owen may well have organized his story and had notes prepared before the writing started; the month in Valparaiso (February 25–March 22) or the two and a half months of the homeward voyage (March 22–June 11) would have given him some time to do that.

The most popular speculation among Nantucket historians conversant with Owen's story is that the ghostwriter was Samuel Haynes Jenks. The speculation does not rest on any solid evidence, but it has a certain amount of logic to commend it. Jenks was a writer with a special interest in whaling; he was some years later reported to be in the process of writing a history of Nantucket's whaling industry.[2] He was conspicuously involved in Nantucket public affairs, and, perhaps most important, he was a journalist: he was the editor of Nantucket's first enduring newspaper, the *Inquirer*.

But there are two considerations that weigh against crediting Jenks with the writing of the *Narrative*. The first is that the *Inquirer* began publication a week and a half after Owen Chase arrived home on the *Eagle*; these were busy days for Jenks, and it is questionable whether he would have had enough time for the book. A more serious objection to Jenks's authorship of the book rests on internal evidence: the more one reads of Jenks's known writings, the more alien to him the style of Owen Chase's *Narrative* comes to seem. Jenks is tolerable when he has a short piece of journalism to compose but, if allowed to go on for long, slips into a self-important and inflated rhetoric. That may be saying no more than that he was a typical journalist of his day, but it would be enough to disqualify him as ghost of Owen's Chase's *Narrative,* for the *Narrative* is too sensitive, imaginative, and timelessly literary to come from such a hand.

There was someone in Nantucket who would pass the stylistic test and who was also a logical writer for someone in Owen's position to turn to. That was Jenks's father-in-law, William Coffin. Coffin was a businessman, barber, wigmaker, and, for a long term, Nantucket's first postmaster. Like several other prominent Nantucketers, he became an object of suspicion and hostility in the wake of the Nantucket bank robbery of June 20, 1795. This remarkable crime and its aftermath had a disastrously divisive effect on the island. As time went by and the crime was not solved, at least not to the point of effective prosecution, suspicion arose that the robbery was an inside job, and the spotlight of accusation moved from one citizen to another, leaving the island in a state like the *hysterica passio* in Thomas Mann's *Magic Mountain*. More than twenty years after the crime William Coffin wrote a pamphlet about it with a view toward exonerating himself and others and suggesting how the police work in the case should have been pursued.

The pamphlet is *A Narrative of the Robbery of the Nantucket Bank. Compiled from Original Documents Collected by William Coffin and Albert Gardner, Esq's.* and was published in Nantucket by Henry Clapp in 1816. Although Albert Gardner's name appears as collaborator, references in the pamphlet and recorded details of events after the robbery suggest that Coffin was the sole author. So much of the pamphlet is given to documentation that the narrative part is relatively short, but from the narrative one may choose almost at random paragraphs that lend themselves to comparison with the text of Owen Chase's *Narrative* on such points as diction, rhythm of phrasing, feeling for comparisons, tone of modifiers, and overall continent handling of exciting material (the last certainly not one of Jenks's characteristics):

> When it was publickly announced that the Bank was robbed, the inhabitants of Nantucket were seized with a consternation, that could not have been much exceeded had they been assured the dead had risen. A degree of horror and alarm was visible upon every countenance, and a great part of the community was agitated with apprehension for their personal safety. The atrocity of the act, and the darkness which inveloped the whole transaction had a powerful influence upon the minds of the inhabitants, not yet familiarized with crimes, to bring into operation a talent for the marvellous, and the wonderful; and never, since the memorable times of the Salem *witchcraft,* did superstition and bigotry wave their sceptre over the human intellect with such unlimitted sway.[3]

Stylistic evidence is never conclusive by itself, but, taken with the limited possibilities of other authorship on Nantucket, it makes a stronger case for Coffin than for anyone else.

It is evident that whoever put the story on paper had seen the letter about the Pollard-Ramsdell rescue attributed to Capt. Aaron Paddack of the *Diana.* The text of this letter in Appendix E is given along with corresponding passages from the *Narrative.* Since this letter apparently played a key role in delivering the shipwreck news to New Bedford and Nantucket, it would have been well known to interested parties and, no doubt, widely accessible. Its use does not give a clue as to who the ghostwriter was.

The publication of the *Narrative* by a minor New York publisher-binder-bookseller is a curiosity. William B. Gilley, an immigrant from the British Isles and a naturalized citizen of the United States, operated a bookstore at 92, later 94, Broadway from at least 1815 to his death in 1830. He was for a while publisher of the *Christian Herald* and was the author of two volumes of light verse, *The Olio* and *Patriotic Effusions.*[4] His offerings as a publisher, to judge by his exchange list for 1819 and other records of titles he published, were a varied selection of current and popular books— Thomson, Southey, Watts, and Smollet, along with a large number of moralistic and didactic works. Gilley had also brought out maritime, even shipwreck, stories and had featured South Sea sketches in the *Christian Herald.* For a variety of reasons Owen Chase's *Narrative* would have been agreeable material for Gilley.

The question arises, though, Who in Nantucket knew of Gilley? Why select him, especially in an age when the publishing business was very localized? "Nationwide" distribution of books was unknown in the 1820s—the only distribution that publishers generally considered was the rather limited one to points accessible by coastal or inland waters, and many publishers contented themselves with the sales available only in their areas.[5]

There are two possible explanations for the choice of Gilley. The first is that an initial approach may have been made not to Gilley but to Gilley's printer, Jonathan Seymour. Seymour was one of the best known printers in New York and was, among other things, the printer of Bowditch's *Practical Navigator.* This volume would have put his name before the eyes of almost every Nantucketer and would have made it reasonable that a Nantucket author should contact him and be forwarded to a publisher with whom he did business.

The other possibility, for which there is just one shred of evidence but an interesting one, is that the book was taken first not to any New York party but to the Philadelphian who more than any other publisher in the country came close to having a national reputation, Matthew Carey. Carey and Gilley had close business ties, and they not only constantly exchanged their own published works—for example, Carey taking a number of books for sale in Philadelphia that Gilley had published in New York in exchange for Gilley's taking a number of Carey-published books for sale in New York—but also exchanged publishing opportunities. On June 26, 1821, for example, Carey wrote to Gilley:

> We have a small parcel of Books in the Euphrates amounting to £3..9.—Capt. Parry's Voyage of Discoveries 4to is contained in this parcel & as we believe it to be the only one in the country you may have it for 40 Copies should you not see proper to accept our proposition pray announce it for Publication by us—[6]

Thus, if Gilley chose to bring out the *Voyage of Discoveries,* he would have sent Carey forty finished volumes of the work on publication by way of payment for the opportunity; if he chose not to bring it out, he would have advertised it as forthcoming and probably carried a number of copies in his own bookstore.

If Owen Chase's *Narrative* was submitted first to Carey, some such swap as this may have taken place. There does not exist in the letters of the two publishers a clear description of such a transaction; however, a letter, undated but apparently of March 8, 1822, from Carey to Gilley suggests that just such an arrangement had been effected:

> Please send us per Mercantile line 50 Sardanapolis 50 Two Foscari 275 law you will much oblige us by sending to Wiley & Halsten per a small bundle and pack it up with them. Please enclose our Journal of the loss of the Whale Ship Essex—[7]

The phrasing of the last sentence is unusual in Carey's letters; "our" is almost nowhere to be found with titles, which are ordinarily preceded only by the number in question. In what sense would Carey call the journal "our"? If he were ordering a copy, it would be, if anything, "your" journal. If he had ordered a copy in a previous letter and was now repeating his order, the "our" might be interpreted as a reference to the initial order, but, as a matter of fact, in precisely such contexts in other letters Carey does not say "our." If, however, the *Narrative* had been a book offered and forwarded to Gilley by Carey, the "our" would be the logical way to refer to it. The sentence can be interpreted as a request either for return of the manuscript or for a printed copy of the book. Carey's reference to it as "Journal" suggests his familiarity with it before it

went to press with its final title. This *may* be how the *Narrative* got
to Gilley.

However it finally got into print, the story of the whale's attack
was being read before the first anniversary of that attack. Gilley's
1821 edition, the only edition of the *Narrative* to appear for more
than a hundred years, was a very limited one and cannot have done
much to serve the purpose Owen Chase announced in the beginning
of the book, "the hope of obtaining something of remuneration, by
giving a short history of my sufferings to the world." But it had
effects that Owen would not have anticipated, for it captivated some
readers, one of whom was going to pass on Owen Chase's name to a
world audience.

HERMAN MELVILLE

Of all the uses and retellings of the *Essex* story, none is more
important than Herman Melville's in *Moby-Dick*. Melville not only
intrudes into his novel in his own persona to tell the *Essex* story in
chapter 45 but draws from the *Essex*'s adventure the climax of
Moby-Dick.

There are some puzzles connected with Melville's knowledge of
Owen Chase and the *Essex,* but there are also some facts that help
explain what Melville knew. (1) Melville learned about the *Essex*
from forecastle conversation on the *Acushnet,* met Owen Chase's
son William Henry some time in 1841 or 1842 in the course of one
of the *Acushnet*'s gams, borrowed from William Henry a copy of
the *Narrative* and read it in one day. All this we know from
Melville's annotations of his copy of the *Narrative*. (2) The *Essex*
story was clear and detailed enough in Melville's mind in 1850 and
1851 when he was writing *Moby-Dick* to indicate that he was rely-
ing on more than the eight- or nine-year-old memory of the story
read at sea. One source that he had in front of him during the last
three or four months of his work on *Moby-Dick* was the copy of
Owen's *Narrative* that his father-in-law had procured for him from
Thomas Macy of Nantucket. (3) In July 1852, a year after finishing
Moby-Dick, Melville traveled to Nantucket, which he had never
visited before, and spoke with Captain Pollard of the *Essex*.

There seems to be no reason to doubt most of what Melville records in his copy of the *Narrative:* he probably did hear the *Essex* talked about on the *Acushnet,* and he probably did meet William Henry Chase and borrow a copy of the *Narrative.* In the same annotations in which Melville speaks of the encounter with William Henry, however, he also mentions seeing Owen Chase himself during a gam with the *Charles Carroll:*

> Somewhere about the latter part of A.D.1841, in this same ship the Achushnet, we spoke the "Wm. Wirt*" of Nantucket & Owen Chace was the Captain, & so it came to pass that I saw him. He was a large, powerful well-made man; rather tall; to all appearances something past forty-five or so; with a handsome face for a Yankee, & expressive of great uprightness & calm unostentatious courage. His whole appearance impressed me pleasantly. He was the most prepossessing-looking whale-hunter I think I ever saw.
>
> Being a mear foremast-hand I had no opportunity of conversing with Owen (tho' he was on board our ship for two hours at a time) nor have I ever seen him since.[8]

The asterisk refers to a note in which Melville corrects his recollection of the name of Owen Chase's ship: "I was doubtful a little at the time of writing whether this ship was the Wm. Wirt. I am now certain that it was the *Charles Carroll* of which Owen Chace was Captain for several voyages."

Melville's whole account of seeing Owen Chase at sea is a puzzle, quite apart from any memory lapse he may have had about a ship's name. The problem is that Owen Chase had returned from his last voyage in February 1840 and had retired from the sea. It was more than ten months later that Melville went to sea on the *Acushnet.* The captain of the *Charles Carroll* on the voyage that coincided with Melville's time at sea was Thomas S. Andrews.

It is possible to find Melville's memory faulty on other occasions—even in his annotation of his copy of the *Narrative* Melville could not recall exactly what year it was he had met Captain Pollard on Nantucket—but to err about having seen someone who was that significant a figure to him is a mistake of a larger order.

Melville said in his annotations of Owen's *Narrative:*

> But what then served to specialise my interest [in the *Essex* story]

at the time [while on the *Acushnet*] was the circumstance that the Second Mate of our ship, Mr. Hall, an Englishman & Londoner by birth, had for two three-year voyages sailed with Owen Chace (then in command of the whaleship "William* Wirt" (I think it was) of Nantucket.) This Hall always spoke of Chace with much interest & sincere regard—but he did not seem to know anything more about him or the Essex affair than any body else.[9]

The asterisk again refers to the note correcting *William Wirt* to *Charles Carroll*. In another annotation a few pages later Melville also credits Hall with telling him the story of Captain Pollard's fate after his second shipwreck.

Hall is central to the puzzle. Suppose that the whole crew of the *Acushnet*, more or less familiar with Owen Chase's story and with the name of Owen's last ship, mistook the visiting captain for Owen Chase, would John Hall, who had sailed for more than six years with Owen, make the same mistake? There can be no question, if Hall was telling the truth about having been out with Owen on two three-year voyages, that the ship he was on was the *Charles Carroll*, for the two voyages on the *Charles Carroll* were the only voyages of three years or more that Owen Chase ever made.

It is always possible that circumstances kept John Hall from seeing the visiting captain during the "two hours at a time" that he was aboard the *Acushnet*. And Hall could have taken the word of some of the men that the visitor was Owen Chase. If John Hall actually did see the visitor, though, and if he did talk about the visitor to Melville (how could he not have?), what did he say? Yes, that's the Owen Chase I remember? One hypothesis that may arise, though I do not support it, is that Hall was not telling the truth about his having sailed with Owen Chase.

What is known of John Hall? His name is a common one, and records from various ships and ports turn up several John Halls. The New Bedford district crew lists describe Melville's John Hall as follows: "age 30, born in England; sailed ship *Acushnet*, Fairhaven Jan. 3, 1841–May 13, 1845; second mate, 1/42 lay."[10] In the same collection of crew lists appears another John Hall, who could have the same birth date: "age 22; born Hallowell; 5´5 1/4˝, light complexion, brown hair; sailed ship *Milwood*, New Bedford, May

15, 1833–April 24, 1834." He is the only one of his namesakes about whom the information is specific enough to suggest that he could be the same as the *Acushnet*'s second mate. But this second John Hall could not have been on the first voyage of the *Charles Carroll,* which was from October 10, 1832, to March 3, 1836, for that would have conflicted with his service on the *Milwood.* Another John Hall was mate of the bark *United States,* out of Westport from June 9, 1846, to October 18, 1849, and received one twenty-fifth lay. This too could have been John Hall of the *Acushnet,* but such an identification would not shed any light on the problem at hand.

If John Hall was, as he claimed, on the voyage of the *Charles Carroll* that ended in 1840, he was one of two John Halls on the ship. The other was a native of the Sandwich Islands; about him Owen Chase noted in the *Charles Carroll*'s log in a space between May 2 and May 15, 1838: "from the 2 of May to the 14 Lying in Owhyhee Harbour of Hedo NE Side after water &. Refreshments W.WSW John Hall Conacka Deserted in this Port." There are other records of this Hawaiian John Hall, and it is clear that he is not the same as the second mate of the *Acushnet.* He is on the crew list of the New Bedford ship *Wilmington and Liverpool Packet* for a voyage that lasted from August 27, 1830, to April 30, 1833, and is described as a black-haired native of the Sandwich Islands.

Wilson Heflin in "More Researching in New Bedford" (*Melville Society Extracts,* September 1980) has noted that Frederick Raymond, who was first mate on the *Acushnet* while Melville was on the ship, had, fourteen years before, served as second mate under Owen Chase on the voyage of the *Winslow* that was cut short by gale damage. This tangible link between Chase and Melville could obviously be significant; among the questions it raises is whether Melville may not have been confusing John Hall and Raymond when he recalled Hall's conversations about Owen and the *Essex.*

It is natural to wonder whether Melville and others on the *Acushnet* may not have mistaken one of Owen's brothers for Owen. Joseph Chase, if we are to judge by the brothers' portraits, looked strikingly like Owen. Joseph had already retired from the sea when the *Acushnet* was out, but Owen's brother Alexander was still out as captain of the *Elizabeth Starbuck,* which conceivably could have gammed the *Acushnet,* although that is among the least likely explanations.

If one goes beyond Owen's brothers to wonder whether or not Melville may have encountered one of the other Chase captains not closely related to Owen, the possibilities are many. Perhaps it was Capt. Peter Chase of the *Eliza* out of Salem, which went to sea six months after the *Acushnet* did. Captain Chase, curiously, ended up as a passenger on board the *Charles Carroll,* something which would very neatly explain how Melville got the impression that *the* Captain Chase was on board the ship, were it not for the fact that Melville was no longer on the *Acushnet* but on land in Honolulu when Capt. Peter Chase, whose *Eliza* had been condemned in Tahiti in July 1843, was taken on board the *Charles Carroll.*[11]

Could a ship that gammed the *Acushnet* have carried some report about Owen Chase that would have been vivid enough to stay in the minds of the *Acushnet*'s people? Melville, for example, speaks of having learned at sea about the infidelity of Owen's wife: "For, while I was in the Acushnet we heard from some whale-ship that we spoke, that the Captain of the "*Charles Carroll*"—that is Owen Chace—had recently rec[eive]d letters from home, informing him of the certain infidelity of his wife."[12] Perhaps some such communication about Owen could have grown into a confused impression that Owen himself had visited the ship? Such an explanation also ranks among the least plausible, but it draws attention to a curious fact: if one examines the list of ships spoken by the *Charles Carroll* on its 1836–40 voyage under Owen Chase and by the *Acushnet* while Melville was aboard, there turns out to be only one ship that spoke the two whalers, and that ship is the *William Wirt,* the one Melville made Owen Chase captain of in his erroneous, later corrected, annotation of the *Narrative.* The *Charles Carroll* spoke the *William Wirt* on February 23, 1839, and again on March 28, 1839; the *Acushnet* first spoke the *William Wirt* over two years later, on May 8, 1841. If the *William Wirt* carried news about Owen, it would not have been fresh news, but it may have been memorable enough to create future associations.

There are more ways than can be traced in which Melville could have come to some knowledge of Owen Chase. We have seen in chapter 4 that Melville served on the *Charles and Henry* with a seaman who had served under Owen's brother Joseph. And Melville was, after all, just a year or two or three behind Owen in a variety of Pacific ports. No speculations, however, satisfactorily explain Melville's belief that he actually had seen Owen Chase at sea.

Determining which ship Owen Chase's son was on when Melville met him is also problematic. It was a Nantucket ship, Melville tells us, and it was gammed by the *Acushnet* near the site of the *Essex* shipwreck and prior to the gam with the ship captained by the assumed Owen Chase. And the *Acushnet* and the other ship sailed together for a few days. Of the approximately twenty ships known to have spoken the *Acushnet* while Melville was on board, the most likely one for Melville to have found William Henry Chase on was the *Lima*. The *Acushnet* gammed it twice, the second time sailing in company with it for several days, August 16 to 18, 1841. Available information makes no other ship suit Melville's description of the gam with William Henry's ship as perfectly as the *Lima*. The *Lima* of Nantucket, Obed Luce, Jr., was out from August 29, 1838, to February 7, 1842.

The Melville debt to Owen Chase's story that is most familiar is almost too obvious to need comment. The climactic moments of the last chapter of *Moby-Dick* are modeled closely on the *Narrative*'s description of the destruction of the *Essex*: all the boats had lowered, two were sent back for repairs, the whale aligned himself for the attack and was watched by the unbelieving crewmen on deck. And then came the attack, as if by Owen Chase's whale:

> Diving beneath the settling ship, the whale ran quivering along its keel; but turning under water, swiftly shot to the surface again, far off the other bow, but within a few yards of Ahab's boat, where, for a time, he lay quiescent.

And, as the boat's crew turned toward the scene of the damage: "The ship? Great God, where is the ship?" The *Essex* did not sink as rapidly or as dramatically as the *Pequod,* nor did it make a maelstrom to engulf the crew, but, that climax apart, the two ships foundered the same way.

Most of the underscorings and marginal markings that Melville made in his copy of Owen's *Narrative* relate to the whale's attack (see Appendix A). Even a detail from the last part of the *Narrative*, a description of a shark snapping at oars, seems to have supplied an image for the chase sequence at the end of *Moby-Dick*. Melville distinctly marked the shark passage in the *Narrative*.

Here and there throughout the Melville corpus a phrase or narrative detail seems to derive from Owen's *Narrative*, like the division of their scanty rations that Tommo and Toby made in chapter 7 of *Typee*, almost as if instructed by the division of bread and water in the three *Essex* boats. These little moments of possible influence are minor, of course.

There are, however, other important debts that Melville may owe to Owen Chase, one of them the figure of Starbuck. More than one Nantucket Quaker whaleman could have posed for the valor-ruined man that Melville placed in opposition to Ahab, but some characteristics of Owen Chase are so suited to a picture of Starbuck and so engagingly expressed in the *Narrative* that Melville can easily be thought to have let his image of Starbuck concretize around them. Above all, Owen Chase combines the probity, religious devotion, courage, and industry that radiate from Starbuck, the virtues that simultaneously awe and sadden the author of the novel. One passage that Melville marked in his copy of the *Narrative* reads, "There was not a hope now remaining to us but that which was derived from a sense of the mercies of our Creator." Melville underscored "mercies of our Creator" and added a question mark in parentheses. This manner of asking, "What mercies?" is of a piece with Melville's challenge to the "permitting stars" that watch Starbuck's attrition and destruction. And in a *Clarel* passage shortly to be quoted Melville describes the mate of a captain clearly intended to be Captain Pollard as "A man to creed austere resigned." This impression is gained from Owen Chase, and the application of it to Starbuck is evident.

Furthermore, in the *Clarel* passage Melville introduces a bit of interplay between the Pollard figure and the Chase figure that suggests a benign version of the Ahab-Starbuck confrontation. The captain believed in his power "to effect each thing he would, / Did reason but pronounce it good." This in its context is a detoxified Prometheanism, an everyday confidence in man's power to measure up to the universe, the boldness of the reasonable and hard-working soul, defiance whittled down to Protestant industry. It is no Ahab, by any means, that is speaking, but even this credo of the captain's is too secular and irreverent for the Starbuck-Chase mate who "held in humble way / That still Heaven's overrulings sway / Will and event." The whole *Clarel* passage (which rearranges a bit the facts of Pollard's disaster) is worth examining:

> For ease upon the ground they sit;
> And Rolfe, with eye still following
> Where Nehemiah slow-footed it,
> Asked Clarel: "Know you anything
> Of this man's prior life at all?"
> "Nothing," said Clarel.—"I recall,"
> Said Rolfe, "a mariner like him."
> "A mariner?"—"Yes; one whom grim
> Disaster made as meek as he
> There plodding." Vine here showed the zest
> Of a deep human interest:
> "We crave of you his history:"
> And Rolfe began: "Scarce would I tell
> Of what this mariner befell—
> So much is it with cloud o'ercast—
> Were he not now gone home at last
> Into the green land of the dead,
> Where he encamps and peace is shed.
> Hardy he was, sanguine and bold,
> The master of a ship. His mind
> In night-watch frequent he unrolled—
> As seamen sometimes are inclined—
> On serious topics, to his mate,
> A man to creed austere resigned.
> The master ever spurned at fate,
> Calvin's or Zeno's. Always still
> Man-like he stood by man's free will
> And power to effect each thing he would,
> Did reason but pronounce it good.
> The subaltern held in humble way

That still Heaven's over-rulings sway
Will and event.
           "On waters far,
Where map-man never made survey,
Gliding along in easy plight,
The strong one brake the lull of night
Emphatic in his willful war—
But staggered, for there came a jar
With fell arrest to keel and speech:
A hidden rock. The pound—the grind—
Collapsing sails o'er deck declined—
Sleek billows curling in the breach,
And nature with her neutral mind.
A wreck. 'Twas in the former days,
Those waters then obscure; a maze;
The isles were dreaded—every chain;
Better to brave the immense of sea,
And venture for the Spanish Main,
Beating and rowing against the trades,
Than float to valleys 'neath the lee,
Nor far removed, and palmy shades.
So deemed he, strongly erring there.
To boats they take; the weather fair—
Never the sky a cloudlet knew;
A temperate wind unvarying blew
Week after week; yet came despair;
The bread tho' doled, and water stored,
Ran low and lower-ceased. They burn—
They agonize till crime abhorred
Lawful might be. O trade-wind, turn!
    "Well may some items sleep unrolled—
Never by the one survivor told.
Him they picked up, where, cuddled down,
They saw the jacketed skeleton,
Lone in the only boat that lived—
His signal frittered to a shred.
    "'Strong need'st thou be,' the rescuers said,
'Who hast such trial sole survived.'
'I *willed* it,' gasped he. And the man,
Renewed ashore, pushed off again.
How bravely sailed the pennoned ship
Bound outward on her sealing trip
Antarctic. Yes; but who returns
Too soon, regaining port by land

Who left it by the bay? What spurns
Were his that so could countermand?
Nor mutineer, nor rock, nor gale
Nor leak had foiled him. No; a whale
Of purpose aiming, stove the bow:
They foundered. To the master now
Owners and neighbors all impute
An inauspiciousness. His wife—
Gentle, but unheroic—she,
Poor thing, at heart knew bitter strife
Between her love and her simplicity:
A Jonah is he?—And men bruit
The story. None will give him place
In a third venture. Came the day
Dire need constrained the man to pace
A night patrolman on the quay
Watching the bales till morning hour
Through fair and foul. Never he smiled;
Call him, and he would come; not sour
In spirit, but meek and reconciled;
Patient he was, he none withstood;
Oft on some secret thing would brood.
He ate what came, though but a crust;
In Calvin's creed he put his trust;
Praised heaven, and said that God was good,
And his calamity but just.
So Sylvio Pellico from cell-door
Forth tottering, after dungeoned years,
Crippled and bleached, and dead his peers:
'Grateful, I thank the Emperor.'"[13]

If Owen Chase lent his traits to the portrait of Starbuck, and if
Captain Pollard played in a different but comparable way the role
of Ahab, *Clarel* has a little light to shed on *Moby-Dick*. It is
retrospective comment, of course, for Melville had not met Pollard
when he wrote *Moby-Dick* and Pollard was not indirectly known to
Melville in any way that would have enabled Melville to draw on
him. Captain and mate in *Clarel* help us appreciate captain and
mate in *Moby-Dick* the way *Billy Budd* helps us to read "The
Town-Ho's Story."

After Pollard and Melville had met, however, this "most
impressive man, tho' wholly unassuming even humble—that I ever
encountered" seems to have affected Melville's imagination

strongly, not so much in the creation of the character to whom he invites the reader of *Clarel* to compare the Pollard figure, namely Nehemiah—for there is too much in Nehemiah that has no bearing on Pollard—but in the creation of a much more important character, Bartleby the Scrivener. The scrivener dwells in the obscurity of a low calling, having left behind what the reader assumes until the end of the story was a more human and worthy life. As a matter of fact, it was more human and worthy, though sad. The most important resemblance between Pollard and Bartleby, that is, between the Pollard figure and Bartleby, is that both of them have survived by exercise of pure will. In Zola's terms they are almost laboratory experiments in the possibilities of will. Bartleby has stripped himself of almost everything except his will and has made a verb of willing his trademark. The Pollard figure, to look back at lines already discussed,

> . . . ever spurned at fate,
> Calvin's or Zeno's. Always still
> Man-like he stood by man's free will
> And power to effect each thing he would.

The spurning at fate is certainly confirmed by Charles Wilkes's report that Pollard's readiness to return to sea after his shipwreck came from a belief that lightning does not strike twice in the same place, but what is most pertinent in these lines to the Bartleby comparison is the inclusion of "Calvin's or Zeno's," a tidy counterpart to "Edwards on the Will" and "Priestley on Necessity" in "Bartleby." The lawyer-narrator of the short story unconsciously comes to grips with the drama of will being played out in front of him and rather comically turns to two authors who, he hopes, can explain to him the working of will—in his perplexity he would be glad to take a cue from any determinism, theological or scientific. It is precisely these two determinisms that the Pollard figure in *Clarel* repudiated and "stood by man's free will." Finally, when the captain in *Clarel* is congratulated for his survival, he replies simply, the emphasis his own, "I *willed* it." The invitation to sit in judgment on human will put to the test is offered many times in Melville's works. The impact on Melville of meeting someone who had gone through the test cannot be underestimated. "Bartleby" was first published about sixteen months after Melville met Captain Pollard.[14]

ACCOUNTS AND BORROWINGS

After Owen Chase's *Narrative* the most important accounts of the shipwreck are those by Captain Pollard and Thomas Chapple (Appendices B and C). After these three accounts come many borrowings and retellings of the *Essex* story in novels, monographs, newspaper and magazine articles, books on Nantucket history, and collections of maritime adventure stories. Rarely does any of them add to the information provided in the three prime sources, and in so many cases that it would be tiresome to point them all out they introduce errors into the story. In the survey that follows no effort has been made to list every mention of the *Essex* in books on the sea or on Nantucket, nor is the listing of newspaper articles complete; works omitted are invariably brief popular renditions of the story or references to it drawn from recognizable published sources.

The uses made of the *Essex* by creative writers other than Melville are slight. In the cases of Edgar Allan Poe and Walt Whitman there is evidence, but not conclusive evidence, that the authors knew and tapped Owen Chase's *Narrative*. Poe's *Narrative of Arthur Gordon Pym* resembles Owen Chase's *Narrative* in several ways, not the least of which is its being told by a Nantucketer, but among the resemblances are some that seem to owe their origin to Poe's reading in other authors exclusively or in other authors as well as in Owen Chase. That part of *Pym* which deals with the long survival at sea contains at least thirteen passages that echo Owen Chase's *Narrative*. Passages dealing with the onset of hunger and thirst, efforts to get supplies by scuttling the decks, building up the gunwales of a boat, attempts to eat leather, attempts to catch sharks, the longevity of tortoises, eating barnacles found on the keel, a seaman dying in convulsions, and the drawing of lots for cannibal sacrifice would strike the reader of Owen's *Narrative*, but at least a third of these details can also be found in the already identified Poe sources.[15]

Walt Whitman incorporates the following line into a catalog of

shameful, vicious, and oppressive human actions in his poem, "I Sit
and Look Out"; "I observe a famine at sea, I observe the sailors
casting lots who shall be kill'd to preserve the lives of the rest."[16]
Since Captain Pollard's boat was not the only place on record
where such lots were drawn, it is not possible to say that Whitman
was thinking of it. The most interesting thing, however, about the
line is the context that Whitman chooses for it: the scene moves the
poet not to sympathize with the victims of famine but to denounce
their sacrifice of one of their own.

But what must count as a link between Owen Chase and Walt
Whitman was established the day that the good gray poet, crossing
the Hudson on the New Jersey ferry, stooped over and kissed little Claudius Tice. That was Owen's great-grandson; Claudius's
daughters tell the story, which it would be churlish to omit in any
event and more than charming to record if Whitman actually had
drawn on Owen's experience.

William Starbuck Mayo, a descendant on his mother's side of the
Nantucket Starbucks but not a Nantucketer himself, put the *Essex*
story before more readers than Owen Chase's *Narrative* did but
without acknowledging that it was the *Essex* story or that Owen
Chase was his source. Mayo was an Ogdensburg, New York, phy-
sician who adopted a literary career after a period of valetudinarian
travel in Europe and North Africa. In his inept and tedious but very
popular novel, *Kaloolah, or Journeyings to the Djebel Kumri* (New
York: G. P. Putnam, 1849), Mayo condensed the *Essex* story into a
paragraph, planted it in the beginning of the novel, and treated it as
an account of an experience of a relative of the narrator. It is not
integrated with the rest of the novel. Since Mayo betrays a certain
study of Nantucket and of whaling, one may ask where precisely he
found the *Essex* story. Phrasing suggests that he did not need any
source beyond Owen's *Narrative*:

> I involuntarily ordered the boy at the helm to put it hard up; intending
> to sheer off and avoid him. . . . I bawled out to the helmsman, "hard
> up!" but she had not fallen off more than a point, before we took the
> . . . shock . . . I was aroused with the cry of a man at the hatchway,
> "here he is—he is making for us again." I . . . saw him . . . coming
> down apparently with twice his ordinary speed. . . . his course

towards us was marked by a white foam of a rod in width. . . . [he] struck the ship with his head, just forward of the fore-chains. . . . I then ordered the signal to be set for the other boats. [Owen Chase, *Narrative*; sentence order changed in places.]

Mayo wrote:

The steersman was directed to put the helm up, in order to give her a sheer out of the way,—but it was too late. Her bows had fallen off but a point or two when the whale struck her, "head on," with tremendous force. . . . It was soon ascertained that no very serious damage had been sustained, when one of the look-outs appalled them with the shout, "Here she comes again!" and down came the whale with renewed fury,—a broad-sheet of white foam attesting the rapidity of her progress. Again she struck the ill-fated vessel in nearly the same place—just forward of the fore chains. . . . Signals were made for the boats to return.

Mayo's use of the *Essex* material is of no historical or literary consequence, but the Melvillean who pursues the matter will notice two other details in *Kaloolah*: first, in the paragraph following the *Essex* paragraph, the story of a too-indomitable-to-be-real whaling captain who lost his leg to a whale, and second, the denial in the preface to the fourth edition that the book was written under the influence of *Typee*.

Joseph C. Hart's *Miriam Coffin; or, The Whale Fisherman* (New York: G. & C. & H. Carvill; Philadelphia: Carey & Hart, 1834) stands between Owen Chase's *Narrative* and *Moby-Dick*, a debtor to the former and creditor to the latter. Vol. 2, chap. 10 of this novel contains a whale-against-ship drama that seems to derive from the obvious *Essex* source, but this climactic moment was not the most useful part of the book for Melville, who drew more on details and references from various other parts of the book. The actual whale attack on the ship described in *Miriam Coffin* differs significantly from the attacks on the *Essex* and the *Pequod*, but it does bring something in *Moby-Dick* to mind, the picture on the wall of the Spouter Inn, described in the beginning of chapter 3 of *Moby-Dick*. What Hart owes to Owen Chase is by and large a knowledge of the reality of a whale attack. Hart, unlike Mayo, was not a mere pirate of Owen's material.[17]

Several early accounts of the *Essex* are indebted to a Nantucket antiquarian and journalist, Fred Sanford. Among these are R. B. Forbes, *Loss of the Essex, Destroyed by a Whale, with an Account of the Sufferings of the Crew, Who Were Driven to Extreme Measures to Sustain Life* (Cambridge: John Wilson & Son, 1884); Gustav Kobbé, "The Perils and Romance of Whaling," *Century Magazine* 40, n.s. 18 (Aug. 1890): 509–525; and L. Vernon Briggs, *History of Shipbuilding on North River, Plymouth County, Massachusetts, with Genealogies of the Shipbuilders, and Accounts of the Industries upon Its Tributaries, 1640 to 1872* (Boston: Coburn Bros., 1889), pp. 49–51. Kobbé describes his source as a "Diary kept by the first mate, Owen Chase, which is in the possession of F. C. Sanford of Nantucket." In fact, it was simply the published version of Owen's *Narrative* that he was drawing on. The Forbes pamphlet and the Briggs passage on the *Essex* are so misinformed and confused as to be thoroughly misleading. Forbes has Captain Downs [*sic*], not Captain Ridgely, arranging the rescue of the three men left on Ducie (when Forbes was writing in 1884 it was clear that the island was Henderson) for $1,000. He has Wright and Weeks returning to Boston on the *London Packet* in June 1822, which is impossible, and he tells the following story, which is irreconcilable with the firsthand reports: "When a black man died in one of the boats, another one partook of his liver, became mad and jumped overboard."[18] In the Briggs book we are told that the *Essex* was built on the North River, Plymouth, which, as we have seen, is not true. Fred Sanford's contributions to the *Inquirer and Mirror*, some appearing over the signature letter "S," touch occasionally on *Essex* matters. Unfortunately his recollections, which a number of writers have taken as authoritative, are not always reliable; he is one of those familiar fountains of information and misinformation that historians must draw on *faute de mieux* and warily. He stored up details of local history lost to the written page and to the recollections of others, but verification was not his forte.

It is curious and perhaps more than coincidental that 1834 and the six or seven years following saw the appearance of a widespread interest in the *Essex*. The sequence of treatments began with a citation of part of Owen Chase's *Narrative* in the *North American*

Review 38 (January 1834). The same month the *Pittsfield Sun* reprinted parts of the *Narrative* (January 30, 1834). It was also in 1834 that Ralph Waldo Emerson, in a journal entry discussed below, spoke of the *Essex,* and in the same year *The Mariner's Chronicle,* already cited, appeared with a short version of the *Essex* story based on the Pollard and Chapple accounts.[19] In 1835 Thomas Beale mentioned the *Essex* in *The Natural History of the Sperm Whale* (London: Effingham Wilson), and Obed Macy gave a short version of the events—minus the cannibalism—in his *History of Nantucket* (Boston: Hilliard, Gray & Co). The next year William H. McGuffey's celebrated readers began telling the nation's schoolchildren of the *Essex; The Eclectic Fourth Reader: Containing Elegant Extracts in Prose and Poetry, from the Best American and English Writers* (Cincinnati: Truman & Smith) contained an accurate version of the adventure but was prefaced by a statement that Captain Pollard was reticent ever to discuss the shipwreck, which, as has been observed, is contradicted by all other descriptions of Pollard.

Also in 1836 appeared a largely erroneous but curious version of the *Essex* story in R. Thomas, *An Authentic Account of the Most Remarkable Events: Containing the Lives of the Most Noted Pirates and Piracies. Also, the Most Remarkable Shipwrecks, Fires, Famines, Calamities, Providential Deliverances, and Lamentable Disasters on the Seas, in Most Parts of the World* (New York: Ezra Strong), 2 vols. in 1, separately paginated. The *Essex* story is in the second volume, pp. 323–25. This book will be discussed below in relation to its evident sources, but its account of the *Essex* may be noted here for one apparently original detail: Captain Downes arranged the rescue of the three left on the island by fitting out a schooner at an expense of $1,200, which schooner returned a month later dismasted, and thereafter by engaging Captain Raine for $300. Captain Downes, as we have seen, did not arrange the island rescue at all, and he was in port only sixteen days, not long enough to learn of the fate of the alleged schooner that returned after a month. The tale of the schooner has to be dismissed if proposed as part of the *Essex* story. Nonetheless, the mention of it commands some attention, for the Chilean schooner *Dolores* did leave Valparaiso while the *Macedonian* was at anchor there and did return leaking on March 21 according to the *Gazeta ministerial de Chile.* Like a stone picked up by a rolling snowball, the *Dolores*'s movements may have become lodged in some account of the survivors' days in Valparaiso told by someone on the scene.

Continuing the survey of 1830s publications about the *Essex,* we come to 1837 and Poe's *Pym.* The year after that a New Zealander, J. S. Polack, included an account of the shipwreck in his book, *New Zealand . . . ,* discussed below. In 1840 Frederick Debell Bennett told the story in his *Narrative of a Whaling Voyage round the Globe from the Year 1833 to 1836* (London: Richard Bentley), and the following year Francis Olmsted reprinted part of Owen Chase's *Narrative* in *Incidents of a Whaling Voyage* (New York: Appleton). Why interest in the *Essex* should have burgeoned during this brief period is hard to explain; the article in the *North American Review* may have prompted at least some of the other treatments.

Ralph Waldo Emerson's comments on the *Essex* in his journal and letters are as interesting as anything written for publication. Emerson had a keen eye and ear for the singular instance and several times jotted down details about the *Essex.* The most interesting note is one in which he records a conversation that inferentially linked Owen Chase with—of all things—a white whale:

> Boston, Feb. 19 [1834]. A seaman in the coach told the story of an old sperm whale which he called a white whale which was known for many years by the whalemen as Old Tom & who rushed upon the boats which attacked him & crushed the boats to small chips in his jaws, the men generally escaping by jumping overboard & being picked up. A vessel was fitted out at New Bedford, he said, to take him. And he was finally taken somewhere off Payta head by the Winslow or the Essex.[20]

The seaman's story certainly owes nothing to *Moby-Dick,* being told seventeen years before *Moby-Dick* appeared, and it is of interest to a study of Owen Chase because it refers not merely to the *Essex* but to Owen's subsequent ship, the *Winslow.* One wonders whether or not some of the white-whale myths in circulation had come to be attached to the *Essex* and to Owen Chase and had been so spoken of in Herman Melville's hearing. When Emerson was on Nantucket in 1847 he noted in his journal that he had seen Captain Pollard, and he also mentioned the sacrifice of Owen Coffin in the boats; as have others, he erroneously referred to Owen Coffin as Pollard's nephew. From Nantucket Emerson also wrote to his daughter Ellen a letter that contained a brief account of the whale's attack on the *Essex*.

Writing later in the nineteenth century, W. Scoresby in *The Whaleman's Adventures* (London: Darton & Co., 1860) draws on Owen's *Narrative* but states that the three crewmen left on Ducie Island were never found again and in a long footnote offers his opinion that the whale's first blow was struck by accident and his second in anger. Another book, *Voyage and Venture; or, The Pleasures and Perils of a Sailor's Life* (Philadelphia: H. C. Peck & Theo. Bliss, 1857), also speaks of the *Essex*.

At this point something may be said about the Australian historiography of the *Essex*. Three Australian sources of the story have been cited in chapter 3, of which Dr. Ramsay's Journal and the Mitchell Library Ms. A131 are the most important, containing as they do eyewitness accounts of the Henderson Island rescue and secondhand accounts of the shipwreck taken directly from the participants. Edward Dobson, the presumed author of Ms. A131, came out from London as a passenger on the *Surry*, ran out of money, and signed on the ship as a crew member when the *Surry* reached Sydney in September 1820. Crew lists give his age as twenty in December 1820.[21] It is Dobson's account that is at the source of almost everything printed in Australia on the *Essex*.

Apparently the first beneficiary of Dobson's journal was the writer of the article in the *Sydney Gazette*, June 9, 1821, which is reprinted in Appendix F. A comparison of the article to Ms. A131 will show how close the article's borrowing is part of the time and how flagrant its misrepresentation of the facts is the rest of the time. Dobson had made it clear that the rescue did not take place on Ducie, but the *Gazette* article ducks the whole question of where the rescue took place and leaves the hasty reader to infer that it was Ducie; the article gives the island's latitude, which is close to Ducie's, but refrains from giving the longitude mentioned by Dobson, which would have made it clear that the island was not Ducie. The article also has eight people, not one, killed in the boats, and has Pollard and Ramsdell drawing lots for the final shooting. When it reaches the survivors' account of the *Essex*'s history the article gives the wrong sailing date for the *Essex* and misdates the shipwreck, though both dates are correctly given in Ms. A131. The article's meaningless expression, "she struck the ship, which was under the cat-head," obviously comes from "the Bows were stove in, under the cathead on the Starboard side." One of the fudged details in the article is the boat "picked up by an American whaler about 60 days after the melancholy occurrence." The details of the story had not been very well absorbed by the author of the article.

The account that the *Sydney Gazette* presented became the duly acknowledged source of an article in the February 1822 issue of the *Wesleyan-Methodist Magazine* (London). This article edited the *Gazette* article a bit and managed to make sense of some of the *Gazette*'s mistakes, for example, "The boat to which these three men belonged, had been picked up by an American Whaler. About sixty days after the melancholy occurrence, another boat, in which were the Captain and the remainder of the crew, soon parted company, and were also fallen in with by another American Whaler, which vessel was the bearer of the intelligence to Valparaiso." This at least is accurate to the extent that the separation of the boats, not the rescue, took place about two months after the shipwreck. This magazine article also corrects the *Gazette* to make sense out of the cathead passage.

The book by R. Thomas, *An Authentic Account of the Most Remarkable Events: . . . Also, the Most Remarkable Shipwrecks,* which was mentioned above, in reporting the *Essex* story repeats the *Wesleyan-Methodist Magazine* article almost verbatim except for its curious inclusion of the dismasted schooner episode already discussed. The Thomas book incidentally, has been identified by Keith Huntress (see n. 15 to this chapter) as a major source of Poe's *Arthur Gordon Pym*; Huntress found that twenty-one accounts of Thomas's were stolen directly from *The Mariner's Chronicle*. Poetic justice was done to Thomas when another book twenty-odd years later stole his account of the *Essex,* dismasted schooner and all: that was the anonymous *Book of the Ocean and Life on the Sea: Containing Thrilling Narratives and Adventures of Ocean Life in All Countries, from the Earliest Period to the Present Time* (Auburn and Buffalo: John E. Beardsley, n.d.).[22] These two American books are clearly part of the Australian transmission of the story.

Also part of the Australian transmission is a book by a nineteenth-century New Zealand author, J. S. Polack, who drew on the *Sydney Gazette* or possibly the *Wesleyan-Methodist Magazine* version for the story he told in *New Zealand: Being a Narrative of Travels and Adventures during a Residence in That Country between the Years 1831 and 1837*, 2 vols. (London: Richard Bentley, 1838). Polack repeats the outstanding errors of the *Gazette* but adds an error of his own—the wreck occurred 47° S. If it had, the survivors could have added pneumonia to their other perils. Polack misread the 47″ in the *Gazette* article (which itself was an error for 47′).

A modern New Zealand writer, who cites Polack as one of his sources, is extremely inaccurate: L. S. Rickard in *The Whaling Trade in Old New Zealand* (Auckland: Minerva, 1965) states that all three of the boats left the island (which he accepts as Ducie); one was never heard from again, one was picked up at sea by Captain Raine "in a New South Wales whaling ship" sixty days after the sinking of the *Essex,* and the third was picked up thirty days after the second by another whaler. Rickard reports that in the third boat, "Day by day, lots had been drawn to decide who was to die and feed his comrades."

Two modern Australian studies of Captain Raine, both already mentioned, are more reliable in their information on the *Essex:* Margaret Fane De Salis, *Captain Thomas Raine, an Early Colonist* (Vaucluse, N.S.W.: Published by the author, 1969), and R. H. Goddard, "Captain Thomas Raine of the Surry, 1795–1860," *Journal and Proceedings of the Royal Australian Historical Society* 26 (1940): 277–317, although the caution about the latter mentioned in n. 37 to chapter 3 should be observed.

In 1935 an anonymous pamphlet, *The Loss of the Essex,* was published by the Inquirer and Mirror Press, Nantucket. It was the fullest study of the *Essex* yet published. In 1950 it was reissued with the name of the author, Edouard Stackpole, and an extensively revised edition subsequently appeared (Falmouth: Kendall Printing, 1977). Mr. Stackpole's account of the *Essex* in his book, *The Sea-Hunters* (Philadelphia: Lippincott, 1953; rep. Westport, Conn.: Greenwood Press, 1972), is a brief version of the story; it has been superseded by the 1977 edition of the pamphlet, but the book unlike the pamphlet has the advantage of footnotes.

In 1974 the most scholarly work on the *Essex* up to that time appeared in a periodical publication of the Melville Society: Deborah C. Andrews, "Attacks of Whales on Ships: A Checklist," *Extracts*, May 1974, pp. 3–17. This annotated bibliography is a natural starting point for students of the *Essex* or of the whole genre of whale attacks.

Among twentieth-century books and articles not already cited in relation to the second section of this chapter several titles may be mentioned. None of them does more than rework the received story—except for those that corrupt it. A good account of the *Essex* is given in Foster Rhea Dulles, *Lowered Boats: A Chronicle of American Whaling* (New York: Harcourt, Brace, 1933). Horace Beck in *Folklore and the Sea* (Middletown, Conn.: Published for the Marine Historical Association by Wesleyan University Press, 1973) treats legendary more than historical aspects of the *Essex* story: "According to legend [Zimri Coffin, captain of the rescue ship *Dauphin*] was the father of Owen Coffin." But the legend, while worth noting as such, should also be corrected, for Owen Coffin's father was Hezekiah Coffin, Jr., not Zimri Coffin. *Folklore and the Sea* also repeats the most strained and unimaginable jest connected with the *Essex* adventure, the remark attributed to Captain Pollard when asked if he had known Owen Coffin, "Know him? Why, young man, I et him." Edwin P. Hoyt devotes a chapter in *Nantucket: The Life of an Island* (Brattleboro, Vt.: Stephen Greene Press, 1978) to the *Essex* and gives a good, compact rendition of the story as told in Owen's *Narrative*.

J. David Truby, "The Turbulent Wars That Whales Have Fought against Men," *Smithsonian* 3 (May 1972), gives a sound, short account of the *Essex*. Elmo Paul Hohman, *The American Whaleman* (New York: Longmans, Green & Co., 1928), tells the

Essex story but misdates it by one year: shipwreck, survival events, and rescue are all dated one year earlier than they actually happened. Hohman was probably misled by the erroneous dates on the title page of the 1821 edition of the *Narrative*. Chapter 2 of Chester Howland, *Thar She Blows* (New York: Wilfred Funk, 1951), is, after a few words of introduction, a quoted and edited-down presentation of Owen Chase's *Narrative*.

Dale Shaw's "The Savage Sea," *True,* October 1958, is a popular but attentively researched telling of the *Essex* story. A. B. C. Whipple's "Three-month Ordeal in Open Boats," *Life,* November 10, 1952, is fairly sound, though it suggests that Captain Pollard knew about Pitcairn Island—which is totally unlikely and unsupported by any evidence—and that in his old age Pollard's mind began to wander; doubtless Whipple is confusing him with Owen Chase. Whipple also tells the "I et him" story. But when Whipple revised the *Life* material for his *Yankee Whalers in the South Seas* (Garden City, N.Y.: Doubleday, 1954) he produced a hysterically overdramatized tale, popular in the worst sense and of almost no historical value. He makes a bibliographical notation (pp. 290–91) calculated to cause considerable confusion for someone tracking down *Essex* sources: he has invented a ghost book on the *Essex* by fusing together elements of the three survivors' accounts. Whipple's *Vintage Nantucket* (New York: Dodd, Mead, 1978) contains the erroneous suggestion that the wife divorced by Owen Chase was his first wife, the one to whom he returned from the wreck of the *Essex*. Only Frank B. Gilbreth, Jr., in *Of Whales and Women* (New York: Crowell, 1956) has done a worse job on the *Essex*; his book is cute, and the account of the *Essex* contains such historical novelties as the return of the five *Essex* survivors from Valparaiso to Nantucket on board the *Hero.* A. A. Hoehling, a disaster specialist, begins *Great Ship Disasters* (New York: Cowles, 1971) with the story of the *Andrea Doria* and follows it with the story of the *Essex*.

Oliver Stuart Chase did a master's thesis on Owen Chase at Columbia University, 1962. Sterling Hayden in his autobiographical *Wanderer* (New York: Avon Books, 1977), p. 143, says that he has written a screenplay on the wreck of the *Essex*.

The editions of Owen Chase's *Narrative* that have appeared following the 1821 first edition are the following: (1) *Narratives of the Wreck of the Whale-Ship Essex of Nantucket Which Was Destroyed by a Whale in the Pacific Ocean in the Year 1819; Told by Owen Chase, First Mate, Thomas Chappel, Second Mate, and George Pollard, Captain of the Said Vessel; Together with an Introduction & Twelve Engravings on Wood by Robert Gibbings* (London: Golden Cockerel Press, 1935); (2) *Narrative of the Most Extraordinary and Distressing Shipwreck of the Whaleship Essex* by Owen Chase, with supplementary accounts of survivors and Herman Melville's notes and introduction by B. R. McElderry, Jr. (New York: Corinth Books, 1963; rep. Gloucester, Mass.: Peter Smith, 1972); (3) *The Wreck of the Whaleship Essex: A Narrative Account by Owen Chase, First Mate,* edited, with prologue and epilogue, by Iola Haverstick and Betty Shepard (New York: Harcourt, Brace & World, 1965).

Copies of the first edition of Owen Chase's *Narrative* are known to be in the Library of Congress, the New York Public Library, the Blunt White Library (Old Mystic, Conn.), the Beinecke Library (Yale University), the Whaling Museum (Nantucket), the Nantucket Atheneum, the Municipal Libraries of Bath (England), the libraries of the American Antiquarian Society, Harvard University, Princeton University, and the University of Virginia, and in the possession of some private parties.

APPENDICES

Appendix A

HERMAN MELVILLE'S ANNOTATIONS AND MARKINGS IN HIS COPY OF OWEN CHASE'S *NARRATIVE*

Herman Melville's copy of Owen Chase's *Narrative* is in the Houghton Library, Harvard University. It is not the copy that Melville borrowed from Owen's son William Henry and read at sea but the copy that Melville's father-in-law, Judge Shaw, procured for him from Thomas Macy of Nantucket and sent to him around April 1851 as he was completing *Moby-Dick*. Thomas Macy apologized for sending an imperfect copy of the *Narrative*—the only one he could find was missing pages 123 to 128 at the end of the volume. Melville made his annotations on sheets of light blue, ruled paper bound into the front and the back of the volume, and he also marked the text of his copy. Immediately inside the front cover is the first of the light blue sheets, blank on both sides, then a sheet with an ink inscription, "Herman Melville / from Judge Shaw / April.1851." This inscribed sheet is blank on the back and is followed by the sheet numbered page 1. The numbering continues without interruption up to page 18 (but page 1 and pages 8 to 13 are blank). Pages 19–20 have been torn out, but a fragment in the binding with a pen marking suggests that there was writing on the page. The next sheet after page 18 is a letter from Thomas Macy to Judge Shaw, which obviously accompanied the gift book. This is the last of the sheets bound in the front of the book; the title page follows. After page 122 the annotations on the blue paper resume, the pages being numbered from 21 to 30 and followed by thirty-four unnumbered blank pages. The page numbering is in pencil and possibly in a later hand. Melville's annotations are in ink except for those on pages 17–18, which are in green crayon. Melville used crayon in his later years when his eyes were failing.

All or most of the annotations except those in crayon were probably written some time in the fifteen-month period between Melville's receipt of the book, presumably April 1851, and his trip to Nantucket in July 1852, for in a comment on page 23 of the annotations he expressed uncertainty as to whether Captain Pollard was still alive, something he would not have done after meeting him July 8, 1852. It is only in the crayon annotation, apparently written in old age, that Melville indicates that he has met Captain Pollard. The annotations, then, seem to coincide with the last months of the writing of *Moby-Dick* or with the writing of *Pierre*.

The annotations are reproduced in full below, facsimile and transcription. Following the annotations, Melville's markings in Owen's text are reproduced.

General Evidences

This thing of the Essex is found (stupidly abbreviated) in many compilations of nautical adventure made within the last 15 or 20 years. ¶ The Englishman Bennett in his exact work ("Whaling Voyage round the Globe") quotes the thing as an acknowledged fact.

¶   Besides seamen several landsman (Judge Shaw & others) acqua[i]nted with Nantucket, have evinced to me their unquestioning faith in the thing; having seen Captain Pollard himself, & being conversant with his situation in Nantucket since the disaster.

What I know of Owen Chace & c
_____

When I was on board the ship Acushnet of Fairhaven, on the passage to the Pacific cruising-grounds, among other matters of forecastle conversation at times was the story of the Essex. It was then that I first became acqua[i]nted with her history and her truly astounding fate.

But what then served to specialise my interest at the time was the circumstance that the

Second Mate of our ship, Mr. Hall, an Englishman & Londoner by birth, had for two three-years voyages sailed with Owen Chace (then in command of the whale-ship "William* Wirt" (I think it was) of Nantucket.) This Hall always spoke of Chace with much interest & sincere regard—but he did not seem to know anything more about him or the Essex affair than any body else. ☐ *See p. 19. of M.S. ☐

Somewhere about the latter part of A. D. 1841, in this same ship the Acushnet, we spoke the

"W<u>m</u> Wirt*'' of Nantucket, & Owen Chace was the Captain, & so it came to pass that I saw him. He was a large, powerful well-made man; rather tall; to all [appearances] something past forty-five or so; with a handsome face for a Yankee, & expressive of great uprightness & calm [unostentatious] courage. His whole [appearance] impressed me pleas[an]tly. He was the most [prepossessing]-looking whalehunter I think I ever saw.

————— Being a mear foremast-hand I had no opportunity of conversing with Owen (tho' he was on board our ship for two hours at a time) nor have I ever seen him since.

But I should have before mentioned, that before seeing Chace's ship, we spoke another Nantucket craft & <u>gammed</u> with her. In the forecastle I made the acquai[n]tance of a fine lad of sixteen or thereabouts, a son of Owen Chace. I questioned him concerning his father's adventure; and when I left his ship to return again the next morning (for the two vessels were to sail in company for a few days) he went to his chest & handed me a complete copy (same edition as this one) of the Narrative. This was the first printed account of it I had ever seen, & the only copy of Chace's Narrative (regular & authentic) except the present one. The reading of this [wondrous] story upon the landless sea, & close to the very latitude of the shipwreck had a surprising effect upon me.

Authorship of the Book

There seems no reason to suppose that Owen himself wrote the Narrative. It bears obvious tokens of having been written for him; but at the same time, its whole air plainly evinces that it was carefully & [conscientiously] written to Owen's dictation of the facts. ——— It is almost as good as tho' Owen wrote it himself.

Another Narrative of the Adventure

I have been told that Pollard the Captain, wrote, or caused to be wrote under his own name, his version of the story. I have seen extracts purporting to be from some such work. But I have never seen the work itself. I should imagine Owen Chace to have been the fittest person to narrate the thing.

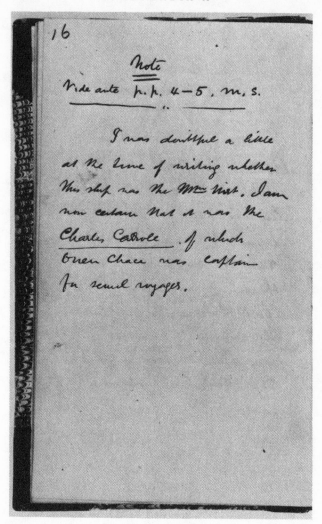

Note
Vide ante p.p. 4–5. m.s.

I was doubtful a little at the time of writing whether this ship was the Wm Wirt. I am now certain that it was the <u>Charles Carroll</u> of which Owen Chace was Captain for several voyages.

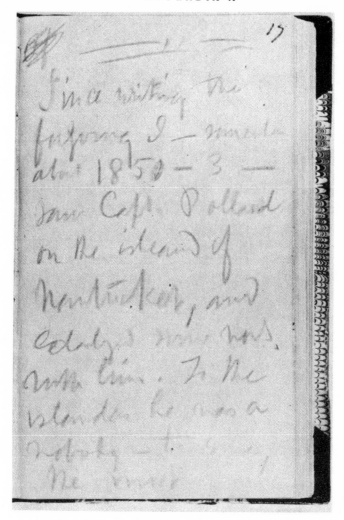

< af >

Since writing the foregoing I—sometime about 1850–3—saw Capt. Pollard on the island of Nantucket, and [exchanged] some words with him. To the islanders he was a nobody—to me, the most

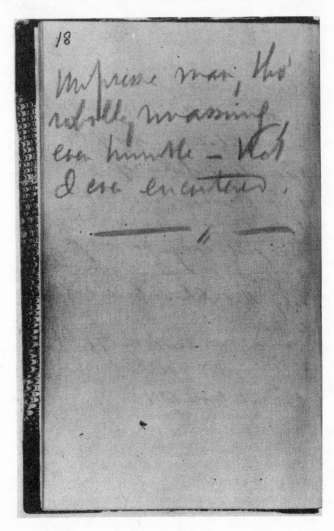

impressive man, tho' wholly unassuming even humble—that I ever encountered

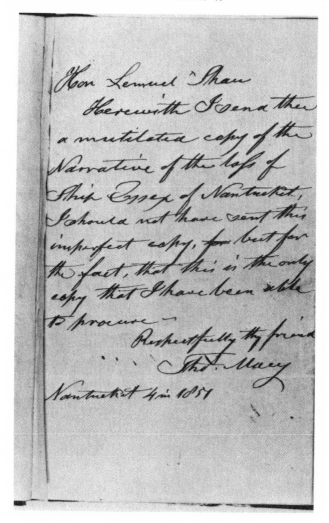

[Page 18 of the annotations is followed by the letter from Thomas Macy to Judge Shaw that accompanied the volume.]

Hon Lemuel Shaw

Herewith I send thee a mutilated copy of the Narrative of the loss of ship Essex of Nantucket, I should not have sent this imperfect copy, ⟨for⟩ but for the fact, that this is the only copy that I have been able to procure—

Respectfully thy friend
Tho.ˢ Macy

Nantucket 4 ṁ 1851

Sequel

—— I can not tell exactly how many more pages the complete narrative contains—but at any rate, very little now remai[n]s to be related.—The boat was picked up by the ship, & the poor fellows were landed in Chili & in time sailed for home. Owen Chace returned to his business of whaling, & in due time became a Captain, as related in the beginning.

Captain Pollard's boat (from which Chace's had become separated) was also after a miserable time, picked up by a ship, but not until two of its crew had died delir[io]us, & furnished food for the survivors.

The third boat, it does not appear, that it was ever heard of, after its sub-separation from Pollard's.

Pollard himself returned to Nantucket, & subsequently sailed on another whaling voyage to the Pacific, but he had not been in the Pacific long, when one night, his ship went ashore on unknown rocks, & was dashed to peaces. The crew, with Pollard, put off in their boats, & were soon picked up by

another whale-ship, with which, the day prev[iou]s, they had sailed in company.—
I got this from Hall, Second Mate of the Acushnet.—

Pollard, it seems, now took the hint, & after reaching home from this second shipwreck, vowed to abide ashore. He has ever since lived in Nantucket. Hall told me that he became a butcher there. I believe he is still living.
A night-watchman
=====

Concerning the three men left on the island;—they were taken off at last (in a sad state <engh> enough) by a ship, which purpos[e]ly touched there for them, being advised of them, by their shipmates who had prev[ious]ly landed ⟨by the sh⟩ in Chili.

——— All the sufferings of these miserable men of the Essex might, in all human probabil[it]y, have been avoided, had they, imm[e]d[iat]ely after leav[in]g the wreck, steered straight for Tahiti, from which they were not very distant at the time, & to which, there was a fair Trade wind. But they dreaded cannibals, & str[an]ge to tell knew not that for more than 20 years, the English missions had been resident in Tahiti; & that in the same year of their shipw[re]ck—1820—it was entirely safe for the Marin[er] to touch at Tahiti.— But they chose to stem a head wind, & make a passage of several thousand miles (an [unavoidably] roundab[ou]t one too) in order to gain a [civilized] harbor on the coast of South America.

Further Concerning Owen Chace

The miserable [pertinaciousness] of misfortune which pursued Pollard the Captain, in his second disast[rou]s & entire shipwreck did likewise hunt poor Owen, tho' somewhat more dilatory in overtaking him the second time.

For, while I was in the Acushnet we heard from some whale-ship that we spoke, that the Captain of the "Charles

Carrol"—that is Owen Chace—had recently rec[eive]d letters from home, informing him of the certain infidelity of his wife, the mother of several children, one of them be[in]g the lad of sixteen, whom I alluded to as gi[vin]g me a copy of his father's nar[ra]tive to read. We also heard that this rec[e]ipt of this news had told most heavily upon Chace, & that he was a prey to the deepest gloom.

HERMAN MELVILLE'S MARKINGS IN HIS
COPY OF OWEN CHASE'S *NARRATIVE*

P. 9 in 1821 edition, *p. 17 in chapter 2 above:*

There are common sailors, boat-steerers,
and harpooners: the last of these is the
most honourable and important. It is in
this station, that all the capacity of the
young sailor is elicited; on the dexterous
management of the harpoon, the line, and
the lance, and in the adventurous positions
which he takes alongside of his enemy, depends almost entirely the successful issue
of his attack; and more real chivalry is not
often exhibited on the deck of a battle-ship,
than is displayed by these hardy sons of
the ocean, in some of their gallant exploits

P. 30, *p. 27:*

We were more than a
thousand miles from the nearest land, and with
nothing but a light open boat, as the resource of
safety for myself and companions. I ordered the
men to cease pumping, and every one to provide
for himself; seizing a hatchet at the same time, I
cut away the lashings of the spare boat, which lay
bottom up, across two spars directly over the quarter deck, and cried out to those near me, to take
her as she came down. They did so accordingly,
and bore her on their shoulders as far as the waist
of the ship. The steward had in the mean time
gone down into the cabin twice, and saved two

P. 31:

quadrants, two practical navigators, and the captain's trunk and mine; all which were hastily

thrown into the boat, as she lay on the deck, with
the two compasses which I snatched from the bin-
nacle. He attempted to descend again; but the
water by this time had rushed in, and he returned
without being able to effect his purpose. By the
time we had got the boat to the waist, the ship
had filled with water, and was going down on her
beam-ends: we shoved our boat as quickly as
possible from the plank-shear into the water, all
hands jumping in her at the same time, and launched off clear of the ship. We were scarcely two
boat's lengths distant from her, when she fell over
to windward, and settled down in the water.

P. 31, *p. 28:*

all appeared to be bound in a spell of stupid con-

P. 32:

sternation; and from the time we were first attacked by the whale, to the period of the fall of
the ship, and of our leaving her in the boat, more
that ten minutes could not certainly have elapsed!

P. 33, *p. 29:*

They had
but shortly before discovered that some accident
had befallen us, but of the nature of which they
were entirely ignorant. The sudden and mysterious disappearance of the ship was first discovered
by the boat-steerer in the captain's boat, and with
a horror-struck countenance and voice, he suddenly exclaimed, "Oh, my God! where is the
ship?" Their operations upon this were instantly

P. 37, *p. 31:*

this sudden and most deadly attack had been made
upon us: by an animal, too, never before suspect-

ed of premeditated violence, and proverbial for its ✕
insensibility and inoffensiveness. Every fact
seemed to warrant me in concluding that it was
any thing but chance which directed his operations; he made two several attacks upon the ship,
at a short interval between them, both of which,
according to their direction, were calculated to do
us the most injury, by being made ahead, and
thereby combining the speed of the two objects
for the shock; to effect which, the exact manœu-
vres which he made were necessary. His aspect
was most horrible, and such as indicated resent-

P. 38:

ment and fury. He came directly from the shoal
which we had just before entered, and in which
we had struck three of his companions, as if fired
with revenge for their sufferings. But to this it
may be observed, that the mode of fighting which
they always adopt is either with repeated strokes
of their tails, or snapping of their jaws together;
and that a case, precisely similar to this one, has
never been heard of amongst the oldest and most experienced whalers. To this I would answer, that
the structure and strength of the whale's head is admirably designed for this mode of attack; the most
prominent part of which is almost as hard and as
tough as iron; indeed, I can compare it to nothing
else but the inside of a horse's hoof, upon which a
lance or harpoon would not make the slightest impression. The eyes and ears are removed nearly
one-third the length of the whole fish, from the front
part of the head, and are not in the least degree
endangered in this mode of attack. At all events,
the whole circumstances taken together, all happening before my own eyes, and producing, at the
time, impressions in my mind of decided, calculat-

    ing mischief, on the part of the whale, (many of
which impressions I cannot now recall,) induce

P. 39:

    me to be satisfied that I am correct in my opinion.|✕

P. 41, *p. 32:*

    cessity of not wasting our time, and of endeavour-
ing to seek some relief wherever God might direct
us. Our thoughts, indeed, hung about the ship,
wrecked and sunken as she was, and we could
scarcely discard from our minds the idea of her
continuing protection. Some great efforts in our

P. 47, *p. 35:*

    [Illegible blotted ink words at top of page, some
lost because of binder's trimming.]

P. 52, *p. 38:*

    hopes and my fears. The dark ocean and swell-
ing waters were nothing; the fears of being swallowed up by some dreadful tempest, or dashed
upon hidden rocks, with all the other ordinary
subjects of fearful contemplation, seemed scarcely
entitled to a moment's thought; the dismal looking wreck, and the horrid aspect and revenge of
the whale, wholly engrossed my reflections, until
day again made its appearance.

P. 59, *pp. 41–42:*

    I immediately aroused myself, and listened a mo-
ment, to hear if any thing further should be said,
when the captain's loud voice arrested my attention. He was calling to the second mate, whose
boat was nearer to him than mine. I made all
haste to put about, ran down to him, and inquired
what was the matter; he replied, "I have been
attacked by an unknown fish, and he has stove my

boat." It appeared, that some large fish had accompanied the boat for a short distance, and
had suddently made an unprovoked attack upon
her, as nearly as they could determine, with his
jaws; the extreme darkness of the night prevented
them from distinguishing what kind of animal it

P. 63, *p. 43:*

> We made a small line from some
rigging that was in the boat, fastened on one of the
fish-hooks, and tied to it a small piece of white
rag; they took not the least notice of it, but continued playing around us, nearly all day, mocking
both our miseries and our efforts.

P. 108, *pp. 65–66:*

On the 15th of January, at night, a very large
shark was observed swimming about us in a most
ravenous manner, making attempts every now and
then upon different parts of the boat, as if he would
devour the very wood with hunger; he came several times and snapped at the steering oar, and
even the stern-post. We tried in vain to stab
him with a lance, but we were so weak as not to
be able to make any impression upon his hard
skin; he was so much larger than an ordinary one,
and manifested such a fearless malignity, as to
make us afraid of him; and our utmost efforts,
which were at first directed to kill him for prey,
became in the end self-defence. Baffled however
in all his hungry attempts upon us, he shortly made
off.

P. 109, *p. 66:*

both body and soul. There was not a hope now
remaining to us but that which was derived from
a sense of the mercies of our Creator. (?) The night
of the 18th was a despairing era in our sufferings;

Appendix B

THE STORY OF THE *ESSEX* SHIPWRECK PRESENTED IN CAPTAIN POLLARD'S INTERVIEW WITH GEORGE BENNET

Daniel Tyerman and George Bennet, who had been sent by the London Missionary Society to survey Pacific and far eastern missions, relate that they had been visiting the Leeward Group of the Society Islands northwest of Tahiti in April 1823 and on April 16 (possibly an error, for they refer to the next day also as April 16) had crossed over from Bora Bora to Raiatea, the largest island in the group. Captain Pollard, whose second shipwreck had occurred two months before, was at the time a passenger on board the U.S. brig *Pearl*, which had tied up at Raiatea. Here Bennet met Pollard and heard the account of the shipwreck which he put down in his *Journal of Voyages and Travels by the Rev. Daniel Tyerman and George Bennet, Esq. Deputed from the London Missionary Society, to Visit Their Various Stations in the South Sea Islands, China, India, &c. between the Years 1821 and 1829.* (London: Frederick Westley & A. H. Davis, 1831, 2 vols.; Boston: Crocker & Brewster, 1832, 3 vols.). James Montgomery, the editor, added a long footnote quoting from Thomas Chapple's account, which footnote is here omitted since Chapple's full account is given in Appendix C. Some discrepancies between Pollard's account and Owen Chase's (for example, Pollard witnessing the whale's attack) will strike the reader but are understandable corruptions in the light of the retellings.

The text of the American edition is followed below except for the final paragraph, which appeared in the British edition only; apart from that paragraph, the two editions differ only in minor matters of spelling and punctuation. The passage below is from 2:22–30 of the British edition, 2:170–73 of the American.

April 16. In the harbor here, we found the American brig Pearl, captain Chandler, which had put in for repairs, having sprung a leak at sea; and on board of this vessel, to our great joy and surprise, we met with our friends, Mr. and Mrs. Chamberlain, from the Sandwich Islands. We never expected to have seen their faces again in this world. They were, however, for reasons which we had known and approved when we parted with them, on their return with their young family to America. They gave us the most gratifying account of the safe arrival and cordial reception of Mr. and Mrs. Ellis, at Oahu, by our American missionary friends there, by the king also, the chiefs, and the people—all of whom rejoiced to welcome them as servants of the Most High God, arrived among them to teach a nation, *without any religion,* the only doctrines under heaven worthy of that name.

There were three captains on board this brig, as passengers to America. The ships of two of these had been wrecked, and that of the third condemned. One of them was captain George Pollard, whose singular and lamentable story, in the case of a *former* shipwreck (as nearly as can be recollected by Mr. Bennet), deserves to be recorded in his own manner. It was substantially as follows:—

"My first shipwreck was in open sea, on the 20th of November, 1820, near the equator, about 118° W. long. The vessel, a South Sea whaler, was called the Essex. On that day, as we were on the look out for sperm whales, and had actually struck two, which the boats' crews were following to secure, I perceived a very large one—it might be eighty or ninety feet long—rushing with great swiftness through the water, right towards the ship. We hoped that she would turn aside, and dive under, when she perceived such a balk in her way. But no! the animal came full force against our stern-port: had any quarter less firm been struck, the vessel must have been burst; as it was, every plank and timber trembled, throughout her whole bulk.

"The whale, as though hurt by a severe and unexpected concussion, shook its enormous head, and sheered off to so considerable a distance, that for some time we had lost sight of her from the starboard quarter; of which we were very glad, hoping that the worst was over. Nearly an hour afterwards, we saw the same fish—we had no doubt of this, from her size, and the direction in which she came—making again towards us. We were at once aware of our danger, but escape was impossible. She dashed her head this time against the ship's side, and so broke it in, that the vessel filled rapidly, and soon became water-logged. At the second shock, expecting her to go down, we lowered our three boats with the utmost expedition, and all hands, twenty in the whole, got into them— seven, and seven, and six. In a little while, as she did not sink, we ventured on board again, and, by scuttling the deck, were enabled to get out some biscuit, beef, water, rum, two sextants, a quadrant, and three compasses. These, together with some rigging, a few muskets, powder, &c. we brought away; and, dividing the stores among our three small crews, rigged the boats as well as we could; there being a compass for each, and a sextant for two, and quadrant for one, but neither sextant nor quadrant for the third. Then, instead of pushing away for some port, so amazed and bewildered were we, that we continued sitting in our places, gazing upon the ship as though she had been an object of the tenderest affection. Our eyes could not leave her, till, at the end of many hours, she gave a slight reel, then down she sank. No words can tell our feelings. We looked at each other—we looked at the place where she had so lately been afloat—and we did not cease to look, till the terrible conviction of our abandoned and perilous situation roused us to exertion, if deliverance were yet possible.

"We now consulted about the course which it might be best to take—westward to India, eastward to South America, or southwestward to the Society Isles. We knew that we were at no great distance from Tahiti, but were so ignorant of the state and temper of the inhabitants, that we feared we should be devoured by cannibals, if we cast ourselves on their mercy. It was determined therefore to make for South America, which we computed to be more than two thousand miles distant. Accordingly we steered eastward, and, though for several days harassed with squalls, we contrived to keep together. It was not long before we found that one of the boats had started a plank, which was no wonder, for whale-boats are all clinker-built, and very slight, being made of half-inch plank only, before planing. To remedy this alarming defect, we all turned to, and, having emptied the damaged boat into the two others, we raised her side as well as we could, and succeeded in re-storing the plank at the bottom. Through this accident, some of our biscuit had become injured by the salt-water. This was equally divided among the several boats' crews. Food and water, mean-while, with our utmost economy, rapidly failed. Our strength was exhausted, not by abstinence only, but by the labors which we were obliged to employ to keep our little vessels afloat, amidst the storms which repeatedly assailed us. One night we were parted in rough weather; but though the next day we fell in with one of our com-panion-boats, we never saw or heard any more of the other, which probably perished at sea, being without either sextant or quadrant.

"When we were reduced to the last pinch, and out of every thing, having been more than three weeks abroad, we were cheered with the sight of a low uninhabited island, which we reached in hope, but were bitterly disappointed. There were some barren bushes, and many rocks on this forlorn spot. The only provisions that we could procure were a few birds and their eggs: this supply was soon reduced; the sea-fowls appeared to have been frightened away, and their nests were left empty after we had once or twice plundered them. What distressed us most was the utter want of fresh water; we could not find a drop any where, till at the extreme verge of ebb tide, a small spring was discovered in the sand; but even that was too scanty to afford us sufficient to quench our thirst before it was covered by the waves at their turn.

"There being no prospect but that of starvation here, we determined to put to sea again. Three of our comrades, however, chose to remain, and we pledged ourselves to send a vessel to bring them off, if we ourselves should ever escape to a Christian port. With a very small morsel of biscuit for each, and a little water, we again ventured out on the wide ocean. In the course of a few days, our provisions were consumed. Two men died; we had no other alternative than to live upon their remains. These we roasted to dryness by means of fires kindled on the ballast-sand at the bottom of the boats. When this supply was spent, what could we do? We looked at each other with horrid thoughts in our minds, but we held our tongues. I am sure that we loved one another as brothers all the time; and yet our looks told plainly what must be done. We cast lots, and the fatal one fell on my poor cabin-boy. I started forward instantly, and cried out, 'My lad, my lad, *if you don't like your lot,* I'll shoot the first man that touches you.' The poor emaciated boy hesitated a moment or two; then, quietly laying his head down upon the gunnel of the boat, he said, *'I like it as well as any other.'* He was soon despatched, and nothing of him left. I think, then, another man died of himself, and him, too, we ate. But I can tell you no more—my head is on fire at the recollection; I hardly know what I say. I forgot to say, that we had parted company with the second boat before now. After some more days of horror and despair, when some were lying down at the bottom of the boat, not able to rise, and scarcely one of us could move a limb, a vessel hove in sight. We were taken on board, and treated with extreme kindness. The second lost boat was also picked up at sea, and the survivors saved. A ship afterwards sailed in search of our companions on the desolate island, and brought them away."

Captain Pollard closed his dreary narrative with saying, in a tone of despondency never to be forgotten by him who heard it—"After a time I found my way to the United States, to which I belonged, and got another ship. That, too, I have lost by a second wreck off the Sandwich Islands, and now I am utterly ruined. No owner will ever trust me with a whaler again, for all will say I am an *unlucky* man."

Appendix C

THOMAS CHAPPLE'S ACCOUNT
OF THE LOSS OF THE *ESSEX*

As we have seen in chapter 3, Thomas Chapple dropped from sight after arriving in Sydney on board the *Surry* June 1, 1821. Nothing is known of him for certain after that date except what can be inferred from the following pamphlet about his experience. There we are told that he returned to London in June 1823, that date apparently being date of arrival. The pamphlet is *An Account of the Loss of the Essex, from Having Been Struck by a Whale in the South Seas; With Some Interesting Particulars of the Sufferings of Her Crew on a Desert Island, and in Their Boats at Sea. From the Narrative of one of the Survivors* (London: Religious Tract Society, n.d.). The pamphlet was in print by 1824 and may have been ready to appear by the end of 1823. The pamphlet was published as number 579 of The Society's (cheaper) "second series." *The Twenty-Fourth Annual Report of the Religious Tract Society,* 1823 (London: Printed for the Society, 1823), lists second series pamphlets up to 583, but next to 579 there is a blank space. The next year's report shows the pamphlet in print in both series. The reader will again be aware that there are minor discrepancies between what he finds here and the main *Essex* story. The only truly puzzling one is the complaint about lack of water, since the spring was known to the men and was constant enough to be still supplying water in the twentieth century. The sailing date of the *Essex* given in the opening sentence is in error, as is the April 5, 1820 date midway through the account.

LOSS OF THE ESSEX

The ship Essex, George Pollard master, sailed from Nantucket, in North America, November 19, 1819, on a whaling voyage to the South Seas.

The Essex was for some months very successful, and procured 750 barrels of oil, in a shorter period than usual.

On the 20th November, 1820, she was on the equator, about 118° west longitude, when several whales were in sight, to the great joy of the crew, who thought they should soon complete their cargo.

The boats were soon lowered in pursuit of the whales; George Pollard, the master, and Thomas Chappel, the second mate, each succeeded in striking one, and were actively engaged in securing them, when a black man, who was in the mate's boat, exclaimed, "Massa, where ship?" The mate immediately looked around, and saw the Essex lying on her beam ends, and a large whale near her; he instantly cut his line and made towards the ship; the captain also saw what had happened, and did the same. As soon as they got on board, to their great astonishment, they found she had been struck by a whale of the largest size, which rose close to the ship and then darted under her, and knocked off a great part of the false keel. The whale appeared again, and went about a quarter of a mile off, then suddenly returned and struck the ship with great force. The shock was most violent, the bows were stove in, and the vessel driven astern a considerable distance; she filled with water, and fell over on her beam ends. The crew exerted themselves to the utmost, the masts were cut away and the ship righted, but she was a mere wreck and entirely unmanageable; the quantity of oil on board alone kept her from foundering. They did not ascertain whether the whale had received any injury, but it remained in sight for some hours without again coming near them.

When the captain found that it was impossible to save the ship, he directed the three boats to be got ready, and they succeeded in saving a small quantity of water, and some biscuit, which was in a very wet state.

As the Essex appeared likely to float for some days longer, the captain remained by her, hoping that some vessel might come in sight. After three days, finding these hopes were not realized, as the wind blew fresh from the east, he determined on attempting to reach the Friendly Islands. They accordingly steered a south-westerly course, and proceeded rapidly for twenty-three days without seeing land. During this time, they had only half a biscuit and a pint of water each man per day. In that warm climate, the scanty supply of water was particulary distressing, but they could not venture on a large allowance, as on leaving the ship their whole stock of provisions was only about one hundred and fifty pounds of bread and fifty gallons of water; occasionally, however, some showers of rain fell, which gave them considerable relief.

On the twenty-fourth day after leaving the Essex, they saw an island, discovered a few years since, and called Elizabeth's Isle. It is about eight or nine miles round, low and flat, nearly covered with trees and underwood.

The shore was rocky, and the surf high; the crew were very weak, so that they did not land without considerable difficulty. Their first search was for water; and their joy was great at finding a spring of fresh water among the rocks; they were, however, disappointed on examining the island, as it was almost destitute of the necessaries of life, and no other fresh water could be discovered. These painful feelings were greatly increased the following day, for the sea had flowed over the rocks, and the spring of fresh water could not be seen, and did not again appear. In this extremity, they endeavoured to dig wells, but without success; their only resource was a small quantity of water which they found in some holes among the rocks.

For six days they continued to examine the island, when finding their situation desperate, the captain and most of the crew determined to put to sea again. The continent of South America was seventeen hundred miles distant, and in their destitute condition they could scarcely expect to reach land: their hopes were rather directed to the possibility of falling in with some vessel.

Thomas Chappel, the second mate, being in a very weak state, thought he might as well remain on the island as attempt such a voyage; William Wright and Seth Weeks also determined to remain with him.

On the 26th of December the boats left the island; this was indeed a trying moment to all; they separated with mutual prayers and good wishes, seventeen venturing to sea with almost certain death before them, while three remained on a rocky isle, destitute of water, and affording hardly any thing to support life. The prospects of these three poor men were gloomy: they again tried to dig a well, but without success, and all hope seemed at an end, when providentially they were relieved by a shower of rain. They were thus delivered from the immediate apprehension of perishing by thirst. Their next care was to procure food, and their difficulties herein were also very great; their principal resource was small birds, about the size of a blackbird, which they caught while at roost. Every night they climbed the trees in search of them, and obtained, by severe exertions, a scanty supply, hardly enough to support life. Some of the trees bore a small berry, which gave them a little relief, but these they found only in small quantities. Shell fish they searched for in vain; and although from the rocks they saw at times a number of sharks, and also other sorts of fish, they were unable to catch any, as they had no fishing tackle. Once they saw several turtles, and succeeded in taking five, but they were then without water, at those times they had little inclination to eat, and before one of them were quite finished the others were become unfit for food.

Their sufferings from want of water were the most severe, their only supply being from what remained in holes among the rocks after the showers which fell at intervals: and sometimes they were five or six days without any; on these occasions they were compelled to suck the blood of the birds they caught, which allayed their thirst in some degree; but they did so very unwillingly, as they found themselves much disordered thereby.

Among the rocks were several caves formed by nature, which afforded a shelter from the wind and rain. In one of these caves they found eight human skeletons, in all probability the remains of some poor mariners who had been shipwrecked on the isle, and perished for want of food and water. They were side by side, as if they had laid down, and died together! This sight deeply affected the mate and his companions; their case was similar, and they had every reason to expect ere long the same end; for many times they lay down at night, with their tongues swollen and their lips parched with thirst, scarcely hoping to see the morning sun; and it is impossible to form an idea of their feelings when the morning dawned, and they found their prayers had been heard and answered by a providential supply of rain.

In this state they continued till the 5th of April following, day after day hoping some vessel might touch at the island; but day after day, and week after week passed by, and they continued in that state of anxious expectation which always tends to cast down the mind and damp exertion, and which is so strongly expressed in the words of Scripture, "Hope deferred maketh the heart sick." The writer of this narrative says, "At this time I found religion not only useful, but absolutely necessary to enable me to bear up under these severe trials. If any man wishes for happiness in this world, or in the world to come, he can only find it by belief in God and trust in him; it is particularly important that seamen, whose troubles and dangers are so numerous, should bear this in mind. In this situation we prayed earnestly, morning, noon, and night, and found comfort and support from thus waiting upon the Lord."

This testimony of the benefits to be derived from religion is exceedingly valuable; hours of trial prove the vanity and uncertainty of all earthly enjoyments, and show the necessity of looking forward for another and a better world. The experience of believers of old taught them that they were but "strangers and pilgrims on the earth," and led them to earnest desires after another and a better country, that is an heavenly. See Heb. xi. Prayer is the means which God has appointed whereby we may draw near to him, asking for the blessings we need. He has promised to hear and to answer us in such a manner as shall be for our good, but let us always remember, that prayer does not consist in merely kneeling down, and uttering our desires with our lips, but prayer should be the earnest expression of the feeling of the heart, filled with a sense of its own misery and wretchedness, not only as to the things of this life, but still more deeply affected as to the concerns of our souls. We may be miserable in this world, and in the world to come also. We may be happy in this life, and miserable hereafter. The one does not depend upon the other, nor are they in any way connected with each other. The prayer of the poor publican, as related in the 18th of St. Luke, was, "God be merciful to me a sinner!" This will always be the first and principal desire of the soul, when awakened to a knowledge of its wretched and miserable state by nature and practice, and we would hope that such was the prayer of these poor men. Our Saviour himself has promised that he will hear and answer such prayers: he graciously declares, "Come unto me, all ye that labour and are heavy laden, and I will give you rest." He has also promised that he will give his Holy Spirit to those that ask him; and the soul that is led by the teaching of the Holy Spirit to draw near to the Saviour, will find support under all the troubles of this life. It will find that peace which the world cannot give.

To return to these poor men. On the morning of April 5, 1820, they were in the woods as usual, searching for food and water, as well as their weakness permitted, when their attention was aroused by a sound which they thought was distant thunder, but looking towards the sea they saw a ship in the offing, which had just fired a gun. Their joy at this sight may be more easily imagined than described; they immediately fell on their knees and thanked God for his goodness, in thus sending deliverance when least expected; then, hastening to the shore, they saw a boat coming towards them. As the boat could not approach the shore without great danger, the mate, being a good swimmer, and stronger than his companions, plunged into the sea, and narrowly escaped a watery grave, at the moment when deliverance was at hand; but the same Providence which had hitherto protected, now preserved him. His companions crawled out further on the rocks, and by the great exertions of the crew were taken into the boat, and soon found themselves on board the Surry, commanded by captain Raine. They were treated in the kindest manner by him and his whole crew, and their health and strength were speedily restored, so that they were able to assist in the duties of the ship.

When on board the Surry, they were told the deplorable and painful history of their captain and shipmates. After leaving the isle, the boats parted company; the captain's boat was sixty days at sea, when it was picked up by an American whaler; only himself and a boy were then alive. Their scanty stock of provisions was soon exhausted, and life had only been sustained by the dead bodies of their companions. The particulars of their sufferings are too painful to relate, but they were confirmed by proofs which could not be doubted. The ship reached Valparaiso, in a few days, when the particulars of the loss of the Essex, and of the men left on the island, were immediately communicated to the captain of an American frigate then in the port, who humanely endeavoured to procure a vessel to go to the island, as his own ship was not ready for sea. Captain Raine, of the Surry, engaged to do this, and sailed without loss of time: he had a quick passage; and, by the kind providence of God, the mate and his companions were preserved till thus unexpectedly relieved.

The sufferings of these men were great, and their preservation remarkable; such circumstances afford instruction to every one. If you are inclined to say, there is no probability of your being similarly situated, remember, that although not placed in a desert island, or in a small boat, destitute of the means of subsistence, yet all are placed in the midst of many and great dangers as to this life. But it is of infinitely more importance to remember, that there is a great and awful danger, namely, of eternal death, to which we are all alike exposed, if ignorant of the Saviour and his salvation. The subject speaks both to seamen and landmen; are you aware of its importance? Pray earnestly to God for the knowledge of his truth; these men prayed earnestly for deliverance from their sufferings; and can you be less earnest respecting your soul? Again, remember that God has promised to give his Holy Spirit to those that ask, and it is only by his teaching that we can be led to a knowledge of our danger, and of the value of that salvation which is so fully and freely offered unto us through Christ, who died for our sins, and rose again for our justification.

To return to our narrative. The mate and two survivors of his boat's crew were picked up by another ship, after sufferings similar to those of the captain; but the third boat was never heard of, and its crew are supposed to have perished for want, or to have found a watery grave.

The Surry proceeded to New South Wales, and the mate, Mr.

Chappel, returned to London in June, 1823, and furnished the details from which this account has been drawn up. He says, "Before I was cast away, I was like most seamen, I never thought much about religion; but no man has seen more of the goodness of the Lord than I have, or had more reason to believe in him. I trust I am enabled to do so." He also bears a strong testimony to the good resulting from the labours of the missionaries in the islands of the South Sea, and the great change effected in the natives; he says, "There are very many among the poor natives of those isles, who know more of religion, and show more of the effects of it in their conduct, than the greater part of our own countrymen."

We meet with many instances of unexpected dangers and remarkable preservations, but few are more worthy of notice than the one which has been related. May it lead the reader to a more earnest and constant attendance upon the means of Divine grace. Above all, remember, that it is not merely hearing of Divine truths, or bending the knees in prayer, that can save from the sentence of "Depart, ye cursed," which will be pronounced at the last day on all evil and wicked doers; nothing but feeling, deeply feeling our lost and ruined state by nature, the evil of sin, and the necessity of a change of heart, can lead us to look to the Saviour, and to trust in him for pardon and salvation.

Again, remember, that ALL, whether seamen or landmen, are passing rapidly along and hastening to eternity! ETERNITY! solemn, awful word! Fearful to those who are pursuing a course of sin and folly, but delightful to the believer in the Lord Jesus Christ; who has been brought out of nature's darkness into marvellous light, and from the power of sin and Satan, to rejoice in the God of salvation; having obtained pardon and sanctification by the blood of the cross, through the influence of the Holy Spirit. And though the believer's course through life may be across a stormy and tempestuous ocean, yet he proceeds with confidence, assured that he shall reach his desired port in safety, because Christ is his Pilot and Saviour.

Appendix D

MARCH 7, 1821, LETTER OF COMMODORE RIDGELY TO THE SECRETARY OF THE NAVY

This letter, written a week and a half after the just rescued Owen Chase was brought into port and a week and a half before Captain Pollard was brought in, re-creates authentically the context of the survivors' arrival in Valparaiso. It complements the account taken from Commodore Ridgely's Journal in chapter 3. This text of the letter is from the copy in U.S. Department of the Navy, Area File (Area 9), National Archives, Record Group 45, M-625, roll 228. Another copy is to be found in U.S. Department of the Navy, Letters Received by the Secretary of the Navy from Captains 1807–84, Letter no. 79 (March 7, 1821), National Archives, Record Group 45, M-125, roll 70. A third copy is in Commodore Ridgely's Letterbook, Naval Historical Foundation Manuscript Collection, Manuscript Division, Library of Congress, Washington, D.C.

U.S.S. Constellation
Valparaiso March 7th 1821

Sir,

By the Macedonian Capt. Downes who arrived here yesterday I have the honor to advise you of the arrival of this ship in the Pacific. By my letter to you of 14th Dec. Ulto. at Rio Janeiro I stated I would sail on the 17th but did not however until the 23rd of that month. I had a passage of forty five days boisterous unpleasant weather but without any accident whatever either to the ship or

Crew. Indeed I have much reason to be very thankful, for although my Crew have been two years on board not a single case of scurvey has appeared nor have I lost a man from sickness or casualty, but all in excellent health. As Capt. Downes has been so long in these seas I beg leave to refer you to him for information relative to the character of this government, as well as that of Peru. He has put in my possession his correspondence with the different authorities which will enable me the better to understand and judge of the most proper mode to pursue in case of a renewal of such flagrant acts against our flag as had been committed within the last two years.

Mr. Hill who goes home in the Macedonian & who has been acting as our consul in this place for the last three or four years, possesses as much useful information relative to this government, and to whom I beg leave to refer you to particularly, he is a respectable intelligent young man. The French Government have a ship of the line and a Frigate in the Pacific & have little or no commerce. The British Government have four ships of War and who with ourselves carry on all the Commerce in this sea. The force of Lord Cochran's fleet is one 60 gun ship, 3 Frigates with some sloops and smaller vessels, he indiscriminately captures all the American vessels he meets with on the coast of Peru takes from them their crews for his fleet & detains them so long either with his fleet or sends them in here for adjudication that when they are cleared their voyage is entirely destroyed, and they are ruined. I shall proceed to Coquimbo on the 7th for the purpose of liberating (if possible) two American ships detained there, they are the Chesapeak of Baltimore with a very valuable Cargo the Warrior of New York. Capt. Downes states to me they are in great distress, and require my immediate assistance. Why he left them in that state I am at a loss to account for, the time for which his men shipped having expired, only prevented my sending him back to their aid. I have taken in as much provisions, water &c as I can carry & shall continue cruising along the coast of Peru to assist & relieve such of my countrymen as I may meet with & who are in want. From Lord Cochran being on that coast & prohibiting all intercourse I fear I shall find many in want. Another frigate and sloop of war would be very useful in the Pacific there would then be no fear of a collision with either Chili or Peru, as such a force would awe them to do that justice to our Commerce that it is entitled to, and from all I can learn whenever they act justly it is from the dread of the consequences that might result if they acted otherwise and not from any disposition to do right. There is a very lucrative and enterprising commerce carried on from China to Chili & Peru by citizens of the U States, which deserves much protection, the whale fishery is not molested at all. Under this cover I send for your consideration the causes which have led to the arrest of Lieut. Randolph Cambreling of the Navy and Lieut. Hall of the Marine Corps and by which I hope you will see the necessity there was of sending them to the U States. This savage and inhuman practice of duelling has arrived to an allarming height in our Navy & beside the injurious to the service materially affects our national character abroad, there is only one way to put a stop to it. That is, that a law should be passed, making it the peremptory duty of all commanders when abroad on foreign service to take the Commission or Warrant from any officer who should fight a duel with a brother officer and dismiss him the Navy ——— Midshipman Murray being desirous to return to the U States, I have permitted him to exchange with Mids^n Gordon of the Macedonian, who prefers remaining out I have also granted permission to Mr Price who has been an acting Lieut. on board this ship, his anxiety to return home is such, that he would prefer resigning rather than remain out, he is a most excellent worthy young man and it would give me great satisfaction if he should receive a Commission ——— A few days since there were brought into this port the Mate & two men of the late ship Essex Capt Geo Pollard of Nantucket, which ship had foundered at sea the 20th Nov last from an attack by a large whale They are in a most distressed situation having been eighty nine days in an open boat and compelled to subsist on the body of one of the crew who died I have afforded them every relief and directed Capt Downes to carry them to the U States, the Capt with part of the Crew are supposed to be on the Island of Esther in latitude 27°9′ S, and 109°35′ West longitude. Three of the men were left on the Island of Ducies, in lat^d 24°40′ S. and 124°40′ W. Long^t. As the latter Island is not inhabited & the former is seldom or never touched at

their surviving and getting to their friends is hardly possible. I am
therefore making arrangements with the Master of an English Ship
at this place to touch at both places and take them off, for which, I
have promised him $500. This sum is but small when the object is
taken into consideration & I feel assured I will meet your approba-
tion. The owners of this ship are Paul Macey, Gideon Folger,
Aaron Folger, and John Smith all of Nantucket, those left on the
Island of Ducies were Wm Wright, Sethe Weeks & Thos. Chappel
Seamen, the two former Americans, the latter an Englishman.
Those that died in the boats were Isaac Cole & Richd Peters
Seaman, Matthew Joy 2nd Mate. The remaining part of the Crew
were with the Captain who separated from the Mate on the 12th
Jany in lat. 32°16´ ̄S and 112° West long^t in a squall ———

I have just heard that the Spanish Government have refused to
ratify the treaty, if war should grow out of it there would be little or
no use for a vessel of war in the Pacific, but I could be of infinite
service off the Philipine Islands & the China seas. There is an
extensive commerce between Mannilla and China ——— As I was
about closing this letter the Mate of an American Whale ship came
in here leaving his ship in the offing becalmed, with the following
information; that the ship is the Hero of Nantucket owned by
Joseph Levi & Simon Starbuck and commanded by Cap. Russel,
that she is out nineteen months taken 1,100 Bbls of Oil, that on the
20th Feby they came to anchor off St. Marys near Conception &
were employed striking whale that they were boarded from some
boats, from a place called Aurauco belonging to the Royalists, that
the Capt was persuaded to land and wait on the Governor, which
he did & was detained in prison with his boats crew of ten men,
that the boats returned armed fired into them, boarded & took
possession & after confining the officers and crew plundered her of
20 Bbl^s of Beef, 12 Bbl^s of flour 4 of Bread, that on the next day
they returned with part of the provisions got the ship underway and
carried her to a port or place called Tubal when they anchored &
took from her more provisions the Capt’ clothes ships papers &c.,
that on seeing a schooner standing in shore, which they supposed
was a patriot vessel, they cut her cables for the purpose of drifting
the ship on shore, and all the Spaniards took to the boats, that the

Mate & Crew took advantage of this, made sail & stood for this port, leaving the Cap.ᵗ and the following men prisoners at Aurauco: Jonathan Burges, Josh Hamblin, Hasiah Pognett, Moses Pognett, Ch.ˢ Perkins, Josh Pease, Frank Major, [   ] Cowett & H.ʸ Boston. The remainder of the Crew with the three Mates are on board the ship—a few days previous to this disaster they spoke the ship Two Brothers of Nantucket the Dauph of do. & the Dianner of New York, on board the latter, was Cap.ᵗ Pollard and a Boy of the late ship Essex & who separated from the Mate who had arrived here, when picked up he had been ninety four days in the boat & all the Crew had died but the boy & himself who subsisted on the flesh of the dead men. I sent out my boats towed her in to anchor, have examined her crew & log book & find all strictly true. Every exertion that I can make shall be done for them, release of the Capt & Crew confined at Aurauco. So long as this coast remains as it now is, one port under the Royalists & the other under the Patriots, another vessel of war is absolutely necessary, as one should always be in Chili while the other is on the coast of Peru, without which any commerce will materially suffer from depradations committed by both parties. A Brig or Schooner of 12 or 14 guns would be very servicable ———

On reflection I have thought it most prudent not to deliver to each of the arrested officers a Copy of the enclosed letter to you relative to their conduct which caused their arrest as they are permitted to go on shore when they please from the Macedonian and are constantly with Mr. Griswold to whom they would communicate the letter & who for obvious reasons should not know its contents. I have therefore enclosed them to Cap.ᵗ Downes to be handed them after getting to sea, or on his arrival in the U States. I enclose a Muster Roll of the Officers & Crew of this ship ———

To the Honb.ˡ
Secretary of the Navy

/ signed

I have the honor
to be Sir
Very Respectfully
Your Ob.ᵗ. Servant

Ch.ˢ G. Ridgely

Appendix E

THE "PADDACK LETTER" ON THE RESCUE OF CAPTAIN POLLARD AND CHARLES RAMSDELL

The following document is copied from a photocopy in the possession of Edouard Stackpole. The original has not been traced. Mr. Stackpole described it as a letter from Capt. Aaron Paddack of the *Diana* written after his gam with the *Dauphin* the day that the *Dauphin* rescued Captain Pollard and Charles Ramsdell. One page is missing on the photocopy. Captain Paddack's account is noteworthy for three reasons: first, it was written the day of the Pollard-Ramsdell rescue and indicates how much of the story—one would assume with the help of notes—Captain Pollard was able to recount immediately after his rescue; second, it is in summary version the story that Captain Paddack passed on to Capt. Zephaniah Wood, who brought the story back to New Bedford; third, it was evidently used by whoever put the text of Owen's *Narrative* on paper. The text of the Paddack document is given below with passages from Owen's *Narrative* that invite comparison inserted in italics.

---

23 February 1821

Off St. Maria

Pacific Ocean

At 5 PM spoke & boarded the Ship Dauphin Capt. Zimri Coffin; on board of this ship I heard the most distressing narrative, that ever came to my knowledge.

Capt. Coffin had that morning taken up a whale boat in which was Capt. George Pollard Jun. & Charles Ramsdell, who are believed to be the only survivors of the crew of Ship Essex* of Nantucket. That ship on the 20th November was in Latitude 40 miles South & Long^d 120 Degrees West of Greenwich, & while two boats were at a distance from the vessell at work on Whales, the ship was attacked in a most deliberate manner by a large spermacetia Whale which made two such violent onsets with his head that the whole bow was stoven & the ship sunk to the waters edge amediately. With great exertions and by scuttling the deck in many places they were enabled to get out 600 [   ] bread & a few Tooles, Nails & other small articles together with as much water as could be taken in the boats

> [*from these casks we obtained six hundred pounds of hard bread. Other parts of the deck were then scuttled, and we got without difficulty as much fresh water as we dared to take in the boats.* (P 30)]

& after laying by the wreck in their three Boats two days, without being able to procure anything more they left her & proceeded Southward. Four days after leaving the ship two of the boats ware near failing by reason of their being heavyly loaded, they ware however strengthened by the Nails ye that had been saved & they continued to make what progress they could to the Southward. On the 28th the Captn^s Boat was attacked in the night by an unknown fish which stove two streaks & split the stern, but was at last beat off by the sprit pole—

> [*he replied, "I have been attacked by an unknown fish, and he has stove my boat." . . . The sprit-pole . . . with which, after repeated attempts to destroy the boat, they succeeded in beating him off.* (Pp 41–42)]

On the 20th December they accidentally fell in with Ducies Island, in Lat^d 24°30′ & Long 124°30′

* with the exception of those on the island (as laid down

[End of page one. Page two:]

on this Island the whole ship's company landed, hauled the boats onto the beach & renailed them, & remained six days. The water they obtained at this Island was very brackish & was found to spring up through a rock at near low water mark. A few fowl & Fish was the only sustinance that could be got & not sufficient to subsist a fourth part of their number. Three of their number chose to remain on the Island & the others (seventeen) again took to the Boats with the hope of being able to reach Easter Island. but by adverse winds & being too much exhausted to make exertions they were drove far south of it.

January 10th 1821 Mathew P. Joy (second officer) Died through debility & costivness & *his corps* was commited to the Ocean.

[*Matthew P. Joy, the second mate, had suffered from debility, and the privations we had experienced. . . . we . . . consigned him in a solemn manner to the ocean.* (P 63)]

The 12th being in Latitude 31°0′ & Longitude about 117°00 the first Officers Boat was separated from the others in the night—the 14th the provisions of the second officers Boat was intirely expended,

[*On the fourteenth, the whole stock of provisions belonging to the second mate's boat was entirely exhausted.* (P 74)]

The 20th one of their crew (a black man) died & became food for the remainder.

[*on the twenty-fifth, the black man, Lawson Thomas, died, and was eaten by his surviving companions.* (P 74, cf. n. 15 to chap. 2.)]

21st the provisions being all gone in the Capt^s Boat, they were glad to partake of the wretched fare with the other crew—the 23^d another (collored) man died in the 3^d boat & was disposed of in the same way.—27th another died in the same boat, & the 28th one died (also black) in the Capt^s Boat and in the night following the 3^d Boat was separated from the other then in Lat 35°00′ and Long^d about 100°00 the 6th of February having intirely consumed the last morsel of sustenance, the Capt & the three others that remained with him ware reduced to the deplorable necessity of casting Lots to see who should be sacraficed to prolong the existance of the others. The lot fell to Owen Coffin, who with composure & resignation submited to his fate,

> [*and on the twenty-third, another coloured man, Charles Shorter, died out of the same boat, and his body was shared for food between the crews of both boats. On the twenty-seventh, another, Isaac Shepherd, (a black man,) died in the third boat; and on the twenty-eighth, another black, named Samuel Reed, died out of the captain's boat. The bodies of these men constituted their only food while it lasted; and on the twenty-ninth, owing to the darkness of the night and want of sufficient power to manage their boats, those of the captain and second mate separated in latitude 35° S. longitude 100° W. On the 1st of February, having consumed the last morsel, the captain and the three other men that remained with him, were reduced to the necessity of casting lots. It fell upon Owen Coffin to die, who with great fortitude and resignation submitted to his fate. (Pp 74–75)]*

then in Lat. 39°00′ & about the Long^d of 90°00′ the 11th Barzillai Ray died being intirely exhausted. by his death the Capt & Ramsdell ware kept alive 'till taken up as before stated

[End of page two. Page three:]

The Essexs Crew at the time of the shipwreck
George Pollard Jun. Master
Owen Chase 1st Officer
Mathew P. Joy 2^d off
Obed Hendricks
Thos Chaplin   3^d & 4th off
Benjn Lawrence
Charles Ramesdell
Barzillia Ray
Owen Coffin
Isaac Cole
Thomas Nickerson
Joseph West
Wm Wright
Seth Wicks & Six Blacks
    In all 20

[Written in sideways:]

At leaving Ducies Island the Crew was disposed of as follows

With the Master	With the 1ˢᵗ Officer	With the 2ᵈ Officer
Owen Coffin	Benj. Lawrence	O Hendricks
Barzillia Ray	Isaac Cole	Jo West
Charles Ramesdell	Thoˢ Nickerson	Wm Bon & Three
& one Black—5	& Richᵈ Peterson	Other
	(Black)—5	Blacks. 7

Left on the Island. Thoˢ Chaplin. Wᵐ Wright & Seth Wicks

[Written in lower left hand corner:]
* who it is needless to and [sic] has
administered in his power to their wants.
NB Capt Pollard, though very low when
   first taken up has amediately
   revived I regret to say that
   young Ramesdell has appeared
   to fail since taken up.

[End of page three.]

REPORT OF THE *ESSEX* SHIPWRECK AND RESCUE IN THE *SYDNEY GAZETTE,* JUNE 9, 1821

This is the first published account of the *Essex* disaster (if one excepts the negligible little paragraph on the *Essex* in the *Gazeta ministerial de Chile,* April 28, 1821) and anticipates by one week the *New Bedford Mercury*'s story on the *Essex.* As has been observed in chapter 5, it destroys any assumption that proximity to events contributes to accuracy of reporting; replete with errors, it has become the tainted source of a number of accounts of the *Essex* in Australia and New Zealand. It is also, however, the source of information that has come to be regarded as accurate, for example, the twenty-first crew member's departure from the *Essex* in Tecamus. And it captures some of the excitement of the fresh news as only a "media job" could.

Just as Captain Raine was on the eve of leaving Valpariso for this part of the world once more, he was informed of a most marvellous affair relating to an American whaler, that had been attacked by a whale at sea in so violent and dreadful a manner as to occasion the vessel to founder, and most of the crew eventually to perish; something of whose disastrous history we have been favored with, and shall present the same to our Readers. Captain Raine received information that there were three men on Ducies Island, who had preferred remaining there rather than venture across the ocean in a boat, to which the crew had been compelled to fly from the ship.

The boat, to which these three men belonged, had been picked up
by an American whaler about 60 days after the melancholy occurrence. Another boat, in which was the Captain and the remainder
of the crew, soon parted company, and were also fell in with by
another whaler of America, which vessel was the bearer of the
intelligence to Valparaiso; and the horrible account given by the
two survivors in this boat was truly deplorable and shuddering.
They had been 90 days at sea before they were fallen in with, and
had experienced the most dreadful of all human vicissitudes; from
the extremity of hunger they had been reduced to the painful
necessity of killing and devouring each other, in order to sustain a
wretched life, that was hourly expected to be terminated.—Eight
times had lots been drawn, and eight human beings had been
sacrificed to afford sustenance to those that remained; and, on the
day the ship encountered them, the Captain and the boy had also
drawn lots, and it had been thus determined that the poor boy
should die! But, providentially, a ship hove in sight and took them
in, and they were restored to existence. Doleful in the extreme as is
it to hear such things, and painful as it is to relate them, it is
nevertheless asserted as a fact by Capt. Raine that the fingers, and
other fragments of their deceased companions, were in the pockets
of the Capt. and boy when taken on board the whaler. The Commander of the Surry becoming opportunely acquainted with those
painful and distressing circumstances, humanely detemined on calling at Ducies Island, and be instrumental in restoring three
unfortunate fellow-creatures to Society, and very possibly rescue
them from a miserable end; particularly as this island was no great
distance out of his track from Valparaiso to New Holland. On
Thursday, the 5th of April, Captain Raine considering himself
within a very short distance of Ducies Island, which is laid down in
Norie's Epitome to be in lat. 24°40′ S. and long. 124°37, W. kept
a good look-out. At about two PM land was perceived, which turned
out to be an island in lat. 24°26′. As the vessel neared the land a gun
was discharged, and shortly after the three poor men were seen to
issue forth from the woods. The boats were presently lowered, Captain Raine taking one himself. On approaching the shore it was
found not only dangerous but utterly impracticable to land, of which

circumstance they were informed, in weak and tremulous voices, by the almost starved and nearly worn-out creatures themselves, who could scarcely, from the miserable plight they were in, articulate a syllable.—One poor fellow summoned up courage to plunge into the waves, and with great difficulty reached the boat; he said one of the others only could swim. After warily backing in the boat as near the rocks as possible, amidst a heavy surf, they proceeded in getting on board, much bruised and lacerated by repeated falls; which object was no sooner effected than each devoutly expressed his gratitude to that benign Being, who had so wonderfully preserved them from sharing in the destruction to which their unhappy shipmates had fallen victims. The whole island appears to be a rock of volcanic matter, and is replete with caves and caverns of considerable extent; in one of which Captain Raine was informed by these men they had discovered the skeletons of eight bodies, on the northwest side of the island; and they further reported, that in several parts there were the signs of people having been there before, such as trees having been cut, and places where fires had been made. They stated that when they first heard the report of the gun, they had just returned from plucking berries, and some of the palm tree, and were lamenting their apparently unrelenting destiny, when the reverberating sounds aroused their attention, which were thought, for the moment, to be distant thunder; but, hope involuntarily arising in the breast of one of them, he cast a wistful eye towards the sea, and joyously beheld a ship, which was destined to release them from a miserable death. Captain Raine conveyed them on board immediately, and it would be superfluous to dilate on benevolence and humanity which is so universally known in New South Wales, suffice it to say, that every precaution and tenderness were observed in regard to their food; and, in a few days, they soon recovered the accustomed cheerfulness of seamen, and were shortly enabled to assist the sailors that had exerted themselves in snatching 3 human beings and fellow mariners from an otherwise inevitable destruction. These men are now with Capt. Raine, and declare their names to be, Thomas Chappel, William Wright, and Seth Weeks; and the following is the account they gave of the distressing circumstance, which we feel no hesitation in declaring, may be numbered with one of those events that are

without a parallel in the history of man. They sailed from Nantucket
in the American ship Essex, of 260 tons, George Pollard master, on
the 19th of August, 1819, on a whaling voyage; they arrived in the
South Seas, where they were pretty fortunate, having succeeded in
procuring 750 barrels of oil, and were in the latitude of 47″ S, and
longitude 118 W. when the accident happened, which was on the
13th of November, 1820. On that day they were among many
whales, and the three boats were lowered down; the mate's boat got
stove, and had returned to the ship to be repaired. Shortly after, a
whale, of the largest class, struck the ship, and knocked part of the
false keel off, just abreast of the main channels. The animal then
remained for some time along-side, endeavoring to clasp the ship
with her jaws, but could not accomplish it; she then turned, went
round the stern, and came up on the other side, and went away a-
head about a quarter of a mile, and then suddenly turning, came at
the ship, with tremendous velocity, head on. The vessel was going at
the rate of 5 knots, but such was the force when she struck the ship,
which was under the cat-head, that the vessel had stern-way, at the
rate of 3 or 4 knots; the consequence was, that the sea rushed into the
cabin windows, every man on deck was knocked down, and worse
than all, the bows were stove completely in, and, in a very few
minutes, the vessel filled, and went on her beam ends. At this
unhappy juncture, the Captain and second mate were fast to a whale
each; but, on beholding the awful catastrophe that had taken place,
immediately cut from the fish, and made for the ship. By cutting
away the masts the vessel righted; the upper deck was then scuttled;
and some water and bread were procured for the two boats, in which
they were compelled to remain, as all thoughts of saving the ship
were given up. In expectation of falling in with some vessel, they
remained three days by the wreck, making sails, &c. but were compelled at length to abandon it, and stood away to the southward, in
hopes of getting the variable winds, experiencing fine weather; but
the wind being constantly from the E. and E.S.E. they made much
lee-way, and were prevented from keeping to the southward, in consequence of which, on the 20th of December, they made the island
from which Captain Raine took them, and which was taken for
Ducies Island; at which place the boat remained one week, but the

island affording hardly any nourishment, in fact exhibiting nothing but sterility, they resolved on venturing for the coast, leaving behind them the three men now on board the Surry, with whose sufferings, and that of their shipmates, we are by this opportunity favored with an account; and, certainly, they are poignant in the extreme. Captain Raine has put into our hands the letter that was left by Captain Pollard on this island, which was enclosed in a tin box, of which the following is a copy:—

"Account of the loss of the ship Essex, of Nantucket in North America, Ducies Island, December 20, 1820, commanded by George Pollard, jun. which shipwreck happened on the 20th day of November, 1820 on the equator, in long. 120 W. done by a large whale striking her in the bow, which caused her to fill with water in about 10 minutes. We got what provisions and water the boats would carry, and left her on the 22d of November, and arrived here this day with all hands, except one black man, who left the ship in Ticamus. We intend to leave to-morrow, which will be the 26th of December, 1820, for the continent. I shall leave with this a letter for my wife, and whoever finds, and will have the goodness to forward it will oblige an unfortunate man, and receive his sincere wishes.

"GEORGE POLLARD, jun."

On the route of the Surry from Valparaiso hither, Captain Raine made Easter Island. The natives swam off to the vessel, which was going five knots, when Captain Raine hove too, and they were soon along-side. Ropes were thrown overboard, which they immediately seized, and with amazing strength and astonishing agility, ascended the vessel; six were taken on deck, as a sufficient specimen of the inhabitants of the island; and the moment they found themselves on board, they actually become frantic with joy, running about jumping, dancing, singing, & beholding every thing at a single glance—curiosity, in fact, appeared to be at its zenith. They manifested not the least disposition to fear; but, on the contrary, declared themselves, by their actions and general appearance, to be an innocent, athletic, and hospitable people. Various presents, mostly consisting of apparel, were distributed among them; which seemed to afford them sincere pleasure. Potatoes and bananas appeared to comprise the principal articles of food on the island. Some seeds of the grape, some wheat, onions, and peach-stones were given them, with signs how they were to be applied, which they seem perfectly to understand. Captain Raine entertained an idea of bringing one of them with him, who seemed anxious to forsake his country and friends; but after mature deliberation, which does credit to our Commander's humanity, he declined following the impulse of the moment, from the circumstance of the poor fellow becoming, in a very short time, dejected at his forlorn condition, and instead of retaining that happiness which he now appeared to possess, he would, in all probability, have been extremely wretched, and that, perhaps, too soon. The native that was selected on this occasion, was not well satisfied with the determination of Captain Raine; on the contrary, he seemed to feel the denial of his wishes rather acutely. A bottle, with the names of the vessel and commander, was secured round one of their necks, and they returned on shore with the same rapidity and ease that they had gained the vessel—the sea appearing to be subservient to their wonderful strength. The island itself has a much more inviting appearance than when Cook visited it, who declares it to be far from being gifted with any external appearance of fruitfulness; but it now wears the cheering aspect of industry, the land seemingly well cultivated, and the fields are laid out with surprising regularity, and the allotments of ground with peculiar neatness. The houses are of singular appearance, and accord with our justly celebrated navigator's description. Only two canoes presented themselves, and they were extremely small. This island is situate in lat. 27°56′ S. and long. 109°40′ W. the variation about 4° East.

Appendix G

TABLE OF ISLANDS FROM BOWDITCH'S *NAVIGATOR*

Some impression of the Pacific as seen by the *Essex* survivors can be had by consulting the table of latitudes and longitudes in the navigational aid they relied on: Nathaniel Bowditch, *The New American Practical Navigator . . .* (New York: E. M. Blount & Samuel A. Burtus; J. Seymour, Printer, 1817). It is not known which edition of the *Navigator* the survivors had, but the table of islands had hardly been revised for more than fifteen years. Henderson Island, which they regarded as Ducie Island when they landed there, is at 24°20′ S/128°18′ W.

From Table 46, "Latitudes and Longitudes" (p. 249; tables, which make up second half of book, have their own pagination): "This Table contains the LATITUDES and LONGITUDES of the most remarkable harbours, islands, shoals, capes, &c. in the WORLD, founded on the latest and most accurate Astronomical observations, surveys and charts."

Pp. 275–76: "Friendly and other Islands in the Pacific Ocean."

Wallis's Island	13°22′	S/176°16′ W
Proby's Island	15 53	175 51
Pylstart's Island	22 22	175 41
Gardner's Island	17 57	175 17
Hoonga-hapee	20 36	175 17
Toofoa	19 46	175 6
Tongatobou, Van Diemen's Road	21 6	175 5
Bickerton's Island	18 48	174 48

Annamoka	20	14	174	50
Eoa (E.P.)	21	24	174	45
Bouhee	19	34	174	29
Haanho	19	41	174	15
Howe's Island	18	32	173	53
Pola (W.P.)	13	32	172	35
Duke of York's Island	8	33	172	4
Calinasse (N.P.)	13	45	171	51
Ilot Plat	13	51	171	48
Duke of Clarence's I.	9	9	171	31
Oyolava (E.P.)	14	3	171	7
Otutuelah	14	30	170	41
Muouna (E.P.)	14	17	170	3
Savage Island	19	2	169	30
Fanfone (E.P.)	14	5	169	18
Leone (S.P.)	14	8	169	16
Opoun (E.P.)	14	9	169	2
Palmerston's Island	18	0	162	57
Whytutakee	18	52	159	41
Hervey's Island	19	17	158	48
Wateeoo Island	20	1	158	15
Mangeea Island	21	57	158	7
Howe's Island	16	46	154	6
Balabola Island	16	32	151	52
Ulietea	16	45	151	31
Ohameneno Harbour	16	45	151	35
Eimeo (Taloo Harbour)	17	30	150	0
Toobouai	23	25	149	23
Huahhine (Owharre Bay)	16	43	151	8
Maurura	16	26	152	33
Otaheite (Oaitipeha Bay)	17	46	149	14
—— Venus Point	17	29	149	36
Osnaburgh or Maitea I.	17	52	148	6
Palliser's Island	15	38	146	30
Adventure Island	17	5	144	18
Furneaux Island	17	11	143	7
Resolution Island	17	23	141	45
Taoukae Island	14	30	145	9
Ohitahoo (Resolution B.)	9	55	139	9
Ohevahoa Island	9	41	139	2

Onateayo Island	9 58	138 51
Magdalena Island	10 25	138 49
Hood's Island	9 26	138 52
Ingraham Island (N. pt.)	8 3	140 48
——— (S. pt.)	9 24	
Carysfort Island	20 49	138 33
Lord Hood's Island	21 31	135 32
Ducie's Island	24 40	124 40
Easter I. (Cook's Bay)	27 9	109 35
Oparo Island	27 36	144 11
Juan Fernandez (S.W.P.)	33 45	79 6
——— (E.P.)	33 41	78 53
Massa Fuero (middle)	33 45	80 38
St. Felix Islands (N.P.)	26 20	79 47
——— (W. point)	26 17	80 4
Gray's Island	26 22	92 30
Gallapagos Islands		
Chatham I. (N.E. part)	0 45	89 9
——— Stephen's Bay	0 53	89 37
Charles I. (S.P.)	1 30	90 33
James' I. Harbour	0 12	90 41
Albermarle I. Christ. P.	0 50	91 25
Cape Berkley	0° 2′ N/	91°31′ W
Abington I. C. Ibetson	0 29	90 43
Redondo Rock	0 15	91 34
Wenman's Island	1 23	91 44
Culpepper's Island	1 40	92 0
Gallego	1 40	104 5
Christmas Island	1 58	157 32
Palmyra Island	5 49	162 28
St. Peter's Island	11 0	178 50
Owyhee (N. point)	20 17	155 58
——— (E. point)	19 34	154 54
——— (S. point)	18 54	155 45
Mowee (E. point)	20 50	155 56
——— (S. point)	20 34	156 12
——— (W. point)	20 54	156 36
Marokinee	20 39	156 27
Tahoorowa	20 35	156 33
Ranai (S. point)	20 46	156 52

Morotoi (W. point)	21	10	157 14
Woahoo	21	43	157 58
Atooi (Wymoa Bay)	21	57	159 40
Oheeheow	21	50	160 15
Oreehua	22	2	160 8
Tahoora	21	40	160 24
Necker Island	23	34	164 32
French Frigate's Shoal	23	45	165 50

Appendix H

CHASE GENEALOGY

The gaps, conflicts, and obvious errors that beset most genealogical records are not wanting in the records that trace the Chase family's descent. Nonetheless, a fairly clear picture of that descent can be drawn from them, and the questionable or missing dates in them seldom prove crucial.

Of the two genealogical charts that follow the first indicates Owen Chase's descent from William Chase, husband of Mary, who came from England with Governor Winthrop in 1630, settled first at Roxbury, then in 1638 in Yarmouth, and died in 1659. The chart is simplified and omits marriages and children not affecting Owen's descent. The second chart shows Owen's marriages and children.

The Chase Family of Yarmouth (Yarmouthport, Mass.: C. W. Swift, 1913) gives the following information on Owen Chase's ancestors: Isaac Chase m. Mary Berry May 23, 1706; m. Charity O'Kelley Aug. 3, 1727. Richard Chase (Mar. 3, 1714/15—Jan. 14, 1794) m. Thankful [Berry] Chase Jan. 21, 1734/35. Archelus Chase (b. May 17, 1740) m. Desire Chase 1764. Desire m. Bachelor (Batchelder) Swain July 30, 1772. George Whitefield Chase, *Genealogy of a Portion of the Descendants of William Chase Who Came to America in 1630, and Died in Yarmouth, Massachusetts, May, 1659* (Washington, D.C., 1886), agrees with these dates, except for that of the marriage of Isaac Chase and Charity O'Kelley (see above, Chap. 1, n. 8). Robert and Ruth Sherman, *Vital Records of Yarmouth, Massachusetts, to the Year 1850* (Providence [?]: Society of Mayflower Descendants, n.d.), give Desire's birth date as March 6, 1741/42.

The following information on the three generations beginning

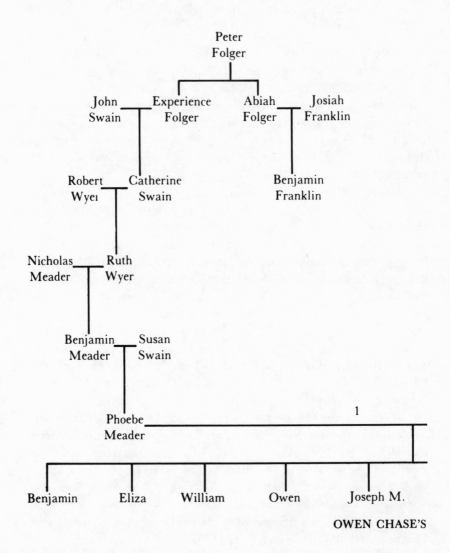

Peter
Folger

John   Experience   Abiah   Josiah
Swain   Folger   Folger   Franklin

Robert   Catherine   Benjamin
Wyer   Swain   Franklin

Nicholas   Ruth
Meader   Wyer

Benjamin   Susan
Meader   Swain

Phoebe _____ 1
Meader

Benjamin   Eliza   William   Owen   Joseph M.

OWEN CHASE'S

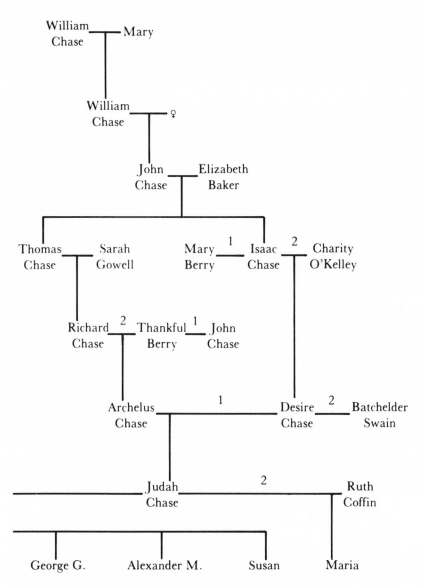

DESCENT FROM WILLIAM CHASE.

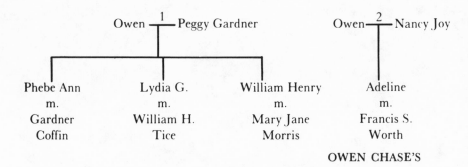

	1			2	
Owen —— Peggy Gardner			Owen —— Nancy Joy		

Phebe Ann	Lydia G.	William Henry	Adeline
m.	m.	m.	m.
Gardner	William H.	Mary Jane	Francis S.
Coffin	Tice	Morris	Worth

OWEN CHASE'S

with Owen Chase's father is from the Nantucket genealogical sources described above in n. 10 to chap. 1 and from the Nantucket Death Records, vol. for 1850–89, in the Nantucket town clerk's office. In conflicts the dates followed are those given in the *Vital Records of Nantucket* unless marked by a superscript [f], in which case they are from the Folger Records in the Peter Foulger Museum, or by a superscript [c], which indicates that they are from the Death Records in the town clerk's office, or by a superscript [b] indicating that they are from the Barney Records. Conflicting dates in the *Vital Records of Nantucket* that cannot be tested by other evidence are given together.

Judah Chase (Jan. 23, 1764–July 23, 1846) m. Phoebe Meader Jan. 31, 1787; m. Ruth Beard Coffin Aug. 25, 1808.
Phoebe Meader Chase (d. Apr. 18, 1806 [Apr. 18, 1808; May 7, 1808]).
Ruth Beard Coffin Chase (b. Apr. 17, 1763 [Apr. 16, 1768; Apr. 17, 1768[f]]).
Benjamin Chase (d. Mar. 10, 1800 [1809])
Eliza Chase Cathcart (b. Aug. 31, 1798 [1791[b]]) m. int. Ariel Cathcart June 7, 1817.
William Chase (b. Aug. 6, 1791 [1794[b]]) m. Lydia Gardner June 25, 1817.
Owen Chase (Oct. 7, 1796–Mar. 7, 1869) m. Peggy Gardner Apr. 28, 1819; m. Nancy Slade Joy June 15, 1825; m. Eunice Chadwick Apr. 5, 1836; m. Susan Coffin Gwinn Sept. 13, 1840. See above chap. 1 n. 10.
Joseph M. Chase (June 15, 1800–June 16, 1855[f]) m. Winnifred Bocot Sept. 2, 1824.

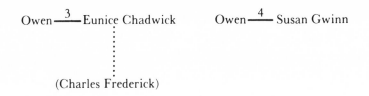

Owen —3— Eunice Chadwick   Owen —4— Susan Gwinn

⋮

(Charles Frederick)

MARRIAGES AND CHILDREN

George G. Chase (b. Sept. 18 [16^r], 1802) m. Rebecca Brown Mar. 19, 1826.

Alexander M. Chase (b. Sept. 2, 1804 [1805^b]) m. Emeline Kilborn June 26, 1831.

Susan Chase Gorham (b. Oct. 10, 1806 [1805]) m. Edward Gorham Jan. 29, 1823.

Maria Chase Fisher (b. Mar. 30, 1812) m. Henry B. Fisher Jan. 19, 1832.

Peggy Gardner Chase (1798–Sept. 26, 1824).

Nancy Slade Joy Chase (Dec. 30, 1798–Aug. 11, 1833).

Eunice Chadwick (Aug. 28, 1808–Apr. 20, 1888^c).

Susan Coffin Gwinn Chase (Aug. 25, 1807^r–Oct. 31, 1881^r).

Phebe Ann Chase Coffin (b. Apr. 16, 1820) m. Gardner Coffin Nov. 28, 1837.

Lydia G. Chase Tice (b. June 1822) m. int. William H. Tice Mar. 15, 1840.

William Henry Chase (b. Sept. 14, 1824) m. Mary Jane Morris May 23, 1847.

Adeline Chase Worth (b. July 1833).

Charles Frederick Chase (b. Jan. 17, 1838).

NOTES

PREFACE

1. See Appendix A. Melville consistently spelled the name Chace, as did some branches of the Chase family, but not Owen's.

2. The *Essex* is the first ship whose loss can unquestionably be attributed to an attack by a whale. About some earlier shipwrecks—most notably that of the *Union* in 1807—the evidence is insufficient to determine whether the ships ran into whales or the whales attacked the ships. See Deborah C. Andrews, "Attacks of Whales on Ships: A Checklist," [Melville Society] *Extracts,* May 1974, pp. 3–17.

CHAPTER ONE

1. From chap. 14, "Nantucket," of *Moby-Dick*, written before Melville had visited Nantucket. *Moby-Dick*, ed. Harrison Hayford and Hershel Parker (New York: W. W. Norton, 1967), p. 62.

2. The sources used here for the history of whaling are Alexander Starbuck, *History of the American Whale Fishery from Its Earliest Inception to the Year 1876* (New York: Argosy-Antiquarian, 1964); Obed Macy, *The History of Nantucket* (New York: Research Reprints, 1970); Alexander Starbuck, *The History of Nantucket, County, Island and Town* (Boston, C. E. Goodspeed & Co., 1924).

3. Reprinted in Starbuck, *Whale Fishery*, 1:39.

4. *Vital Records of Nantucket to the Year 1850: Published by the New England Historical Genealogical Society at the Robert Henry Eddy Memorial Rooms at the Charge of the Eddy Town Record Fund* (Boston, 1928), 1:204, 2:527.

5. Recollections of James Chase recounted to his daughter-in-law, Irene Chase.

6. Scrapbook, "Nantucket Heroes of the Sea," kept by Will Gardner and assembled by the Nantucket Historical Association, 1955; in Peter Foulger Museum. No pagination; quote is from section on Walter Nelson Chase, Owen's grandson.

7. The Yarmouth Chase genealogies are taken from *The Chase Family of Yarmouth* (Yarmouthport, Mass.: C. W. Swift, 1913) and George Whitefield

Chase, *Genealogy of a Portion of the Descendants of William Chase, Who Came to America in 1630, and Died in Yarmouth, Massachusetts, May, 1659* (Washington, D.C., 1886).

8. Here appears a remarkable discrepancy between *The Chase Family of Yarmouth* and George Whitefield Chase: The latter gives June 28, 1707, as the marriage date of Isaac Chase and Charity O'Kelley, a date that is unlikely, to say the least, if Desire's birth date—on which the two volumes agree—is correct: she was probably not born thirty-four years after her parents were married.

9. He is described as "yeoman" or "husbandman" in a variety of deeds: *County of Nantucket Unregistered Deeds*, liber 12, p. 294; liber 26, p. 5, etc. In the Death Records of the Nantucket town clerk's office he is described as a yeoman (vol. for 1843–49, p. 168).

10. There is unusual confusion over Owen Chase's birth date, part of it arising from the classic error of transposing the numbers indicating day and month, and part arising from conflicting reports of the year. The Folger Records and one of the entries in the *Vital Records of Nantucket* give July 10, 1796, as the date (the 1840 Nantucket census gives merely July 1796). The 1850 Nantucket census and another entry in the *Vital Records of Nantucket* give October 7, 1797 (the 1855 census merely gives the year 1797). The 1821 crew list of the *Florida* gives Owen's age as twenty-four, indicating a 1797 birth date. Owen himself has resolved the October 7 vs. July 10 conflict by noting in the 1836–40 log of the *Charles Carroll* under October 7, 1836, that that day was his birthday. The date that has secured the most support as Owen's birth date is October 7, 1796; it is the date indicated by the earliest record of Owen's age, Obed Macy's 1810 census records, and the last record of his age, his obituary in the *Inquirer and Mirror*, March 13, 1869. It is also the date indicated by the 1830 and 1865 Nantucket census. The census records cited are found both in the Nantucket town clerk's office and in the Peter Foulger Museum, except for Obed Macy's 1810 records and the 1855 census, which are in the Peter Foulger only. See Appendix H for some conflicts in birth dates of Owen's brothers and sisters.

11. Grace Brown Gardner, Scrapbook #39, "Nantucket Schools, General," in Peter Foulger Museum.

12. In the Peter Foulger Museum.

13. Baptist Church Records for 1839 ff., the only volume of these records that falls within Owen Chase's life; the Record Book of the Methodist Episcopal Church for 1830 ff.; and assorted records of the Congregational Church and the North and South Quaker Meetings are in the Peter Foulger Museum.

14. Recollections of Charlotte Simkin Lewis.

15. About Joseph Chase's first going to sea: "My father shipped (as they used to say) at the age of 15 years as Boatswain and was steadily promoted untill at the age of 24 when he and Mother were married he was first Mate of a large ship." Letter of Joseph Chase's daughter, Winifred Chase Smith, Aurora, N.Y., Dec. 31, 1917;

in possession of Mrs. Isabell Burnett. The crew lists of the *Winslow*, giving the ages of the young seamen, are in the National Archives, Record Group 36.

16. Wharf Book of the *Essex*, Whaling Museum, Nantucket. Starbuck, *Whale Fishery*, 1:222–23, differs slightly on return date of the ship and oil totals.

17. Bureau of Customs, Newburyport, Mass., Certificates of Registry, 1789–1801. Register #64 issued at Newburyport Oct. 11, 1799. National Archives, Record Group 36.

18. Permanent registers were issued when ships were registered in their home ports. Temporary registers were issued by ports other than home ports—in this case by Newburyport, for the new ownership of the *Essex* indicated that it was now a Nantucket ship. This temporary register is cited in *Ship Registers of the District of Newburyport, Massachusetts, 1789–1870, Compiled from the Newburyport Customs House Records, Now on Deposit at the Essex Institute,* with an introduction by Stephen Willard Phillips (Salem, Mass.: Essex Institute, 1937), p. 67.

19. Register #18 issued at Nantucket June 18, 1815. Document not located; information as cited in Register #24 (1815), which replaced it.

20. National Archives, Record Group 41, Bureau of Marine Inspection and Navigation Register #24 issued at Nantucket, June 21, 1815. New registers were issued when a ship changed owners, specifications, name, type of trade, or district.

21. Ibid., Register #21 issued at Nantucket, Aug. 10, 1819. Document partly deteriorated; some words lost.

22. In *History of Shipbuilding on North River . . .* (Boston: Coburn Bros., 1889), p. 49, L. Vernon Briggs says that Pollard "was an officer on Fulton's steamer in 1807." Briggs gives as his source a pamphlet by R. B. Forbes, *Loss of the Essex, . . .* (Cambridge: John Wilson & Son, 1884); Forbes in turn gives as his source Fred Sanford of Nantucket. These accounts are discussed in chap. 5. Pollard would have been sixteen when the *North River* made the world's first steam voyage. He would certainly not have been an officer, and there is no record of his having been on the ship in any capacity. There was a steward named George, but he is known to have been a black man. There may have been a deck boy or two whose names do not appear on any extant records, so it is not strictly impossible that Pollard was on the ship—nor is it impossible that he was later connected with Fulton in some way—but the general unreliability of Briggs makes the story unconvincing.

23. The text is that of the 1821 first edition. No silent corrections have been made except as called for by a list of errata in the front of the 1821 volume. The changes thus made are: p. 23, line 2, "are now" was *one vows*; p. 34, line 11, "none" was *one*; p. 40, line 18, "heeled" was *keeled*; p. 63, line 1, "Matthew" was *Mather*; p. 65, line 23, "it" had to be inserted after *ourselves*; p. 44, line 26, "mommentary" was *momentous*. One change called for by the errata list was not made: read "and" for *of* on p. 40, line 24; the original was no erratum at all but more precise than the suggested emendation.

The reproduced title page of the volume itself contains an error: "1819 & 1820" should, of course, be "1820 & 1821."

CHAPTER TWO

1. For the effect of the War of 1812 on Nantucket whaling, see Edouard Stackpole, *Whales and Destiny* (Amherst: University of Massachusetts Press, 1972).

2. The "patriots" and "royalists" were the parties to the wars of liberation under way in South America at the time the *Narrative* was written. The *Essex* survivors' contact with these hostilities is explained in chap. 3.

3. At this point in the 1821 edition, the errata list described in chap. 1, n. 23, above, follows on a separate page.

4. The whale chart that Herman Melville spoke of in chap. 44 of *Moby-Dick* as forthcoming was published the same year as *Moby-Dick*, 1851. It was prepared by the celebrated oceanographer Matthew Fontaine Maury and represents graphically the distribution of whales in the world's oceans. It can be found as an endpaper in Starbuck's *Whale Fishery*, 1964 reprint.

5. At the time of the shipwreck the crew was twenty men, not twenty-one. Captain Pollard in one of the messages left on Henderson Island said that one of the crewmen left the ship in Tecamus. This letter of Captain Pollard was printed in the *Sydney* (Australia) *Gazette*, June 9, 1821. See Appendix F.

6. Azores.

7. I.e., Flores. A few months later the *Essex* would not have been permitted to make the stop. Around January 1820 the authorities in the Azores began quarantining (refusing landing rights to) American ships on report of yellow fever raging in the United States. See U.S. Department of State, Despatches from United States Consuls in Fayal, Azores, Mar. 4, 1795–Nov. 28, 1832, National Archives, Record Group 59, T203, roll 1, especially letters from John B. Dabney, consul, and Thomas Hickling, vice-consul for St. Michael.

8. For the significance of St. Mary's Island, see chap. 3.

9. "Decamas" is Tecamus.

10. If "spissy" is a neologism, it is a good one: *spissus* in Latin means dense or thick. In the copy of the *Narrative* that belonged to Owen's father, Judah Chase, "spissy" is crossed out and "pitchy" written in. (Judah Chase's copy is in the Nantucket Atheneum.)

11. The island was not Ducie but Henderson, as is explained in chap. 3.

12. Owen Chase's *Narrative* was in print before word of the rescue of Wright, Weeks, and Chapple reached Nantucket.

13. This conclusion is examined in chap. 3.

14. The Paddack letter (Appendix E), reporting Captain Pollard's account, places the separation at 31°S/117° W.

15. Some dates in this paragraph conflict with dates given elsewhere. Lawson Thomas may have died on the fifteenth or the twentieth rather than the twenty-fifth. A cursive hand popular when the *Narrative* was written makes the 2 look very much like the 1; curiously this is the case with the hand in which the Paddack letter is written (it seems at first glance to be misdated). It would be easy for a printer to read 25 for 15. It is also logical to read fifteenth since the boat's food supply was exhausted on the fourteenth; what would the men have stayed alive on for eleven days if Thomas did not die until the twenty-fifth? The Paddack letter places his death on the twentieth. Both fifteenth and twentieth fit the sequence of dates in the *Narrative*, but twenty-fifth does not. The date given below for the separation of the captain's boat and the third boat, the twenty-ninth, contradicts the date given in the previous paragraph, the twenty-eighth. The Paddack letter says that the casting of lots that led to Owen Coffin's death took place on February 6, not February 1.

16. Owen Coffin was Captain Pollard's first cousin, not, as often reported, his nephew. Owen Coffin's grandfather was Hezekiah Coffin, said to be the first man to heave tea overboard at the Boston Tea Party.

17. James is an obvious misprint for George. The names of two of the survivors are variously spelled in Nantucket records: Ramsdale is also Ramsdell, and Nicholson is also Nickerson. The latter form in each case is adopted elsewhere in this book as being the more common in general Nantucket usage and in subsequent reference in town records to the two men themselves.

CHAPTER THREE

1. Positions of these ships are taken from the 1820–23 log of the *Coquette* in the Peter Foulger Museum.

2. Anderson, *Melville in the South Seas* (New York: Dover Publications, 1966), p. 107.

3. There are many accounts of seamen killed by Pacific natives. J. N. Reynolds collected a number of them in *Address on the Subject of a Surveying and Exploring Expedition to the Pacific Ocean and South Seas Delivered in the Hall of Representatives on the Evening of April 3, 1836* (New York: Harper and Bros., 1836), p. 46 ff. Cf. the following instance, which occurred not long after Herman Melville left the Marquesas: "New Bedford July 18, 1845 . . . one other of s^d Ships Crew Antone Fauncis was killed by the Natives at the Marqueese Islands about the Middle of Jany 1844." Deposition with crew list of the *Rousseau*, 1841–45, National Archives, Record Group 36.

4. Starbuck, *Whale Fishery*, 1:225, on the *Equator* and *Balaena*. Also: "The first American whalers—the *Balaena* and *Equator*, of New Bedford [the *Equator* was actually from Nantucket]—arrived in 1819. It was found that no other place was so convenient for the semiannual refitting, repairing, and provisioning of these

vessels, and the transhipping of oil and bone, and the islands soon became the rendezvous for whalers of all countries." William Fremont Blackman, *The Making of Hawaii: A Study in Social Evolution* (New York: Macmillan, 1899), p. 188.

5. In many editions from the end of the eighteenth century to the present day; one likely to have been used by the *Essex* was published in New York by E. M. Blount & Samuel A. Burtus, 1817. See Appendix G.

6. Ducie was apparently given the tentative names of Luna Puesta and Anegada before Quiros settled on Encarnación. For the discovery and naming of these islands, see Clements R. Markham, ed., *The Voyages of Pedro Fernandez de Quiros 1595 to 1606*, Hakluyt Society Works, 2d ser. no. 14 (London: Printed for the Hakluyt Society, 1904); Herman A. Friis, ed., *The Pacific Basin: A History of Its Geographical Exploration* (New York: American Geographical Society, 1967); Edward Edwards and George Hamilton, *Voyage of HMS Pandora . . .* (London: Francis Edwards, 1915); George Hamilton, *A Voyage Round the World in His Majesty's Frigate Pandora . . .* (London: Printed for the Bookseller, 1799); Andrew Sharp, *The Discovery of the Pacific Islands* (Oxford: Clarendon Press, 1960); Ernest S. Dodge, *Beyond the Capes* (London: Gollancz, 1971). Dodge, apparently following Captain Beechey (n. 7, below), erroneously credits the discovery of Henderson to the crew of the *Essex*. For approximate dating of Captain Henderson's visit to Henderson Island, see his articles about his stop at Pitcairn in *Calcutta Government Gazette*, May 6 and July 22, 1819.

7. Capt. Frederick William Beechey, R.N., *Narrative of a Voyage to the Pacific and Beering's Strait to Co-operate with the Polar Expeditions: Performed in His Majesty's Ship Blossom . . . in the Years 1825, 26, 27, 28*, 2 vols. (London: Henry Colburn & Richard Bentley, 1831), 1:59-61.

8. Ibid., pp. 61-64.

9. *Field Monograph of Tuamotu Archipelago and Henderson Islands,* ONI-87, Office of Chief of Naval Operations Division of Naval Intelligence, June 30, 1942, p. 8.

10. Robert McLoughlin, *Law and Order on Pitcairn Island* (Auckland, N.Z.: Government of Pitcairn, Henderson, Ducie and Oeno Islands, 1971), pp. 69-72.

11. Journal of Capt. Joseph Mitchell II on the *Three Brothers,* July 7, 1846, to July 15, 1851, in the Peter Foulger Museum.

12. Beechey, *Narrative*, 1:48-50.

13. Ibid., p. 65.

14. For the medical analysis of the survivors' condition I am indebted to Charles Paddack, M.D.

15. Principal sources for the following Chilean history are Luis Galdames, *A History of Chile* (Chapel Hill: University of North Carolina Press, 1941); Benjamin Vicuña Mackenna, *Historia jeneral de la Republica de Chile desde su independencia hasta nuestros días*, 5 vols. (Santiago: Impr. nacional, 1866-82); Diego Barros Arana, *Historia jeneral de Chile,* 16 vols. (Santiago: R. Jover, 1884-1902).

16. The story is told in the *New Bedford Mercury* (June 15, July 20, 1821, and February 15, 1822); in Edouard Stackpole, *The Sea-Hunters* (Westport, Conn.: Greenwood Press, 1972), pp. 310–13; and in passing in various books on whaling and on Nantucket. Captain Russell and a cabin boy were eventually murdered by their captors.

17. Charles Murphey, *A Journal of a Whaling Voyage on Board Ship Dauphin, of Nantucket* (Mattapoisett, Mass.: Atlantic Publishing Co. 1877), p. 9.

18. Ibid., p. 10.

19. The June 7 arrival date is from Starbuck, *Whale Fishery,* the June 9 from the *New Bedford Mercury.* The June 15 issue of the *Mercury,* which carried Captain Wood's story, added before it went to press the news about the rescue of those in Owen Chase's boat. This news it obviously received on June 12, when the *Eagle* arrived in Nantucket, or the day after.

20. Henry Hill, *Recollections of an Octogenarian.* (Boston: D. Lothrop & Co., 1884), passim.

21. Biographical data on Commodore Ridgely are from ZB file, Operational Archives, Naval Historical Center, Washington Navy Yard. A note on titles: "A captain . . . who had commanded a company of ships was privileged to call himself a commodore. . . . Commodore was not a commisioned rank but a courtesy title." Leonard F. Guttridge and Jay D. Smith, *The Commodores* (New York: Harper & Row, 1969), p. ix.

22. Australia.

23. Journal of Capt. Charles Goodwin Ridgely, Naval Historical Foundation Manuscript Collection, Manuscript Division, Library of Congress, Washington, D.C. Pages unnumbered; these would be pp. 32–36 if numbered.

24. Muster Roll, U.S.S. *Constellation,* vol. 2 (1814–20), National Archives, Record Group 45.

25. *Gazeta ministerial de Chile,* April 28, 1821, p. 4.

26. U.S. Department of the Navy, Letters Received by the Secretary of the Navy: Captains' Letters, 1805–61, 1866–85, Letter no. 56 (May 16, 1821), National Archives, Record Group 45, M-125, roll 71.

27. Ibid., Letter no. 78 (Mar. 7, 1821), roll 70. There is an interruption in the National Archives microfilm copy of this letter (pp. 2 and 3 are missing); the remainder of the text given here up to the arrest of the three officers is from a different copy of the same letter, this one in Captain Ridgely's Letterbook in the Naval Historical Foundation Manuscript Collection, Manuscript Division, Library of Congress, Washington, D.C.

28. Ridgely, Journal; pages would be 29–30 if numbered.

29. Letters Received by the Secretary of the Navy from Captains, Letter no. 78 (Mar. 7, 1821).

30. U.S., Department of the Navy, Log of the U.S.S. *Macedonian* (1818–21), National Archives, Record Group 24. The Almendral was the suburb that stretched along the north and northeast sides of Valparaiso Bay.

31. Ibid., Mar. 15, 1821.

32. "Narrative of the Loss of the Ship Essex," State Library of New South Wales, ML DOC 348. This three-page ms. is well informed and precise on the *Essex* story.

33. Margaret Fane De Salis, *Captain Thomas Raine, an Early Colonist* (Vaucluse, N.S.W.: Published by the author, 1969), is a full-length biography.

34. Abstract Log of the *Surry,* from a transcription by the Hon. E. P. T. Raine, C.B.E., E.D., the log's owner.

35. The Abstract Log of the *Surry* and the Journal of Dr. Ramsay are in the possession of Judge Raine, who transcribed them for use in this book. Mitchell Ms. A131, which has been given the title *"Journal of a Voyage from London to New South Wales and V.D.'s Land,"* is attributed by the Mitchell Library with reasonable certitude to Edward Dobson, a passenger on and subsequently a crew member of the *Surry.* There are minor discrepancies in the three *Surry* documents. The Abstract Log has the *Surry* arriving at Henderson (referred to by Captain Raine as Incarnation—there is no question, however, that it is Henderson, for an observation is given and the ship had just come from Ducie) at 12:30 on Apr. 9; Ramsay and Ms. A131 have it arriving at 2:00 PM. The Abstract Log gives an observation of 24°58′ S/130°18′ W for the next day, Apr. 10, which would mean that the *Surry* had not only reached but gone around the west end of Pitcairn that day. The other two accounts say that the *Surry* took the men off the island on the afternoon of Apr. 9, stood off the island overnight, sent a boat ashore the next day for the papers left on the island, and in the afternoon (A131 says 4:00 PM) set sail for Pitcairn arriving there Apr. 11. There is a dating error in the Ramsay Journal: "Sunday 9th April 1821"—Apr. 9 was a Monday.

36. The text of the Pollard letter given here differs from that in the *Sydney Gazette* (Appendix F). Whether there were two public letters or whether one or both were edited is unknown. The version in the *Sydney Gazette* was the one that became known back on Nantucket.

37. Captain Raine's account was published in *Australian Magazine* 1 (1821): 80–84, 109–14. Some of its wording closely corresponds to that of Mitchell Ms. A131. Dr. Ramsay's account is the continuation of the Journal already quoted. It can be found, after a fashion, in appendix A of R. H. Goddard, "Captain Thomas Raine of the Surry, 1795–1860," *Journal and Proceedings of the Royal Australian Historical Society* 26 (1940):277–317. Goddard has taken parts of the Abstract Log of the *Surry* and interlarded them into the Ramsay Journal without explanation; the reader has no way of knowing which he is reading. Ramsay and *Australian Magazine* both spell Quintal with an *r*, Quintral (or Quintrel).

38. *Australian Magazine* 1 (1821):114.

39. Sir Charles Lucas, ed., *The Pitcairn Island Register Book* (London: Society for Promoting Christian Knowledge; New York and Toronto: Macmillan, 1929), pp. 10–15.

40. Records of Wright's and Weeks's service on the *Surry* are to be found in the Ship's Musters taken Aug. 23, 1821, and Jan. 29, 1822, Archives Office of New

South Wales, 4/4772, p. 44, and 4/4773, pp. 15–16. Governor Macquarie also gives the crew list in his "Journal of a Voyage from New South Wales to England in 1822," Mitchell Library, A775, p. 21.

41. *The Twenty-Fifth Annual Report of the Religious Tract Society, M.DCCC.XXIV* (London: Printed for the Society, 1824), p. xvi.

42. Plymouth Register of Electors, 1834. Information supplied by Olive M. Riding, Devon Record Services.

43. The chest came into the possession of a ship's carpenter, John Taber, whose son-in-law, James Norton, donated it to the Nantucket Historical Association. Its full story is told in the *Ravenna* (Ohio) *Republican*, Mar. 5 and Sept. 10, 1896, and the Nantucket *Inquirer and Mirror*, Aug. 22, 1896.

CHAPTER FOUR

1. The date is taken from Owen's *Narrative* and differs from the June 12 date given by Starbuck. One- or two-day discrepancies in arrival dates reported in logs, newspapers, journals, and Starbuck are common.

2. Gustav Kobbé, "The Perils and Romance of Whaling," *Century Magazine* 40, n.s. 18 (Aug. 1890):509–25.

3. Crew list of the *Florida* in New Bedford Free Public Library. Nantucket *Inquirer,* Dec. 9, 1823.

4. *County of Nantucket Unregistered Deeds,* liber 28, p. 309: "I Judah Chase . . . yeoman in consideration of seven hundred & twenty five dollars paid by Owen Chase of Nantucket . . . sell and convey unto the said Owen Chase . . . a certain tract of land bounded as follows viz! on the south by Meader [sic] Lane West by land formerly belonging to Davis Gorham & others, North and East by land owned by John Gorham & Davis Gorham, said land admeasuring fourteen rods hereby meaning & Intending to sell all that tract of land which I bought of Resom Taber and no more, as will appear by his Deed to me together with the Dwelling house standing on the same." On p. 311 follows a legal instrument of a kind then commonly in use on Nantucket and amounting to a mortgage held by Judah Chase on the property; it was a deed of the property from Owen to Judah to be voided on payment of $500 by a fixed date.

5. Crew list of the *Winslow*, National Archives, Record Group 36. Nantucket *Inquirer*, July 28, 1827.

6. *County of Nantucket Unregistered Deeds*, liber 28, p. 311, marginal note: "Nantucket August 2, 1827 then Received of Owen Chase five hundred Dollars in full Discharge of this Mortgage Deed—Judah Chase."

7. Crew list of the *Winslow*.

8. Nantucket *Inquirer,* Oct. 27, 1827.

9. Crew list of *Winslow*. Nantucket *Inquirer,* July 10, 1830, lists ships spoken by the *Winslow*.

10. Log of the *Catherine*, 1835–38, in possession of Mr. and Mrs. Howard Chase.

11. *Seaman Register Ship Index Mar. 14, 1834–Aug. 15, 1843,* p. 64, New Bedford Free Public Library.

12. A vivid, and to some extent comic, account of a South American earthquake is given by that most engaging chronicler, Capt. Basil Hall, in *Extracts from a Journal Written on the Coasts of Chili, Peru, and Mexico, in the Years 1820, 1821, 1822* (Edinburgh: Archibald Constable & Co.; London: Hurst, Robinson & Co., 1824; rep. Upper Saddle River, N.J.: Gregg Press, 1968), 1:51.

13. Albert F. Ellis, *Ocean Island and Nauru: Their Story* (Sydney: Angus & Robertson, 1935), pp. 136–37. The explanation for the tardy exploration of Makatea by the commercial interests is doubtless that there was no incentive to open up new phosphate mines until the twentieth century, because so much phosphate was available, first in western Europe and then in the eastern United States. I am indebted to Prof. Richard Ropp, Rutgers University; Mr. A. J. G. Notholt, Institute of Geological Sciences, London; and Mr. G. H. Lording, office of the British Phosphate Commissioners, for information on Makatea's phosphate deposits.

14. Charles Wilkes, *Narrative of the United States Exploring Expedition during the Years 1838, 1839, 1840, 1841, 1842* (Philadelphia, 1849), 2:1–60; and *Autobiography of Rear Admiral Charles Wilkes, U.S. Navy, 1798–1877* (Washington, D.C.: Naval Historical Division, Department of the Navy, 1978), pp. 423–28.

15. Herman Melville, *Omoo: A Narrative of Adventures in the South Seas* (Evanston and Chicago: Northwestern University Press and Newberry Library, 1968), p. 100.

16. David Jaffe, *The Stormy Petrel and the Whale: Some Origins of Moby-Dick* (Baltimore: Privately printed, 1976).

17. Wilkes, *Narrative,* 2:55.

18. *Records of the Supreme Judicial Court, Commonwealth of Massachusetts, Nantucket Ss.,* 1838–43:52–53 (in office of court clerk, Nantucket).

19. Ibid.

20. Nantucket *Inquirer and Mirror,* Jan. 5, 1907. The *Berkeley Daily Gazette* for Dec. 21, 1906, reported, "Joseph P. Chase, aged 75 years, of 2109 Fourth Street, West Berkeley died today. Deceased was a native of Portugal, had resided in California for forty-three years, thirty-one of which he had spent in West Berkeley."

21. *County of Nantucket Unregistered Deeds,* lib. 26–59, passim, and *County of Nantucket Tax Assessment Records,* 1861 ff.

22. Letter in special collections of the Nantucket Atheneum, inserted in Judah Chase's copy of Owen's *Narrative.*

23. Log of the *Catherine,* 1835–38, entry for May 31, 1838.

24. Log of the *Franklin,* 1828–30, in possession of Mr. and Mrs. Howard Chase, entry for Nov. 6, 1829.

25. Log of *Catherine,* 1835–38, entry for Jan. 3, 1837.

26. Obed Macy, Journal, 6:53; ms. in Peter Foulger Museum, Nantucket.

27. Log of the *Catherine*, 1835–38, entry for Mar. 14, 1838.

28. Macy, Journal, vol. 6, entry for June 16, 1839.

29. In possession of Mr. and Mrs. Howard Chase. Ariel is Owen's brother-in-law Ariel Cathcart, Phoebe probably Owen's daughter Phebe Ann Coffin, Susan Owen's wife, and Sister Worth probably Owen's daughter Adeline Worth. A period should probably be inserted between "cousin" and "Susan." The result would be to make the references to relatives logical, but it would put into Susan Chase's mouth the "O *my head*" exclamation, which seems to be Owen's—Susan may have been quoting Owen.

30. *Nantucket Probate Records* 28 (1867–84):44–45.

31. Transcribed from the ms. in the Manuscript Division of the Library of Congress, Washington, D.C. Since this transcription was made, the *Autobiography* has been published (n. 14, above).

32. Ms. in Peter Foulger Museum with notation "From Copy W$^{\underline{m}}$ Randall." The date on the ms. is erroneously given as 1822.

33. *New York Daily Times,* Dec. 14 and 15, 1853; and Harrison Hayford, "The Sailor Poet of White-Jacket," *Boston Public Library Quarterly* 3 (July 1951):221–28. The Pease marriage, which was brought to my attention by Wilson Heflin, is recorded in *Vital Records of Edgartown, Massachusetts, to the Year 1850* (Boston: New England Historical Genealogical Society, 1906), p. 166.

34. Obed Macy, noting the good results of appointing a night watch, says, "In addition to the Town watch there is also one or two watches established by individuals whose limits are prescribed by those who employ them." Journal, Feb. 4, 1821.

35. The Folger Records are ampler on Ramsdell than the *Vital Records of Nantucket* or the Barney Records.

36. Starbuck does list a Ramsdell, no first name, for that voyage. Cf. Edouard Stackpole, *The Loss of the Essex* (Falmouth: Kendall Printing, 1977), p. 32.

37. More or less the same information is to be found in an *Inquirer and Mirror* article, Apr. 5, 1879, on the occasion of Lawrence's death.

38. Dates of the *Surry* are from the London maritime newspaper, *Lloyd's List,* July 5, 1822. Dates of the *London Packet* are from *Lloyd's List,* Feb. 22, July 2 and Aug. 9, 1822. Information supplied by C. J. Ware, National Maritime Museum, Greenwich.

CHAPTER FIVE

1. Annotation in Owen Chase's *Narrative*. See Appendix A.

2. Starbuck, *Whale Fishery*, 1:1.

3. P. v. For a history of the bank robbery, see Emil F. Guba, *The Great Nantucket Bank Robbery Conspiracy and Solemn Aftermath; or, The End of Old Nantucket* (Waltham, Mass.: Published by the author, 1973).

4. *The Olio, Being a Collection of Poems, Fables, Epigrams, &c.* (New York: Published by the author, 1823). Bob Short [pseud. of William B. Gilley], *Patriotic Effusions* (New York: L. & F. Lockwood, 1819).

5. The American publishing scene during this period is well described in William Charvat, *Literary Publishing in America 1790-1850* (Philadelphia: University of Pennsylvania Press, 1959).

6. Letter 1194, Matthew Carey Letterbook, Mar. 1821–Sept. 1821, in Lea and Febiger Collection, Historical Society of Pennsylvania, Philadelphia.

7. Letter 805, ibid., Jan. 1, 1822–June 11, 1822. The reason for assuming that the date is Mar. 8, 1822, is that the letters immediately preceding and following are of that date.

8. Appendix A.

9. Ibid.

10. Card Index to Seamen, New Bedford Free Public Library.

11. Nantucket *Inquirer,* Dec. 9, 1843.

12.   Appendix A.

13. Text is that of the first edition: *Clarel: A Poem and a Pilgrimage to the Holy Land* (New York: G. P. Putnam's Sons, 1876), canto 37; 1:132–35.

14. The most fundamental book someone studying the relationship of Melville and Owen Chase can consult is Jay Leyda, *The Melville Log,* 2d ed. with additional material (New York: Gordian Press, 1969). Jay Leyda pointed out to me his erroneous placement of the *Essex* shipwreck under 1819 rather than 1820. (The title page of the 1821 edition of the *Narrative,* as has been noted, first made this mistake, giving 1819 and 1820 for 1820 and 1821.) Charles Roberts Anderson, *Melville in the South Seas,* cited earlier, is eminently helpful on its subject. Among the important pieces of scholarly discovery that Wilson Heflin has contributed to Melville studies, the student of Owen Chase will be most interested in "Melville and Nantucket," *Moby-Dick Centennial Essays,* ed. Tyrus Hillway and Luther S. Mansfield (Dallas: Southern Methodist University Press, 1953). Charles Olson's *Call Me Ishmael* (New York: Reynal & Hitchcock, 1947) was the first work to discuss at length Melville's annotations of Owen Chase's *Narrative.* Henry F. Pommer, "Herman Melville and the Wake of the *Essex,*" *American Literature* 20 (Nov. 1948):290–304, studies Melville's use of the *Essex* story. Wilbur S. Scott, Jr.'s Princeton dissertation, "Melville's Originality: A Study of Some of the Sources of Moby-Dick" (1943), treats Owen Chase as one of Melville's sources (pp. 218–22). Many other biographical and critical works on Melville speak of Owen Chase in passing.

15. "Chapter I and a part of Chapter II,, of *The Narrative of Arthur Gordon Pym* appeared in *The Southern Literary Messenger* for January, 1837; the remainder of Chapter II, all Chapter III, and a part of Chapter IV, in the February number of the same magazine. No more was published serially but the entire work was issued in book form in both England and America in 1838." *Narrative of Arthur Gordon Pym* (New York: Limited Editions Club, 1930), bibliog. note, p.

xvii. Poe's sources are treated in R. L. Rhea, "Some Observations on Poe's Origins," *University of Texas Bulletin* 10 (1930):135–44; D. M. McKeithan, "Two Sources of Poe's *Narrative of Arthur Gordon Pym,*" *University of Texas Bulletin* 13 (1933):127–37; J. O. Bailey, "Sources for Poe's *Arthur Gordon Pym,* 'Hans Pfaal,' and Other Pieces," *PMLA* 57 (June 1942):513–35; Keith Huntress, "Another Source for Poe's *Narrative of Arthur Gordon Pym,*" *American Literature* 16 (1944):19–25.

16. *Leaves of Grass* (New York: W. W. Norton, 1965), p. 273.

17. For Melville's use of *Miriam Coffin,* see Leon Howard, "A Predecessor of *Moby-Dick,*" *Modern Language Notes* 49 (May 1934):310–11.

18. Forbes may have been drawing on a vague recollection of a passage in Archibald Duncan, *The Mariner's Chronicle* (Philadelphia: James Humphreys, 1806), 2:192. The episode described there is not connected with the *Essex,* obviously.

19. (New Haven: R. M. Treadway, 1834), pp. 398–402; a rev. one-vol. ed.

20. *The Journals and Miscellaneous Notebooks of Ralph Waldo Emerson,* ed. Alfred R. Ferguson (Cambridge: Harvard University Press, 1964), 4:265. A twentieth-century account also has the *Essex* being sunk by a white whale, but this story is merely the result of confusion between the *Essex*'s adventures and *Moby-Dick*: Estuardo Núñez, "Viajeros norteamericanos en el Pacifico Antes de 1825," *Journal of Inter-American Studies* 4 (July 1962):329.

21. Letter of Edward Dobson to his father, May 7, 1820, Mitchell Library; passenger list of *Surry* on arrival in Sydney, *Sydney Gazette,* Sept. 16, 1820; ships' muster lists for *Surry,* Dec. 1820, Mitchell Library. Information furnished by Suzanne Saunders, Mitchell Librarian.

22. The date has to be 1857 or after. See Karl Kabelac, "Book Publishing History. . . ," Auburn (N.Y.) *Citizen,* July 4, 1976, p. 22, for dates of this publisher.

INDEX

About the Author

Thomas Farel Heffernan, a Melville enthusiast, discovered Owen Chase by chance on a farm in Aurora, New York, near the family home where Heffernan spent his childhood. His wife, Carol, noticed an old sea chest in a neighbor's kitchen: the sea chest belonged to Owen Chase's brother. "That was the day the Owen Chase book was born," he says. He has since published several articles on Melville and related subjects.

Heffernan, now associate professor of English at Adelphi University in Garden City, New York, received his B.A. from Fordham University and his Ph.D. from Columbia. He has lived and studied in Quebec, Dublin, Oxford, and various places in Italy.